Ken Lussey

FRIEND OR FOE?

Other books by Ken Lussey

Thrillers featuring Bob Sutherland and Monique Dubois
and set in Scotland and beyond during World War Two:
Eyes Turned Skywards
The Danger of Life
Bloody Orkney
The Stockholm Run
Hide and Seek
The Eye of Horus

Contemporary thrillers featuring Callum Anderson:
The High Road
A Tangled Web
Thicker Than Water

For younger readers:
The House With 46 Chimneys

First published in Great Britain in 2025 by
Arachnid Press Ltd
91 Columbia Avenue
Livingston EH54 6PT
Scotland

www.arachnid.scot
www.kenlussey.com

Paperback ISBN: 978-1-0686257-5-6

Cover design by Carolyn Henry Photography
Cover photograph by Maureen Lussey
The cover photograph is of Galloway House
Printed and bound in Great Britain by Flexpress Ltd,
6 Coal Cart Road, Interchange, Birstall, Leicester LE4 3BY.

For my grandson Alistair,
who's been waiting for me to finish this book.

PROLOGUE

Grace had told him on the telephone that when he had the front of Galloway House fully in view he should turn right onto a road that stayed well clear of it. After following this into a wood and past the walled garden he would find Broom Cottage on his right.

The cottage was made of stone and, on this warm and sunny June day, it looked as if it had come straight off a postcard, with a window on either side of the blue front door and two dormer windows set into the grey slate roof. The left-hand end was partly covered by a strong growth of pink climbing roses and there was a small stone-walled garden between it and the road.

Adrian Somerset felt oddly nervous as he brought the borrowed vehicle to a halt. There was no reason why he should. Since he was old enough to notice them, girls and then women had always found him extremely attractive. His physical presence, blue eyes, blond hair and dashing moustache worked strongly in his favour. Add the uniform of an RAF flight lieutenant, a pair of pilot's wings and a ribbon showing he had been awarded the Distinguished Flying Cross and his amorous advances were seldom rejected. As often as not he found himself able to pick and choose amongst the women who pursued him.

Yet Grace Sullivan wasn't like any of the women he'd known before. With red shoulder-length curly hair, freckles and piercing green eyes, she had an assured presence that unsettled him. He'd got off to a bad start with her. When she'd come into the consulting room to look at the swelling on the side of his head caused when he'd ducked into rather than away from a swiftly bowled cricket ball, he'd asked how long the doctor would be.

Grace had simply stood and looked at him as if he were a specimen in a petri dish until he belatedly realised the implications of her white coat and the stethoscope around her neck. His embarrassment and apologies were genuine and the smile she rewarded him with lit up the room.

She'd said that Adrian needed to spend the night at Galloway House, under observation, to ensure he wasn't suffering from concussion. She arranged to have him placed in a private room rather than in one of the men's wards on the hospital's ground floor.

Adrian had assumed this was because of his status as an officer. That night he discovered that Dr Grace Sullivan had put him in a private room for an altogether different reason and that her idea of 'observation' was probably not normally recognised as best practice in medical textbooks.

That had been the previous Saturday night and there had been no sign of Grace when Adrian awoke the next morning. It had been a different doctor, the squadron leader who served as the medical officer at RAF Wigtown and explained that he helped out at Galloway House, who had seen him on the Sunday. The squadron leader discharged him and arranged for him to be driven back to the airfield.

Adrian had telephoned Galloway House on the Monday and again on the Wednesday, asking to speak to Dr Sullivan. He was beginning to wonder if the bang on his head had caused him to imagine the whole encounter and was relieved to find that she was on duty the second time he rang.

He asked if he could see her again and was delighted to hear her soft Irish voice suggesting they might go for lunch in Garlieston together. He agreed to pick her up on the Friday, two days later, when they would both be off duty.

Adrian opened the garden gate as Grace came out of the cottage, closing the door behind herself. She was wearing a plain green summer dress that set off her red hair beautifully and her smile was enough to remove any doubt in Adrian's mind about the reality of what had happened between them the previous Saturday night.

'You're looking beautiful,' he said.

'Thank you,' said Grace. 'And you are looking very handsome. I'm pleased you spared no expense when selecting our carriage.'

Adrian laughed. 'Grace, I'd like you to meet Tilly. I'd have picked something more sporty for the occasion but this Standard 12 utility vehicle, known to everyone as Tilly, was all I could get my hands on.'

The vehicle combined the bonnet and front seats of the car it was based on with a canvas-hooded back end. It was painted in RAF blue grey. As far as Adrian knew, the utility vehicles found fulfilling bridesmaids' roles on just about every British military base were always called Tilly, whatever car they were originally based on, a name not very imaginatively derived from 'utility'.

Adrian walked round and opened the passenger side door for Grace, who kissed him on the cheek as she got in.

'There's a lane that leads directly past the stables and into the village,' she said. 'Sadly the gate at the bottom, where it comes out onto the road round to the harbour, is closed to vehicles as part of the security cordon there. It's still the best way to walk into the village but as we're driving we'll have to return the way you came in.'

Adrian found his way back through the estate and they drove into Garlieston from the west.

'I'm new in these parts,' said Adrian. 'Where's the best place for lunch?'

‘Just about the only place is the Galloway Arms Hotel. Turn right when we get to the sea. The hotel is on South Crescent.’

‘Assuming these chaps let us through,’ said Adrian, pulling to a halt at a checkpoint on the edge of the village manned by three men wearing khaki uniforms and carrying rifles.

The man who looked at Adrian’s identification returned it, then stepped back and saluted. A second man who had gone around the other side of the vehicle smiled when he saw Grace and declined her offered identity card.

‘You seem to know the right people,’ said Adrian as he eased the vehicle back into motion.

‘I encountered that young man professionally last week,’ said Grace. ‘I’ll spare you the details but he was referred to the hospital at Galloway House for treatment of a minor but embarrassing ailment so I think he felt we were well enough acquainted to wave me through.’

‘Why are they here?’ asked Adrian. ‘You talked about a security cordon. What is there to protect in what seems a very sleepy backwater that’s about as far from the action as it’s possible to be?’

‘I suspect that’s the point,’ said Grace. ‘It’s all very hush-hush. No one is saying anything but military activity and associated security has been getting increasingly intense. The harbour at the far end of the village has been a focal point but the whole of the coastline from here down to Cairn Head and the Isle of Whithorn has been taken over by army engineers supported by the Royal Navy. When you came in with that bump on your head saying you’d only just arrived in Scotland I assumed the RAF was playing its part in whatever is going on.’

‘Not as far as I know,’ said Adrian. ‘I’m a flight

commander on 175 Squadron and we're currently getting to grips with a new aircraft type. I'm leading the advance party setting up a training deployment at RAF Wigtown that we and our sister 174 Squadron can rotate pilots through to help with that process. Both squadrons are based in southern England and there's a real benefit to being able to train up here without having to constantly watch out for enemy aircraft. Maybe the army and navy have the same idea?'

'Perhaps,' said Grace. 'Though I didn't know they were quite so open about what they're doing as they appear to be today.'

They had reached a T-junction formed by the road into the village and one running along the seafront. As Adrian turned right he saw that Grace was pointing to their left, towards a large vessel in the bay.

'I think that's a tank landing craft,' he said. 'More importantly, I'm assuming that they serve good lunches at the Galloway Arms?'

'The best in the area,' said Grace. 'It's the favourite haunt of local farmers and as a result the place never seems to be short of anything. You'd hardly believe there was a war on if it wasn't for what we've been discussing.'

Adrian parked just beyond the hotel. The front door was open and three men were standing on the opposite side of the road, by a low stone wall. One wore a shirt and tie while the other two were dressed as farmers and carried part-filled pint glasses.

'It appears the navy has an audience,' he said. 'Should we take a look at what's going on?' He saw a look of doubt on Grace's face. 'Come on, Grace. If anyone asks I've got the uniform and the RAF vehicle.'

He led the way across the road and stood a little distance

away from the three men. Grace stood close beside him but he quelled the instinct to put his arm around her waist, worried that it might not be what she wanted. Beyond the stone wall was a muddy and partly seaweed-covered beach that looked as if it was submerged by the sea at high tide. The water was a little way out but Adrian had no way of knowing if the tide was coming in or going out.

The tank landing craft was some distance away, in the northern corner of the bay, so he and Grace were looking at it side-on. There were two smaller boats in attendance. The landing craft had come to a halt some way offshore and its large bow door had been lowered into the sea.

What was extraordinary was that a narrow strip of what appeared to be slatted roadway extended from the front of the landing craft across the water in front of it and then across the muddy sand as far as a fringe of greenery where a group of khaki-clad figures were standing. As Adrian watched, a lorry was driven out of the landing craft and onto the roadway. Even at this distance, it was possible to see parts of the roadway sink into the sea as the lorry crossed each segment, only to recover when it had passed. At the landward end, the lorry drove up onto the shore, then did a multi-point turn and began the return journey back to the landing craft.

This didn't go so well. Activity at the rear of the landing craft suggested something had gone wrong and the vessel moved slowly towards the beach as the lorry neared it, sinking segments of the roadway ever more deeply into the sea as the vehicle crossed over them. When the lorry was perhaps thirty yards from the landing craft it became obvious that it was sinking, taking part of the roadway with it. One of the small boats came alongside the lorry and Adrian was relieved to see the driver climb out of his cab and get aboard.

'I think the show's over,' said a voice from behind them.

Adrian turned to see the man in the shirt and tie looking at him.

'I hope the driver of the lorry is all right,' said Grace.

'I'm sure he will be, miss. This is the third time this week they've tried that, each time with different unsuccessful results. I think the landing craft pulled its anchors free this time, which removed the tension from the stretched-out Swiss Roll and allowed it to sink under the weight of the lorry. The tide's on its way out so they'll recover the lorry and roll up the roadway and doubtless try again in a day or two.'

'Come on Adrian,' said Grace. 'You promised me lunch.'

The man in the shirt and tie smiled. 'Ah, customers! I can guarantee you'll not be disappointed.'

The food was excellent but Adrian found Grace hard work. She was happy to talk about the area and her work in the auxiliary hospital at Galloway House, but she deflected his attempts to find out more about her as a woman. She also sidestepped his efforts to agree on ways of furthering their sexual relationship, though in the quiet dining room where he had the sense they might easily be overheard by the few other customers, these had to be very subtle.

After lunch, they emerged from the relative darkness of the Galloway Arms into a beautifully warm and startlingly bright afternoon.

Grace looked at her watch. 'It's been lovely, Adrian, but I need to get back to the cottage.'

He put on his most winning smile. 'Are you going to invite me in when we get back?'

'I'm sorry, Adrian. I hope you don't think I've been

leading you on, but I share Broom Cottage with my mother, who's had a stroke and spends quite a lot of time in bed. When I'm not looking after other people at the hospital I spend most of my time looking after her at the cottage. It was wonderful to spend Saturday night with you at the hospital, and I'm flattered that you wanted to see me again. But I don't think I'm the right person for you at the moment.'

Adrian smiled, though rejection wasn't something he was used to. 'Perhaps I could spend more time with you if I found other ways of getting sent to the hospital?'

Grace frowned. 'You're a pilot, Adrian. Please don't even joke about that.'

After Adrian had turned the utility vehicle around, they drove in silence back along the road alongside the shore. As they approached the junction where they needed to turn inland, an army Jeep coming the other way pulled across the road ahead of them, blocking it. It was driven by a sergeant who got out and ran over to Grace's side of the vehicle.

'Are you Dr Sullivan? I was told you were in the village.'

'Yes, I am,' said Grace. 'What's wrong?'

'Would you mind following me, ma'am?'

Adrian saw Grace look at him and he shrugged. The sergeant turned the Jeep in the road and Adrian followed it around the bay to where the strip of roadway from the landing craft came to an end. More of the roadway was now on sand or mud that had been exposed by the receding tide and the far end had been detached from the landing craft, which had moved further out into the bay.

A group of men in khaki were gathered a little way out, just beyond the reach of the gently lapping waves and on the far side of the roadway.

Grace got out as soon as Adrian brought the Tilly to a halt behind the Jeep.

'It's this way, ma'am,' said the sergeant, who then turned and hurried down a grassy slope and onto the muddy sand.

'I'm not walking on that in these shoes,' said Grace. She bent down to take them off then threw her shoes into the front passenger footwell before following the sergeant in bare feet.

After a moment's indecision, Adrian went after her, more slowly and carefully to try to preserve his service shoes. As he approached the gathering on the beach he saw her crouching down beside a body lying on its back.

Adrian stood a little way away for a few minutes but didn't feel he belonged there. He turned and walked back to the Tilly and got in, then lit a cigarette. He only got back out when he saw Grace returning.

'Are you all right?' he asked.

'I am, but that poor bastard isn't,' she said. 'This never gets any easier. Have you got a cigarette?'

Adrian offered Grace one and lit it for her before lighting another for himself. Then he retrieved her shoes and offered her a blanket to dry her feet. He'd put this in the back of the vehicle earlier, with an altogether different use in mind.

'Is it the lorry driver?' he asked.

'No, I hope he's fine. It's a man in an army uniform. He looks like he's been in the water for a couple of days. They found him snagged on the side of the roadway when the tide went out. It's difficult to be sure after his time in the water but I think he was strangled with a cord of some sort.'

‘He’s been murdered? God, I’m sorry you had to deal with that, Grace. And you’ve got mud on your lovely dress. Can I run you back to the cottage?’

‘No, thank you, Adrian. The military police are on the way and they’ll want to talk to me. Don’t worry, someone will give me a lift back. I think you should cut your losses and go back to RAF Wigtown.’ She smiled. ‘For what it’s worth I did enjoy lunch and I’m sorry the afternoon hasn’t ended in the way you had in mind.’

CHAPTER ONE

'You told us it would be lively, Anne. You certainly weren't wrong!' Connie Bright had to raise her voice to be heard over the hubbub as she placed her empty pint glass back on a small circular table whose ill-sorted collection of beermats was struggling to absorb the accumulating spillage.

Anne Saunders had been born and brought up in Blackburn, only a few miles to the east, so knew the area well. She'd said that a friend had told her that Ye Olde Hob Inn had become a more interesting pub than most in the area so they'd decided to pay it a visit.

Anne had drawn the short straw when they came in and was sitting on a red plush-covered stool with her back to the bar. Connie sat next to Felicity on a matching seat that curved around a corner on the other side of the table, facing out past Anne and across the smoky room whose ceiling, presumably once white, was nearly dark enough to blend in with the exposed wooden beams.

Connie looked around the busy bar. The Three Musketeers, as they referred to themselves when they thought no one else was listening, had been lucky to find a free table when they'd arrived.

Anne leaned forwards and smiled broadly. 'It's not like England at all. Isn't it exciting!'

'It does make a pleasant change,' said Felicity. 'That's the bell for last orders. Sadly, I think it's my round. Are you both up for another pint of bitter?'

Bombardier Felicity Brunt, by a narrow margin the most senior of the three women, stood up and walked over to the bar. It struck Connie that Felicity never seemed aware of how attractive she was and how well her Auxiliary Territorial Service uniform showed off her figure. Though the pub was very busy, the crowd parted like the biblical Red Sea to allow Felicity unimpeded access to the near end of the bar. A few of those waiting to be served were elderly locals, old enough to be exempt from military service but not so old they couldn't appreciate a fine example of the female form. A couple more were British servicemen in uniform. But most of those pressing up against the bar were young black US servicemen in their much smarter and better-tailored uniforms. Connie watched as Felicity was served immediately and one of the Americans helped her carry the drinks back to the table.

Connie expected him to deliver some sort of chat-up line with the beers and felt both relieved and slightly disappointed when he simply smiled at the three women before returning to his place amongst those waiting to be served.

'That was painless,' said Felicity, picking up her pint. 'If I'd tried that in a pub in Preston I'd have made myself very unpopular with the unwashed masses of British squaddies from Fulwood Barracks.'

'The Americans seem to know how to behave like gentlemen,' said Connie.

'I don't know about all of them,' said Anne. 'But I heard this place is popular with men from a US Army Air Forces supply unit based in the village. The enlisted men and non-commissioned officers of the unit are all black and they've made a great impression on the locals. As you say, Felicity, it's a very refreshing change after drinking in Preston.'

The beer in Ye Olde Hob Inn was as good as the ambience and the three women settled down to enjoy their drinks.

‘The problem with beer is the effect it has on the bladder,’ said Connie. ‘I’m just off to the loo.’

It wasn’t her first visit but Connie knew it would be her last of the evening. They needed to leave quite soon. It was a little less than half a mile to Bamber Bridge railway station and they needed to keep enough time in hand to ensure they caught the last train to Preston. That was only six minutes up the line and then they would have to take their chances on the availability of transport to get them back to Fulwood Barracks and avoid a two-mile walk.

When Connie returned to the bar she realised that the atmosphere had changed completely. The pub had gone quiet and all attention was focused on the seating area facing the front of the bar, where two white men in the uniforms of American military policemen, complete with white helmets and black armbands, were standing over a group of seated black soldiers.

‘What’s going on?’ she asked quietly as she sat down.

‘It appears that one of the Americans hasn’t got a pass to be off the base and is wearing the wrong uniform,’ said Felicity. ‘The MPs want to arrest him.’

The discussion was becoming heated with insults being traded and three of the seated US servicemen stood up. The rest of the pub remained silent.

‘I’ve had enough of this,’ said Felicity. She stood up, shaking off Connie’s attempt to grab her arm, and walked towards where the confrontation was taking place. ‘They’re not doing anything or bothering anyone,’ she said, loudly. ‘Why don’t you leave them alone?’

One of the military policemen, a corporal, turned towards Felicity. ‘Stay out of this, miss. It’s got nothing to do with you.’

‘It has when you start using language like that and ruin

what was a nice night out for me and my friends. You're guests in my country and you should behave accordingly.'

'You tell them, love!' said an old man in a tweed jacket standing at the near end of the bar.

Someone beyond the bar shouted 'Hear, hear!' and then other cries of encouragement and a ripple of applause went around the pub. More of the seated soldiers stood up and the other military policeman, a private, took a step backwards before drawing a revolver from his holster and holding it up in the air.

A black man in a US uniform with sergeant's stripes on each arm who had been standing beyond the confrontation raised his hands and walked slowly towards the two military policemen. 'Enough! Put your gun away. Everyone else, sit back down. What the lady said was right. This isn't our country. You've heard what the people who live here think. The two of you should leave peacefully and we can all pretend this never happened.'

From where she was sitting, Connie could see the uncertainty on the faces of the two MPs. She could also see fear, which she thought was far more dangerous. One of the MPs, the corporal, tapped the other on the shoulder, who holstered his revolver. The two men then left the pub, to the accompaniment of cheers and jeers.

A moment later, despite the sergeant's attempts to stop them, a group of the men who had been at the heart of the argument followed the MPs out of the pub.

Connie looked at her watch. 'I think we should be heading to the railway station, don't you, ladies?' she said.

Felicity had returned to their table but was still standing. She bent down to pick up her glass before taking a drink. Connie could see she was shaking.

'I've still got half a pint left,' said Anne. 'But after what just happened I don't feel like drinking it. Let's go.'

Connie was startled by the bright daylight outside the pub. It was well after 10 p.m. but the tops of the trees on the green across the road from Ye Olde Hob Inn were still catching the last of the sun's rays. Wartime double daylight saving in the summer was something she'd grown used to, like everyone else. But there still was a strangeness about walking out of a pub at closing time into daylight.

A group of US servicemen was disappearing out of sight round the corner onto the road that led to the station, and another was gathering outside the pub.

The young man who had helped Felicity carry the beers back to the table detached himself from the second group and came over to join them. 'Hello again, ladies. I'm sorry if that spoiled your night out, but I'm sure I'm speaking for all of us when I thank you for your support.'

'It's what anyone would have done,' said Felicity.

'I'm not so sure. I should introduce myself. I'm William Thompson, from Brooklyn, New York.'

Connie introduced the three of them.

'So, you're a corporal, Felicity, and you're both lance corporals, am I right?' said William.

Connie smiled. 'Close, but not quite. We're members of the Auxiliary Territorial Service, which you can think of as the female part of the British Army. We're serving with the headquarters of the No. 4 Anti-Aircraft Group at Fulwood Barracks in Preston. Because our unit comes under the Royal Artillery, two stripes are worn by a bombardier rather than a corporal and one stripe means a lance bombardier.'

'Can I walk you anywhere?'

'Thanks for the offer,' said Felicity. 'But we're only going as far as the railway station and we'd not want to separate you from your friends.'

‘I’m going that way anyway. We’re with the 1511th Quartermaster Truck Regiment of the Eighth Air Force and we’re based at Adam Hall, or Air Force Station 569, on Mounsey Road, which isn’t far from the railway station. Let me walk you along Station Road at least. You made those MPs look very stupid and I’m not sure it’s safe for you to be on your own in Bamber Bridge tonight.’

‘You think we’re at risk from the US military police?’ asked Felicity, smiling. ‘Do me a favour! You need to improve your chat-up lines, William.’

The other US servicemen had disappeared out of sight onto Station Road and the three women followed, with William accompanying them by default.

‘I’m being serious, Felicity,’ said William. ‘It might be hard to understand when seen from this side of the Atlantic, but US military units are racially segregated. As you’ll have noticed, mine is black. All the men and one of the officers, anyway. The rest of the officers are white and it’s not seen as a prize posting so we don’t get the best of them.

‘Meanwhile, the 234th US Military Police Company is an all-white unit based on the north side of Bamber Bridge. It’s fair to say the two units don’t get on. The MPs are responsible for the pressure that’s been applied to pubs in Bamber Bridge to introduce segregation. You may not have noticed, but all three pubs have responded by declaring themselves "Black Troops Only", which only applies to US troops and has gone down really badly with the MPs.

‘The MPs are pretty unhappy anyway because they believe that the local English population favour us over them and that English women prefer going out with us rather than with them. I don’t think that’s down to skin color. I think it’s that we say “please” and “thank you” more often.

‘Things have gotten worse because of race riots in Detroit earlier this week. I doubt if the full story has come out yet but, from what we’ve heard, many people were killed and injured and many more were arrested. You should also know that when the MPs drove away just now, one of the men who followed them out of the pub threw a beer glass that hit their Jeep. I don’t think the MPs will let things rest.’

Station Road was very quiet. There were a couple of civilians on foot and a bus passed by heading south, going to Leyland according to the destination blind on its front. The brick houses and shops along both sides of the road all seemed to have been closed down in preparation for darkness, even though that was still some way away. People were so used to blackout precautions by now that most complied without thinking about it.

Connie could see the second group of US servicemen ahead of them, walking along the pavement on the right-hand side of the road. Felicity seemed on edge and Connie linked arms with her, getting a grateful smile in return. William and Anne followed.

There were shouts from the men ahead as a Jeep coming in the other direction drove past them. Connie recognised the markings of the US military police and as it passed she could see four men in white helmets, who all seemed to be looking directly at her and Felicity, sitting in it. The Jeep carried on along Station Road before disappearing out of sight around the corner near the pub they’d been drinking in.

‘I told you they’d not let things rest,’ said William. ‘It looks like they’ve collected two friends.’

Connie felt Felicity pull her arm as she twisted to look behind them.

‘They’ve turned round and are coming back,’ said Felicity. ‘I don’t like this.’

The Jeep passed them again, this time on the opposite side of the road, and carried on.

Connie saw it pass the group of men walking ahead of them, to the accompaniment of more shouts. It then stopped, she guessed opposite the leading group of US servicemen walking back to their base. She saw the four MPs jump out and walk across the road. The shouting took on a greater intensity and, after a moment’s disbelief, she realised that men were fighting in the street. It looked like some of those on the pavement were picking up stones from the small gardens in front of the houses on the right-hand side of the road and throwing them at the MPs.

‘I’m sorry ladies,’ said William. ‘Unless you want to walk through the middle of that, I think you can forget about catching your train. Let me take you to the regimental base at Adam Hall. You’ll be safe there. If we take this road on the right, this side of the MacKenzie Arms, we can cut across a playing field behind the houses on Station Road.’

‘We need to get back to Fulwood Barracks,’ said Felicity.

‘In the circumstances, I’m sure we can drive you there after this is over,’ said William. ‘Our job is transporting things and your barracks is probably no more than four miles in a straight line from here. Right now the important thing is ensuring that the three of you are safe.’

Connie thought Felicity was about to argue but then two gunshots rang out somewhere ahead of them on Station Road.

‘All right,’ said Felicity.

As they moved out of sight of the fighting further along

the road, Connie heard two more shots. Afterwards, she wondered if she had been in shock after hearing the gunfire because she remembered little of walking to the US base at Adam Hall except that she had been very frightened, that William had urged them to move as quickly as possible, and that it had seemed less far than she had expected.

Once there, William introduced them to a white officer, a major who said he was the acting commanding officer of the 1511th Quartermaster Truck Regiment in the absence of the colonel. He assured the women that they'd be provided with transport back to their barracks as soon as it was safe. He asked them to wait in the colonel's office and told William to get them coffee.

William was gone for quite some time and when he returned with coffee he looked grim. 'It's bad. The MPs shot and badly injured a friend of mine. That was one of the gunshots we heard. The fighting got worse after that and we've got a few walking wounded. I'm told some of the MPs were injured too. Most of the men are back at Adam Hall but stories are circulating that the MPs are hunting for some of the others who are still in the village and intend to kill them.

'Some of the men have armed themselves and gone to look for the MPs and more shooting has been heard. Other men say they intend to defend the base in case the MPs attack in force. Our only black officer, a lieutenant, has helped the major calm things down a little but it's still very tense.' He looked at his watch. 'It's 11.15 p.m. now and it's getting dark outside. Give it until midnight and if nothing else has happened I'll ask permission to drive you to your barracks myself.'

There was a worn brown leather sofa and matching armchair in one corner of the office and Felicity and

Connie shared the sofa while Anne sat in the chair, all covered by blankets that William provided.

Connie awoke with a start with Felicity tapping her on her shoulder.

William was standing by the office door. 'Everything seems quiet and I've been given permission to take you back to your barracks. I've got the keys to a staff car. We'll be driving in the blackout of course, but it shouldn't take long to get there.'

'Thank you,' said Felicity. 'It will be a great relief to get back. I can't remember when I last said that about Fulwood Barracks!' She smiled but then her expression changed. 'I'm sorry, William, your friend was injured tonight and that must have seemed very insensitive.'

'Don't worry,' said William. 'Getting you back is the least we can do in return for your support in the pub earlier.'

The regiment's vehicles were lined up in an open area to one side of the buildings and in the dark William led the three women to a car. Then he stopped.

'Can you hear anything?' he asked.

'Vehicles,' said Anne. 'They're getting closer.'

'They're coming along Mounsey Road,' said William. 'Keep down.'

In the light of the half-moon, Connie saw four darkened vehicles come to a halt on the road where it passed the gate into the base. Three were Jeeps, each carrying several men. The fourth was a larger vehicle with men standing in the back.

Someone shouted out a challenge. 'Halt or I'll fire.'

The response came over a megaphone. 'Lay down your arms and surrender.'

'Wait! I want to talk to the senior officer present.'

‘That’s the major,’ said William, quietly.

Several lights came on around the main gate to the base and from her position crouched behind the bonnet of the car, Connie could see three men standing next to the leading Military Police Jeep, talking.

‘My God! They’ve got a Browning machine gun mounted in the back of the fourth vehicle,’ said William. ‘If anyone starts shooting, run for the door we came out of from the headquarters block. This car will give us no protection at all.’

Connie found it hard to breathe and felt a deep sense of relief when the meeting appeared to end peacefully. The rear vehicle, the one carrying the machine gun, reversed back along Mounsey Road away from the base, while the Jeeps turned around in the road.

But then there was more shooting. Connie wasn't sure who fired first, but it quickly became obvious that both sides were taking part.

‘We need to get back inside,’ said William.

Inside the headquarters building, men were rushing around without any obvious purpose. Then Connie saw one group collecting rifles and ammunition from two men who were laying them on a table in a corridor. The three women returned to the regimental colonel’s office, to the sound of sporadic gunfire from outside.

William came in with more coffee a short time later. ‘The MPs have pulled back and a lot of the men have armed themselves and gone after them. Others have set up a defensive perimeter around the base. I think the MPs’ withdrawal is a trap designed to lure us out but no one is inclined to take any notice.’

‘We’re not going to get back to Fulwood Barracks any time soon, are we?’ asked Anne.

‘No, we’re not,’ said Felicity, ‘but that may be the least of tonight’s problems. William, do you know if the phone on the colonel’s desk is connected to a public switchboard?’

‘We have a telephone switchboard on the base which ought to be manned but might not be given the circumstances. The colonel may also have an outside line. I don’t know. Who do you want to call?’

‘The most senior officer I can find on duty tonight at Fulwood Barracks. The outside world must know by now that something dreadful is happening here but I’ll wager no one has the slightest idea what it is.’

CHAPTER TWO

Monique looked at her watch as the car was allowed through the main gate of RAF Northolt. It was 12.30 a.m. and now the adrenaline had left her she felt exhausted. She glanced across at where Bob was sitting, on the other side of the rear seat of the car.

He must have seen her movement, even in the darkness of the blackout. 'Not long now and we'll be home in Edinburgh,' he said.

Monique could hear in his voice that he was smiling and smiled back. 'You said something very like that when we landed here with Maurice earlier. It didn't work out quite that way, did it?'

*

The truth was that their plans had already been knocked well off course by the time their Avro Anson had landed at Northolt some hours before. The intention had been to spend part of a second day with Amanda Ewing at her home on the coast south-east of Plymouth, have an early dinner with her there and then drive with Maurice Cunningham to RAF Roborough, where Bob had arranged for an aircraft to fly them first to RAF Northolt near London to drop off Maurice and then to RAF Turnhouse near Edinburgh. They should have been home hours ago with, Bob had promised her, a three-day weekend ahead of them to catch some breath before telling anyone they were back on Monday.

Only there had been a mix-up and there was no aircraft waiting for them. Bob became quite angry, clearly feeling that a failure on the part of the RAF reflected badly on him in front of his boss, Commodore Maurice Cunningham. When an Avro Anson did eventually arrive from another airfield to pick them up it was trailing black smoke from one wing and was immediately grounded pending an engine change.

To Monique's relief, in the face of profuse apologies from RAF Roborough's station commander, Bob did finally see the funny side of the situation.

He was less amused later when, on arrival at RAF Northolt, the pilot taxied the aircraft to a parking spot close to the control tower and shut down the engines.

Bob clambered to the front of the passenger compartment, where he could speak to the pilot. 'The plan was to keep the engines going while we dropped off the commodore and then head directly to Turnhouse,' he said.

'I know, sir,' said the pilot. 'But I've been instructed to park here.'

Monique could see that Bob was prepared to argue the point.

'Hang on, Bob,' said the commodore. 'Look over towards the control tower.'

Monique looked and saw a figure standing on the concrete, watching them. It took a moment for her to recognise him as Major General Sir Peter Maitland, the Director of Military Intelligence, looking stern and wearing his full dress uniform.

'Bloody hell! That's all we need!' said Bob.

'My thought exactly,' said Maurice. 'Though as a navy man, I might have put it more strongly. Let's go and face the music. I want both of you to back me up when I tell Sir Peter that this whole thing was my idea. That's the truth, after all, and I don't want either of you throwing away your promising careers through any sense of misplaced loyalty to me.'

Monique caught Bob's eye as they made their way to the aircraft door, which had been opened from the outside. She found it difficult to interpret the look on his face.

The three walked over to where Sir Peter was standing and both Maurice and Bob saluted.

'I would imagine you are all surprised to see me here,' said Sir Peter. 'I've arranged a room in the control tower where I can explain my presence. Would you follow me, please?'

The room Sir Peter led them to was large enough for a wooden meeting table with eight matching chairs around it. It was oblong and an end wall had the room's only window, criss-crossed in sticky tape to minimise blast damage in an air raid. Most of the two longer walls were covered in maps of southern Britain.

'Let's not stand on ceremony,' said Sir Peter. 'Can you all sit down? Thank you.'

'Can I say something, Sir Peter?' asked the commodore.

'I think it might be better if I start, Maurice. I do have a very particular reason for driving out here to meet the three of you, which I will come to in a moment. But first, I would be grateful if you could indulge a little idle curiosity on my part.

'Thank you for the invitation to your wedding, Monique and Bob, and I should apologise again for not being there. I did think of you both on the day and wished you well. I'm sure you can imagine my surprise when, less than a week after your wedding in Edinburgh and only a few days after you left for your honeymoon in the Highlands, I read a report that the German intelligence service, the Abwehr, had identified the two of you arriving in Gibraltar while en route to Malta.'

'I can explain, sir,' said the commodore.

'I'm sure you can, Maurice. Am I right in thinking that you have a nephew serving in Malta?'

'Until recently, yes. He's missing, presumed dead.'

'I'm very sorry to hear that, Maurice. Is that why the three of you have been visiting your sister Amanda Ewing, the young man's mother, in Devon?'

'Yes, it is,' said the commodore. 'You need to know, Sir Peter, that the entire venture was my idea and Bob and Monique only became involved through loyalty to me. The fault is entirely mine and you will have my resignation as head of Military Intelligence, Section 11, on your desk first thing in the morning.'

'Thank you for the offer, Maurice. Your resignation is rejected, so save yourself the trouble of writing it. I believe it was Napoleon Bonaparte who said something like, "I'd rather have lucky generals than good ones". I don't agree that one should have to choose between those characteristics, but I do share his view of the value of good luck.

'Maurice, what you did in sending Bob and Monique off on a personal quest to Malta was ill-considered, unfair to them and disloyal to me. But we all know how that quest ended. On Tuesday, I was asked to go to Downing Street to discuss what happened with the prime minister. He congratulated me on the progress I had made in coordinating the activities of the various sections of my Directorate of Military Intelligence and was especially fulsome in his praise of the way a joint operation between MI5, MI6 and MI11 achieved such a happy result in Malta.

'I refrained from telling the prime minister that MI11 should never have been in Malta at all. I also failed to mention that the result he was so pleased about was down to sheer good luck, combined with some excellent work on the ground by the two of you, Bob and Monique.

'Against the background of my meeting with Winston, I obviously cannot accept your resignation, Maurice. I must admit that pleases me because I would hate to lose you. I will say this, though. Please don't ever underestimate me or try to pull the wool over my eyes again. I won't be so forgiving a second time. And, with that out of the way, I would like to congratulate all three of you on what MI11 achieved in Malta.'

'Thank you, sir,' said the commodore. 'And I am truly sorry.'

'Apology accepted,' said Sir Peter. 'Now let me change the subject. There's something else I urgently need to talk to the three of you about. We all know that thanks to our ability to intercept Abwehr communications we have made it virtually impossible for them to run agents inside the UK without our knowing in advance that they are coming and dealing with them when they arrive.'

'Bob and Monique are both cleared to know about Ultra, sir,' said Maurice Cunningham.

'I'm fully aware of that, Maurice,' said Sir Peter, 'or we'd not be having this conversation. Learning about your jaunt to Malta hasn't been my only recent surprise. I was contacted this morning by the head of the NKVD office in the Soviet embassy in London, a gentleman called Yevgeny Popov. He said he had something urgent to tell me and asked to meet me in Kensington Gardens. This sounded like something written by John Buchan but, having discussed it with colleagues and taken steps to ensure I would not be compromised or in danger, I met with Mr Popov.

‘He, of course, is not cleared to know about Ultra. But, as you are all aware, the Soviets have a good idea of what we’re doing even if, thanks to you, Monique, they’ve never been able to get their hands on the fine detail. At our meeting, he told me that the NKVD had uncovered evidence of a German agent we appear not to know about. They believe that this agent, a man they call the Karakatitsa, has already visited Scotland and, though he isn’t there now, intends to return.’

‘Why do they call him the Cuttlefish?’ asked Monique.

‘Because it changes colour to conceal itself,’ said Sir Peter. ‘Apparently, this agent is a master of disguise. Mr Popov is a fan of Conan Doyle and said that the Cuttlefish’s ability to assume disguises and characters would put Sherlock Holmes to shame. I understand that he is operating from a base in Dublin and ensures his security by completely isolating himself from his handlers while he is in the field and never relying on radio communications, even when in Dublin. He only makes reports on paper via secure diplomatic channels. If that is true, then it might help explain why MI5 knows nothing about him.’

‘On the other hand, he might be a Soviet invention for some reason we’ve yet to discover,’ said Commodore Cunningham.

‘That’s true, Maurice, but we have to take what they say seriously until we are sure, one way or the other.’

‘If what the Soviets are saying is correct, how can we hope to catch him?’ asked Bob. ‘Some bloke with a German accent and hairy legs dressed as a nun and acting suspiciously might be spotted by the people he’s interacting with, but we’re never going to find him unless he makes a mistake that gets him noticed.’

‘That’s where it gets interesting,’ said Sir Peter. ‘It

seems that a lady called Katerina Komarova, who is nominally a first secretary in the Soviet embassy in Dublin, actually earns her keep as a senior member of the NKVD office there. Miss Komarova had previously worked for the NKVD in Madrid. Mr Popov told me that while she was there, she had encountered a Sicherheitsdienst or SD agent she unsuccessfully tried to recruit to work for the Soviets. Popov wasn't specific but I got the impression there was a real or feigned romantic entanglement involved.

'Anyway, on Monday she saw the same man across a street in Dublin without, she believes, him seeing her in return. She spent the next two days doing some discreet background digging and then flew to London yesterday evening to talk to Popov. That was what prompted him to contact me this morning.'

'What did her digging unearth?' asked Monique.

'The Cuttlefish's preference for acting independently and his avoidance of the use of a radio in the field may have prevented MI5 from becoming aware of him, but it also means he needs to travel back to Dublin to make written reports. Miss Komarova's source, presumably within the German embassy in Dublin, appears well-informed. They told her that he had landed from a U-boat in the west of Ireland at the beginning of the month and that he spent last week in Scotland before returning to Dublin.'

'Which is why Katerina Komarova was able to spot him on a Dublin street on Monday,' said Monique.

'Indeed,' said Sir Peter. 'Miss Komarova's source also told her that the Cuttlefish is planning to return to Scotland, for a longer period this time, probably at the end of next week.'

'The implication of what you are saying, sir, and the fact you're discussing it with us, is that you want to catch this spy through a joint operation between MI11 and the NKVD,' said Monique. 'The hope is that if Katerina Komarova has shared a bed with the Cuttlefish, she will recognise him, whatever disguise he's using.'

'Yes, that's right,' said Sir Peter.

Bob and Maurice both started to speak at the same time.

'Hang on, both of you,' said Sir Peter. 'I, too, have wondered if this is an elaborate device to expose Monique to revenge by the NKVD for the death of Helena Berdyaev.'

'It's not just her, is it, Sir Peter?' asked Monique. 'Yes, Captain Darlington and I killed Helena Berdyaev in April. But I also shot and seriously wounded Sergei Avdonin in Leith last October. Remember, too, that Lieutenant Commander Dixon shot and killed Maxim Kozlov on a London street when he tried to kill Bob and me with a submachine gun. And that's before you consider our successes in stopping the NKVD's operations at X Base in Gruinard Bay and at Bletchley Park, which must have hurt them badly. This may not be about revenge against me, it might be an operation aimed at MI11 as a whole.'

'Yes, Monique, I do understand the risks,' said Sir Peter. 'It gets even more complex because Mr Popov is insisting that a second agent is involved to watch Katerina Komarova's back, presumably because he doesn't trust us either. The name he mentioned was Major Nikolay Malinovsky.'

'The Soviet Air Force officer we encountered at RAF Errol?' asked Bob. 'The man the stolen anthrax spores were meant to go to?'

'That's the one,' said Sir Peter. 'You were sure he was with the NKVD at the time and this simply confirms that he is.'

‘This all seems highly suspect,’ said Maurice Cunningham.

‘I agree,’ said Sir Peter. ‘And you’ve not heard the best part yet.’

‘What’s that?’ asked Monique.

‘The plan is that I make a telephone call after we’ve had this discussion and then we go together to the Soviet embassy in Kensington Palace Gardens so we can meet Mr Popov, Miss Komarova and Major Malinovsky.’

Monique saw Bob catch her eye again. This time she knew exactly what he was thinking.

‘That means we’ll effectively be on Soviet territory,’ said Bob. ‘Isn’t that asking for trouble?’

‘It is,’ said Sir Peter. ‘But the Soviets know that if they try anything untoward, especially in the presence of Maurice and I, they’d be calling into question the very basis of the alliance between the United Kingdom and the Soviet Union.’

Monique smiled at Bob and shrugged.

‘Just so long as you know that if they do try “anything untoward” I’m going to start shooting,’ said Bob.

‘I’d expect nothing less of you,’ said Sir Peter. ‘I’m also armed and I’m sure Maurice is too.’

Monique saw Sir Peter look at Maurice Cunningham, who nodded.

CHAPTER THREE

Bob thought they must have looked an odd bunch as they stood in the reception area of the Soviet embassy in Kensington Palace Gardens. An army officer, a navy officer and an air force officer, like something out of the start of a joke, plus Monique.

Sir Peter Maitland wore his major general's uniform with the ease of a man who knew he truly belonged amongst the most powerful in the land. Bob and he had got off to a poor start when Sir Peter had tried to force Bob to take the job of deputy head of Military Intelligence, Section 11, when all that had been needed was something a little nearer to 'please'. They had since got on rather better.

Commodore Maurice Cunningham was Bob's immediate boss. Aged in his late forties, he had black hair and a black beard that was just starting to go grey at the sides. His impeccably pressed naval uniform, which always made Bob feel a little shabby in comparison, was up to his usual standards despite the disrupted travel arrangements and delays.

And then there was Monique. She was wearing a plain dark grey jacket and matching skirt over a white blouse. The way her handbag hung confirmed that she was also armed. Bob assumed this hadn't been mentioned at Northolt because everyone present knew she would be.

Bob caught her eye and winked, raising a smile. As always, he was struck by her remarkable presence, even here in a place that had such obvious dangers. Monique spent much of her life trying unsuccessfully to blend into the background. The truth was that she'd have stood out in a crowd wherever she was and whatever she was wearing.

Monique's dark hair framed a face that was classically beautiful, but oddly flawed in a way that he found intensely attractive. Her eyes were a similar shade of brown to his own but too often he'd seen them take on a dark, haunted look, as if they'd seen things their owner wished they hadn't. She was 30, some seven months younger than him. She'd packed a lot of living into that time and Bob knew she carried more than her fair share of ghosts with her. Despite the weirdness of the situation and the danger of the surroundings, he felt a surge of pure joy at the realisation that he was now married to her.

A man in a suit came through a side door and asked them to follow him to a lift. They emerged from it into a fine wood-panelled corridor complete with framed pictures of Stalin, Lenin and other, Bob assumed, Soviet heroes, plus Soviet flags and small statues of soldiers and factory workers placed on wooden tables.

The room they were led into was large and by any standards opulent. It had chairs arranged around the walls, which were covered in more wood panelling and decorated with more paintings that Bob felt might be better appreciated by someone who understood Soviet history and iconography. There were three large windows, or at least three large areas of heavy curtain that Bob assumed covered windows.

Looking rather lost in the middle of this large room was a highly polished and very fine wooden meeting table. Bob realised that the table had four chairs on either side and two at each end, so couldn't be called small. It simply seemed out of place in such a large room, surrounded by acres of what looked like very expensive carpet on every side.

Three people were sitting on the far side of the table when Sir Peter and his party entered, and all stood up.

The man who came round the table to greet them looked very familiar to Bob. He was wearing a dark suit with a waistcoat and had a largely bald head with a dark moustache and goatee beard. Especially striking were his piercing dark eyes. Sir Peter introduced him as Yevgeny Popov and as Bob shook his hand he realised why Popov looked so familiar. He was the spitting image of Vladimir Lenin, the man depicted in at least one painting in the corridor outside and another in the meeting room.

He smiled when he saw Bob's surprise. 'When Sir Peter and I met yesterday he was polite enough not to ask if a resemblance to Comrade Lenin has been a help or a hindrance in pursuing a career in the NKVD. I can only say it's not been a problem so far.' His English had only the slightest trace of an accent.

Sir Peter sat down and Maurice Cunningham sat beyond him. Bob sat to the left of Sir Peter with Monique on his left. Sir Peter introduced them, using Monique's MI11 working name of Monique Dubois rather than the name she used in MI5 in London or her married name.

Popov sat down opposite Sir Peter and introduced his colleagues. The chair on his right, opposite Bob, was occupied by Major Nikolay Malinovsky. He looked much the same as he had when Bob briefly met him at RAF Errol the previous November and he wore the same full Soviet Air Force uniform, complete with riding breeches and boots. He was of about average height and in his thirties. He was unremarkable apart from eyes that had an unsettling sense of hardness. Monique had spent a little more time with him at Errol and formed an intense dislike of someone who seemed wholly intent on undressing her with his eyes.

Sitting next to Malinovsky, opposite Monique, was

Katerina Komarova. Bob had been unsure what to expect, perhaps someone a little like Monique. In the event, it seemed to be his day for finding lookalikes because in his mind Katerina Komarova had a strong resemblance to Marlene Dietrich. He wasn't sure how old Marlene Dietrich was, but then he couldn't be sure about Katerina Komarova's age either. If pushed, he'd have said she was in her thirties, possibly her early thirties, but he could be well out. She wore a blue dress with a black leather belt around the middle and no obvious jewellery.

Bob noticed that no refreshments had been offered. Perhaps this was because their Soviet hosts realised how awkward it might become if the guests all refused to eat or drink anything to avoid running the risk of being poisoned. That was a precaution the British contingent had agreed on before leaving Northolt.

'Thank you all for coming,' said Popov. 'I should start by clearing the air. We all know that relations between the NKVD office in the embassy here and British military intelligence, and by that I mean your Section 11 in particular, have been less than ideal. That's a diplomatic euphemism for catastrophically bad. I am deeply unhappy that one of my officers tried to kill two of you in a London street, and I am also very sad that two of my officers have been killed and another man badly injured by agents of MI11.'

He paused, as if to give Sir Peter Maitland space to express reciprocal regrets. Bob was grateful that Sir Peter said nothing.

As the pause started to feel awkward, Popov continued. 'That is all now water under the bridge, as you say. I hope that your side can put our past misunderstandings behind us just as we are trying to do.' He paused again.

This time Sir Peter did respond. 'Our nations are allies and you can take it from me that my officers will act in a way that gives effect to the spirit of that alliance.'

Sir Peter was treading warily and Bob realised he wasn't the only one who'd noticed when Katerina Komarova said something in Russian under her breath to Major Malinovsky.

Popov banged a fist down on the table hard enough to cause Bob to jump.

'That's enough! We need some rules. On my side, I insist that all conversation is in English unless only Russian speakers are present. There will be no use of Russian to exclude anyone from any conversation. There is little point trying anyway as I believe Madame Dubois is a fluent Russian speaker.'

'Thank you, Yevgeny,' said Sir Peter. 'My knowledge of the language is nothing like as good as Monique's but I have to acknowledge that perhaps I was being a little pompous just now, as Miss Komarova pointed out. Let me be more straightforward. My officers will behave professionally towards yours if yours do the same towards mine. The recent history between us is, as you say, far from ideal and I am sure you feel as wary about working with us as we do about working with you. But I would like to think we can put that behind us and my colleagues are aware that I expect nothing less from them. You can take our coming here tonight as a token of our willingness to work with you in our mutual interests.'

'Thank you, too, Sir Peter,' said Popov. 'I did not know you spoke Russian. Perhaps we should move on to the real business of the evening. I've asked Miss Komarova to brief us on what we know about the man we refer to as the Karakatitsa, or the Cuttlefish if you prefer.'

Katerina Komarova's English was very good, though not quite as good as Yevgeny Popov's. Bob listened while she gave a slightly fuller version of the story that Sir Peter had told them earlier. He noticed that she slid quite smoothly over the details of her relationship with the Sicherheitsdienst agent she had met in Madrid and he had the impression she was holding things back in her account of seeing the man again in Dublin.

When she finished, Bob spoke first. 'What I'm unclear about is how we start looking for a man who is a master of disguise, who doesn't use any form of communication that might compromise him while in the field, and whose only obvious weakness is that he is well-known to you, Miss Komarova. Simply wandering around Scotland with you in the hope you see a familiar face isn't going to achieve very much.'

Komarova smiled. 'We do have one advantage. I have been told that on his first visit to Scotland, he established a forward base close enough to the town of Stranraer, where the steamers from Northern Ireland land, to allow him a chance to escape if he is compromised when he returns. That means we can narrow our search for him considerably.'

'What can you tell us about the Cuttlefish?' asked Monique. 'How good is his English, for example? Has he got a noticeable accent that might help give him away?'

Bob saw Katerina Komarova smile again.

'Not in the way you might hope,' she said. 'He has an Irish accent. We know nothing for certain, but when I met him in Madrid he told me that his father was German and his mother Irish and that he'd grown up near Dublin before studying at a university in Germany. The name I knew him by was "Edward Daly" but I strongly suspect that's an alias. He is still using the same name. Beyond that, I can tell you he is of average height and build, has black hair and brown eyes, and is around 35 years old. He has a scar about 10cm long across the top of his right thigh that he says he acquired in a sabre fight. That's not going to help identify him when he's clothed, of course.'

Bob could see from the expressions on the faces of the men on the opposite side of the table that he wasn't the only one to think that Edward Daly was very lucky not to have a more serious reason to remember his encounter with a sabre.

Sir Peter Maitland snorted. 'He's using the name of the man who commanded the Irish Volunteers in Dublin during the 1916 Easter Rising and was one of those we executed in its immediate aftermath. Does that mean there's some sort of Irish dimension to whatever the Cuttlefish is doing in Scotland?'

'We don't know,' said Popov. 'But if he is presenting himself as Irish rather than German it might mean he can find fellow-countrymen prepared to help him amongst the many engaged in war work in Scotland.'

'Do you have a photograph of this man?' asked Sir Peter.

'I'm afraid not,' said Popov.

'If he's so secretive, what's your source for your information about the Cuttlefish's plans?' asked Monique.

It was Katerina Komarova who replied. 'The Abwehr, the German intelligence service, has a well-staffed unit attached to the German embassy in Dublin. The SD or Sicherheitsdienst, on the other hand, has a very small office a little distance away. You are probably aware of the animosity between the Sicherheitsdienst and the Abwehr. The Sicherheitsdienst, whose full name is the

"Sicherheitsdienst des Reichsführers-SS" or the Security Service of the Reichsführer-SS, can be thought of as the intelligence agency of the SS and the Nazi Party and they are in a serious power struggle with the Abwehr. Despite this, some information appears to pass between the two agencies' offices in Dublin.'

'And someone in the Abwehr office is working for you?' asked Monique.

'I'm sure you'd not answer that question if I asked it of you in similar circumstances, Madame Dubois.'

'Let's consider how we should proceed,' said Sir Peter. 'I agree we should narrow our geographical focus as you suggest. MI11 will travel to the area early next week to look for evidence of what the Cuttlefish was doing during his first visit and in particular try to find the base you say he has established. I suggest that Miss Komarova and Major Malinovsky join them there. Commodore Cunningham will take the lead on my side and liaise directly with you, Yevgeny. I will ensure that security is stepped up on both sides of the North Channel. The steamer connection between Larne and Stranraer is an obvious means of travel from Ireland to Scotland, but it's not the only one. If he poses as an Irish republican, then I can see ways the Cuttlefish might make the crossing courtesy of a sympathetic fisherman, for example.'

'That all seems reasonable,' said Popov. 'For our part, Miss Komarova will return to Dublin before she and the major join MI11 in Scotland to see whether we can find out anything else that might help catch the Cuttlefish.'

After a little more discussion about practicalities, the meeting ended cordially.

Bob breathed a deep sigh of relief as they walked out of the Soviet embassy and got into Sir Peter's car for the drive to his office in Whitehall.

When they arrived, Sir Peter broke out his best coffee for the occasion and Bob realised how nervous even he had been at the Soviet embassy.

There was a moment's silence after they sat down around Sir Peter's meeting table, which he broke. 'Thank you for not revealing the depth of our knowledge about the animosity between the Abwehr and the SD. Part of me was wondering what our Soviet friends' reaction would have been, Bob, if you'd dropped into the conversation that you'd been discussing that very thing with Admiral Canaris in Stockholm only recently. On the whole, I think it's better if we tell our new colleagues as little as possible while working with them. Remember that we still have very little idea about their true agenda.

'With that in mind, I will ask MI5 and MI6 to see what they can discover about the man who calls himself Mr Edward Daly. If we can work out whether he is a real person or a Soviet invention, it will give a lot more certainty to our dealings with our allies. If he is real, it might help immeasurably to know about his background and associates. A photograph might come in handy, too.'

After further discussion of what had happened at the Soviet embassy and the next steps, Sir Peter's driver took Bob and Monique back to Northolt.

They didn't say much in the car on the way, though Bob did ask what exactly Katerina Komarova had said under her breath at the meeting.

'She called Sir Peter a pompous old fool,' said Monique. 'Did you know he could speak Russian? It was a surprise to me.'

'It was a surprise to Yevgeny Popov, too,' said Bob.

'I can tell you one thing,' said Monique. 'There's a lot

that Katerina Komarova didn't say at the meeting about her relationship with the Cuttlefish. Yes, her knowing about his scar confirms their relationship was intimate but I wonder how much of the real detail even Popov knows. I'd like to find out more because I think that may be the key to tracking this man down.'

'Are you suggesting she might obstruct the search?' asked Bob.

'No, that would be inconsistent with her being the one to alert us to his presence in Dublin in the first place. But if she is hiding anything, perhaps because she thinks it's embarrassing or a danger to her career or not relevant, then we need to know. Changing the subject, doesn't she look like Marlene Dietrich?'

'I'm glad I'm not the only one to have seen the likeness,' said Bob. 'We can't be far from RAF Northolt now. Maurice said he'd telephone ahead so the pilot ought to be ready to go as soon as we get there.'

CHAPTER FOUR

Bob had never been a great fan of Robert Burns, perhaps because one of his teachers at George Heriot's School in Edinburgh had admired Scotland's National Bard a little too much. Having to read out loud, in unison, a different poem expressed in barely accessible language each morning was hardly likely to engender enthusiasm amongst a class of twelve or thirteen-year-old boys though that, presumably, had been the teacher's intention.

Nonetheless, some of it had stuck. After the Avro Anson took off from RAF Northolt the pilot turned to pick up their northerly heading and Bob saw the airfield lights go out to comply with the blackout regulations. It was a clear night and, in the light of the half-moon, Bob could pick out some features on the ground despite the absence of artificial lights.

He quickly gave up trying to work out where they were and sat back in his seat, reaching across the aircraft to take Monique's hand and closing his eyes. Completely unbidden, a quote from one of Burns' poems came into his head: '*The best laid schemes o' Mice an' Men gang aft agley'*. It had been a very strange day and since they'd left Amanda Ewing's house almost nothing had gone to plan. He knew how Burns, and the mouse the poem was about, must have felt.

Monique woke him by touching his arm. He leaned over towards where he knew she was in the darkened aircraft cabin.

'We've turned and are descending,' she said over the sound of the aircraft engines. 'We've made good time.'

Bob looked at his watch. They'd taken off from RAF

Northolt shortly after 1 a.m. It was now coming up to 2.30 a.m. and he couldn't think of any way that the Avro Anson could have covered the distance to RAF Turnhouse in that time.

'Hang on, Monique.' Bob got up and made his way to the front of the passenger cabin where it gave access to the aircraft cockpit. He reached across to tap the pilot, sitting in the left-hand seat, on the shoulder.

The pilot looked around and shifted his leather flying helmet so his ear nearest Bob was uncovered. 'I'm sorry, sir. There's been another change of plan.'

'What's happening?' asked Bob.

'We were over Bradford when I was ordered to turn west. We're due to land at Samlesbury Aerodrome in a few minutes. Would you mind going back to your seat?'

'Do you know whose idea this is?' asked Bob.

'I was told you'd ask, sir. You'll be met when we land and should then contact Sir Peter Maitland, who will explain everything. They've switched on the airfield lights so we're quite close. You need to return to your seat, sir.'

Bob complied.

Monique leaned across. 'I can't wait to get into our own bed,' she said.

'I'm sorry, my love, but you may have to. We're about to land in Lancashire and I've no idea why.'

As Bob felt the aircraft touch down the Robert Burns quote came to mind again.

*

Bob sat for a moment to collect his thoughts before following Monique out of the Anson. The door was held open by a police sergeant and as Bob exited the aircraft the man saluted. Bob returned the salute. In the muted lights that illuminated the aircraft parking area, he could see Monique standing next to a police car a short distance away and talking to a man in a dark suit.

'Hello, Bob. This is Inspector James Carmichael who tells me he is with Lancashire Constabulary's Special Branch. Inspector, this is Group Captain Robert Sutherland, deputy head of Military Intelligence, Section 11.'

The inspector was a tall man with dark hair. 'I'm pleased to meet you, sir.'

Bob shook his hand. 'I'm told I need to contact Sir Peter Maitland, presumably at his office in Whitehall. Is there a secure phone I can use?'

'Yes, sir, there's one in the operations office in the control tower. This isn't an RAF airfield, it's owned by English Electric, who manufacture Handley Page bombers here, but they can still offer a secure line.'

'Can you give me a clue what this is about?' asked Bob.

'Sorry, sir, I've been told to get you to a phone as soon as you land.'

The operations room turned out to be an office with radio equipment on a table built onto one long wall.

The inspector stayed outside in a corridor and Monique closed the door and came over to stand close beside Bob as the call was connected.

There was a grunt on the other end of the line after the phone was picked up.

'Hello, is that Sir Peter?'

'Yes, sorry Bob, I'd dozed off waiting for your call. Maurice Cunningham is with me and has suggested I ask you about your honeymoon.'

Bob had no idea what Sir Peter wanted to know and Monique reached out to turn the handset slightly in his hand so she could also be heard.

'Hello, Sir Peter, it's Monique. Tell Maurice it's a shame that we drank the hotel dry of champagne before he arrived.'

'Thank you. Maurice has nodded to assure me that you are indeed you. I assume you can both hear me? That's good. I'm sorry to break into your journey home a second time but something extremely worrying has occurred and I need the two of you to act as the eyes and ears of British military intelligence on the ground.'

'Why us, sir?' asked Bob.

'You're in the right place at the right time,' said Sir Peter. 'Though you may think of it as the wrong place at the wrong time. Hear me out and I'll tell you what I need you to do. You are at Samlesbury in Lancashire. About five miles south-west of you is a village called Bamber Bridge. It's also a couple of miles south-east of Preston, which you are more likely to have heard of.

'A few hours ago an incident in a pub at closing time escalated very seriously and, as a result, two United States military units are currently engaged in what amounts to a shooting war with one another in a British village and with British villagers caught in the crossfire.

'One of the units is a transport regiment whose men are all black, though most of their officers are white. The other is a military police company whose men are all white. There appear to be clear racial overtones to the conflict which comes at an especially difficult time in the wake of serious race riots in the USA. I would imagine the two of you have been too busy travelling to read about them. The US military authorities tell us that this is a case of mutiny by a small number of disaffected troops and that the fault lies entirely with the men of the transport regiment.

'We have access to an independent source of information which suggests that the truth is rather more complex and there is fault on both sides. The US authorities are trying to get a grip on the situation and, in case they fail, we are taking steps to ensure it is at least geographically contained for the moment.

'My concern, however, is that there are racially segregated units of the US armed forces stationed pretty much anywhere you care to look in the UK. If what is happening in Bamber Bridge were to spread more widely we'd end up with something a little like a re-run of the American Civil War here in Britain with all that might imply for the Allies' capacity to pursue the war against Hitler.

'The British response is being coordinated from Fulwood Barracks in Preston. I want the two of you, acting as my representatives, to go there to be briefed on the latest developments and then, if possible without exposing yourselves to an unacceptable level of risk, find out what's happening on the ground.

'I need you to telephone me by 6.30 a.m. with a preliminary assessment because I will need to contact Downing Street by 7 a.m. at the latest so they can brief the prime minister when he wakes up.'

'Yes, of course, sir,' said Bob, still not quite believing what he was hearing. 'We'll go to the barracks immediately.'

'Thank you,' said Sir Peter. 'And take care. You've both dodged German and Soviet bullets before. Remember that a bullet made in the USA could be just as fatal if you get in its way.'

*

Monique sat with Bob in the back of the police car while the inspector sat in the front and the sergeant drove. They went far faster than Monique felt was safe in the blackout, even with the police bell sounding out to warn of their approach.

After passing through a security gate they drove into Fulwood Barracks through an arch in a two-storey stone building. Beyond, in the glare of floodlights, Monique had an impression of a large open rectangular area surrounded by ranges of buildings. There were a couple of other vehicles in view but the place felt oddly quiet, even at this time of the morning.

'Someone's decided to disregard the blackout tonight,' said Bob.

'I think it was so the army could get everyone mobilised earlier, sir,' said the inspector. 'When we left to meet you this place was full of lorries loading up with men. We're going to the headquarters building.'

'Who are we meeting?' asked Bob.

'The commanding officer of the barracks is Brigadier Lockwood. He's also the man running things from here.'

Monique, Bob and the inspector were taken to an upper-floor meeting room that looked like it doubled as a regimental dining room on other occasions. Glass cases around the room displayed beautifully lit collections of silverware and there were large oil paintings of battle scenes on the walls. Even though it was June, there was a vigorous fire blazing in a marble fireplace at one end. A large table in the centre of the room was covered in unfolded maps and several men and two women were gathered around it.

A heavily built man in a brigadier's uniform was standing on the far side of the table and looked up as they entered. ‘Hello. I take it you are Group Captain Sutherland?’

‘Yes, sir. And this is Monique Dubois, who also works in Military Intelligence, Section 11.’

‘I’m pleased to meet you, though I would have preferred it to be in less trying circumstances. I’ll not introduce everyone here, but you do need to know that this is Senior Commander Berresford, the officer in charge of the ATS contingent in the headquarters of the No. 4 Anti-Aircraft Group. I’ll explain the significance of that in a moment.’

He gestured towards a blonde woman in an army major’s uniform who was standing next to him. She looked up at Bob and Monique and smiled.

The brigadier stubbed out a cigarette in an ashtray. ‘I understand, group captain, that you are here at the behest of Major General Sir Peter Maitland, the Director of Military Intelligence, who outranks all of us. What can I do for you?’

‘I’ve been asked to find out what’s happened and what’s still happening, sir. Sir Peter has asked me to report to him by 6.30 a.m. so he in turn can brief Downing Street. He is aware of racial overtones to the trouble in Bamber Bridge and hopes to find out if this is an isolated incident or whether US units elsewhere in the country are about to start shooting at one another.’

The brigadier looked at his watch. ‘That gives you perhaps three and a half hours before you need to return here to call the major general. Let’s not waste any time. I take it you have some idea of what’s going on?’

‘A mainly black US transport unit fell out with a completely white US military police unit and it’s escalated to the point they are shooting at each other,’ said Bob. ‘The US military authorities are telling us that there’s been a mutiny by black troops but we know it's more complex than that.'

'That will do for a start,' said the brigadier. 'While Sir Peter Maitland is concerned about the spread of armed conflict between US units to other parts of the country, I've been more concerned to contain the fighting that's still going on, now rather sporadically, within Bamber Bridge itself. The reason why Fulwood Barracks might have seemed a little empty when you arrived is that I've got everyone I can maintaining a cordon around the village.

'It's bad enough that we've got US troops shooting each other. It would be far worse to have US and British troops in armed conflict. My soldiers are under strict instruction not to fire on anyone unless by doing so they save someone's life. Instead, we are simply holding position and whenever anyone from either US unit bumps into our cordon we are as gently as possible disarming them and taking them into protective custody. This has not gone down well with the US military police, who see themselves as wholly in the right but, to my mind, every armed US serviceman we remove from the streets of Bamber Bridge is a step in the right direction.

'More casualties may emerge when it starts to get light at around 5 a.m. but, as far as we are aware, there has so far been one death and a number of men wounded, with all the casualties being US servicemen. Given the scale of the conflict, this figure is miraculously low and, in a second miracle, we are unaware of any British casualties. The gunfire on the streets has lessened considerably in intensity over the last hour or so. If you feel up to it, you might want to talk to the officers of the 1511th Quartermaster Truck Regiment at their base at Adam Hall, which is here on the map, and those of the 234th US Military Police Company, who are currently operating out of Bamber Bridge police station, which is here, north of the railway station. The British civilian police might also be able to offer useful insights.'

'You also need to talk to my ladies,' said Senior Commander Berresford.

'I'm sorry, Joan,' said the brigadier. 'I should have mentioned them myself. Can you explain?'

'Of course, brigadier. This all erupted because of an incident in a pub called Ye Olde Hob Inn, which is here on the map.' She leaned over the table to point.

'It escalated while the black troops were walking back to their camp, which as the brigadier said is here. Three junior non-commissioned officers of the ATS were drinking in the pub and afterwards set out to walk to Bamber Bridge railway station, which is here. Their way was blocked by a fight in the street, and then the shooting started. They sought refuge at Adam Hall and have been there ever since. We only began to realise the scale of what was happening in Bamber Bridge when one of them rang me here at the barracks at about 12.20 a.m. The story they tell is rather different from the one we've been told by the US military authorities and while their version may reflect their particular experience of what happened, you do need to talk to them.'

'The only question is how you get to Adam Hall and Bamber Bridge police station when there is still shooting on the streets,' said the brigadier. 'I have a Daimler Armoured Car I could lend you, with a driver, but the ATS bombardier who's been speaking to us from Adam Hall says that it was when the MPs turned up there with a machine gun mounted on a truck that the fighting intensified. An armoured car might do more harm than good.'

'Perhaps there's a better way,' said Monique. 'We came here in a police car with its bell ringing. That's about as uniquely British as you can get. Let's simply drive to Adam Hall in the same car with the bell still ringing. If Senior Commander Berresford can contact the ATS bombardier in the meantime, she can warn the men at Adam Hall we are coming and reduce the scope for misunderstandings when we arrive.'

Monique turned to look at Inspector Carmichael. 'Can we borrow your car, inspector?'

'There's no need, ma'am. I'd be very pleased to go with you, and I'm certain that Sergeant Mathers will be more than happy to drive. He knows the area and won't get lost.'

'Are you sure?' asked Bob.

'If the two of you are prepared to risk it then so am I, sir.'

Monique wondered if the sergeant's driving might be more of a danger to them than the armed Americans, but just smiled. 'Thank you. Let's go.'

*

Bob was put through to Sir Peter Maitland at 6.20 a.m. after a high-speed drive in the police car from Bamber Bridge to Fulwood Barracks. Once again, Monique shared the call with him.

'What do I tell the prime minister, Bob?' asked Sir Peter.

'Let me start with the headlines, sir. Although what happened last night has highlighted wider problems, I don't believe that it will be remembered as the start of a re-run of the American Civil War in Britain.'

'Thank God for that!'

‘The second piece of good news is that casualties have been very light, though the family of the young man serving with the transport regiment who was shot and killed last night might not view the outcome quite so positively. There appear to have been no casualties amongst the resident British population and there’s less property damage reported than might have been expected. As far as US servicemen are concerned, as well as the one death there have been several injuries from street fights or gunfire, some of them serious. Given the scale of what’s been going on it’s amazing that things are not far worse.

‘But while the two headlines are good, every other conclusion I have reached is bad. It seems to me that what happened here exposes serious problems in the way our American friends organise and manage themselves.’

‘What do you mean?’ asked Sir Peter.

Bob paused to gather his thoughts before speaking. ‘To my mind, there are two fundamental causes of the conflict that took place here. The first is the racial segregation of US units. It’s asking for trouble and last night trouble decided to answer the call. There were some particular issues at work too, especially tensions raised by the Detroit race riots. But at its heart, it’s a system that appears designed to exacerbate racism and prejudice. I talked to several members of the white US military police unit involved and was frankly shocked at the way attitudes I found sickening were aired as if it was only natural that I should share them. Meanwhile, there’s a lot of bad feeling amongst members of the military police company about what they see as British civilian prejudice against them and in favour of the mainly black unit. I’m told this does exist, but largely due to the MPs “acting as if they own the place” according to a British policeman we spoke to. This led to pressure being put on local pubs by the MP unit to introduce racial segregation and all three in the village responded by refusing to serve white US troops. You can imagine how that was received by the military police.'

'And the second main cause?' asked Sir Peter.

'It's associated with the first. Almost everyone Monique and I talked to, from officers and men of the military police company to British civilian police to the three Auxiliary Territorial Service non-commissioned officers who were caught up in what happened, commented on the very poor quality of the white officers serving in the 1511th Quartermaster Truck Regiment. We got the same view, in veiled form, from the only black officer in the regiment and even from the white major who was the acting commanding officer last night.

'A Lancashire Constabulary police inspector, not the Special Branch man, called them "bloody useless" and a lieutenant in the US military police company used a much stronger expression. It would appear that it was white officers of the 1511th Quartermaster Truck Regiment who first made a complaint to the MPs about the behaviour of black troops of their own regiment in the pub where the problem arose. When the trouble spilled out onto the street the same officers took a step backwards when asked for help by the MPs and that led directly to the fight in which the shooting started. One of the ATS women said that the young man who'd helped her and her two friends get to safety had told her that the regiment, and black units more widely, are not seen as prize postings by white officers, so don't get the best of them.'

'Is that everything?'

'Nearly, sir,' said Bob. 'A US Army Air Forces general turned up at the base of the 1511th Quartermaster Truck

Regiment an hour or so ago. His main focus was on accounting for the weapons that were taken without authority last night. That's fair enough, but I get the sense he is sold on the idea that the best way to deal with this is to throw the book at the black soldiers involved and ignore the wider issues I've just talked about.'

'Thank you, Bob, that's helpful to know. Are you and Monique going to Edinburgh now?'

'Yes, sir. I stood the pilot down after we spoke to you from Samlesbury Aerodrome so he could get some sleep. That gives Monique and I time to find out if the officers' mess here is serving breakfast yet and get back to the aerodrome at 8 a.m. to resume the flight to Turnhouse.'

'That's good, Bob. I promise not to disrupt your trip home a third time. The two of you should get some sleep when you get back.'

'We will, sir,' said Monique.

CHAPTER FIVE

Monique had trouble working out where she was when she awoke. Then she smiled as she remembered that they were back at the bungalow in Featherhall Crescent. Home at last! Finding out what time it was proved trickier. She could hear Bob breathing next to her and rolled carefully away from him so as not to wake him. The alarm clock on the bedside table was showing 8.30, though whether a.m. or p.m. she had no idea. They only had the lightweight curtains drawn, not the heavier blackout blinds, but at this time of year the muted daylight entering from outside gave no clue. Then she realised the clock wasn't ticking because it hadn't been wound since before their wedding nearly three weeks earlier.

Monique carefully reached out for her wristwatch and saw that it was showing twenty past two, which had to be in the afternoon given the light outside. They'd slept for nearly four hours and she felt better for it.

It was warm in the bedroom and when Monique turned over towards Bob she saw that he was lying on his back, uncovered by the bedding. Monique always enjoyed looking at Bob in the way an art lover might enjoy looking at a marble statue sculpted by one of the great masters. She thought he was a beautiful man.

Bob's beauty was more than just skin deep. She'd spent much of her adult life, and adulthood had started very early for her, moving from one bastard to another and she'd known from the start that Bob was different. For a while she did have doubts, mainly because she thought he might be just too different from all the others and far too good for her.

Her greatest concern had been his lack of any discernible killer instinct. Bob had been a highly successful fighter pilot in the Battle of Britain. But with his feet on the ground he was different. When faced by a man with a gun in Orkney, he lowered his pistol so he could try to talk sense into his opponent and was nearly killed as a result. That all changed in Stockholm a couple of months earlier. He pulled off a feat she thought would have been beyond her. With just six rounds fired from his Walther PPK, he shot and killed three German agents, caused the death of a fourth and wounded a fifth. In the process, he saved her life.

By then they were engaged to be married and she realised that the man she wanted to spend her life with loved and cared for her; looked great; was better in bed than he realised; and when the need arose he could protect her at least as ably as she could protect him. Bob was as near her perfect partner as she was ever likely to find. She glanced down at the engagement and wedding rings on her finger and smiled. She'd retrieved them from their hiding place in the kitchen and put them on as soon as she got home that morning.

As she looked at Bob's body a thought took hold of her and she quietly got out of bed and went to the bathroom. Now they were no longer sharing the bungalow with anyone else the need to don a dressing gown for excursions beyond the bedroom had disappeared.

When she got back into bed, she saw that Bob's eyes were open and that he was smiling at her. She smiled back. When she looked into his lovely brown eyes it was easy for her to forget that he was only seeing through one of them. If you knew where to look you could see the scar on his left temple, where he'd been wounded when he was shot down in late 1940. He'd recovered from his other injuries but the damage to the optic nerve on that side was permanent. She sometimes thought that an injury that had ended his career as a fighter pilot might also have saved his life, but she'd never said so to him. Bob coped very well with his loss of depth perception, of three-dimensional vision, and of peripheral vision on his left side, but he still avoided driving at night when he could and he never flew an aircraft in the dark.

Her gaze moved down from his eyes to take in the rest of his body and she knew it was time to turn her thoughts into actions. She leaned over to kiss him on the mouth and gently slid her body over his, then straddled him as she felt him respond.

When she broke the kiss, Bob's smile broadened. 'This is a lovely way to be woken up, but what about…'

Monique gently touched his lips with a finger.

'Shush. I sorted it when I went to the bathroom.'

*

Bob seemed restless when they got up and Monique thought she knew why before he said anything.

'I know I said we should keep our heads down until Monday and not let anyone in the office know we're back,' he said. 'But even though Maurice's people are doing most of the work we need to get ourselves organised for next week. I think I should go in this afternoon.'

Military Intelligence, Section 11, had offices in a fine country house at Craigiehall, west of Edinburgh. It never took long to drive there from the bungalow in Corstorphine and as Bob had borrowed an RAF car on arrival at Turnhouse, they wouldn't need to ask to be picked up and driven.

Monique could see Bob's point but could also see problems that might arise.

'If you go then I'm coming with you,' she said. 'But if you do go, remember that despite Joyce Stuart's best efforts to minimise it, there will be a three-week high pile of paperwork waiting for you. That's going to divert you from what you want to do and once you've made a start on it, stopping will be hard. I can see us losing our whole weekend to your paperwork and I think we both badly need a couple of days to relax.'

Joyce Stuart was Bob's extremely efficient secretary. But even she couldn't deal with everything in Bob's absence. Monique had chosen her grounds for objecting carefully. She knew that paperwork was the part of his job that Bob liked least.

'If I don't go in, it will mean we've lost three days by Monday,' he said.

'How about a compromise?' asked Monique. 'Ring in, say we're back, and ask Michael to call in here on his way to the flat at the Haymarket Station Hotel. He can brief you on anything urgent and we can talk to him about our Soviet friends and the Cuttlefish.'

'That's reasonable,' said Bob. 'I'll give him a call.'

The telephone was in the hall and Monique went through to the kitchen to make two cups of tea while Bob talked to Michael. Lieutenant Commander Michael Dixon was Bob's second-in-command. He was in his mid-twenties and had been promoted into the post on Bob's recommendation late the previous year.

Monique knew Michael well. After he had become engaged earlier in the year to an Orcadian girl, Betty Swanson, Michael and Betty moved into the spare room in the bungalow on Featherhall Crescent.

Betty had previously helped run her late father's hotel in Orkney and, on moving south to be with Michael, successfully applied for a deputy manager's job at the Haymarket Station Hotel. A staff flat had become available in the hotel in the middle of May and she and Michael jumped at the chance of having their own place, leaving Bob and Monique to theirs before their wedding, and moved into it from the bungalow.

Monique realised they had no milk and their teas would have to be black, a thought she found very unappealing. They needed to do some shopping. She wondered about suggesting to Bob that once Michael had gone they should get a taxi to the North British Hotel on Princes Street for dinner and champagne. They'd spent their wedding night there, and the one after it, and there seemed a nice circularity about returning now.

Bob came into the kitchen with a worried expression on his face.

'What's wrong?' asked Monique.

Bob looked at his watch. 'Michael said he was in a meeting but that he'd be here by 4.00 p.m. He also said that he was no longer living in the hotel flat but was happy to come here anyway. He's moved back to the officers' accommodation at HMS *Lochinvar*, the Royal Navy shore base at Port Edgar on the River Forth.'

'What's happened?' asked Monique.

'He said he'll tell us the full story when he gets here but it seems Betty broke off their engagement the day after you and I got married.'

'Oh no!' said Monique. 'They seemed so happy together. What's Betty doing?'

'I don't know. He says he moved his belongings out of

the hotel flat that same day and he's not seen her or heard from her since.'

'I feel for both of them,' said Monique. 'But Betty's pretty much alone in the world and I'm worried about her. I'm sure she'll know people at the hotel but, outside of her work, I may be the only friend she's got in Edinburgh.'

'I'm sure Michael will tell us more,' said Bob.

'I think you should see him on your own,' said Monique. 'You don't need me for the conversation about the Cuttlefish and it might be helpful if I'm not around when you talk to him about Betty. Find out everything you can. I was going to suggest we dine at the North British Hotel but that will keep. Perhaps you should take him to eat at the officers' mess at RAF Turnhouse?'

'I feel a little like I did when I knew you were going to do something I'd not approve of in Malta,' said Bob. 'What have to got in mind? You're not going to interfere, are you?'

'Unless you object, I'm going to borrow the RAF car we've got outside and take it into Edinburgh. I feel like I'm three weeks too late but I have to see Betty. I'm not going to interfere, but I can provide a sympathetic ear.'

Monique saw Bob look at her.

'Thank you for not asking, Bob. Yes, I also need to talk to Betty to find out if I'm to blame for her breaking up with Michael.'

Bob smiled grimly. 'I'm sure RAF Turnhouse won't miss their car for now. The key is next to the phone in the hall.'

'Thanks, Bob.' Monique looked at her watch. 'I'm sorry to do this to you, but you've got time before Michael arrives to walk to St John's Road to do some shopping. We need a pint of milk and a loaf of bread, and probably butter too. Make sure you take a ration book. Do you have any British pounds? We've not needed money for anything since leaving Malta on Monday.'

'I'm glad you remembered. Government of Malta notes printed only on one side might not be viewed very kindly here. I've got some British cash in the bedroom.'

'You'd better give me some too,' said Monique.

CHAPTER SIX

The elderly gentleman behind the reception desk in the Haymarket Station Hotel said that Betty Swanson was due to come on duty as night manager at 9 p.m. He didn't know if she was in her flat or not.

Monique wasn't sure what to expect when she knocked on the door to the flat but feared she might have some difficult explaining to do. She was surprised when the attractive blonde girl who opened the door smiled broadly and then hugged her.

'Monique! You're back! I'm so pleased to see you. Come in. You didn't get that suntan in Kyle of Lochalsh, did you?'

Monique followed her into the flat. She had forgotten how beautiful Betty's Orcadian accent was. 'No. We only spent a few days there before something came up and Bob and I had to go to Malta.'

Betty's smile disappeared. 'According to the newspapers, the Mediterranean is a pretty dangerous place to be.'

'It had its moments, but we're both fine. Look, Betty, I came to see you as soon as I heard about you and Michael. Are you all right?'

'What have you heard?' asked Betty.

'Just that you broke off the engagement the day after Bob and I got married and that Michael moved back to Port Edgar.'

Monique saw Betty take a deep breath.

'It's a long story,' said Betty. She looked at her watch. 'I'm not on duty until 9 p.m. I'm happy to talk but I don't want to keep you if there's something you need to do.'

'I've nothing more important I want to do,' said Monique. 'Do you fancy getting something to eat? I'll treat you. It's been a funny day. I had an early breakfast in Preston and am very aware of how long it's been since I last ate.'

'That would be nice,' said Betty. 'How did you get here?'

'I borrowed a car.'

'There are plenty of places to eat in this part of the city, but would you mind if we went somewhere else? Edinburgh is a lovely place but it can get a little overwhelming for someone who has never lived anywhere bigger than Kirkwall before.'

'Do you have anywhere in mind?' asked Monique.

'A few weeks ago I heard someone talking about an amazing fish and chip shop in a place called Bo'ness, on the south shore of the Firth of Forth beyond Queensferry. I'm not sure how far it is or what their opening times are. But there must be a good chance they'll be open at tea time on a Friday.'

Monique had parked the RAF car just round the corner from the hotel and once they'd got in she looked in the glove compartment.

'Just as I'd hoped, a road map!' She unfolded it. 'Bo'nes is only about as far again from Queensferry as Queensferry is from here. Looking at this, I think we should take the main road that goes past RAF Turnhouse and follow it as far as Linlithgow, then turn right and head due north to Bo'ness. I'm sure I can find the way, even in the absence of any roadsigns, but could you keep an eye on the map, Betty?'

It was a beautiful June afternoon and they were approaching Linlithgow when Betty started to talk. 'Is

Michael all right?'

'I'm sorry, Betty, I don't know. Bob talked to him on the phone this afternoon to ask him to call in at the bungalow so they could discuss work and Michael told him what had happened. I think Bob plans to take him out for something to eat. But I only know what I've already told you, and that was second-hand. Do you mind my asking you what happened?'

Out of the corner of her eye, Monique saw Betty turn to look across the car at her.

After a pause, Betty spoke. 'In a funny sort of way, I suppose you could say that Ruth Woodburn happened.'

Monique had met Leading Wren Ruth Woodburn, a Royal Navy driver, when visiting Kyle of Lochalsh earlier in the year. She'd persuaded Bob to recruit Ruth to fill a vacancy for a driver in MI11 and Ruth had also acted as an assistant to Monique in her liaison work with MI5. More recently there had been talk of Ruth gaining a commission in the Royal Navy, something Commodore Cunningham was pursuing.

When Monique first spoke to Bob about Ruth he highlighted the dangers of an attractive young female on the team catching the eye of Michael Dixon, who had earned a reputation as a ladies' man before he met and became engaged to Betty.

'I'm so sorry, Betty,' said Monique. 'Bob warned me that Ruth might cause problems between you and Michael when I asked him to take her on. It doesn't help, but this is entirely my fault.'

Monique looked across to see a puzzled expression on Betty's face.

'It's me who should apologise for not being clear, Monique. I'm not talking about anything happening between Michael and Ruth, not as far as I know, anyway. It's Ruth's effect on me that I'm talking about.'

Monique wasn't sure how to take that and was startled when Betty laughed out loud.

'Oh my God! I've realised how that must have sounded. Let me try again. I've got to know Ruth a little and been envious of the life she's led. It's not her expensive schooling or well-connected parents I envy, it's the fact that she's made her own decisions in life and done exactly what she wanted, and to hell with everybody else.

'You're the same, Monique. Michael's never betrayed any confidences about you but I know that you are your own woman and you've always taken the path you wanted to take. Yes, you're now married, but it's obvious that's because you want to be.'

It took Monique a moment to frame her reply. 'I suspect it's not all been sweetness and light for Ruth and I know for sure it's not been for me. You might be surprised to hear that Bob is my third husband. My first was an impoverished Russian count who I married when I had just turned 18. He turned me into a spy and a cocaine addict and after I left him he tried to kill me. He was later shot by the Soviets as a spy. In 1937, when I was 24, I married a senior officer in the German intelligence service, the Abwehr, who wasn't far short of 60 at the time. He was killed in a car crash in Berlin in 1940 and I became a full-time field agent for the Abwehr.'

'Are you pulling my leg, Monique?' asked Betty.

'No, I'm not. The part of the story I missed was that after I left my first husband I was recruited by the British Secret Intelligence Service, or MI6, and operated as a double agent for them when married to my second husband and when working for the Abwehr. I'll not go into the detail of how I came to meet Bob Sutherland but my life took a distinct upward turn at that point and I'm enjoying being married to a man I truly love for the first time.'

'Why are you telling me this, Monique? I'm just a hotel manager. Couldn't I be a security risk?'

'I don't think so. And I'm not telling you because I want to persuade you that marriage is necessarily good or bad. It's just that if you want to take your own decisions you have to learn to live with the consequences, both good and bad. Is this Bo'ness?'

'According to the map, it must be. It's not quite what I expected from a seaside town.'

Monique was driving down a steep and twisty road that offered partial views ahead over the Firth of Forth to hills beyond its far shore.

The views were partial because Bo'ness itself appeared to be an extremely active industrial town and clouds of smoke and steam billowed from factories that lined the near shore of the Forth. Monique had caught a glimpse of a pit winding wheel as they had started their descent into the town and what she could see of the heart of Bo'ness suggested it had busy docks too. Further down, the road passed below a graveyard set on an improbably steep slope.

'At least we didn't come for the scenery,' said Monique. 'Do you know how to find the fish and chip shop you were told about?'

'No. I just know it's called Corvi's. I get the impression that the centre of the town is a bit to our right. If you turn right at the bottom of the hill I'll ask someone.'

Monique turned onto a much broader street.

'There's no need to ask,' she said. 'That's Corvi's over there on our right.'

There was a sign on the wall inside Corvi's saying that it

had been established in 1896 but that the current building was more recent. It had certainly been there long enough for word about it to get around. There was a queue waiting to be served at the counter on one side that extended out of a door and onto the street, while the seating area was also extremely busy, perhaps because it was late afternoon on a Friday.

Monique saw two young men in naval uniform stand up from a table and steered Betty in their direction, smiling brightly at one of them as she sat down in what had until a few seconds earlier been his chair. Betty followed her lead and took the seat the other man had vacated.

When their meals were served, they were every bit as good as Betty had promised.

'I don't think I've ever seen fish or chips cooked as well as this,' said Monique.

'There's a chippie in Kirkwall that runs it close,' said Betty. 'But I'm here and that's hundreds of miles away. Right now, I think this is as near perfection as I've ever eaten.'

On the way back to Edinburgh, Monique followed a road that ran parallel to the shore through Bo'ness before turning inland and climbing a hill past a ruined church. This finally took them out of the smoky atmosphere of the town and into the clearer air and blue skies of a lovely summer's evening.

'This road should take us back to Edinburgh via Queensferry,' said Monique.

Betty smiled. 'I'll keep an eye on the map again.'

'We were too busy expressing our admiration for the food to finish our conversation about women who make their own decisions in life,' said Monique.

Betty said nothing for a while, and when she did speak

Monique struggled to hear her over the noise of the car. ‘When you interviewed me in Kirkwall I told you the sorry story of my parents and that I was born in September 1919. I’ll be 24 in a few months. Have you ever wondered why I was able to work in my father’s hotel in Kirkwall rather than be called up for war work? By rights, I should have been caught up in it when they changed the rules in December 1941.’

‘Not really,’ said Monique. ‘I suppose I just assumed that there was a good reason and left it at that.’

‘I told you that my mother died of cancer in 1938 and that while she was on her death bed my father was sleeping with the wife of a ship’s captain and feeding Kirkwall’s gossip-mongers. What I didn’t tell you was that after my mother died I decided I’d had enough, of everything. One day I turned on the gas oven in the kitchen of our accommodation at the rear of the hotel and put my head inside. If one of the hotel staff hadn’t come in to clean I’d have killed myself and blown up the hotel.

‘It tells you everything you need to know that my father was much more upset about the possible loss of the hotel than about the possible loss of me.’

‘I’m sorry,’ said Monique.

Betty smiled ruefully. ‘When it became likely that I’d be called up for war work my father decided he needed to find a way of getting me out of it. Without asking what I wanted, he arranged for me to see a local doctor. Based on my suicide attempt years earlier, this doctor concluded that I was unfit to be called up on psychiatric grounds. It won’t surprise you to know that I think the doctor was in my father’s pocket.

‘This was perfect for my father because by then I was helping run the hotel and was very cheap labour. I suppose

I didn't object because I accepted that what he wanted must be right. I just smiled and got on with it.

'But then I met Michael and the rest of you; my father was killed; I became rich when I inherited and then sold my father's three-quarters of the hotel; and I got engaged to Michael and moved to Edinburgh.'

Monique glanced across the car and caught Betty's eye before looking back at the road ahead. 'I think I can see where this is going. But to be sure, tell me why this mattered when you met Ruth Woodburn and got to know me.'

Betty's smile disappeared. 'Ruth isn't much different to me in age but, unlike me, she's living a life that matters. She's making a real contribution to what you're doing in MI11 and Michael's told me there's talk of her being commissioned. The world is in turmoil and when in years to come her children ask her what she did in the war, she'll have interesting and exciting things to tell them.

'Do you remember me telling you in Kirkwall that when I was about 10 a teacher showed my class a poster produced during the last war that depicted a little girl sitting on her father's knee asking, "Daddy, what did you do in the Great War?" I've always remembered it because I never in my whole life sat on my father's knee. I told my father about the poster and asked what he'd done in the war. He said that he'd not been able to join up because of flat feet, so had done his bit by arranging shipping to help keep the country fed.

'What am I going to tell my children in years to come when they ask what I did in this war, Monique? Am I meant to tell them that after I'd tried to kill myself because my mother died and my father cheated on her, I was deemed unfit to serve on psychiatric grounds and spent my war as a hotel manager, making sure people had somewhere comfortable to stay?'

'What have you done, Betty?' asked Monique.

'A couple of weeks before you and Bob got married I was standing in for a member of staff behind the bar in the hotel. It was a quiet night and I got talking to an elderly gentleman who said he was a professor in the medical school at the University of Cambridge and that he specialised in psychiatry. He was visiting Edinburgh to attend a conference at the university.

'He was in the bar again the following night and again we talked. He told me about his two sons in the RAF and I told him what the doctor in Kirkwall had done and how I felt about it. He said that I should take time to think about it, but that if I was very sure I wanted a second opinion he would put me in touch with a contact in Edinburgh. I told him I had thought about it for long enough and was very sure. A few days later I went to see an eminent psychiatrist at the Royal Infirmary of Edinburgh. The result is that I'm no longer medically exempt from being called up for war work and expect it to happen soon.'

'And what about Michael?' asked Monique.

'I love Michael. I always will. I like to think that perhaps we can meet again after the war is over and live happily ever after. But I know that's a stupid idea. He will move on and perhaps I will too.'

'Have you talked to him about any of this?' asked Monique.

'He knows about my suicide attempt and the medical exemption. But I've never told him how I feel about it. I certainly didn't discuss the idea of getting a second opinion with him. He's gentle and caring but he'd still have found a way of talking me round, even if he didn't mean to. And if I now tell him that the medical exemption has been removed, he's noble enough to say that he'll pause his life and wait for me, or that we should get married immediately and then live apart. I don't want either of those things. I want him to live his life without being tied to a promise to me that was made under very different circumstances.'

'So you just told him that the engagement was over, without offering any explanation?'

'It sounds brutal, but I honestly believe it was the best way for both of us.'

Monique felt torn. She was friends with both Michael and Betty and wanted the best for both. 'Will you promise to keep in touch with me, Betty?'

'Yes, of course, Monique. You've been a good friend and I don't want to lose you. Thank you for not trying to change my mind.'

Monique bit back the reply that it was far too late for that. She wondered if things might have been different if she'd not been so tied up with the preparations for the wedding and had paid more attention to Betty back when her options were still open.

Monique dropped Betty off outside the main entrance of the Haymarket Station Hotel and drove back to the bungalow.

CHAPTER SEVEN

'I'm glad I found you!'

Bob had just walked out of the main entrance of the officers' mess at RAF Turnhouse with Michael Dixon close behind him when a familiar voice stopped him in his tracks.

Michael was quicker off the mark. 'Hello, Monique. You're looking very well.' He walked past Bob and embraced Monique, who had come to a halt a few yards ahead of him on the paved path leading from the road.

'Oi! You can't park there!'

The bellow came from somewhere to Bob's left and he turned so he could see the source with his right eye. A figure in an RAF uniform was standing in front of a building perhaps a hundred and fifty yards away and waving a stick in the air.

'It's the station warrant officer,' Bob said. He looked beyond Monique to a car parked on the side of the road behind her. 'Is that the car we borrowed?'

'Yes,' said Monique. 'I didn't want to miss you.'

'Let's all hop in and drive to the car park. We can talk there.'

'I thought you outranked everyone at RAF Turnhouse, including the station commander,' said Monique. 'You told me he's a wing commander.'

'Bernard Spencer is a wing commander and I do outrank him,' said Bob. 'But I don't want to spoil the working relationship or the friendship I've got with him, and no one wants to upset the station warrant officer, who you can think of as the personification of God on Earth, or the small part of Earth occupied by RAF Turnhouse, anyway.'

Bob waved in acknowledgement in the direction of the

man who had shouted and walked with the other two to the car. Monique got into the driver's seat and Bob sat next to her with Michael in the back.

'The car park is just over there,' he said, pointing. 'It doubles as a parade ground if someone very important is visiting. Michael's car is next to the verge on this side.'

Monique stopped next to the staff car Michael was using. 'Can I park here without being shouted at?'

'Yes, this is fine,' said Bob.

'Does he shout at everyone like that, or was it because I'm a woman in civilian clothes?'

'Station warrant officers tend not to discriminate,' said Bob. 'It would have been no different if I'd parked on the road. Anyway, it's good to see you, but I'm afraid you've missed dinner if that's what you had in mind.'

'No, that's fine, I've eaten,' said Monique.

Bob noted the 'I' and decided it was a sign Monique didn't want to tell Michael she'd been to see Betty. He realised how difficult this could become.

'I came to find you because when I got back to the bungalow the phone was ringing. It was Maurice Cunningham. He said he needs to talk to you on a secure line. I told him I'd track you down.'

'I'm sure we could ring from here,' said Bob. 'But we might be better going to Craigiehall. It's no distance at all and we could kill two birds with one stone by returning RAF Turnhouse's car before leaving and picking up my staff car when we get there.'

'What about the pile of paperwork that's going to be waiting for you?' asked Monique. 'MI11 owes us both a weekend off.'

'It's all right,' said Michael. 'I've been telling Bob that because we had no idea when he would be back, we've been managing his paperwork between us. There's very little that needs his attention and none of it is urgent.'

'Craigiehall it is, then,' said Monique. 'Bob, you return this car and Michael and I can follow in his.'

*

As Bob had said, Craigiehall was only a short distance from RAF Turnhouse. It was also quite close to Cramond, where Bob's parents had settled when he was ten. At that time the grand house was empty and abandoned and Bob, like many local children, played in the grounds. When Bob was about fourteen the house was renovated and reoccupied, and access became much more tricky. His parents had told him when Craigiehall was converted into a hotel in 1933, and a year or two before the war he stayed there with a young lady he'd met through the Auxiliary Air Force. He chose the location because he wanted to know what the interior of the house was like but found the two-night stay extremely uncomfortable. There was nothing wrong with the hotel itself, it was just that he spent the whole time worrying that a fellow guest or member of staff might recognise him and tell his parents that he'd been in the area without calling in on them.

Bob smiled at the memory as Michael stopped the car and showed his pass to the guard at the main gate, who stood back and saluted. Craigiehall had been requisitioned by the army at the start of the war, and the main house had been joined by assorted Nissen huts and wooden buildings. That meant that MI11 didn't need to worry about mundane matters like security, catering and accommodation for the junior staff in the office.

Once past the gate, Michael drove to the grand entrance

of the house itself. Much of the main house was used as a headquarters by anti-aircraft and anti-shipping artillery units whose operational elements were scattered along both banks of the Firth of Forth and on islands in the river. Bob's predecessor had been an army colonel and had negotiated the use by MI11 of a series of first-floor rooms in an extension added to the original house in the 1820s. Bob felt that the accommodation worked well and the location suited him and Monique perfectly.

The MI11 offices were deserted, as Bob had expected at this time on a Friday evening. Michael was able to put the call through from the desk of Bob's secretary and then walk through to Bob's office to join him and Monique after making that end of the connection.

'Hello, is that Bob?'

Bob recognised the voice of Commodore Maurice Cunningham.

'Yes, sir,' said Bob. 'I called back as soon as I could. Monique is with me, as is Michael Dixon, and I've connected my phone to a speaker.'

'You didn't get much sleep last night. I hope you've caught up today.'

'Yes, sir, we have. When you spoke to Monique, you said you needed to talk on a secure line.'

'That's right,' said the commodore. 'I managed to get more sleep than you did last night, even if it was in an armchair in Sir Peter Maitland's office. That meant I was able to get things moving this morning. Against the background of what our Soviet friends told us about the Cuttlefish, I've had my people contact military units on the ground in south-west Scotland as well as the police in the area and people in the War Office, Air Ministry and Admiralty. We asked everyone we talked to if they knew of any unusual activity or odd incidents, especially during the week when we believe the Cuttlefish was in Scotland.'

'I'm guessing you've found something, sir,' said Bob.

'Enough to worry both Sir Peter and I,' said the commodore. 'I'll tell you why in a moment. First, I'll give you the broader picture. I'm sure you've experienced this yourself, but if you start asking for examples of suspicious happenings, almost everyone will have something to tell you.

'The range of stories we were told about incidents in the area was intriguing. Several sources we spoke to told us that an MI5 agent was roaming the area dressed as a tramp to test the security of military installations, though not necessarily during the week we are most interested in. We have checked with MI5 and they know nothing about him, and if he exists at all he's certainly nothing to do with MI11. There are also stories of lights seen at night as enemy agents send signals to submarines we can be pretty sure don't exist.

'Rather more seriously, we were told about the disappearance of an RAF officer during the week we believe the Cuttlefish was in the area. Flight Lieutenant James Thorn is an engineering officer on a flying boat servicing unit based at RAF Wig Bay, on the west shore of Loch Ryan north of Stranraer. On the evening of 16th of June, last Wednesday, and during the time we believe the Cuttlefish was in Scotland, Flight Lieutenant Thorn told a colleague he was going into Stranraer to meet a lady friend and didn't return, which was totally out of character. The RAF Police have established that the lady is real and that the flight lieutenant spent the evening with her, then left to cycle back to RAF Wig Bay, but never arrived.

'That's worrying in itself, but it's something that

happened the night before that is causing us the most concern. On the night of the Tuesday into Wednesday a young soldier, Private Stanley Young, disappeared while on guard duty in a coastal lookout about eight miles south of Wigtown.

'Last Friday his body turned up a couple of miles north of where he'd disappeared, in Garlieston Bay. He was found because he caught on a piece of equipment being used to test ways of getting vehicles ashore from a tank landing craft in tricky tidal conditions. He'd been garrotted, which to my mind speaks more of a sentry being surprised by an intruder than it does of a disagreement over a game of cards or a girl.'

'The west side of Wigtown Bay is being used for some very hush-hush testing, isn't it, sir?' asked Michael. 'I'm aware of a recent build-up of military activity there, but haven't yet visited myself.'

'Yes,' said Commodore Cunningham. 'This afternoon I heard someone at the War Office describe what's going on there as, in military security terms, the "crown jewels". Let me tell you why. You know as well as I do that, at some point, the Allies are going to need to land an army on the coast of mainland Europe. The main problem with mounting any large-scale invasion will be getting huge numbers of men and huge quantities of equipment and material ashore quickly when, we must assume, the Germans will have rendered all the ports unusable. Work is underway to find ways of resolving that problem and much of it is taking place on the west side of Wigtown Bay under the code name "Mulberry". If security there has been breached it could have appalling consequences for the plans for an invasion.'

'Do you think that's why the Cuttlefish is in Scotland,'

sir?' asked Michael. 'To report back on Allied preparations for an invasion?'

'I don't know, and neither does Sir Peter,' said the commodore. 'And I'm not sure how the disappearance of a flight lieutenant at RAF Wig Bay could tie in with that. But we would like you to treat the protection of the work on Mulberry as your highest priority, especially if we are unable to prevent the Cuttlefish from returning to Scotland. The added complication is that our Soviet friends are hopefully in blissful ignorance of Mulberry and you should try to avoid enlightening them.'

'That might be awkward,' said Bob. 'What you're saying is that you want us to work in partnership with the Soviets while avoiding revealing to them how worried we are about the Cuttlefish stealing what you've called the crown jewels?'

'Precisely that,' said the commodore. 'I will keep my people here trawling for leads over the weekend to see if we can come up with anything more. But I think we should plan on you basing yourself somewhere nearby. I know you feel at home on airfields so I'm thinking that RAF Wigtown might be as good as anywhere. When I spoke to Monique earlier she told me very firmly that the two of you need the weekend off, and I share that view, up to a point at least. I suggest that the three of you telephone me again late on Sunday afternoon with a view to finalising arrangements for you to travel south-west the following day, Monday. We'll organise accommodation from here. How many should we plan for from your side?'

Bob looked at Michael. 'It would be helpful to have a runway available, sir, so RAF Wigtown might be ideal. Lieutenant Commander Dixon and I talked about who to involve earlier when I told him about the Cuttlefish. I understand that the head of my RAF team, Flight Lieutenant Buchan, is training the new head of your RAF team by undertaking a series of joint visits to airfields and other installations in north-east England over the coming week. I think we should let that arrangement stand. It's unreasonable to expect my secretary to run the office with only junior staff in support indefinitely, however good she is. I therefore propose to leave my army team here, so Captain Darlington will be in charge.

'That means that Monique and I will be accompanied on this trip by Michael, with the junior members of my naval and RAF teams providing support. I'm in two minds about involving a driver. One of ours is laid up with a broken ankle at the moment. Where do things stand with Leading Wren Woodburn?'

'I was going to mention her,' said the commodore. 'I received news this morning that she is likely to be called for officer selection within the next week. From what you've said and from my limited first-hand knowledge of her, I would expect her to be successful. That means that she will in due course reappear at Craigiehall as Third Officer Woodburn as you have said you will keep her on in a different role and she is happy with that.'

'That's excellent news, sir,' said Bob. 'In that case, Michael, Petty Officer MacDonald and Sergeant Bennett will drive down in three cars, while Monique and I fly. That way we can be sure we'll be self-sufficient in transport, even assuming the Soviets don't have a car available, and I'll have the Mosquito in case I need to get back here quickly for any reason. Hopefully, security at RAF Wigtown will be good enough to ensure that Major Malinovsky isn't tempted to revive the Soviets' ambitions from last year to steal one.'

‘There would be no need,’ said the commodore. ‘I saw a memo yesterday that said the Air Ministry has agreed to give the Soviets a Mosquito for testing purposes. I gather it’s due to be flown to their base at RAF Errol within the next few weeks by an instructor who will teach them how to fly it. I’m sure a copy of the memo will find its way to you in due course.’

‘That’s darkly ironic in the circumstance,’ said Bob.

‘It is,’ said the commodore. ‘But I’m sure there have been many needless and pointless deaths in this war. The unfortunate man who was shot while trying to steal a Mosquito for the Soviets was just one more.’

After Bob ended the call he looked at Monique and Michael, who had both drawn up chairs on the other side of his desk. ‘I suggest we reconvene here at 4 p.m. on Sunday afternoon to see if the commodore has turned up anything else and finalise arrangements to head south-west on Monday morning.’

Michael stood up. He paused for a moment, as if uncertain what to do next. ‘Monique, can I ask, did you see Betty this afternoon?’

Bob got the sense that Monique had been expecting the question.

‘Yes, I did, Michael.’

‘Whatever she might think and whatever she told you, I’ve been completely faithful to her. There’s been no one else since I met her.’

‘I know, Michael,’ said Monique. ‘She knows it too. And she’s also been faithful to you. Knowing that may not make you feel any better about the situation.’

‘It doesn’t,’ said Michael. ‘I’ve respected Betty’s wishes for a clean break and not tried to see her. Would it make any difference if I did talk to her?’

'I don't think so,' said Monique.

'Thank you, Monique. It's hard, but I'll stay away from her. Changing the subject, Bob, I'd planned to spend this weekend with Andrew MacDonald, making unannounced visits to assess security at naval installations along the Firth of Forth. I've tried to keep myself busy at weekends since Betty ended things and with Commodore Cunningham making the running on our visit to the south-west I see no reason why I should change my plans.'

'I disagree, Michael. When did you last have a day off?'

'On the Sunday, the day after the two of you got married.'

'You told me that was the day you moved your belongings out of the hotel flat,' said Bob. 'That means you've not had any time off in nearly three weeks and I assume the same goes for Petty Officer MacDonald?'

Michael nodded.

'I would like you to ask Andrew MacDonald and Peter Bennett to join us in the office on Sunday evening so we can finalise our plans after the three of us have talked to the commodore. Can you also make sure that we've got three cars fuelled up and checked so there are no hitches on Monday morning?'

'Yes, of course, Bob.'

'But I would also like both you and Andrew to have the day off tomorrow. I understand that you don't want to sit in your room at HMS *Lochinvar* and think about what might have been with Betty. But I'm sure that if you ask, Andrew and perhaps some of the others will be happy to join you on a tour of Edinburgh's pubs tomorrow evening.'

Michael smiled. 'Is that an order, Bob?'

'It is.'

After Michael had gone, Bob and Monique left the main

house and walked to where Bob's staff car was parked.

'Did Betty swear you to silence when you spoke to her?' asked Bob.

'No, she didn't,' said Monique. 'You drive us home and I'll tell you why she broke up with Michael.'

On the drive back to Featherhall Crescent, Monique gave Bob a summary of what Betty had told her.

'It's like something out of a Shakespearian tragedy,' said Bob. 'Part of me thinks you should tell Michael. It will stop him torturing himself over whether this is somehow his fault.'

'I'll give it a fortnight,' said Monique. 'If he's still grieving as badly then, I'll tell him.'

'That will be too late for him to make any difference,' said Bob.

'It was too late from the moment Betty got her second opinion and her exemption from call-up was removed,' said Monique. 'I'll be completely honest with you, Bob. After Betty told me, I felt guilty. I wondered if I might have been able to help if I'd not been so self-absorbed before the wedding. But now I've had a chance to think about it, I'm beginning to believe that she might have done the best thing for her and, possibly, for Michael too. I'm almost grateful that I was spared the responsibility of being able to advise her while she could still have changed her mind.'

CHAPTER EIGHT

When Monique awoke the next morning she could smell bacon frying. The alarm clock, now wound up and working properly, told her it was a minute or two before 10.00 a.m. She couldn't remember when she'd last slept for so long. Bob's side of the bed was empty, which was perhaps as well as it would have been worrying if it wasn't him who was cooking.

Monique put on a dressing gown and went through to the kitchen. She burst out laughing when she saw Bob wearing his uniform trousers and shirt under a floral kitchen apron that had obviously been designed with someone more feminine in mind.

'Where did you find that?' she asked.

'It was on the back of the kitchen door when we moved in,' he said. 'I got it filthy cleaning out the boiler and fires before our second trip to Stockholm and Mrs Grant must have found it during one of her Thursday morning cleaning visits and laundered it. I discovered it just now in the drawer over there.'

'Are we having a fried breakfast?' asked Monique.

'I was going to bring you breakfast in bed, but it might be easier to eat at the kitchen table. I've got bacon, eggs, square sausage and black pudding, and I'm toasting some bread under the grill. I hope you're hungry.'

Monique smiled. 'It sounds lovely. When I reminded you to take a ration book with you to the shops yesterday, I didn't intend for you to blow what sounds like a month's worth of rationed foodstuffs for both of us on one meal.'

Bob looked serious, then smiled back at her. 'It might not have been very socially responsible, but with the dining out and at military messes we do, not to mention the fish and chips we eat, we need to buy rationed items so rarely it's not going to matter. And there's enough bacon to ensure we can have sandwiches tomorrow morning, so it's not just one meal. The bread, bacon and butter should last until then, despite the warm weather. You talked yesterday about dinner at the North British Hotel on Princes Street. I suggest we go this evening, by taxi so we can make the most of their champagne.'

'That sounds lovely,' said Monique. 'But right now, this breakfast sounds even better.'

Breakfast was wonderful. Afterwards, they decided they should go out as it was another fine day.

'It's your city, Bob, where should we go?'

'When I was younger and living with my parents, I'd have jumped at the chance of going to Portobello on a day like today. The beach there is the best near Edinburgh, though it used to get crowded as a result. A few years before the war they built a huge outdoor pool which I've only been to once. They even had plans for a pier and pavilion and were about to start building when Hitler decided to invade Poland.'

'It might be nice to see what's still there,' said Monique.

'I'm guessing, but I suspect that what might be there now is an excess of barbed wire to deter beach landings.'

'So where, then?'

'Do you remember that after our first trip to Stockholm, we visited Cairnpapple Hill?' asked Bob.

'I do. But that was the low point of our time together and I don't want to be reminded of how I was feeling by going back to it.'

'I'm sorry Monique. That wasn't a very sensitive way of making a suggestion. Not far beyond it is a little village called Torphichen, which we can get to without going via Cairnpapple. There's an ancient church there called Torphichen Preceptory. I went there once with Dad when I was still at school. It's one of those places with an amazing story though it's not a well-known one.'

'I'm happy to go anywhere, well, almost anywhere, so long as it's with you, Bob. What's so special about this place?'

'It was one of only two bases in Britain, with the other being in London, of the Knights Hospitaller of the Order of St John of Jerusalem.'

'Wasn't that the religious order that built so many of the defences in Malta?' asked Monique.

'The very same. It was while we were there that I remembered Torphichen Preceptory. The Order of St John established it in the early 12th century. Early in the following century, they took over the Scottish properties of another order of fighting monks, the Knights of the Temple or the Knights Templar after that was dissolved by the pope. The Reformation of 1560 brought an end to the preceptory as an active religious foundation, though the roofless tower and transepts of its church still stand, attached to a parish church built in the 18th century on the site of what was originally the nave of the preceptory.'

'You get very enthusiastic about history, don't you, Bob?' asked Monique, smiling.

'I think I told you once that the family plan was for me to study history or modern languages at the University of Edinburgh. That was of course before I spoiled things by chucking in studying, moving to London, then walking from the Hook of Holland to Rome before returning to Scotland to join the City of Glasgow Police.'

'You did tell me that.'

‘I sometimes wonder what my life would have been like if I’d stayed in Edinburgh and studied history, or perhaps archaeology,’ said Bob.

‘For a start, we’d not be having this conversation because we’d never have met,’ said Monique. ‘I’m very glad you gave up studying when you did.’

‘Me too,’ said Bob, smiling. ‘But perhaps, when all the fighting is over, I could go to university and see if there’s anything of that “other me” that I might explore?’

‘Do you think “all the fighting” will ever be over?’ asked Monique. ‘Yes, we can now look forward with confidence to a time when Hitler is defeated. But you and I already spend some of our time fighting the war after this one, the war against the Soviets.’

‘That’s frighteningly true,’ said Bob. ‘And it adds a real edge to the thought of working with the NKVD to catch the Cuttlefish.’

*

Monique thoroughly enjoyed their trip to Torphichen. Not because of the place itself, though it was interesting enough, but because Bob’s enthusiasm was infectious.

Afterwards, they returned to the bungalow in Featherhall Crescent and went to bed, though not to sleep.

That evening they telephoned for a taxi to take them to the North British Hotel on Princes Street. Bob and Monique were well known at the hotel, especially after spending the first two nights of their honeymoon there, and they were shown to their favourite table in the dining room.

The food, as ever, was good, though with wartime regulations controlling the maximum price of restaurant meals, Monique imagined that the quality had probably been better before the war. And perhaps it would be again afterwards, she thought, which was something to dream about. There were no wartime controls over the maximum price of alcohol, which meant that the champagne on offer at the hotel was always superb.

For Monique, the Saturday was something of an oasis of calm after Malta and Bamber Bridge and before whatever awaited them in the hunt for the Cuttlefish. She got the sense that Bob felt the same and that if she'd not suggested a second bottle of champagne after dinner, he'd have done so himself.

Monique didn't find Sunday quite so relaxing because she knew they would have to switch back to their official personas for the return to Craigiehall and the planned telephone call to Commodore Cunningham. After a breakfast of bacon sandwiches prepared by Bob, they drove to the Royal Botanic Garden and spent a few hours just walking and talking and enjoying the warm sunshine. Afterwards, they had a late lunch at Bob's parents' house in Cramond, catching up on what Monique and Bob had been up to since the wedding.

At Craigiehall, the arrangements for the telephone call mirrored those on the Friday evening, with Bob, Monique and Michael in Bob's office, gathered around the speaker on the desk.

'RAF Wigtown is expecting your team of five to arrive tomorrow,' said the commodore. 'Yevgeny Popov tells me his people are likely to join you a couple of days later. I'm hoping you can do what you need to do about Mulberry and refocus on Stranraer before the Soviets arrive and before the Cuttlefish is supposed to be returning to Scotland. That gets around any problems arising from the Soviets wondering why we are paying so much attention to the west side of Wigtown Bay. You can play that by ear, but please keep me in touch with your plans, Bob, so I can manage Mr Popov.

'You should also know that we've heard about a second military officer who has gone missing. A captain in the Royal Engineers arrived back in Stranraer on the steamer from Larne on the Friday of the week we believe the Cuttlefish was in Scotland, the 18th of June. He is based at Cairnryan where he has something to do with operating the military railway serving the port that's been built there. He disappeared that evening.'

'That means he's been missing for over a week,' said Bob. 'And the flight lieutenant from the flying boat base has been gone for two days longer. We'll certainly make reviewing security surrounding Mulberry our highest priority, but I think we also need to find out what we can about the investigations into the disappearances of the two men. One missing officer while the Cuttlefish was in the area might be a coincidence. Two feels much more worrying.'

'I agree,' said the Commodore. 'But, as I said, make sure you keep me in touch.'

CHAPTER NINE

'We need to watch out for the high ground.' said Bob. 'There's plenty of it about.'

'That's Newton Stewart ahead of us,' said Michael Dixon, looking at the map he was holding. 'If we turn to head south from here, we can keep the mass of Cairnsmore of Fleet on our left and descend while we're over the valley of the River Cree and Wigtown Bay. There's a hill called Cairnharrow that rises to nearly 1,500 feet not far inland from the bay's north-east side but so long as we stay over the water we'll be fine. RAF Wigtown is on the west shore of the bay and given what you said about the winds, our approach to the main runway will be from the north-east.'

'Thanks, Michael. Mountains are rarely a problem on cloudless days like today when the visibility is endless. Imagine how this would feel on a typical murky November day with the base of the clouds only a few hundred feet above the sea. Then imagine it's pouring with rain, blowing a gale and, if you want to add even more interest, that the sun set an hour ago. We'd know there were mountains in the area but not exactly where and we'd get very little clue about where we were from settlements on the ground because of the blackout. We'd never have seen Newton Stewart just now.'

'You make it sound terrifying, Bob.'

'It can be.' Bob turned slightly to look across the snug cockpit of the Mosquito at Michael, whose navigator's seat was to the right of and set back a little from his, leaving just enough room for their shoulders when the rear of Bob's was touching the front of Michael's. In the distance he caught a glimpse of a shape against the blue sky, and then a second. 'Hello, we've got company. Look, two aircraft.'

Michael followed the direction of his gaze. 'They're fighters and seem to be descending towards us. They've got black and white stripes on the bottoms of their wings. I'm hoping you're going to tell me they're friendly?'

Bob was surprised by how nervous Michael sounded, then remembered that the cockpit of a Mosquito was a very alien environment for him.

'Don't worry, Michael, they're Hawker Typhoons. The type is still quite new and from some angles can look like a German Focke-Wulf Fw 190. The stripes under the wings are an attempt to avoid being shot at by our own side. They seem to be coming to take a look at us. Can you keep an eye on them and give me a running commentary on where they are?'

Bob saw Michael twist around as far as the straps attaching him to his seat permitted then he looked ahead to focus on their descent towards RAF Wigtown.

'They're still closing in,' said Michael. 'Now they've gone round behind us. Is that safe?'

'So long as I don't do anything sudden,' said Bob. 'And I promise I won't.'

'They've closed right in and are a little behind us on your side,' said Michael, who had turned towards Bob.

It was Bob's turn to twist around in his seat so he could see the two Typhoons from his good right eye. The lead aircraft came into close formation on the left of the Mosquito with the second a little further out and behind it. Bob saw the pilot of the nearest aircraft turn his head to look at him. He was easily close enough for Bob to see he had his oxygen mask covering the lower part of his face while his goggles were over the brow of his leather flying helmet. The man gave an approximation of a salute with his right hand and when Bob waved in response the outer Typhoon banked sharply away and turned to the left, to be followed a few seconds later by the nearest aircraft.

'They just wanted to say hello,' said Bob.

'Does that mean I can breathe again?' asked Michael.

'Up to a point,' said Bob. 'Looking ahead I can see half a dozen aircraft in the circuit of the airfield or on longer approaches to land. It looks like RAF Wigtown is a busy place. I'll call up the tower on the radio.'

*

'It is a very busy place,' said Michael as Bob turned the aircraft left off the far end of the runway onto a taxiway that led back towards the hangars and control tower. 'I recognise most of the aircraft we saw in the air and parked on the ground as Avro Ansons. What are the odd-looking ones with high wings?'

'Westland Lysanders,' said Bob. 'They're used for target spotting for the army, and some are used to land on rough fields in occupied Europe at night in support of our friends in MI6 and the Special Operations Executive. The idea is to get people in and out without the Germans noticing and it appears to work. It's not a job I'd have fancied even when I could fly in the dark. Lysanders are also used for training, which I assume is why there are some here. I don't know if you noticed them, but I also saw four Typhoons parked on the south side of the airfield as we were landing.'

'I'm not sure where we can park,' said Michael. 'The grass along the inner side of the taxiway is pretty much lined with aircraft.'

'They've asked me to taxi back to the control tower,' said Bob. 'That will take us past the hangars.' Bob watched out for any parked aircraft starting to move. The last thing he wanted was a ground collision on a crowded airfield. 'We're being waved onto the grass at the end of this line of Ansons, short of the control tower.' Bob brought the aircraft to a halt where directed by the airman marshalling them, then shut down the engines.

Michael squeezed through the hatch in the floor of the cockpit first and Bob followed.

'Group Captain Sutherland?'

Bob saw that an RAF squadron leader was standing beside Michael, who was struggling to remove his Mae West life vest and flying jacket.

Michael waved towards Bob and the squadron leader approached him and saluted.

'Hello, sir. I'm Flight Lieutenant Talbot, the junior engineering officer. I will act as your liaison here at RAF Wigtown. Group Captain Belmont has asked me to pass on his regards and is happy to meet when it suits you. I understand that you want to visit the army engineers at Cairn Head first and that we can get you settled in afterwards?'

'That's right,' said Bob. 'I've got three more people driving down from Edinburgh who will be here in due course. The army said they'd send a car for me.'

'Yes, sir. It's just over there.' Talbot pointed towards a car that had driven onto the grass at the back of the Mosquito.

'Thank you, Flight Lieutenant Talbot, and please pass on my thanks to Group Captain Belmont. We'll leave our gear in the Mosquito and can sort out the domestic arrangements when everyone has arrived.'

*

Bob and Michael sat in the back of the army staff car.

Bob looked at his watch. 'I'm not sure what time the others will get here.'

He saw Michael smile.

'Stop worrying, Bob. You saw how Monique reacted when she thought you were doubting her ability to drive one of the cars down here. We agreed it made sense for you and me to make the initial visit to Cairn Head and she's every bit as good a driver as I am, if not better. Besides, the three of them are in convoy, which gives some fallback in case of mechanical problems.'

'That's all true,' said Bob. He saw they were coming into a settlement. 'Where is this, driver?'

'It's Whithorn, sir. We've followed the main road south and we turn left here onto a minor road that takes us to the coast.'

The name rang a bell with Bob. 'Isn't there an ancient church here?'

'I'm sorry, sir, I don't know. But if you want to visit a church, there's one beside the back road that runs down the coast from Garlieston that is guaranteed to get the hairs on the back of your neck going. It's surrounded by trees in the middle of a field and is as spooky as you like.'

'Thank you, I'll bear that in mind.'

Not far beyond Whithorn, the driver stopped at a checkpoint manned by three soldiers carrying rifles. After Bob and Michael had shown their passes and explained the purpose of their visit, they were allowed through.

'Do all the roads leading to Cairn Head have checkpoints?' asked Michael.

'I'm sorry, sir, I don't think I'm allowed to tell you that.'

'That's fair enough.'

Bob was looking out at the passing countryside and

realised that they were approaching the coast. After a second checkpoint, the road turned to run behind the shore of a rocky bay. Ahead of them, at the far end of the bay, a substantial roadway extended out from the shoreline for perhaps a hundred yards or more into the sea. It was supported by a series of pontoons whose hulls ran at right angles to the roadway and made the structure look like a temporary bridge.

Only this bridge didn't cross a river, it extended from the shore to an offshore platform that was perhaps fifty yards wide and had tall metal supports at each corner that extended well above its deck. Bob could see what looked like the superstructure of a large boat protruding above the platform as if it were moored to the far side.

'I don't suppose you can tell me what that is, can you, driver,' said Michael.

'That's right, sir,' said the driver.

Just beyond the landward end of the roadway, the road they were following turned inland. A gateway on the left with more armed guards gave access to a camp of Nissen huts and wood or concrete buildings set on land behind the south shore of the bay.

The driver stopped the car outside one of the concrete buildings. 'This is the unit headquarters, sir. Major Avery should be waiting for you.'

After they'd shown their passes to a sentry outside the door, and another at a desk just inside it, Bob and Michael were taken to a small office towards one end of the building.

An army major looked up as they entered, then stood up and saluted. 'I assume you are Group Captain Sutherland, sir?' The man was in his forties and had a grey moustache that didn't match his black hair.

‘Bob showed the major his security pass. ‘That’s right. And this is Lieutenant Commander Dixon, who is my deputy in the Edinburgh office of Military Intelligence, Section 11.’

‘Welcome to Cairn Head. I’ve asked for three teas. We might even be able to run to a biscuit or two. Please take a seat.’

The major’s office was large enough to house a desk, a chair behind it and two more in front of it. The far end wall was taken up with shelving on which were piled papers and books, while the largest wall was partly covered by a map of what looked like the local area. The door filled part of the second end wall and two locking filing cabinets occupied much of the rest of it. Behind the major’s chair was a window whose glass had been taped over in a criss-cross pattern to prevent flying shards in the event of an air raid. As he sat down, Bob saw it gave a view out over the rocky bay and the bridge-like structure that had been built in it.

‘I’m grateful to you both for coming,’ said Major Avery, after tea had been served by an army private. ‘I’m told you have information about a possible security breach. As you’ll have noticed, we take security very seriously and any breach could be very damaging.’

Bob sipped his tea.

Michael looked down at his notebook. ‘We’re told that on the night of Tuesday, the 15th of June, one of your men went missing while on guard duty and that his body was found on the Friday of that week in circumstances that make his death look suspicious.’

‘Yes, that’s right. He was one of two men on duty in a lookout post we’ve got above the shore at a place called Cruggleton Point.’ The major stood up. ‘If I can squeeze past, I'll show you on the map.'

Bob vacated his chair to allow the major access.

'Look, it's here. If you follow the minor road south from Garlieston, you pass the track leading to Cruggleton, which is little more than a farmstead. There's a church marked beside the road here and a short distance to the east, above the shore, the Ordnance Survey has marked a castle, which in reality amounts to a very fragmentary ruin. Our lookout post is close by. It's perhaps thee miles north of here.'

'What happened?' asked Michael.

'We have two men stationed there on a rolling basis, four hours at a time, before being relieved. It's an important location because it commands views north along the coast to Garlieston and south in this direction. That night, Private Stanley Young and another man were on guard duty from midnight until 4 a.m. About thirty minutes before they were due to be relieved, Private Young told the other man on duty that he needed to go for a pee. He left the other man in the lookout post and didn't return. The other man says he started looking for Private Young about 15 minutes after he went out, and when the two relief lookouts arrived at 4 a.m. all three men searched for him. Two continued to do so while one returned here to raise the alarm. We then mounted a full search of the area. You have to remember that it was getting light by this time, but we found nothing more than Private Young's rifle, wedged between two rocks just above the shoreline.

'When Private Young was found on the Friday, it emerged that he had been garrotted with something like a length of braided telephone handset cord and that his body had probably gone into the sea very shortly after he disappeared.'

'An obvious possibility is that he argued with the other

man and was killed by him,' said Michael.

'Yes, as you say, that's an obvious possibility. I talked to the other man, Private Spencer, about his account of what happened. I found what he had to say totally believable. I should add that he has a reputation for being what you might call a gentle man. He volunteers for anything, happily does more than his share of chores, is supportive of those around him and is universally liked by everyone in the unit. I don't believe he killed Private Young and I don't think you'll find anyone else at Cairn Head who believes it either. You are, of course, welcome to talk to him yourself.'

'Thank you,' said Michael. 'I would like to return with two colleagues this afternoon to look at security at Cairn Head and Garlieston and will talk to Private Spencer then.'

'I was told that MI11 believes there may be another explanation for Private Young's death,' said Major Avery.

'That's right,' said Bob. 'We've had information that suggests that a Geman spy might have spent the week in which Private Young was killed in south-west Scotland. When we heard about Private Young's killing, we added two and two. Whether four is the right answer remains to be seen, but I'm told the War Office regards what's going on here as, in military security terms, the crown jewels. If our information is correct, this spy plans to return to the area. That means we have to do everything possible to protect what's being done here.'

'That's rather disturbing,' said the major. 'It would be a catastrophe if the Germans were to work out what we are doing here and why we are doing it. It's flattering that the War Office regard us as on a par with the crown jewels, but the truth is that what's happening here is much, much more important than that. Has anyone told you what we are doing?'

‘Only in very general terms,’ said Bob. ‘Simply that when an invasion of mainland Europe takes place the Allies will need to land men and material in very large quantities even though the enemy will have destroyed the ports. You are working on ways of solving that problem.’

‘That’s a fair summary, sir,’ said the Major. ‘We are developing a range of landing techniques but at their core are the components of what we hope will form “Mulberry harbours”. These will be temporary harbours whose components can be towed to wherever they are needed and then quickly assembled in situ to give as much landing capacity as a fair-sized port.

‘If we can make the harbours work they will have a huge impact on the course of the war. Without them, very large-scale amphibious landings on the coast of mainland Europe are much less likely to succeed. In an invasion, the speed of the build-up will be critical to success. Unless we can get men and tanks and fuel and food and ammunition and everything else ashore faster than the enemy can reinforce their defences, then we will be driven back into the sea. It’s as simple as that. The Mulberry harbours could make all the difference.’

‘And the fear is that if the enemy learned about them in advance they could focus their defensive efforts on them when the day arrives?’ asked Bob.

‘Yes, though it’s worse than even that makes it seem. I’ve heard the idea of the Mulberry harbours compared to that of the Trojan Horse. The Trojan Horse was a completely novel idea whose success was down to it being so unexpected. Once it had been done, no one in history could ever do it again. What makes the possibility of a security breach so worrying is that it’s not just the details or the technicalities of the Mulberry harbours that need to remain secret, it's the very idea itself.'

Bob put his teacup down. 'What you are saying is that a German spy wouldn't need to break into this building and steal some blueprints to succeed, he'd simply need to understand the principle of what you are trying to achieve.'

'That's it, exactly,' said Major Avery. 'You've got a head start because you are aware of the overall aim, group captain, but if an enemy spy saw what we've got out there in Portyerrock Bay at the moment, how long do you think it would take him to work out what we're trying to do?'

'Does that mean there's a chance the crown jewels might already have been stolen?' asked Michael.

'This spy of yours, if it was him who killed Private Young, wouldn't have needed to come much further south along the coast to see the pierhead and floating pier we've got parked out there, which would have been enough to give the game away to anyone of even average intelligence. It was in the bay at the time that Private Young disappeared and that night the weather was clear and the moon was nearly full. On the other hand, if you believe this spy is going to return to Scotland, it suggests he may not have seen enough to work out what's planned during his first visit.'

'That makes it all the more important that we catch him,' said Bob. 'As Michael mentioned, it might be helpful if he returns this afternoon with two colleagues to go over your security arrangements in detail and see if we can offer any advice on tightening them up.'

'Of course, sir. I've been told to assist you in every way.'

CHAPTER TEN

'Stranraer looks like a nice enough place,' said Monique, sitting in the front passenger seat of the car.

'We're looking for the Wigtownshire Police Headquarters,' said Bob. 'I'm told it's on Lewis Street, the main road leading into the town from the south.'

'Turn left at the next junction,' said Monique, looking at a street map they'd been given at RAF Wigtown. 'It ought to be on the right.'

Having been in quite a few, from Kirkwall in the north to, now, Stranraer in the south, Monique was getting used to the idea that Scottish police stations all had something in common. Bob, who had been in many more than her, had once said that they all smelled the same and that might have been part of it. Whatever it was, she'd have known that the headquarters of Wigtownshire Constabulary in Stranraer was a police station from the moment she walked in, even if she'd been blindfolded.

A dark-haired young woman in the uniform of a constable of the Women's Auxiliary Police Corps was sitting behind the front desk reading a newspaper and she looked up as Bob led the way into the reception area beyond the front door from the street. It took her a moment to register the significance of the braid on Bob's peaked cap and then she stood up.

'Can I help you, sir?'

'Inspector White is expecting us. I'm Group Captain Sutherland and this is Madame Dubois. We're with Military Intelligence, Section 11.'

'Yes, of course, sir. Would you follow me, please?'

Monique had expected them to be taken to an interview

room to meet the inspector. Instead, she and Bob were led up a set of stairs to the first floor and shown into a fine office with mainly wood-panelled walls and a fireplace. Two glass-fronted bookcases full of cloth and leather-bound books stood against one wall and a framed map of the area hung on another. In front of the window was an imposing wooden desk inlaid with a green leather top. Bob and Monique were invited to sit on two chairs on the near side of the desk.

'Can I get you both tea?' asked the constable.

'Yes, please,' said Monique, smiling.

The constable returned a short time later with a tray on which were two mugs of tea and a plate of plain biscuits. 'Inspector White is on the telephone. He'll be with you as soon as possible.' Then she left, closing the office door behind herself.

Monique watched as Bob took a biscuit. 'I didn't ask, have you had anything to eat since you left home?'

'Michael and I had corned beef sandwiches from a NAAFI wagon we came across when we got back to RAF Wigtown from Cairn Head. Otherwise, no. How about you? You had an earlier start than me. I'm sorry, I didn't think to ask when the three of you arrived.'

'Andrew, Peter and I stopped for breakfast in a very nice café we found in a place called Thornhill on the drive down. The portions were generous and I suspect I've eaten better than you have, Bob.'

At that point, the office door opened and a grey-haired man in his fifties wearing the uniform of a police inspector came in, carrying a mug of, Monique assumed, tea.

'Hello, I'm sorry to have kept you both waiting. Could I start by asking to see your identity papers?'

He smiled when he returned them. 'Sorry, but you can't

be too careful.'

'I'd expect nothing less,' said Bob.

The inspector sat down on the chair behind the desk and took a sip from his mug. 'In case you are wondering, this is not my office. Lieutenant Campbell, the deputy chief constable, thought his office would be more suitable than an interview room. He sends his apologies for not seeing you himself. He had to accompany the chief constable to a meeting in Glasgow today.'

'Please pass on my thanks,' said Bob. 'We're here to find out what we can about the disappearance of two military officers, Flight Lieutenant James Thorn and Captain William Evans. I understand both were last seen in Stranraer before vanishing on Wednesday and Friday of the week before last.'

The inspector leaned forwards to place his mug on a circular cork coaster on the desk. 'The RAF has a strong presence in Galloway and the RAF Police flight at RAF Wig Bay is taking the lead on investigating Flight Lieutenant Thorn's disappearance. I am aware they interviewed the woman he spent the evening with on the day he was last seen but other than that I know little about what they've been doing.'

'I've got a meeting arranged with Flying Officer Dugdale a little later this afternoon,' said Bob.

'That's good,' said the inspector. 'The army has less of a presence in the area so we've been taking the lead on the disappearance of Captain Evans. That all changed earlier today, however, and the reason I couldn't see you when you arrived was that I was on the phone with a major in the Corps of Military Police based in Belfast. He has agreed to take over the case.'

'What's happened to bring that about?' asked Bob.

‘The young lady you met when you arrived, who is frankly wasted doing the sort of receptionist and secretarial jobs she’s limited to in the Women’s Auxiliary Police Corps, asked a question this morning that the rest of us should have asked as soon as Captain Evans disappeared. What emerged as a result is both very helpful and rather embarrassing and certainly changes our working theory about what has become of the captain.’

‘Let me guess,’ said Monique. ‘She asked whether you’d looked at passenger lists for the steamers sailing from here to Northern Ireland in the period after Captain Evans was last seen.’ Monique laughed at the expression on the inspector’s face. ‘You did give us a strong hint when you said the military police in Northern Ireland have taken over the case.’

The inspector smiled back. ‘Let me explain the background a little. Captain Evans commands a small unit of railway engineers that operates the Cairnryan military railway. That’s a network of railway lines that have been established to service the port they’ve built at Cairnryan on the east shore of Loch Ryan and which connect to the London, Midland and Scottish Railway main line from Stranraer to Dumfries.

‘Captain Evans and one of his men, Warrant Officer Yardley, travelled by steamer to Larne on Tuesday the 15th of June. They spent their time in Northern Ireland looking at railway operations in the Belfast and Larne areas. The two men travelled back on the afternoon sailing from Larne to Stranraer on Friday the 18th of June. On arrival, it was met by an army vehicle. This took Warrant Officer Yardley back to the base the Royal Engineers have established near Cairnryan. Captain Evans, with another Royal Engineers officer, is staying in the old RAF Stranraer officers’ mess at

North West Castle. That's not far from the steamer pier and Captain Evans said that as it was a nice afternoon he would walk to his accommodation and be on duty the following morning as usual. The driver of the army vehicle dropped the captain's bag off there while the captain walked.

'That evening, Captain Evans had dinner at North West Castle with his junior colleague, Lieutenant Cochrane. When I spoke to him after the captain was reported missing the following day, Lieutenant Cochrane told me that Evans had appeared nervous over dinner. He thought he had been followed from the steamer pier to North West Castle by a naval officer, a lieutenant, who had again seemed to be following him when he went out for a pre-dinner walk.

'I wasn't able to find anyone else who had noticed a naval officer hanging around the steamer pier or North West Castle. Meanwhile, Captain Evans had simply disappeared off the face of the Earth between having dinner with his colleague on the Friday evening and failing to report for duty in Cairnryan on the Saturday morning. His travel bag was in his room at North West Castle, as if he'd only partly unpacked it after returning, and there was no indication that any of his belongings were missing.

'That was where things stood until Woman Auxiliary Police Constable Franklin asked about passenger lists this morning. It didn't take long to establish that Captain Evans sailed on the 6 a.m. mail steamer from Stranraer to Larne on Saturday the 19th of June, which meant he arrived in Larne at about the same time as he was missed at Cairnryan. He is a man with an impeccable record but, in the circumstances, the Corps of Military Police is now looking for him in Northern Ireland as a possible deserter.'

'Does he have any Irish connection?' asked Bob.

'None that we know of, sir,' said the inspector. 'I'm told

he comes from Kent.'

Monique caught Bob's eye and could see exactly what he was thinking. 'Did anyone give you a description of Captain Evans?' she asked.

'He's 32 years old, has black hair and a moustache and brown eyes. He's of average height and build. I can see the two of you think that's significant in a way that's escaped me.'

It was Bob who answered. 'What's worrying us is the thought that the man who travelled to Larne on the Saturday morning might not have been Captain Evans. We believe that a German agent based in Eire was operating in the area during the week that the captain disappeared. The limited description we have for him matches the description you just gave us for Captain Evans quite closely, though without the moustache.

'Perhaps this agent did harm to Captain Evans later on the Friday evening and took his uniform and identity papers, and added a fake moustache, so he could board a steamer to Larne the following morning? We know the agent was in Dublin two days later so if I'm right there's no point looking for Captain Evans in Northern Ireland.'

'That suggests we should carry on looking for the captain here, or perhaps more likely his body,' said the inspector. 'How sure are you of this?'

'It has to be a strong possibility,' said Bob. 'Am I right in thinking that you need special permission to travel on the steamers between Stranraer and Larne?'

'Yes,' said Inspector White. 'Again let me start with the background. Before the war, the service was excellent. But things then changed significantly. Northern Ireland is extensively used for troop training and there is a lot of military traffic back and forth across the North Passage. A variety of ships are called into service for this and one of the pre-war steamers, the *Princess Maud*, is exclusively used as a troopship on the route. That means that all other users have to sail on the only other steamer, the *Princess Margaret*. Because this carries the mail it leaves Stranraer early each morning to make the crossing to Larne, then makes the return trip each afternoon.

'The other factor to take into account is the one you identified, group captain. There are quite stringent restrictions on who can travel between Great Britain on the one hand and Northern Ireland or Eire on the other. Only passengers with a Travel Identity Card are allowed to book passage on the steamer. The card is effectively a passport. Look, I'll show you.'

The inspector reached into an inside pocket and then passed over to Bob a green card-covered folded document. Monique watched as Bob opened it, revealing an intricately printed interior carrying the inspector's photograph on one side and information about him on the other.

'We know that Captain Evans must have one of those,' said Monique, 'because he was able to travel to Larne and back that week.'

'That's right,' said the inspector.

'If I wanted to travel to Northern Ireland and I didn't have a Travel Identity Card, then the best way to find someone who did have one would be to watch who got off the steamer from Larne,' she said. 'Obviously, I'd pick someone who looked like me so the photograph was a reasonable match and if I wanted to adopt a military identity I'd pick someone wearing a uniform that would fit me. Then I'd keep track of them until I had a chance to relieve them of their uniform and their identity documents, both the Travel Identity Card and their military identity papers and anything else they had, perhaps a ration book or a driving licence.'

'So I probably am looking for a body,' said the inspector. 'What about the missing flight lieutenant? He also disappeared during the week you say the German agent was here.'

'We don't know,' said Bob. 'But two missing military officers in three days in the same town is a hell of a coincidence. I'll ask Flying Officer Dugdale to liaise with you if we think it's likely the two cases are connected when we've talked to him.'

'One thing puzzles me,' said the inspector. 'You said this German agent was based in Eire. If he needed to steal a Travel Identity Card to get on board the steamer from Stranraer to Larne, how was he able to cross the North Passage to Scotland in the first place?'

'That's a good question,' said Bob, 'and one we need to answer.'

CHAPTER ELEVEN

RAF Wig Bay sprawled along a considerable length of the west shore of Loch Ryan a few miles north of Stranraer. To Bob, the most striking aspect of the establishment was the large number of Short Sunderland flying boats either moored in the loch or pulled out of the water on slipways or in parking areas.

Security was very tight. Bob wondered whether that was normal or because they were expecting a visit from Military Intelligence, Section 11. At the third checkpoint manned by bored-looking men of the RAF Regiment, they were told the station headquarters could be found amongst a cluster of buildings at the end of a length of concrete roadway on a natural raised shelf that stood back from and above the shore of the loch.

Flying Officer Dugdale commanded the RAF Police flight at RAF Wig Bay. He received Bob and Monique in an office whose door carried a sign stating that it belonged to 'OC Engineering', perhaps because he felt it conveyed a better impression or offered more space than his own.

The flying officer was in his early twenties and very nervous. When Bob and Monique politely refused his offer first of tea and then of cigarettes, it only made him more so.

Bob tried to put him at ease. 'You seem to be on top of security here if our experience is anything to go by. The geography of the base must give you problems.'

'Yes, sir, it's long and narrow, running along the shore. That gives us a considerable length of land perimeter to protect on the west side and it gives us a lot of water to protect in Loch Ryan. It's of some help that our neighbours at the military port on the far side of the loch also take security very seriously, while to our immediate north is the RAF Marine Craft Training School. But sometimes I envy men I trained with who were posted to ordinary airfields with three runways and a roughly circular boundary fence.'

'Yes, I can understand that,' said Bob. 'As you know, we're here to ask about Flight Lieutenant Thorn. We've talked this afternoon to Inspector White in Stranraer about the army captain who disappeared two days after Thorn and are trying to establish if their disappearances might be connected. Can you summarise where you've got to?'

'Not very far, sir, if I'm honest,' said the flying officer.

'Could you start by describing the flight lieutenant?' asked Monique.

'Of course, ma'am. He's 37 years old. He comes from Alnwick in Northumberland and has a wife and three children there. He ran a garage and sold cars before the war and is a highly respected engineer on 1 Flying Boat Servicing Unit, which is the main unit based here, though next month they will be joined by 11 Flying Boat Fitting Unit.'

'A casual glance around suggests your main business is servicing Short Sunderlands,' said Bob.'

'That's right, sir. I saw a memo this morning that said we have sixteen Sunderlands being serviced here at present and another twenty-eight fully serviceable aircraft in reserve, to be supplied to operational squadrons as needed.'

'We were talking about Flight Lieutenant Thorn,' said Monique.

'Sorry, Monique,' said Bob.

'Yes, ma'am. I think I told you most of what I know.'

'What's he like physically?'

'He's unexceptional. Normal sort of height and build, with black hair and brown eyes. He's a nice man who is well-liked. I can see why he was successful selling cars.'

'Have you been able to come up with any reason for his disappearance?' asked Monique.

'None at all, ma'am. It was on the Wednesday evening, the week before last. Though married, he had formed a close friendship with a lady who manages one of the shifts at the telephone exchange in Stranraer, Mrs Margaret Abercrombie. She's a war widow who lives in a small terraced house in the centre of the town. He says he visits her so they can listen to music together on her gramophone and because they enjoy each other's company. I'm not sure many of his friends believe that's all there is to it, but that's no one else's business except his wife's.

'The flight lieutenant cycled into Stranraer that evening and spent about two hours with Mrs Abercrombie. She told me that he then set off to cycle back, just as he normally would. The weather was good, it was still full daylight and they'd not drunk any alcohol. There was no reason why he shouldn't return to his room in the officers' mess here, but he didn't.

'He was reported missing the next morning. I talked to Mrs Abercrombie not long afterwards and had no problem getting plenty of volunteers to mount a search. We combed every inch of the road from Stranraer to Wig Bay, plus ditches and hedgerows, plus the fields on the inland side of the road and the shoreline of the loch which, as you'll have seen, the road closely follows. We were looking for the flight lieutenant or any trace of him, or his bicycle. We found nothing.'

'Could he have argued with Mrs Abercrombie?' asked Monique.

'She asked me to search her house when I first went to see her,' said Dugdale. 'She said she had nothing to hide or be ashamed of so two of my men gave the place a thorough but gentle going-over. There was no indication of foul play. We also spoke to the neighbours. It appears the party walls are not very thick. They can hear the music she plays, and don't object to it as she never plays it late or very loud. But they heard nothing to help explain Flight Lieutenant Thorn's disappearance.

*

At Bob's request, Flying Officer Dugdale contacted Mrs Abercrombie at the telephone exchange in Stranraer and arranged for Bob and Monique to visit her at home after her shift finished at 4 p.m.

The house was one of a terrace leading from the centre of the town towards the south end of Loch Ryan. Bob had agreed with Monique that she should take the lead.

It was obvious to Monique that Mrs Abercrombie had been crying. She was a blonde woman in her late thirties and, red-rimmed and puffy eyes aside, was very attractive.

'It's about James, isn't it?' she asked.

'Yes, we're trying to find out where he is,' said Monique. She introduced herself and Bob and accepted Mrs Abercrombie's invitation to go through to the front room. She also accepted an offer of tea and cake on behalf of both of them.

The room was small but impeccably clean. There was silence for a moment after the tea and cake had been served.

'Can you tell us what happened that evening?' asked Monique. 'We don't need to know how you spent the evening, just whether there was anything out of the ordinary that happened.'

‘James is dead, isn’t he?’ asked Margaret Abercrombie.

‘We don’t know,’ said Monique. ‘We need your help to find out.’

‘We were just good friends, whatever the neighbours think,’ said Margaret. ‘We met in the corner shop at the top of the road a few months ago and he said something about music. The next time we met he was on his bicycle and nearly ran me over in the street close to the Castle of St John. We got talking about music and I told him about my record collection. He’s been visiting about an evening each week since then.’

There was another silence.

‘It wasn't just the neighbours who had the wrong idea. James joked about his friends thinking there was more to him visiting me than just the music. Listen to me. I’m even talking about him as if he’s dead. The truth is that he loves his wife. That’s wonderful in one way and desperately sad in another. James is everything that my late and unlamented brute of a husband never was and, well, hope springs eternal, as they say. I don’t know why I’m telling two complete strangers this, perhaps because I know I can never tell James, even if he’s alive.’

She started crying again. Monique moved from the armchair she’d been sitting on to the sofa, next to Margaret, and put her arm round her.

‘Was there anything out of the ordinary about that evening, Margaret?’

‘James did behave a little oddly when he arrived. He said he’d had to swerve to avoid a naval officer who’d stepped off the pavement just before he’d turned into the street and the two men had exchanged mild insults. He said he thought that the man had then seen him come to the house. He looked out of the front window a couple of times while he was here, down towards the loch, and did say he thought the officer he'd bumped into was watching the house. When I went to look I couldn't see anyone. He even went to the upstairs front room once to look in that direction. I don't think he saw anyone. I was more worried that one of the neighbours would see him in the window of my bedroom.'

'But apart from that, it was an ordinary evening of talk and music?' asked Monique.

'That's right. And then he left and I've not seen him since.' Margaret burst into tears again.

'Did he say anything else?' asked Monique. 'Anything about the naval officer?'

'He said he was a lieutenant and that he had a strong Liverpool accent.'

'Thank you, Margaret, we're very grateful to you for talking to us.'

'Will you let me know if you find out what's happened to James?'

'Yes, of course.'

*

'You've just caught me. I was about to go off duty.'

Monique had followed Bob into the reception area of the Wigtownshire Police Headquarters and could see Inspector White standing at the foot of the staircase to the upper floor of the building.

'It won't take long,' said Bob. 'A couple of things have come up that we need to discuss with you.'

'Follow me up to the lieutenant's office,' said the inspector.

'Should I make tea?' asked Woman Auxiliary Police

Constable Franklin, from behind the front desk.

'Thank you, but no,' said Monique, smiling. 'We've just had some and we won't be here long.'

'What can I do for you?' asked the inspector once they'd sat down in the lieutenant's office.

Bob leaned forwards in his seat. 'You said that Captain Evans told his colleague over dinner that he thought he had been followed by a naval lieutenant from the steamer pier to North West Castle, and then again when he went out for a pre-dinner walk.'

'That's right,' said the inspector.

'We've just been to see Mrs Abercrombie.'

'The woman the RAF flight lieutenant spent the evening he disappeared with?'

'Yes,' said Bob. 'When Monique asked her whether there was anything unusual about his visit, Mrs Abercrombie said that the flight lieutenant had an altercation with a naval lieutenant who stepped out into the road in front of his bicycle not far from her house. During his visit, he was concerned that the man was watching the house, though when she looked out of the window she wasn't able to see him.'

'I'm not a great believer in coincidence,' said Inspector White.

'No, me neither,' agreed Bob. 'It would help if you could get your officers to ask around to see whether anyone noticed a naval lieutenant acting strangely in or around the town during the week the two officers disappeared. What I've not told you is that we believe this German agent, who we know as the Cuttlefish to reflect his ability to disguise himself, intends to return to Scotland and that, during his first visit, he established a base here. It would be especially helpful to know if anyone let a room or a property to a naval lieutenant during that week.'

'Yes, of course,' said the inspector. 'Captain Evans didn't give his colleague a description of the naval lieutenant. You talked earlier of a man who matched the captain's appearance quite closely. Am I right in recalling that the missing flight lieutenant is of similar appearance to the captain and to the German agent?'

'Yes, he is,' said Monique.

'Did Flight Lieutenant Thorn tell Mrs Abercrombie anything else that might help?'

'He told her that the naval lieutenant had a strong Liverpool accent,' said Monique. 'We believe the man we are looking for naturally has an Irish accent and may have been covering that up. However, we have heard him described as a "master of disguise" so he may be able to deploy a variety of accents. We are also told he has a long scar across the top of his right thigh, but that won't help identify him in normal circumstances.'

The inspector raised his eyebrows. 'I've seen no reports of a missing naval lieutenant. But there does seem to be a pattern developing here so I wonder whether I need to ask more widely.'

'That's a good idea,' said Bob. 'When we arrived earlier you were talking to a major in the Corps of Military Police based in Belfast. If you have equivalent contacts on the naval side of things in Northern Ireland, I think it might be worth asking them whether they have a missing lieutenant.'

'Yes, I'll do that,' said Inspector White. 'It feels to me as if someone has been collecting identities and the naval officer's might have been the first to be acquired. If that was done in Northern Ireland then it might answer the question I posed earlier, about how this German agent of yours crossed the North Channel in the first place.'

‘My thought exactly,’ said Bob. ‘Presumably, he wanted to use a different identity on the steamer back to Larne, which is why Captain Evans disappeared. It doesn’t explain why he needed Flight Lieutenant Thorn’s identity, though, assuming that’s what’s happened.’

‘At least you know two of the names he’s likely to be using if he does try to return to Scotland,’ said the inspector. ‘And if we can track down a missing naval officer then that will give you a third.’

Monique wasn't sure it would be that easy and she could see that Bob thought the same.

CHAPTER TWELVE

Group Captain Donald Belmont was a tall man in his mid-forties with dark hair that matched his impressive handlebar moustache. 'I wondered where you'd gone to, Bob. Last time we met, you were in command of 55 Operational Training Unit at RAF Annan.'

Bob smiled. 'And you landed there in a Blackburn Botha that had suffered an engine failure. That was a memorable night in the mess bar. I suppose I'd still be training young men to be fighter pilots if fate hadn't taken a hand. I was made deputy head of Military Intelligence, Section 11, last October, and haven't looked back since.'

'And a promotion, too. Congratulations!'

Bob was meeting the group captain in the manager's office of the officers' mess at RAF Wigtown.

'I'm sorry that I'm seeing you here, Bob, rather than at the station headquarters. You'll have noticed that the domestic site is the better part of a mile away from the technical site and the airfield so the mess is the best bet at this time of the day. The arrangement must have made sense to someone when the place was built but I shudder to think how much fuel we use shuttling people back and forth or how much it costs to provide and maintain the large fleet of bicycles we have, all just to get our men and women between where they live and where they work.'

'How many people do you have here?' asked Bob.

'It varies from day to day, obviously, but at the end of last week I had 244 RAF and 12 Women's Auxiliary Air Force officers on the books, plus 491 RAF and 12 WAAF senior non-commissioned officers and 1,240 RAF and 468 WAAF other ranks.'

'I'm grateful to you for accommodating us at short notice, Donald.'

'How long are you likely to be with us?'

'Unhelpfully, I don't know,' said Bob. 'We may move on as early as tomorrow or Wednesday but it does depend on how our investigation goes. I'm sorry to be so vague. Still worse, I know my people in London mentioned that we might be joined by a Soviet Air Force officer and a woman from the Soviet embassy. I'm afraid I don't know whether that will happen or not.'

'That's not a problem.'

'I was struck by how busy the airfield was when I arrived.'

'It usually is,' said Belmont. 'I'm sure you know from your time at Annan that we are part of Flying Training Command. The main unit based here is the awkwardly named No. 1 (Observer) Advanced Flying Unit. We take in newly qualified navigators and bomb aimers, many freshly returned from training in Canada, and prepare them for operational flying in UK and European conditions. It's a very intensive process. I have sixty-five Avro Ansons and nine Westland Lysanders based here and last month we managed to achieve over 3,700 flying hours, including over 1,000 at night.'

'That's impressive,' said Bob. 'How do your pilots respond to flying routine training sorties day after day?'

'That's a very perceptive question,' said Belmont. 'A good proportion of them are young Canadian sergeant or flight sergeant pilots who would prefer to be posted to operational squadrons, while others are on rotation from operational units. I suspect that none of them chose to become pilots so they could provide what they regard as taxi-driving services to wet-behind-the-ears navigators and bomb aimers.'

'That must cause problems,' said Bob.

'Bored pilots and flight safety don't go hand in hand. We have more accidents than we should, and the high ground to the east and north doesn't help. In the first three weeks of August last year, we had four fatal accidents causing seventeen deaths. We've managed to improve things since then but we still get episodes of unauthorised low flying and what we ask our young men to do is inherently dangerous to start with.'

'I was greeted by two Typhoons when I arrived and saw more on the ground,' said Bob. 'I can't imagine they have any part in training navigators or bomb aimers.'

'You're right,' said Belmont. 'For the next couple of months, we're playing host to Typhoons from 174 and 175 Squadrons. Both squadrons exchanged their Hurricanes for Typhoons in April and are sending groups of pilots up here to hone their ground attack skills where they can count on not being distracted by the need to mount defensive patrols against hit-and-run raids by Focke-Wulf Fw 190s. Anyway, should we go for a drink? I just need to make a quick phone call, but I'll join you in a couple of minutes.'

*

Monique found her way without difficulty to the bar in the officers' mess. The bedroom the RAF had provided for her was in an upper-floor corridor that carried large signs proclaiming it to be for 'WAAF officers only' and 'out of bounds to all male personnel'. She wondered if anyone took any notice.

Since meeting Bob, Monique had been in the bars of enough RAF officers' messes to realise that this one was fairly typical. It was also fairly quiet, perhaps because it was still quite early in the evening.

Monique looked around, hoping that Michael had returned to RAF Wigtown or that Bob had finished his meeting with the station commander. Neither was there. Two women in the uniforms of WAAF officers were sitting at a table in one corner and several other tables were occupied by men, smoking and drinking, and by a group playing dominoes.

Two officers were standing and talking at the bar and Monique went a little further along from them and asked the elderly barman for a gin and tonic. She wasn't entirely surprised to be asked to prove who she was. After all, she was wearing civilian clothes and had a foreign accent. She showed the man her MI5 identity card, feeling it would be simpler not to have to explain what MI11 was. In the event, she still had to tell him that MI5 was an arm of British military intelligence, and that was enough to persuade him to sell her a drink.

Monique took a sip of her gin and looked around the room again, trying to decide whether to introduce herself to the two WAAF officers or go and sit at an empty table and wait for Bob or Michael.

'Hello, I've not seen you here before.'

Monique realised that one of the two officers who had been talking at the bar had approached her. He was a tall and extremely attractive young man with blond hair, blue eyes and a moustache, wearing an RAF flight lieutenant's uniform with pilot's wings.

She smiled, instinctively. 'Hello. That's because I've never been here before.'

'I couldn't help but overhear you telling the barman that you are with MI5. That must be fascinating work.'

Monique thought the young pilot had to be in his early twenties and wondered whether he'd misjudged her age while she was talking to the barman. Surprisingly, the look of doubt or second thoughts she'd expected when he could see her more clearly never crossed his face. In another life, not so very long before, she'd have been flattered by his obvious interest, perhaps flattered enough to respond positively.

'I'm Adrian, what's your name?'

'My name's Monique, Adrian. Please don't be offended if I suggest that I may be a little too old for you.'

Adrian smiled. 'I beg to differ, Monique. You intrigue me and I'd like the chance to get to know you better.'

'You're not easily put off, are you Adrian? It's not just my age. I think I'm also a little too married for you.'

'I've never found that to be an insurmountable obstacle. There's a war on, and husbands are usually a long way away from their wives.'

Monique smiled. 'Would it make a difference if I told you that my husband was just behind you?'

Bob had walked into the bar and was a little further away than she'd suggested but still close enough to realise something was going on. He had a puzzled but slightly amused expression on his face.

The flight lieutenant whirled around.

'Hello Bob,' said Monique. 'Can I introduce you to, sorry, Adrian, you didn't tell me your second name.'

'It's Flight Lieutenant Somerset, sir.'

'Flight Lieutenant Somerset was just explaining to me his theory about lonely wives,' said Monique. 'Adrian, this is my husband, Group Captain Bob Sutherland.'

'I'm pleased to meet you, sir. Look, I'm sorry to both of you for my misunderstanding and I hope I've not offended either of you.'

There was a pause. Adrian Somerset had his back to Monique but she got the sense he was trying to work out how to escape from the situation he'd created. She could see that the two WAAF officers in the corner of the room were watching what was going on and smiling broadly. One of them caught Monique's eye and raised her glass. Monique smiled back.

Then something changed in the way the flight lieutenant was standing.

'Hang on, sir, you're the Mosquito pilot, aren't you? There was a group captain's pennant painted on the nose, so it has to be yours.'

'That's right. Was it you who welcomed me in a Typhoon this morning?'

'Yes, sir. You've also got 22 kill markings on the nose of your aircraft, haven't you?'

'That's right,' said Bob. 'By my count, it's 24, but it was better only to mark confirmed kills on the Mosquito.'

'It's now 23 and 25,' said Monique. 'You've forgotten the aircraft you shot down when we were on that landing craft in Malta. Everyone in the harbour witnessed what happened so it must count as "confirmed".'

'That's true, but I wasn't flying at the time,' said Bob, smiling. 'I see you've got a Distinguished Flying Cross, flight lieutenant. May I ask what that was for?'

'I got lucky on one of our early anti-intruder patrols in the Typhoon last month, sir. I shot down two Focke-Wulf Fw 190 a little inland from Hastings after they'd surprised us and got my flight commander. He baled out and survived but then it was me against them and thankfully they made a muck of it. I also shot down a Messerschmitt Me 410 at the beginning of this month, but I've got a very long way to go before I'm in your league, sir.'

'Being lucky is a big part of it,' said Bob. 'How is your flight commander?'

'He's facing up to life without a lower right leg, sir. I've taken over his role on 175 Squadron. I could have wished to get the promotion in another way if I'm honest.'

'We've all felt that,' said Bob, 'but in time it passes. It's good to meet you, Flight Lieutenant Somerset.'

'You too, sir.' The flight lieutenant turned to smile at Monique. 'And you, Mrs Sutherland.'

Monique smiled back as Adrian Somerset made his escape, leaving the bar entirely. He was followed out of the room by the pilot officer he'd been talking to when Monique had entered.

A moment later a tall man in a group captain's uniform entered and walked over to the bar.

'Can I buy you a drink, Bob?'

'Thank you, Donald, a gin and tonic, please. May I introduce you to Madame Monique Dubois, who is on secondment from MI5 to work with me in MI11? Monique, this is Donald Belmont.'

'I'm very pleased to meet you, Madame Dubois,' said Group Captain Belmont.

'And you, group captain. Please call me Monique.'

'Donald, to avoid any misunderstandings, you also need to know that Monique and I were married at the beginning of the month.'

'Congratulations! If I'd known, we'd have changed the room arrangements.'

'I don't want to put you to any trouble,' said Bob.

'We do have some twin rooms and could probably find one for you. It would be a net saving of a room from our point of view.'

'Thank you, group captain, that would be perfect,' said Monique.

'Call me Donald, please.'

'Thank you, Donald.'

'Your drink is almost gone, Monique, let me buy you both one. Choose a table, I'll have them brought over.'

The drinks were carried to the table on a tray by the barman, with Group Captain Belmont following.

Donald sat down. 'The barman tells me you encountered Flight Lieutenant Somerset, Monique. I hope he didn't offend you.'

'Not at all,' said Monique.

'He arrived a few weeks ago as the officer commanding the advance party setting up the Typhoon deployment. I'm told he's a fine pilot, but I'm also told that he's broken hearts while he's been here, both amongst the WAAF contingent on the base and in the wider community. I'm sure you can look after yourself, Monique, but you do need to be careful around him.'

Monique could see that Bob was trying not to laugh.

'What's so funny?' asked Donald.

'I think it's Flight Lieutenant Somerset who needs to be careful,' said Bob. 'Monique has an uncompromising approach to men who try to take liberties with her.'

CHAPTER THIRTEEN

The manager of the officers' mess was happy for Bob to use a small staff restroom adjacent to the kitchen, from which the smell of breakfast being cooked was emanating. The aromas of bacon and sausages did not sit well with the stale tobacco smell in the room itself, which was perhaps partly due to the two metal ashtrays on the table, both full of cigarette ends. A poster on the wall beside the door reminded staff of the importance of washing their hands before serving food. Having seen and smelled the room, Bob was pleased he'd already had his breakfast. It wasn't the sort of place that promoted a healthy appetite.

As he often had in the past, Bob wondered about the sense behind a military class system that dictated that Petty Officer Andrew MacDonald and Sergeant Peter Bennett were excluded from the 'front of house' parts of the officers' mess simply because of their rank.

'So this is how the other half live,' said Peter, after they had sat down around the scarred wooden table. 'It makes me grateful for the delights of the sergeants' mess.'

Bob smiled. 'Was the accommodation all right?'

'Andrew and I shared a twin room, sir, but otherwise it was fine. The bar was full of trainee aircrew who seemed keen to get their drinking done today in case there's no tomorrow.'

'If you consider that many of them will go on to become navigators and bomb aimers on heavy bombers flying over Germany, you've got to have some sympathy,' said Bob.

Bob was sitting at one end of the table with Monique and Michael Dixon to his right. To his left were Petty Officer Andrew MacDonald, who normally supported

Michael on visits to naval bases, and Sergeant Peter Bennett, the junior member of his RAF team.

A mess orderly brought in teas and Sergeant Bennett helped distribute them around the table.

Bob took a sip of his and then resumed. 'I spoke to Maurice Cunningham this morning. There's still no news of our Soviet colleagues and I thought it would be useful for the five of us to catch up before we head off in different directions for the day. As you know, Monique and I were in Stranraer yesterday afternoon.' He went on to give a brief account of what they'd found there. 'We intend to return this morning to ensure the police are doing everything possible to track the movements of the mysterious naval lieutenant with the Liverpudlian accent. Until we come up with anything better, we have to assume that he's the Cuttlefish and if he has established a forward base in or near Stranraer as our Soviet friends suggest, then finding it before he returns would be a huge step forward.'

'Does that mean you are now confident that he is real rather than a Soviet invention?' asked Michael.

'As you know, I thought it best to keep an open mind on that,' said Bob. 'However, the disappearance of two military officers during the week the Soviets say the Cuttlefish was in Scotland with the only thing linking their disappearances being a man who matches the description we have for him does appear highly significant. Yes, I accept that quite a lot of men would match the same description, but the fact that the missing captain, or someone carrying his identity documents, travelled by steamer from Stranraer to Larne the morning after he was last seen also appears to tie in with the idea that the Cuttlefish is real. How did things go yesterday with you, Michael? I didn't see you when you got back last night so I assume you made the most of the daylight?'

Michael Dixon put his teacup down in its saucer. 'Andrew, Peter and I spent the afternoon and early evening taking a detailed look at the security in place to protect the work on the Mulberry harbours, especially at Cairn Head and Garlieston. I should come clean and tell you that didn't take the entire time because we found a very nice hotel in Garlieston that served good food. After we'd eaten we spent an hour or so sitting on the nearby sea wall while enjoying a couple of beers and discussing what we'd found where no one could overhear us.

'For the most part, they're doing a pretty good job, though Major Avery believes that they need more men to ensure security on the approaches to the area and along the coastline. We agree with him. Given we've now identified a specific threat to security, the major is going to pursue the question of reinforcements when his two senior officers, a colonel and a brigadier, pay a pre-planned visit to Cairn Head by seaplane this afternoon. I gather they intend to inspect progress on Mulberry before staying overnight to watch a demonstration of the use of the pierhead and floating pier early tomorrow morning.

'Major Avery asked if one of us could attend at least part of the initial meeting after these men arrive to emphasise MI11's support for more manpower.'

'I'll go,' said Bob. 'Monique and I should be able to get back from Stranraer in time.'

'I'm sure the major will welcome that,' said Michael. 'When we finish here, I'll telephone him to let him know and see if there's been any update on the time these men are due to arrive. It's worth mentioning that Andrew, Peter and I also discussed the situation at Garlieston while enjoying our beers. The harbour and bay there are in full view of the village and are where some of the development work is being done on Mulberry. The area is already designated a "Protected Area" under the 1939 Defence Regulations, so civilians living or travelling there need special passes, in addition to their National Registration Identity Cards. Short of evacuating the village entirely, which would seem likely to raise interest in the place rather than suppress it, even with control over what the press can publish, there's not much that can be done to tighten things further, beyond ensuring the major has all the men he needs.'

'Thank you, Michael. What are your priorities for today?'

'As you and I discussed on the flight down yesterday, Bob, we need to learn more about the stories Commodore Cunningham's people uncovered about an MI5 agent dressed as a tramp who has been testing the security of military installations in the area. We need to find out if we're dealing with actual incidents or something someone heard in a pub that then grew in the telling. Our first port of call will be at No. 2 Heavy Anti Aircraft Practice Camp, which is at Burrow Head, at the southern tip of the peninsula south of Whithorn.

'We will then pay a visit to the police stations in Whithorn and Wigtown, both of which reported the rumour when Commodore Cunningham's people were ringing round. Then we're heading to an explosives factory at a place called Carsegowan Moss just off the main road a couple of miles north of Whithorn. After that we need to drive west, to visit RAF Castle Kennedy, beside the road to Stranraer, and then to RAF Wig Bay, north-west of Stranraer. The final stop on our Cook's Tour will be a bombing range at Braid Fell, in the hills to the east of Cairnryan. As well as trying to get to the bottom of the story of the mysterious tramp, we will take the opportunity to form a quick impression of security more generally at the military installations we visit, again as you and I discussed. I think that should keep us busy.'

'That's an eclectic collection of locations for this supposed MI5 officer to be taking an interest in,' said Bob. 'Has there been any mention of him testing security at anywhere associated with Mulberry?'

'No,' said Michael. 'I specifically asked Major Avery about that yesterday afternoon. We also have no feel for the timeframe in which this is all meant to have happened. If any of these incidents are real, then knowing if they took place when we believe the Cuttlefish was in Scotland would be a great help. Looking ahead, do you want to return here tonight, Bob?'

'That seems best for the moment,' said Bob, 'though it might help to keep our options open. We can leave the Mosquito and one of the cars here but let's pack our bags in the other two, just in case. We should try to keep in touch during the day. I noticed you managed to get radios fitted in the cars while Monique and I were away. Do we have any idea how effective they are?'

It was Andrew MacDonald who replied. 'In general terms, sir. When you first asked about this, you were keen to look at the system the City of Glasgow Police had been using in their cars since before the war. I think you know we also looked at the army's Wireless Set No. 22. Neither system was what you might call elegant and both meant giving up the space in the boot to batteries and radio equipment.

'With a powerful base transmitter and receiver, the Glasgow police equipment, which they sourced in the USA, could manage ranges of up to 15 miles for voice and 25 for

Morse, with a red light on the dashboard illuminating to alert a car to an incoming message. The range between cars is nearer 10 miles for voice and 20 for Morse. The army's Wireless Set No. 22 can manage similar ranges between vehicles but relies on a much more unwieldy aerial arrangement. That, combined with your initial preference, was why we went for the Glasgow police system.

'We've done some initial tests, both between cars and using a base transmitter and receiver at Craigiehall. These suggest the theoretical ranges I've just given assume a flat Earth with no topography. In practice, if you transmit or receive while on top of a hill, you do rather better, but if you use the radios in a valley you do much worse. It follows that if both cars are on top of hills you get more than the theoretical range. On the other hand, if the two cars are in valleys you are lucky to get much more than a line of sight between them.'

'When we were coming back from Stranraer last night we worked out it's not far short of 30 miles away from here,' said Monique. 'That suggests the radios may not be much use today.'

'That's true,' said Bob. 'I think we'll need to rely more on the old-fashioned approach, of phoning Joyce Stuart at Craigiehall and coordinating what we're doing via her.'

CHAPTER FOURTEEN

The front door of the Wigtownshire Police Headquarters in Stranraer was propped open with a curling stone. Monique assumed this was to allow a flow of air to give some relief from what was becoming a very hot day. Woman Auxiliary Police Constable Franklin was again on duty at the front desk and Monique wondered if she spent her whole working life there.

'Hello. Inspector White's been trying to get hold of you at RAF Wigtown but no one knew where you were.'

'What's happened?' asked Bob.

'Two young women with the Women's Timber Corps were marking trees for felling in a remote forested area west of here when they found the bodies of two men earlier this morning. The bodies had been there for some time. That's all I can tell you, I'm afraid.'

'Can you show us on a map where this is?' asked Bob.

'There's no need, sir. I know the area well. I'll get someone to cover the desk and show you how to get there myself.'

Monique was about to say that dead bodies that had been in the open for any length of time in warm weather would not make for a pleasant excursion but bit the comment back. It was probably the sort of thing Constable Franklin heard from her male colleagues every day and she deserved better from another woman.

The constable went into an office and a short time later was followed back out into the reception area by an elderly Police War Reserve constable who acted as though he had better things to do.

She then led the way out into the sunshine with Monique

following and Bob bringing up the rear.

'You must be pleased to get out of the office,' said Monique.

'Yes, ma'am. I see more of that front desk than I'd like.'

'Call me Monique, please.'

'Of course, Monique. I'm Dorothy.'

Monique drove while Dorothy gave directions from the rear seat.

'This is the way we went to RAF Wig Bay,' said Bob.

'Yes, it would be, sir. We take a left turn inland just along here. It's uphill from there.'

They took another left and then a third, this time onto a very minor road that continued to climb and had vegetation growing so densely that at times it brushed against the sides of the car.

The narrow confines of the road made progress seem very slow to Monique. 'Is it much further?' she asked.

'No,' said Dorothy. 'We've passed Knock Hill and Slewscinnie Hill, both on our left. The road now passes the top of Rawer Hill, which you can see ahead of us. On the opposite side, on the right of the road, is an area of dense woodland with a track leading into it. We turn onto the track.'

Monique turned as instructed and followed a rough track with a central strip of tufted grass. Even at a very slow speed, the bumps in the surface tested the suspension.

'There's a clearing ahead, with vehicles parked in it,' said Bob.

In the heat of the morning, they had the car windows wound down and Monique could smell death even before they reached the clearing. She stopped between two parked police vehicles, a car and a van. A little further beyond was another police car. Two police constables were standing to one side and one of them approached as the car came to a halt.

'Is Inspector White here?' asked Bob.

'He's with the bodies, sir. The first is fifty yards past the police car over there. It's best not to go any closer than here without a gas mask on. Do you have one with you?'

'It's been a while since I carried a gas mask everywhere with me,' said Bob.

'We've got some in the back of the van, sir, help yourself.'

Monique saw Bob look at her. 'If you like, I'll go and look at the bodies, Bob. You should wait here. I suggest you do too, Dorothy.'

Monique got the impression that Constable Franklin was about to argue, before she had second thoughts.

'It's going to be horrible, isn't it?' she asked.

'Yes,' said Monique. 'It's best to avoid giving yourself nightmares when you don't have to. Besides, the fewer people tramping around the area the better.'

'I'll see if I can help here.' Dorothy walked over towards where the other police constable was standing.

Monique took a gas mask from the back of the police van and put it on, tightening the straps in a way that would once have been very familiar. She felt her face start to prickle with sweat almost immediately.

The police car had been left on a continuation of the track through the clearing and she had no problem finding her way on foot, even with her vision restricted and blurred by the gas mask.

She found Inspector White and another man, both wearing gas masks, standing on the track looking off to one side of it, towards a dense stand of nettles that had been partly beaten down. As she followed their gaze, Monique could see there was something on the ground in the heart of the nettles. The air was still and she heard the buzz of flies even before she saw a cloud of them around whatever was there. Monique assumed this was where one of the bodies had been left but it was hard to tell given how little was visible because of the nettles.

Both men turned as she approached.

'Hello, Inspector, it's Monique Dubois of Military Intelligence, Section 11.' Monique held out her pass, knowing she would be unrecognisable in the gas mask.

'Hello, Madame Dubois. This is Dr Maxwell, the police doctor in Stranraer.'

'I take it that's one of the dead men?' asked Monique.

'Yes. The other is about fifty yards in that direction.' The inspector pointed off to the other side of the track. 'Both were concealed in dense vegetation. The two young women who found this first body noticed the smell and thought it was a dead deer or badger before realising it was human when they looked more closely. They telephoned us from the nearest farm. It was only when the first of my men arrived that they realised there was a second body.'

'Do you mind if I take a look?' asked Monique.

'It's not pleasant. But if you stick to the already disturbed path into the nettles and don't touch anything, be my guest,' said the inspector.

Monique had seen some grim things in her time but the body in the nettles was as bad as anything she could remember. She thought it must be a man rather than a woman from the amount of body hair she could see amongst the maggots that thickly covered the visible parts of the corpse. He appeared to be naked and was lying face down with his arms held together behind his back. Bloating caused by decomposition was so bad that Monique couldn't be sure if his hands had been tied, but it seemed likely from his posture. It also looked like he had been savagely attacked, but then Monique realised she might be seeing the effects of wild animals feasting on the body.

She returned to where the doctor and inspector, now joined by a sergeant and a constable, were standing.

'Is it possible to say how he died?' she asked.

'It will be easier to talk without the gas masks,' said the inspector. 'Unless you want to see the other body I suggest we go back to the cars.'

'I think I should,' said Monique.

*

Monique and the inspector both looked drained when they took their gas masks off. Bob had been agonising over his decision to allow her to do a job that should have been down to him as the senior officer present. But she had a much stronger stomach than him and it was too late for second thoughts now.

'How are you?' he asked.

'Better than the poor bastards back there,' said the inspector.

Monique smiled. 'I'm fine, Bob, though that sort of thing never gets any easier.' She turned as a man in wellington boots, tweed trousers and an open-necked shirt approached. 'This is Dr Maxwell, the police doctor.'

'Is there much we can learn from the bodies at this stage?' asked Bob.

'Not much, I'm afraid,' said the doctor. 'I'll need to take a closer look in a more controlled environment, which I'm not especially looking forward to. I can tell you that the bodies have been there for long enough for decomposition to be very well advanced, but you'll have worked that out for yourself from the smell, even this far away.'

'Are you talking about a few days, or a week, or what?' asked Bob.

'It's difficult to say, especially as the weather has been so warm lately. I know from the inspector that you have been looking for two men who went missing the week before last. These bodies could have been here since then.

'I can also tell you that the bodies are unclothed and neither has military identity discs. Your colleague asked about the cause of death. Because of decomposition, insect larvae and animal interference, I simply have no idea at present.'

'Thank you, doctor,' said Inspector White. 'Can you let me know when you've got anything more definite?'

'Of course,' said the doctor. 'It wouldn't be the normal course of action, but I suggest we try to move the bodies first, having marked their positions. That will allow me to make a start on a full examination. It will also mean that your men can conduct a proper search for remaining evidence without the need to wear gas masks.'

Bob stood with Monique while the inspector and the doctor went to talk to a police sergeant who had appeared on the side of the clearing nearest the bodies.

'How did the dead men look to you?' he asked.

'Quite far gone,' said Monique. 'Even simple identification will be hard without reference to fingerprints. I did once read that you can get quite good fingerprints from decomposing bodies.'

Monique paused for a moment before continuing. 'The doctor was right, it is too early to be sure, but I'll put money on the men being killed in the same way, and the killer taking care not to get any blood on their uniforms.

Either they were bloodless killings while the men were clothed, or they were forced to strip before being killed.'

'Because blood would prevent the killer from wearing their uniforms when he used their identities?' asked Bob.

'That's it, exactly.'

The inspector rejoined them. 'We can't be certain but I suspect that's two of the missing military officers accounted for.'

'I'm only aware of two,' said Bob. 'Are there more?'

'Not on this side of the North Channel,' said Inspector White. 'But I heard first thing this morning that the Royal Navy is short of a lieutenant who went missing from a minesweeper moored in Belfast docks on the night of Sunday the 13th of June.'

'That could tie in with when the agent we're looking for travelled to Scotland on his first visit,' said Bob. 'Do we know if the missing man in Belfast had a Travel Identity Card that allowed him to travel on the steamer from Larne to Stranraer?'

'I asked that and he did,' said Inspector White. 'We also now know that the killer must have had access to a vehicle. He drove it here, perhaps twice, to dump those bodies.'

'It might have been easier to bring them here alive,' said Monique. 'Then they wouldn't need to be carried into the woods. If each was brought here individually they could probably be forced to walk from the killer's vehicle. Perhaps he even forced them to strip before killing them, which would mean he didn't need to worry about getting blood on their uniforms when he pulled the trigger, assuming that's what he did. Does anyone live near enough to have heard gunshots?'

'There are a few scattered farms and other properties within a mile or two, though the nearest is some distance away. I suspect you could shoot someone here without it being noticed beyond the woodland.'

'Thank you,' said Monique.

'I do find the location very odd, though,' said the inspector.

'In what way?' asked Bob.

'I appreciate it's wrong to jump to conclusions,' said the inspector. 'But there does seem a good chance that the man who dumped these bodies here is the German agent you've been looking for. How would someone who had only just arrived in the area, in the country for that matter, know of this place? You would both have seen how out of the way it was when you drove here. I can't think of anywhere more remote within an easy distance of Stranraer. If the two WTC women hadn't been here marking trees for felling, and if the recent warm weather hadn't caused the smell of decomposition in the area to be so bad, there's every chance that these men's bodies might have gone undiscovered for much longer.'

'What conclusion do you draw from that?' asked Monique.

'It appears to me there may be a link between the killer knowing about this place and what you said about the German agent establishing a base in the area. The Wigtownshire Constabulary only has limited manpower, but I put in some overtime after we spoke yesterday. I've had people knocking on doors last evening and this morning, until I had to send everyone I could spare here, looking for anyone who might have let property to a naval lieutenant during the week you say he was in the country. We didn't find anything useful, but I'm now wondering whether he knew of this place because he'd set up a base somewhere near here.

‘And before you say anything, yes, I know that there would be a risk involved in dumping dead bodies on your own doorstep, but perhaps it seemed a lesser risk to dump them somewhere he’d had a chance to visit in advance? I don’t know. What I do know is that as soon as I can, I will get men talking to the people who live in this area. As I said, there aren’t that many of them.’

‘Thank you, inspector,’ said Bob. ‘That would be very helpful. What’s the name of the naval lieutenant who went missing in Belfast?’

The inspector produced a notebook. ‘Lieutenant John MacKinlay, originally from Glasgow, which is why he had a Travel Identity Card. I’ll let you know if anything helpful turns up, group captain.’

‘Would it be possible to get someone to check the passenger lists for the steamer from Larne to Stranraer for the days following Lieutenant MacKinlay’s disappearance?’ asked Bob. ‘If we assume the Cuttlefish used his identity to make the crossing, then his name ought to show up.’

‘Of course, group captain.’

Bob saw Monique frown. ‘If you don’t mind, inspector I’d like to go and see Margaret Abercrombie, either at home or at the telephone exchange, wherever she is at the moment. I promised I’d let her know if we found out what had happened to Flight Lieutenant Thorn. I appreciate we don’t yet know if one of the bodies here is his but, in a small town, news that something has been found is going to get around very quickly. I owe it to her to tell her what we do know.’

‘That’s one less distressing job for me or one of my officers to do, Madame Dubois. Thank you.’

CHAPTER FIFTEEN

Monique spoke with Margaret Abercrombie in the manager's office of the Stranraer telephone exchange while Bob waited in the car. She emphasised that the identities of the bodies still had to be established and was thankful that Margaret didn't offer to help with the process. Perhaps she understood the implications of the passage of time and preferred to remember her friend as she last saw him.

Margaret took the news calmly, almost as if she was relieved that the uncertainty and fear that had been hanging over her for nearly two weeks looked to be coming to an end.

In the car afterwards, Monique wondered how she would feel in the same situation. She thought she'd prefer to keep open the possibility of a favourable outcome for as long as possible, but recognised that not everyone was the same.

She wasn't sure how long she'd been lost in her thoughts when Bob spoke.

'Are you all right, Monique?'

'I've had better mornings if I'm honest, Bob.'

'I'm sorry. I should have gone to find the inspector and view the bodies when we arrived in the woods.'

'And vomit up your breakfast in your gas mask when you got near enough to see the first corpse? No, it was the right thing for me to go. It just wasn't a wonderful experience.' Monique smiled. 'Do you want to know the oddest thing?'

'What's that?'

'I feel ravenously hungry, despite having had a good breakfast.'

Monique saw Bob take his left hand off the steering wheel to look at his watch. This meant moving it across to where he could see it with his right eye. She sometimes wondered why he didn't wear his watch on his right hand to make it easier to see with his good eye, but had never found the right moment to ask. She didn't think this was it, either.

'Michael talked about a hotel in Garlieston that has good food,' said Bob. 'I wonder if we can get there before they stop serving lunch? We've got plenty of time in hand before we need to be at Cairn Head. I'd intended to return to RAF Wigtown on the way to ring Maurice Cunningham on a secure line, but that can wait until later.'

They stopped at an army checkpoint a few miles short of Garlieston and at another as they entered the village. At the second checkpoint, Monique asked how to find the hotel. The young private she asked, sweating profusely in a khaki battledress that looked far too hot for the weather, was happy to direct her. She thanked him and smiled as Bob pulled away.

The Galloway Arms Hotel was still serving lunch when they arrived, and a very good lunch at that. Afterwards, they took glasses of tonic water outside and sat on a stone wall that separated the road that ran past the hotel from the beach.

'The tide is a long way out,' said Monique.

'It is,' agreed Bob. 'I'd suggest a walk on the sand but it looks to be mainly mud. It's easy to see what Michael meant about the bay and the harbour being in full view of people in the village. You'd not get much sailing into the bay at the moment, because of the tide, but there are some quite interesting vessels and other structures in the harbour. If you set yourself up with a telescope in an upper-floor room of any of the houses along this road you'd have a grandstand view of everything going on there.'

Monique looked at the houses along the road that overlooked the bay. 'That's true. I also think Michael was right in saying that evacuating the place would risk drawing attention to it. Besides, that lunch was excellent and evacuation would mean closing the hotel.'

Bob looked at his watch. 'I don't know about you, Monique, but I'm getting too hot in the sun. We've still time in hand. Perhaps we should drive down to Cairn Head? You've not seen what they are doing there and it's only when you do see it that you can fully understand the need for security.'

'That sounds like a good idea,' said Monique. 'I'll drive.'

They encountered another army checkpoint at a junction not far south of Garlieston, where Bob, having consulted the map he was holding, said they needed to turn left onto the road that ran parallel to the coast.

A little further on, Monique was struck by the sight of a dense growth of trees within a stone-walled enclosure set a little way off to the left of the road and slightly uphill from it.

'Can we stop, Monique?'

'What's wrong, Bob?

'Nothing's wrong. The last time I went to Cairn Head, the army car that took me there from RAF Wigtown, and the one that took me back, used a main road further inland. But one of the drivers did talk about a church near this road that is surrounded by trees and in the middle of a field. I think that must be it. I know it's hot but it's not far to walk, and you can pull the car off the road near the wooden gate we're coming to. Do you fancy taking a look?'

Monique was happy to indulge Bob's interest in old buildings and stopped the car.

Bob got out, then took a folded map out of his tunic pocket and looked at it. 'The sign on the gate says this is Cruggleton Old Church. There's a faint track leading up through the crop, which I think is barley. We can follow that to the corner of the stone enclosure, then along its front to the gate in the wall.'

'I think we can probably find our way without the map, Bob,' said Monique, smiling.

'I was just looking at the wider area. The Ordnance Survey shows the church as a small anonymous cross and then the ground gently rises, as we can see, before descending to a castle marked as being on the coast, which we can't see. It's not marked on the map but just north-east of the castle, which Major Avery said was no more than a fragmentary ruin, is Cruggleton Point, which is where the private who later turned up dead was on guard duty when he disappeared. There's no obvious track I can see beyond the church and across the field, so I assume the army access their lookout from Cruggleton, which is a farmstead a little to the north.'

'I don't think we've got time for serious exploration of the area,' said Monique.

'No, you're right, I just want to get it straight in my head.'

Bob held open the wooden gate for Monique to pass through and then closed it behind them.

'I'm going to have to take your word that this is a church, Bob. The trees are so dense it's impossible to see a structure amongst them.'

As they approached the corner of the stone wall surrounding the church, which Monique could now begin to see set within the heart of the clump of trees, she felt a gust of cold wind from her right. The contrast with the baking hot day was so striking that she stopped walking. The hairs on her arms stood up and she felt a shiver run down her spine.

Bob stopped and turned towards her. 'That's odd. There's a sudden chill in the air. Let's walk along the wall as far as the gate. If it's locked there's a stone step stile just this side of it.'

A thought crossed Monique's mind. 'Bob, what did the driver tell you that got you so interested in this place? Is there something you're not telling me?'

'It seemed silly, to be honest. He said it was spooky and got the hairs on the back of your neck going. It's certainly doing that for me. We can go back to the car if you prefer.'

Monique smiled. 'Not a chance, Bob. This was your bright idea and I think we should go through with it. Or do you want me to tell the team that we went to see a church but you backed out because it felt spooky?'

Bob caught her eye and laughed. 'If you're making it into a personal challenge, then I'm not giving up before you do. Besides, this is the first time today that I've felt any relief from the heat.'

The gate in the wall was formed from vertical iron rods and held in place by a chain that could be unclipped. Bob pushed it open. Beyond the gate, and some of the trees, and a dense mass of vegetation growing to waist level or higher, was the end wall of the church.

'I can't remember ever seeing anywhere quite so densely overgrown,' said Bob.

'I can,' said Monique. 'Only the last time I saw somewhere like this, someone had used it to hide two dead bodies. Look, we're not the first to have been here since all this vegetation flourished. There's a faint track leading round to the right of the church. And while there's a cold wind, at least it's not carrying the smell of death.'

Monique was happy to let Bob lead. She still felt a chill in the air and she still had goosebumps, but she didn't feel threatened in any way. It was a very odd sensation.

The south side of the church was very austere. Monique could see a round-arched door set in a grey stone wall that was relieved only by a couple of high-level slit window openings. The door was made from ancient-looking broad wooden planks that carried rusty decorative iron straps and nails. If ever a door was intended to tell visitors to go away, it was this one.

Bob came to a halt in front of the door.

'Should we see if we can get in?' asked Monique, reaching around him to turn the door handle. The handle turned but the door wouldn't move. 'You give it a go, Bob.'

It wouldn't open for him either despite his much harder shove. 'If I'm honest, I'm not sorry about that,' said Bob. 'There's another door further along, where the building narrows to form the choir of the church. The track through the nettles goes that way.'

The second door wouldn't open either. They then made their way through the vegetation around the far end of the church to its north side. Here there was just one door and no windows. The door was built as strongly as those on the south wall and was also locked.

'At least we tried,' said Bob.

Monique continued to feel the cold wind from the south until a few yards before they reached the gate to the road, where they'd parked the car. Then it dropped to nothing and she was suddenly aware of the heat of the sun again.

'I think "spooky" is a very good word for this place,

Bob. It was interesting to experience but I'm not sorry we're leaving. Get in this side of the car, I'll drive to Cairn Head. Even though we left the windows open, it's going to be like an oven inside.'

*

Brigadier Bishop and Colonel Hawkins arrived on time, courtesy of an RAF Catalina flying boat that alighted in the bay to the north of Cairn Head. They were brought ashore by boat and then met Major Avery, Bob and Monique in the major's office. The two men struck Bob as the sort of army officers he liked, intelligent and flexible and not in thrall to centuries of regimental tradition. Given the threat posed by the Cuttlefish and the murder of Private Young, the two officers took little convincing of the need to provide the major with the additional men he needed to tighten the physical security around Mulberry. Still better, they promised to have them there within 24 hours.

Bob also raised with them and Major Avery the situation in Garlieston, and the three men shared MI11's assessment that evacuating the village would be counterproductive. After a meeting of no more than half an hour, including the time to serve tea, the two senior officers were led away by Major Avery to visit the pierhead and floating pier. The major was happy to allow Bob to use a phone before he and Monique left Cairn Head.

Bob's call was put through by Maurice Cunningham's secretary immediately.

'Hello, Bob. I take it you've picked up the message I left for you at RAF Wigtown to get in touch?'

'Sorry, sir, no. Monique and I are at Cairn Head and this simply seemed a good opportunity to bring you up to date on a secure line.'

'Never mind, I've got you now. Yevgeny Popov called me earlier this afternoon. It appears that there have been what he called "unexpected developments" in Dublin. He wouldn't give details when I asked but I get the impression that the quest by Miss Komarova and Major Malinovsky to find out more about the Cuttlefish's intentions may not be going to plan. As a result, the two of them were flying to London to meet Popov this afternoon and will be joining you at RAF Wigtown this evening.'

Bob was holding the telephone receiver so that Monique, who had pulled up a chair close beside his, could listen in to the conversation. He glanced at her and she raised her eyebrows.

'You were hoping that we could complete our work on security around Mulberry and move somewhere closer to Stranraer before the Soviets joined us,' said Bob. 'I think we have now done all we can for Mulberry, for the moment at least, but I can only say that because of a meeting that took place here a short time ago.'

'That's good to know. It may not matter too much. When I told Popov that you were currently at RAF Wigtown he didn't appear concerned by the distance from Stranraer. I got the sense he was worried about whatever had happened in Dublin and not thinking any further. I'm sure you'll find out more when the Soviets join you. When you do discover what's going on, you are the one best placed to decide whether to stay in Wigtown tomorrow or move your base nearer Stranraer. Keep me in touch, though. My people here can help make any arrangements you need.'

'Yes, of course, sir,' said Bob.

CHAPTER SIXTEEN

They parked the three cars at the end of the hangar closest to the control tower and Bob, Monique and Michael got out and went to stand at the corner of the building that gave the best view over the airfield.

Bob had told her that a lot of night flying took place here and things didn't seem to Monique to be slackening off as the day became evening. RAF Wigtown was still busy with men and women walking and cycling, with vehicles coming and going, and with aircraft taking off, landing and circling the area.

'At least we proved the radios work,' said Michael.

'You were on your way back here anyway,' said Bob. 'But given where you say you were, I think we must have beaten the 10 miles claimed range for voice communications. When we have time, we need to organise some Morse code training. Mine is very rusty.'

Michael looked at his watch. 'If they're running to time, they ought to be here in ten minutes.'

'Could they be ahead of time?' asked Monique, looking out beyond the control tower. There's an aircraft coming our way that looks different to the others.'

'That could well be them,' said Bob.

Monique watched as a sleek twin-engined aircraft landed, then carried on past them to the far end of the runway. It was completely white, apart from a red stripe along the side that resolved into lettering on the rear fuselage.

'What is it?' asked Michael.

'It's an Airspeed Envoy with a British civilian registration,' said Bob. 'It carries a pilot and, if I remember correctly, up to six passengers. It's been a while since I last saw one.'

'Can you identify every aircraft type that there is?' asked Monique, smiling.

'When my job was to make split-second decisions about whether or not to shoot down any aircraft I encountered, it helped to be very sure which were friendly and which weren't. That sort of knowledge becomes ingrained.'

The aircraft taxied back towards them and after it had passed where they were standing it turned sharply left onto the grass not far from the control tower. It came to a halt beside Bob's Mosquito.

Bob walked towards the rear of the aircraft and Monique followed with Michael. Nothing happened for a few moments after the engines stopped. Then a door opened in the side of the rear fuselage and Major Malinovsky jumped down to the grass before turning back to lift out a step from the aircraft which he placed on the ground. Katerina Komarova then got out, taking the major's hand for balance as she used the step.

Bob and the major exchanged salutes.

'You both know Madame Dubois. This is Lieutenant Commander Michael Dixon, my deputy in the northern arm of Military Intelligence, Section 11.'

More salutes were exchanged before Michael shook hands with Major Malinovsky and Katerina Komarova. The woman bestowed a dazzling smile on Michael. Monique wondered if she'd ever been so unsubtle herself.

Sergeant Bennett had driven one of the cars over to the back of the aircraft.

'We've arranged accommodation for you at the officers' mess, which is also where we're staying,' said Bob. 'That's a little distance away and I thought it might be helpful if we could first discuss developments since some of us met at the Soviet embassy on Thursday evening.'

'That would suit us, group captain,' said Katerina Komarova.

'Sergeant Bennett is a member of my team and will drive you to the station's engineering squadron headquarters, where I've borrowed a meeting room. It's not far and we'll follow in our cars.'

It was only about two hundred yards to a single-storey building almost hidden amongst a cluster of similar buildings behind the hangar furthest from the control tower.

Bob hadn't exactly appeared nervous before the arrival of the Soviets, but Monique had felt a tension in him, a concern to ensure that no part of the arrangements he was responsible for went wrong. She knew that was why he had checked the meeting room before they'd gone to wait for the Soviets' aircraft and spoken to Flight Lieutenant Talbot before he went off duty.

The three cars stopped outside the front of the building and their occupants got out. Monique wondered if anyone was going to shout at them for their choice of parking place, then realised that Bob would have cleared this with the flight lieutenant.

He'd also arranged for a choice of tea or coffee in a room whose eight-seat wooden table was just about large enough to accommodate everyone. One long wall had two windows whose panes were covered by the obligatory criss-crosses of sticky tape to reduce blast damage while all of the other long wall, apart from the door, was covered in a large blackboard with a chalk grid that looked to Monique's inexpert eyes as if it might be used to track servicing work on aircraft.

The Soviets occupied two of the three chairs on the

window side of the table while Bob took the centre seat on the other side, flanked by Monique and Michael, with Peter and Andrew at the ends of the table.

'Thank you for the coffee,' said Katerina Komarova. 'I don't suppose you could manage a brandy to add to it, could you? The weather might be beautiful but the flight here from RAF Hendon was rather bumpy.'

Monique caught a flicker of irritation on Major Malinovsky's face before he saw her watching him.

'Once we've got business out of the way I suggest we have a drink at the bar in the officers' mess,' said Bob. 'I'm sure they can offer a choice of brandies. That gives us an incentive not to prolong this meeting. In the interests of being fully open with our Soviet allies, let me begin by talking you through developments on our side since Thursday evening.

'I'll start with what seems most important. We believe that the Cuttlefish's first visit to Scotland resulted in the disappearance of two military officers in Stranraer. We suspect he killed them and dumped their bodies in a remote location west of the town.'

'Why do you think it was him, group captain?' asked Katerina Komarova.

'The emerging evidence seems to tie too closely with what we already know about him to be coincidence,' said Bob. 'As I see it, Edward Daly attacked and probably killed a Royal Navy officer, Lieutenant John MacKinlay, in Belfast on the night of Sunday the 13th of June. He stole the lieutenant's uniform and identity documents and subsequently travelled to Scotland. The police are checking the passenger lists for sailings of the steamer from Larne to Stranraer.

'On the evening of Wednesday the 16th of June, we

believe Daly, while posing as the Royal Navy lieutenant, abducted and subsequently killed RAF Flight Lieutenant James Thorn in Stranraer. On the evening of Friday the 18th of June, we believe he did the same thing to Royal Engineers Captain William Evans, again while wearing the uniform of the naval lieutenant and again in Stranraer. Someone using Captain Evans' identity and documents, and presumably his uniform, travelled on the steamer from Stranraer to Larne early the following morning. I believe that was Edward Daly returning to Dublin.

'It feels to me as if Daly probably made his first trip to Scotland to gather the identity documents and uniforms of men who looked like him. He acquired the persona of a naval lieutenant in Belfast before coming here and used that to help him add an RAF flight lieutenant and an army captain to his collection. This morning we found two bodies. They are yet to be identified, but I think we will find that they are the flight lieutenant and the captain who disappeared in Stranraer.

'It's worth adding that we've followed up on your suggestion that Daly used his first visit to establish a forward base in or close to Stranraer and the police there have been making enquiries. They've not yet come up with anything useful, but they have suggested that Daly may have known where he could dump the bodies because he was setting up a base close by. The police inspector who raised the possibility acknowledged that would mean Daly dumping dead bodies on his own doorstep, but said he would check properties in the area.'

'Edward Daly is arrogant enough to see no problem using the same area for both purposes,' said Katerina Komarova. 'He'd never believe anyone else could be intelligent enough to think of the possibility.'

'That sounds like a serious weakness,' said Monique.

'It is,' said Katerina Komarova. 'He is extremely good, but he does suffer from an excess of self-belief and an overdose of vanity.'

'That's helpful to know,' said Bob. 'That's not been our only line of enquiry. I'd like to ask Michael to report on what he's found about stories we've heard from several sources of an MI5 officer dressed as a tramp checking security at locations in the area.'

'There's not a lot to report,' said Michael. 'We have now visited several of the units where this was meant to have happened and could find no one who had personally seen or interacted with this alleged MI5 officer. A lot of people had heard the story, but it was always someone on the other shift who it happened to or someone manning the next gate along. The more people we talked to, the more it felt like a piece of folklore in the making. I know that Andrew and Peter feel the same way.'

'That's right,' said Andrew MacDonald. 'There's also the question of timing. We were told that these stories have been doing the rounds for months, since long before we believe the Cuttlefish first came to Scotland. And we picked up no specific reports of this happening during the week he was here.'

Katerina Komarova put her coffee cup down on its saucer. 'Comrade Popov told us that he believed you had established an initial base here at RAF Wigtown because it is close to where amphibious landing trials are taking place, on the coast south of here. You will appreciate that the Soviet Union has as much interest in the successful opening of a Second Front as the other Allied nations. Have you uncovered anything that suggests the Cuttlefish is taking an interest in the work that's going on there?'

Monique wished they'd thought about this possibility in advance and been able to discuss it.

'Perhaps,' said Bob. 'I told you what we believe we know about the Cuttlefish's activities while he was in Scotland. A possible addition to the list I gave you took place in the early hours of the morning on Wednesday the 16th of June, in other words much earlier on the day we believe Daly abducted the flight lieutenant in Stranraer.

'A soldier on guard duty at a coastal lookout south of here disappeared. When he was found washed up further up the coast two days later it emerged that he had been garrotted and dumped in the sea.'

'Can I assume you weren't going to mention that if I hadn't asked? That is hard to reconcile with, how did you put it, "being fully open with our Soviet allies".'

'The story was complicated enough as it was,' said Bob. 'We've done all we need to do about security around the activities you have in mind and were proposing to relocate nearer to Stranraer tomorrow, pending your arrival. After all, if we succeed in catching the Cuttlefish when he arrives, it won't matter what he was hoping to achieve. He will have failed. I think that brings us to your earlier-than-expected arrival in Scotland and what Commodore Cunningham described to me on the telephone as "unexpected developments" in Dublin. What's happened?'

Komarova smiled. 'Very well. I think I told you in London that the Abwehr has a well-staffed unit attached to the German embassy in Dublin while the Sicherheitsdienst or SD has a very small office a little distance away. I also referred to the animosity between the two organisations.

'After I saw Edward Daly on a street in Dublin, and having cleared what I proposed to do with my colleagues to protect my position, I made contact with a source within the Abwehr office in the German embassy who has been of help from time to time in the past. Dublin is the capital city of a neutral country, nominally neutral, anyway, and things can work in unexpected ways there. The man I contacted is in a senior position in the Abwehr office. He has in the past told me he is acting without the knowledge of anyone else there but I don't believe him. While he wants me to believe that I've turned him into a Soviet asset I am sure he's not working for me in the sense you might think. I believe that he simply gives me information the Abwehr as an organisation thinks it useful to pass to the NKVD.

'When I met him on the Tuesday morning, my Abwehr contact said he had never heard of Edward Daly and knew of no one who matched his description with the SD in the city. I believed him. We met again that evening and he confirmed that Edward Daly was in Dublin. He said he was trying to find out why and asked to meet me again the following day.

'It was when we met for the third time that he was able to tell me about Edward Daly's arrival in Ireland and the timing of his visit to Scotland. He also told me that Daly intended to return here at the end of this week. That evening I flew to London to talk to Comrade Popov. You know the rest.'

'What happened when you went back to Dublin?' asked Monique.

'Nikolay flew me there on Friday afternoon and I tried to make contact that evening and again on Saturday with my Abwehr source. You will understand that even though I suspect his meetings with me are officially sanctioned by the Abwehr, I can't simply leave a message for him with a colleague asking him to get in touch. The arrangement we have is that if I need to make contact I call him at his office or home from a public telephone box posing as a florist. I am sure that calls to his home and the German embassy are monitored by G2, the Irish Directorate of Military Intelligence, so we need to be discreet.

'I was able to reach him at home on Sunday evening and we agreed he would pick up a fictitious bouquet yesterday at noon. We met in Amiens Street Station in the centre of the city and my source was uncharacteristically jumpy. He said he'd had a long weekend away with a friend, I assume a mistress. He said that he had tried yesterday morning to get an update on Edward Daly's intentions but that his source within the Sicherheitsdienst or SD office in Dublin was concerned they had been compromised. I got the sense that this source was in touch with one of my Abwehr contact's colleagues rather than with him directly.

'We agreed to meet today, again at noon. We did so and he told me that the SD plan was now for Edward Daly to travel to Belfast tomorrow night, crossing the border into Northern Ireland under cover of what little darkness there is at this time of year, and then to catch the steamer that leaves Larne for Stranraer on Thursday afternoon. I intended to pass this information on to Comrade Popov in London so that he in turn could alert Commodore Cunningham, which would give MI5 and the Royal Ulster Constabulary a chance to increase security in the hope they might catch the Cuttlefish en route or at Larne, however unlikely that might be given they won't be able to recognise him.'

'What's changed?' asked Monique.

Katerina Komarova sat back in her chair. 'At about the time I met my contact, there was an explosion followed by a small fire in a long-established printer's shop in a run-down part of Dublin. I heard about it perhaps three-quarters of an hour after I returned to my office in the Soviet embassy, just as I finished writing my telegram to Comrade Popov. I learned of it when I received a telephone call from my Abwehr contact. He was calling from his office in the German embassy, something that broke the procedures we had agreed and undermined his pretence to be acting alone.

'Given how recent an event it was, he was incredibly well-informed. He told me that the fire had been confined to a storeroom at the rear of the premises and was quickly put out. The Garda Síochána, or Irish police if you prefer, found the body of Paul Burke, the elderly man whose business it was, in the upstairs printing area. He'd been attacked and suffered serious head injuries.

'A second victim, a young man, was found dead in a car outside. He had identity papers linking him to the German embassy and my Abwehr contact said that he had been their agent within the SD office. Remember that he knew this was on an open line that was probably being listened to by G2, so I think his message was intended as much for the Irish authorities as it was for me. He went on to say that Mr Burke was known to forge identity and travel documents and the Abwehr believed that Edward Daly had used his services and probably killed him to prevent him from revealing anything about the identities he had provided. That is consistent with Daly trying to burn the place down. His killing of the Abwehr agent in the SD office suggests he knew the Abwehr was on to him.

'My contact went on to say that the Abwehr believed that Edward Daly would try to leave Eire as quickly as possible. He might abandon his mission and try to find a boat to take him to France or Norway. But the Abwehr thought he would instead head for Northern Ireland with all speed and then travel to Scotland earlier than previously planned. The steamers from Larne to Stranraer leave at 2 p.m. daily and there was no chance of his making today's sailing given the timing of the incident in Dublin. The Abwehr therefore believed Edward Daly would try to board tomorrow's steamer, in other words, a day earlier than he had intended.'

'There's a lot to digest there,' said Bob. 'Can I assume that Mr Popov will have given Commodore Cunningham enough information to allow MI5 and the RUC to step up their security in Northern Ireland and at Larne as you suggested? We also need to bear in mind the possibility that the Cuttlefish will find another way of making the crossing to Scotland.'

'Yes, he has,' said Katerina Komarova. 'And the Soviet embassy in Dublin also contacted the authorities in Northern Ireland, as well as G2 and the Garda Síochána. In a way, it's helped that the Cuttlefish has killed two men in Dublin. That makes it a simple murder hunt and we can leave the additional deaths in Scotland and the matter of the rivalry between the Sicherheitsdienst and the Abwehr out of it.'

'That brings me to something that I'm very unclear about,' said Monique. 'We've discussed the enmity between the SD and the Abwehr, but have you any idea why the Abwehr in Dublin want to take this to the point that they are prepared to work with you against an SD operation in Scotland? That seems rather extreme.'

'It does,' said Katerina Komarova. 'But that is what they have been doing. Perhaps we will know more when we find out what the Cuttlefish is trying to achieve in Scotland beyond killing military officers and stealing their uniforms and papers.'

'Assuming the Abwehr assessment of Daly's intentions

is correct, we have less than a day in hand before tomorrow's steamer arrives in Stranraer,' said Bob. 'We need to ensure that security at all ports and any other possible entry points is as tight as possible but, to my mind, our best bet now is to decide how to maximise our chances of you, Miss Komarova, identifying Edward Daly and ensuring he is prevented from landing in Scotland if he does board that steamer.'

'I agree,' said Katerina Komarova. 'We discussed that with Comrade Popov in London. We propose that we divide our resources, with some of us flying to Northern Ireland in the morning and boarding the steamer ourselves, while the rest of us ensure that security at Stranraer is extremely high in case we miss him on the steamer. That might involve holding everyone on the ship after it lands until I can personally clear each passenger and member of the crew, and if necessary searching the ship. It would be much better if I could identify the Cuttlefish en route.'

'That runs the risk of him identifying you, too,' said Monique.

'I will take steps to change my appearance to minimise the chance of that happening, but yes, that is a risk.'

'Who should go and who should stay?' asked Michael Dixon.

'I think the group captain would stand out too much on the steamer because of his rank,' said Katerina Komarova. 'I think the same is true for Major Malinovsky, because of his unusual uniform. He does have the civilian suit he wore in Dublin but he might still be better waiting for the steamer in Stranraer with the group captain.

'Otherwise, I think that the more support we have the better, so I would suggest that the lieutenant commander and your two other men travel to Larne with Madame

Dubois and me.'

'I'd imagine that any young women on the steamer will be in uniform,' said Michael Dixon. 'Even if you are in disguise, Miss Komarova, your civilian clothes won't help you blend in. Nor yours Monique.'

'What do you suggest, lieutenant commander?' asked Katerina Komarova.

'Could we get the RAF to help out? There must be a uniform store here.'

'That's a good idea,' said Bob. 'I'll talk to Group Captain Belmont.'

'You will need transport,' said Major Malinovsky. 'I am happy to fly the five of you to Northern Ireland in the morning.'

Monique very much disliked the idea of being in a plane flown by the major. Even with Michael and the others with them, and even if they had truly found a common cause with the Soviets, she still deeply distrusted both Katerina Komarova and Major Malinovsky.

'That's a kind offer, major, but I have a better idea,' said Bob. 'The RAF has sixty-five Avro Ansons based here and I am sure they can spare one of them, plus a pilot, to fly our five colleagues to Northern Ireland in the morning. That avoids any risk of your Airspeed Envoy becoming unserviceable at the wrong time or in the wrong place and making it difficult for you to be with me in Stranraer when the steamer arrives.'

It was obvious to Monique, as she was sure it was to everyone else in the room, that this was Bob's way of sidestepping the question of their trust, or lack of it, in the major. It was an elegant solution and she was very grateful, though she tried not to show what she was feeling in front of the Soviets.

CHAPTER SEVENTEEN

Bob brought Commodore Cunningham up to date via the telephone in the mess manager's office, which was connected to the secure switchboard on the airfield main site. Bob wanted a variety of arrangements put in place for the following day and the commodore was happy to have his people set them up overnight and in the morning. The commodore also seemed untroubled by the news that the Soviets knew about amphibious landing trials in the area, pointing out that from what Bob had said their knowledge was quite vague. He suggested that Bob should try to keep it that way. Bob then walked the short distance to the entrance hall of the mess. He'd timed it just right, as Michael and Monique were coming down the stairs together as he arrived. Major Malinovsky was already there, resplendent in a Soviet Air Force uniform that looked as if it had been freshly pressed and attracting curious glances from RAF officers coming into or leaving the mess.

Katerina Komarova made them wait five minutes before she put in an appearance in a striking red dress, causing Malinovsky to look impatiently at his watch. Bob caught Monique's eye and smiled as the woman appeared at the top of the stairs. Before he'd left their room to telephone the commodore, Monique had said that Miss Komarova would make them wait. She'd also predicted that the Soviet woman would dress to impress.

Monique was in her usual dark jacket and skirt with a white blouse. Bob noted that the two women did have one thing in common. Like Monique, Miss Komarova had a handbag that hung from its shoulder strap as if was carrying more weight than its designer intended. He wasn't surprised that she was armed.

'Good evening everyone,' said Bob. 'As this is a social occasion, may I suggest that we use first names? As a token of our welcome, you should know that MI11 has opened a mess bar account. Drinks are on us. Food is of course on the RAF and can be ordered and eaten in the bar or the dining room. I've reserved a table in the bar, but if the two of you prefer the dining room, now is the moment to say so.'

'The bar, definitely,' said Katerina Komarova. 'I'm not sure my stomach has recovered from the flight yet but I'll have no problem with a brandy or two.'

Bob had the sense that Malinovsky would have chosen differently, but the major said nothing.

'Are the two other men who were at our meeting earlier not joining us, group captain?' asked Katerina Komarova.

'Come on, Katarina,' said Malinovsky. 'Please spare us the socialist ideology. You know as well as I do that if this was a Soviet Air Force base, non-commissioned officers would never dine or drink in the officers' mess.'

To Bob's surprise, Komarova laughed. He wondered if she had asked her question specifically to embarrass or irritate the major.

As they walked along the corridor towards the door to the bar, the hubbub of conversation grew steadily in volume, suggesting that it was busier than it had been the previous night. When they entered, he realised that it was, considerably so.

Bob smiled wryly as their entrance stilled the noise for a moment before it resumed at a lower level than before. He had known that the arrival of his very odd group would give rise to considerable interest. He'd grown used to the cautious surprise that invariably greeted the arrival of an unknown group captain in a bar like this. But when you added two women in civilian clothes, a major in a Soviet Air Force uniform and a Royal Navy officer, they probably formed the most exotic group the occupants of the bar had seen in some time.

Bob hoped to find Group Captain Belmont in the bar but there was no sign of him. He did see a table large enough to accommodate them carrying a handwritten 'reserved' sign in an alcove on the far side of the room.

'I think that's ours,' he said.

'I'm going to get that brandy,' said Katerina Komarova, turning towards the bar.

'Tell the barman to charge it to Group Captain Sutherland,' said Bob.

'I'll come with you, Katerina,' said Malinovsky, following her.

'You do know this could get expensive, don't you Bob?' said Monique, smiling.

'Maurice Cunningham kindly agreed to foot the bill when I spoke to him just now.'

'That was very generous of him.'

'I put it to him that getting our new Soviet friends properly relaxed might be the best way to find out if they are being honest about their agenda. I reminded him that the same approach worked well when I wanted one of your agents to tell me what you were up to in Scotland last October.'

'Ouch! Touché.' Monique smiled again as they sat down at the alcove table.

'Given that's the plan, is it all right if we drink too, Bob?' asked Michael. 'As our guests are looking after themselves, I can get drinks for the three of us without a problem.'

‘That’s fine, Michael. Have what you want. I’ll have a tonic water disguised as a gin and tonic, please.’

‘I’ll have the same,’ said Monique.

Michael set off for the bar and Bob glanced around the room again.

Monique tapped him gently on the arm. ‘Look at that, Bob! They’re trying to conceal it but from the way they’re standing and the expressions on their faces it looks like our Soviet friends are arguing. I bet the barman doesn’t speak Russian, which is a shame.’

Bob could see what Monique meant. ‘She does most of the talking in any meeting but, in other ways, he doesn’t act as if he’s her junior.’

‘They appear to have made up and are heading this way,’ said Monique. ‘Let’s not let them know we’re watching.’

Michael joined them a short time later with two fake gin and tonics and a pint of beer.

*

After they’d eaten, there were more rounds of drinks. Monique wondered if Maurice Cunningham was going to regret his generosity. She’d tried to keep track of how much brandy Katerina Komarova had consumed, but stopped bothering when it got to ‘a lot’.

Major Malinovsky didn’t attempt to keep up but was alternating between beer and Scotch whisky, while Michel drank several beers, though not enough to have an obvious effect on him. Bob and Monique continued to nurse tonics masquerading as something more potent.

Monique saw Major Malinovsky, quite literally, bump into Flight Lieutenant Somerset while getting drinks at the bar and he was then drawn by the flight lieutenant into a group of RAF pilots gathered around a piano in the far corner of the room. Monique wasn't sure if the piano had been there the previous night but was grateful that the officer playing it was more interested in classical music than drinking songs. So far, at least. Surprisingly, Michael Dixon then also joined the group while on his way back from the toilets.

'Group Captain Belmont has come in,' said Bob. 'The barman said he was expected. I need to ask him about borrowing an Avro Anson and a pilot to get you to Northern Ireland tomorrow and about kitting the two of you up in WAAF uniforms. Excuse me.' Bob picked up his drink and stood up.

'That leaves just you and me, Monique.'

'It does, Katerina.'

'I think you're trying to get me drunk. It's not going to work, you know.'

'I don't think anyone's trying to get you drunk, Katerina,' said Monique, smiling. 'And if I were, I'd have given up by now.'

'You're not drinking, are you? I tried your gin and tonic when no one was looking and I don't think there's any gin in it. I've been wondering why you might want to get me drunk while staying sober yourself.'

'What conclusion have you reached, Katerina?'

'I can only think of two possible reasons. The first is that you like me and want to get to know me better.'

Monique thought that Katerina Komarova was quite attractive in a rather hard-edged Marlene Dietrich sort of way but this possibility simply hadn't crossed her mind. Perhaps the brandy was affecting Katerina after all?

'You are a beautiful woman, Katerina, and there was a time when I would have liked to get to know you much better.’ That was a lie, there was something not far beneath Katerina Komarova's superficial attractiveness that slightly repelled Monique. But this didn’t seem the moment to say so.

‘I can tell that you are about to say “but”, Monique.’

‘Yes, I am. The “but” is that I am very happy with someone else.’

‘Are you and the group captain…? There is something about the way you look at each other.’

Monique instinctively shied away from the idea of giving any personal information to the Soviets in case it was subsequently used against her, Bob, or MI11. But she had agreed with Bob before he left their room to telephone the commodore that if the question came up, they had no option but to be honest.

‘Yes, we are,’ she said. ‘We were married in Edinburgh on the fifth of the month. And before you ask either of the obvious questions, I don’t wear a ring when I’m working and I don’t use my married name either.’

‘That’s a shame. That puts both of you out of bounds. He would have been my next choice after you.’

Monique thought it was time to change the subject. ‘What about you and Nikolay?’

‘I only met him for the first time after I flew to London last Wednesday. He’s a bully and a peasant, despite his fancy uniform and high opinion of himself. I don’t know if he’s married or not but, if he is, I think he’s the sort of man who beats his wife. He is unhappy with me because I rejected his advances in the bar of our hotel in Dublin on Saturday night. In his eyes, because I am working with him I should also be sleeping with him.’

‘That must be awkward for you,’ said Monique.

‘I told him that if he tries it on with me again I’ll cut his dick off. He can't make up his mind whether I'm bluffing and that doubt is enough to ensure he keeps his hands off me.'

Monique smiled. She felt herself warming to the woman, despite herself. 'From your description of him, it sounds as if someone might have tried to cut off Edward Daly's dick at some time. The sabre wound you mentioned must have come very close.'

'Ah,' said Katerina. 'This is the second possible reason I thought you might be trying to get me drunk, so I would tell you more about the Cuttlefish. I'd have been happy to do so sober, just as I'd have been happy to share a bed with you sober.'

'So what can you tell me that might help us catch him?' asked Monique.

'My glass is empty. Now I've drunk this much brandy I need to drink more, just to stop myself from falling asleep.'

'That's no problem. I'll get more drinks,' said Monique.

'Why not put some gin in yours this time?' asked Katerina.

'I will.'

Monique made her way to the bar.

Bob had finished talking to Group Captain Belmont and came over to join her. 'I saw you deep in conversation with Katerina and thought it best to steer clear. How's it going?'

'She propositioned me and then backed off when I told her that you and I are married. We were just getting to the interesting part about the Cuttlefish when she noticed she was out of brandy.'

'I'll leave you to it then. I'll go and see how Michael and Major Malinovsky are getting on with the Typhoon pilots.'

'You should know that the major tried his luck with

Katerina in Dublin over the weekend. He's leaving her alone because she threatened to emasculate him if he tried again, but he's not happy about his enforced celibacy.'

'That's useful to know,' aid Bob. 'I see you've turned your pretend G&T into the real thing. I think I'll do the same.'

Monique returned to the table and put the brandy glass down in front of Katerina. 'You were going to tell me more about Edward Daly.'

'And you were going to put gin in your drink. Did you?'

'Yes, I did,' said Monique. 'Here, taste it for yourself.'

'No, thanks. Gin is disgusting stuff. But thank you for properly keeping me company.'

'At the meeting in London, you said that you met Edward Daly in Madrid and got to know him well enough for him to tell you about his family background and for you to learn about the scar on his thigh. You also said that he was with the SD at the time and you unsuccessfully attempted to recruit him to become a Soviet agent.'

'That is a fair summary,' said Katerina. 'It happened late last year, from October into November. We were lovers for perhaps three weeks and I think I might have been falling for him when something he said in a bar one night struck a false note. I'm not sure what it was, it was almost subliminal. But it rang alarm bells. After that, I paid much closer attention to the details of anything he said, even the casual or inconsequential things that lovers say when they're in bed together. I think he realised that something had changed. We met on a street corner one night and he told me that we should never see each other again because the next time we did, one of us would have to kill the other. I concluded that while I had been trying to recruit him as an agent, he had been trying to do the same with me and had realised it wasn't going to work. My senior officers were fully aware of everything that had been going on. It was decided that it would be best if I left Spain immediately as the SD and the Germans had much more support there than the NKVD and the Soviet Union, given what happened in the Civil War and Franco's sympathy for the Nazis.'

'And that was the last you saw or heard of him until you spotted him across a street in Dublin last Monday?' asked Monique.

'That's right. It was quite a shock.'

'How sure are you that he didn't recognise you in return?'

'Very. He was on the sunny side of the street with the sun shining on his face. I was on the shaded side. I saw him well enough to be certain it was him, then turned away to look in a shop window. I didn't attempt to follow him in case that gave me away. I simply made contact with my Abwehr source as I've told you before and asked what he knew.'

'And there's nothing else you can tell me that might help us identify Edward Daly when he tries to return to Scotland?' asked Monique.

'I'm sorry. If this conversation has been to allow you to identify some fatal weakness in him that you can use to ensure his downfall, I've got to disappoint you.'

'Mainly it's been to get to know you better,' said Monique. 'Though not so well that we end up in bed together.'

Katerina laughed and some of the hardness left her face, just for a moment.

*

‘Hello, Group Captain Sutherland,’ said Adrian Somerset. ‘Can I get you a drink?’

Bob held up his glass. ‘No, I have one, thank you.’

The group of pilots standing around the piano had succeeded in getting the pianist to inject the occasional popular song into his repertoire. He now started up on a number whose lyrics revolved around disparaging references to Adolf Hitler’s genitalia.

The flight lieutenant raised his voice. ‘Sorry, sir, it’s getting noisy here. Could you spare me a moment, perhaps over by the bar?’

Bob followed the young man to a space at one end of the bar.

‘What can I do for you, flight lieutenant?’

‘How much do you know about your Soviet colleague, Major Malinovsky?’

‘Not a lot, to be frank. I know he’s had a career flying with the Soviet Air Force and that he now works in the Soviet embassy in London for the NKVD, which you can think of as approximately equivalent to MI6. Why?’

‘Do you know if he’s any good as a pilot, sir?’

‘My only direct experience is seeing him land an Airspeed Envoy earlier this evening. I can tell you that his previous post was with a Soviet Air Force unit based at an airfield between Perth and Dundee where, although also working for the NKVD, he taught young men how to fly the Armstrong Whitworth Albemarle aircraft we have given the Soviets. His commanding officer described him as a good pilot who did his job well. Why are you asking?’

‘We were talking about the Typhoon’s ground attack capabilities, sir, and he was telling me how he flew the Ilyushin Il-2 in the autumn and winter of 1941 after the German invasion.’

‘That’s a Soviet two-seat ground attack aircraft, isn’t it?’ asked Bob. ‘It’s supposed to be highly effective.’

‘That’s what I thought, too. Apparently, the early versions were single-seaters because of the limited power of the engines at the time. To hear him talk he’s wiped out entire panzer divisions by himself and he also said he has six confirmed air-to-air kills, three Junkers Ju 87 Stukas and three Henschel Hs 126 reconnaissance aircraft. To be frank, that is more believable than his claim he destroyed hundreds of German tanks and vehicles.

‘To cut a long story short, he asked if it would be possible to fly a Typhoon so he could make a direct comparison with his memories of the Il-2. He said he unexpectedly had the morning free tomorrow and could do it then. I said I’d let him know. I’m in command of the advance party setting up the Typhoon deployment here so it’s my decision. I’m asking for your advice, sir, as someone in military intelligence. Do you see any problem with Major Malinovsky flying a Typhoon?’

‘I’d raise a couple of caveats, but see no problem in principle. Last year he was involved in a plot intended to steal a Mosquito and fly it to the Soviet Union. Make sure that you only put enough fuel in the Typhoon you give him to allow him to fly the sortie you have in mind, plus a reasonable margin. And you should insist in advance that he agrees to write a report comparing the Typhoon and the Il-2. Who knows, he might produce some worthwhile insights. I’d also ask that you avoid allowing him to fly over the coast south of here, especially around Cairn Head. Things are going on there that I’d prefer him not to see.’

‘The whole coastal area from Garlieston down to the Isle of Whithorn is out of bounds to us anyway, sir, so that’s no problem, and I’ll make sure we restrict the amount of fuel we put in his aircraft. There's another thing I want to ask you. Major Malinovsky mentioned that you were also free tomorrow morning. Do you fancy flying a third aircraft, with the major and me in the other two?'

Bob paused for a moment, realising he should have seen this coming. 'Don't take this the wrong way, flight lieutenant, but do the tails still fall off Typhoons if you sneeze too hard while flying one?'

'No sir, the structural problems are all behind us, if you'll excuse the bad taste pun.'

'What about carbon monoxide poisoning?'

'That's more problematic. There has been a fix of sorts, but we still find it better to use our oxygen masks from before engine start-up to after engine shut-down. But flying the Typhoon is no more tricky than flying any other single seater. What did you fly when you were operational?'

'Spitfires and later Hurricanes.'

'You'll be fine, sir,' said Flight Lieutenant. 'We converted from the Hurricane to the Typhoon in April and it was a reasonably smooth process.'

'The major and I will both be occupied until about 10.00 a.m.,' said Bob. 'Would 10.30 a.m. work for you?'

*

They'd pushed the two single beds in the room together. Bob was surprised by how ardent Monique was after a day that had at times been very unpleasant. Perhaps this was her way of putting that out of her mind.

Afterwards, Monique lay partly across Bob while she talked him through her conversation with Katerina Komarova. They then talked about what the next day might bring, both on the steamer and in Stranraer. Bob had scheduled a meeting with the full team at 9.00 a.m. but it helped to run through ideas with Monique first.

Then there was a silence and Bob wondered if Monique had fallen asleep and, if she had, how he could extricate himself from under her without waking her up.

But she wasn't asleep. 'You're getting better at hiding things from me, Bob,' she said. 'Which is good, in case you're wondering. You will remember my concern in Stockholm about the imbalance in our relationship, which meant you had to trust me while I could read you like a book without trust entering the equation.'

'Yes, I do. What's changed?'

'I'm not sure, but right now I've got the strong sense there's something you've been building up to telling me that you think I'm not going to like.'

Bob told her about his conversation with Flight Lieutenant Somerset, only omitting any reference to their discussion of the Typhoon's early failings.

Monique turned on the bedside light and sat up.

'Is that a good idea, Bob?'

Then he saw her smile.

'If this is Adrian Somerset's way of removing an inconvenient husband from the scene it's not going to work. If he turns me from a wife into a widow after just a month I'll kill him.'

Bob laughed. 'Your faith in my abilities is touching. I'm sure it won't come to that, Monique, and it is an interesting opportunity.'

'To think about what might have been if your flying career hadn't been brought to a sudden end?'

'Yes. Though as we've discussed, I prefer the path that led me to you. Do you want to know the thing about this that matters most to me?'

‘What’s that, Bob?’

‘Tonight was the first time since I was shot down that I’ve discussed the possibility of flying without feeling I had to bring up the subject of my vision. I didn’t even think about it until afterwards.’

Monique looked at him in silence for a moment and then hugged him. ‘That’s really important to you, isn’t it, Bob?’

Bob struggled to hold back tears. He didn’t want anyone, not even Monique, to know just how important it was to him.

CHAPTER EIGHTEEN

Although Group Captain Belmont had sixty-five Avro Ansons available at RAF Wigtown, most were fitted out for training navigators and bomb aimers and only three were intended to carry passengers. He had been happy to make one of them available to MI11 and it was waiting on the grass beside the control tower, not far from where Bob's Mosquito and Major Malinovsky's Airspeed Envoy were parked.

Bob stopped the lead car near the hangar closest to the control tower and looked across at Monique. 'You do look very sexy in that uniform, you know. I can't wait to help you take it off later.'

She laughed. 'It was good of them to dress us as officers. As I've got two stripes around each cuff, I assume that a flight officer in the Women's Auxiliary Air Force is equivalent to a flight lieutenant in the RAF?'

'That's right.'

'It does feel very strange to be wearing it. I wonder if they're going to ask for it back afterwards? It might be useful to keep it in my wardrobe for other occasions when a change of look is needed.'

'I can see the value in that,' said Bob. 'For the same reason, I think I need to make sure that Katerina Komarova returns hers. Doesn't she look different in that black wig? Anyway, the others are getting out of their cars, so we should too. Please take care, my love.'

'You too, Bob. I'll see you later in Stranraer.' Monique leaned across the car to kiss him.

There wasn't a cloud in the sky and the morning was already uncomfortably warm as the group walked across the grass to the Avro Anson. The two women boarded, followed by the three men who were travelling with them to Northern Ireland. After the door in the side of the fuselage was closed, Bob moved a little distance away, where he was joined by Major Malinovsky. The aircraft engines were started and the aircraft's control surfaces waggled as the pilot completed his checks. Then two airmen removed the chocks from under the main wheels and a moment later the aircraft began to move, turning to trundle along the concrete perimeter track that would take it around the airfield to the north-east end of the main runway.

'Do you want to wait for them to take off, group captain?' asked Malinovsky.

'No, but I do need to get my flying jacket and helmet from the Mosquito. Do you have your kit with you?' asked Bob.

'Only my leather jacket, which I left in the Envoy. Hopefully, Flight Lieutenant Somerset can loan me the rest of what I need.'

'We can leave the other two cars here for the moment, though we'll need to take one of them to Stranraer later to ensure we can all get back. I'll drive us round to the south side of the airfield where the Typhoons are based. Get your jacket and meet me at the car.'

When they arrived, half a dozen Typhoons were parked in a line on the grass, facing out onto the airfield just beyond a single-storey grey building with a corrugated roof. Bob parked between a lorry and a utility vehicle, both painted RAF blue grey, outside the building.

A corporal who was emerging from the building saw Bob getting out of the car and turned to go back inside. A moment later Flight Lieutenant Somerset came out and saluted. He was wearing a leather flying jacket with a faded yellow life vest over it and carrying a soft flying helmet like the one Bob had with him.

'Hello, sir. It's another perfect day for flying. Good morning, Major Malinovsky.'

'Good morning, flight lieutenant,' said Bob. 'The Typhoon is quite a beast when you get this close to it.'

'It will seem even more of one when you climb into it, sir. But don't let that deceive you. I've yet to hear anyone call the aircraft dainty or pretty, and I doubt if I ever will. But I'm not the only one on the squadron who wouldn't swap it back for a Hurricane. The Napier Sabre engine can be awkward to start in some conditions, but once it's going it's got twice the power of the Merlin engines in the Hurricanes we had before, and the top speed is 100 m.p.h. faster.

'They designed it as a medium to high-altitude fighter, which is ironic given it has achieved its best results at low-level, where it's become a very successful defence against Focke-Wulf Fw 190 intruders.

'It's also come into its own in the ground attack role. The four 20 mm cannons you can see sticking out of the leading edges of the wings give it tremendous impact and because it is such a beast, to borrow your description, it can carry two 1,000 pound bombs, one under each wing. Looking ahead, they reckon we'll be able to carry four 60 pound rockets under each wing within a few months. It's claimed that will give each Typhoon more firepower than a broadside from a Royal Navy destroyer.'

'What have you got in mind for us this morning?' asked Bob. 'It's a long time since I've flown anything with bombs attached and I don't think this is the moment to renew my acquaintance with them.'

'No, sir, I agree, though I did promise Major Malinovsky the chance to compare the Typhoon and the Ilyushin Il-2. I'll show you on a map inside, but I suggest we take off and head north at around 5,000ft and stooge around for a while, to give you both a chance to get used to flying the aircraft, perhaps doing some aerobatics and simulated dive attacks.

'Then we'll come in from the north to overfly the ranges at the north end of Luce Bay from the landward side. I will point out the targets we use for cannon attacks and if I'm sure you've correctly located them, we can swing round to the east before coming in to make live attacks, one at a time, on the targets. If there's time we can make more than one run, then return here. How does that sound?'

'Will there be any chance to simulate dogfighting?' asked Major Malinovsky.

'I'm sorry major, but no,' said Flight Lieutenant Somerset. 'History records too many cases of accidents caused by pilots forgetting that their weapons are armed in the excitement of getting on the tail of their simulated opponent and pressing the button. I felt that the opportunity to experience a live attack on a ground target would be more useful for you.'

'Thank you, I agree,' said the major.

'If you follow me into the crew room I'll get you kitted out. I see you've both got flying jackets. The cockpit of a Typhoon tends to be warm rather than cold, except at high altitudes, and as today is already quite hot you might prefer not to wear your tunics under your jackets. You can take them off when we get inside and I'll have someone put them in your car.'

Flight Lieutenant Somerset led them into the building and then along a corridor to a room that had a range of wooden lockers along one wall. Bob took off his uniform tunic at the same time as Major Malinovsky. It didn't surprise him to see the major was also wearing a shoulder holster.

'What pistol are you carrying, group captain?' asked the major.

'A Walther PPK. Not very patriotic, perhaps, but it has saved my life more than once. What about you?'

'I carry a Tokarev TT-33,' said Malinovsky. 'It's larger and heavier than your PPK and I have to admit I'd swap with you in a moment if I didn't think I'd be criticised for carrying a German-made pistol.'

Bob could see that Flight Lieutenant Somerset was amused to be witnessing such a bizarre conversation.

Bob donned his flying jacket and a life vest and picked up his helmet and oxygen mask. 'I'm ready,' he said. 'Over to you to talk us through the route on the map, flight lieutenant.'

After the briefing, Adrian Somerset led Bob to one of the Typhoons parked on the grass outside and made sure he was properly strapped in and his oxygen mask was working, then talked him through the aircraft controls. They were not hugely different from those of the Hurricane or Spitfire. A pilot officer was detailed to do the same for Major Malinovsky.

An airman stayed with Bob while Somerset went to get into his own aircraft, then helped with the start-up procedure. Once the canopy was closed, Bob knew he was on his own and he could feel the adrenaline flowing and hear his heart pounding.

'Raise a hand when you're ready.'

Bob complied, then saw Adrian Somerset's aircraft roll forwards. After it turned onto the perimeter track, Bob followed cautiously, zig-zagging to keep a view ahead past the bulk of his aircraft's nose.

As they approached the north-east end of the main runway there was another message over the radio from Somerset. 'We've got clearance for take off. I've pulled out of the way on the right. You go first Blue 2. Remember, keep the flaps set at 15 degrees and increase the throttle smoothly and she'll fly off without much tendency to swing to starboard. Don't let the tail lift too much or you risk the propeller striking the ground. Once airborne, keep straight ahead until you've cleaned up the aircraft, then turn due north and climb to 5,000 ft. Watch out for any traffic in the circuit.'

Bob got the aircraft into the air with no dramas and once he was climbing north, he started to look behind for any sign of Adrian Somerset's aircraft. After a short time, Somerset came past on Bob's right. Major Malinovsky, flying as Blue 3, was already tucked in closely just behind and to the right of Somerset.

What followed was glorious fun. Bob had never flown a single-seat aircraft with anything like as much power as the Typhoon and it was a sheer joy to fly. It might have looked like a beast on the ground, but it had an agility he found both exciting and rewarding.

'If you both feel comfortable with the aircraft, we'll head south-west before turning south over the high ground to the east of Cairnryan. Keep a good lookout, both of you. Before we reach the ranges we'll be passing over RAF Castle Kennedy and just to the east of RAF West Freugh, both busy training bases. The endless visibility today helps, but you still need to remember we're approaching a very crowded area of sky and flying into another aircraft will spoil your day and give me lots of forms to fill in. We'll descend to make our first run on the range once we're beyond Castle Kennedy.'

Again, Malinovsky was able to maintain a tight formation with Somerset that left Bob feeling rusty. Bob saw several other aircraft, alerting the other two when he did so. They also saw some he'd missed.

Somerset came back on the radio. 'I've made contact with the range controller and there's no one else playing at the moment, so we've got the place to ourselves. We'll orbit here, roughly equidistant between the two airfields, and then make our first approach at 2,000ft without using our weapons. I want to fly at a steady 240 m.p.h., which is slow enough to give you both plenty of thinking time. If we were attacking a train or an airfield in northern France we'd be flying at well over 400 m.p.h. Blue 2 should aim to fly 15 seconds behind me, which equates to a one-mile separation at our speed. That should be plenty. Blue 3 should stay a similar distance behind Blue 2.'

Bob waited for Flight Lieutenant Somerset to turn south from their orbit. He then counted to fifteen seconds before turning to follow.

'The reflection of the sun off the sea can be distracting, but look out for a broad grassy strip aligned with the direction of our approach between areas of sand dunes. Then look for the large white concrete arrow set into the grass, pointing towards the targets. Finally, you will see the targets themselves, four of them set upright in a line just before the grassy area becomes a beach. You will know this very well, major, but for Group Captain Sutherland's benefit, I would suggest you give yourself plenty of room to make your run and then pull up after firing before you get too low. Please remember the danger of target fixation. If you fly your aircraft into the ground in your enthusiasm to hit the target it will again give me lots of forms to fill in, and I hate forms. Once you've fired at a target I want you to break away to the left as quickly as possible and return to the north, to where we were orbiting.'

Bob had to squint slightly to keep Flight Lieutenant Somerset's aircraft in sight against the glare from the surface of Luce Bay. But he was pleased to be able to maintain what felt like the right distance from the aircraft ahead and then identify the range itself, the white arrow, and finally the targets.

'Did you both see the targets?'

Bob confirmed he had, and the major said that he had too.

'Maintain your separation from the aircraft in front and we'll circle round and come in for a live run on the targets. Don't worry which one you go for, just try to get one of them.'

Bob could feel his heart rate climbing. He again kept what seemed the correct distance behind Somerset's aircraft and watched as he dived towards the targets, then saw a cloud of dust appear from the one on the right-hand end of the line. Then he watched Somerset climb and turn to the left. Bob suddenly realised that he should have started his own dive towards the targets sooner and he pushed the nose of his aircraft hard forward. He did briefly see one of the targets in his gunsight but knew he was attacking too steeply.

'Pull up, group captain!' Either Somerset had turned his aircraft sufficiently to watch Bob's attack or someone on the ground had told him it wasn't going to plan. Bob pulled back hard on the control column without firing his cannons. He then followed Somerset around to the left. He tried to look over his left shoulder to see if Malinovsky was able to hit any of the targets but the lack of sight in his left eye made it impossible.

'Well done, Major Malinovsky. I'm told you destroyed the target you went for. But you've done this many times before so I expected nothing less. Not a bad effort for a first attempt, Group Captain Sutherland. The range controller said that you started your dive too late and never gave yourself a chance to hit the targets.

'I suggest the two of you have a second run while I loiter to the east to talk you in, group captain. I'm sure you'll do better with a little coaching.'

Bob found it easier when he didn't have to maintain a set distance from an aircraft ahead of him. He had no problem seeing the range and then the large white concrete arrow on the ground.

'Start your dive now, Blue 2, but back off on the throttle to maintain your speed at 240 m.p.h. That's it. You should see the targets, just pick one and move your aircraft to place your chosen target in your gunsight. When you're happy, give it a nice long burst with the cannons.'

Bob did as instructed. The physical recoil from the four cannons was much greater than he'd expected and shook the whole aircraft. He was gratified to see the tracer rounds included in his loadout converge on his chosen target and dust and sand being kicked up around it.

'Blue 2, pull up hard now!'

Bob thought he'd managed his attack well but complied instantly. As he did so, he saw the streaks of tracer rounds coming from somewhere behind him pass immediately to his right, just beneath his wing, and then carry on down towards the targets on the ground.

'Blue 3, cease fire!'

Bob realised that Malinovsky must have been much

closer than he should and had fired at him from behind.

Bob had heard the phrase 'red mist' before but until now he'd never experienced it, not even on that night in Stockholm. Instinct kicked in and he pushed the throttle as far forward as it would go and banked to turn the Typhoon as hard as he could to the left without bleeding off too much speed. He saw Somerset's aircraft ahead of him for a moment and continued to turn. As he came around further he saw that the second Typhoon had turned to the east as it was supposed to and was climbing. As much by luck as judgment, Bob's aircraft was now behind Malinovsky's and travelling faster than it. Bob corrected his heading as they closed, so he could bring the Typhoon into his gunsight.

'Group Captain Sutherland! Hold your fire!'

Bob realised his thumb was resting on the gun firing button set into the circular grip on top of the control column and that it would take only a tiny amount of extra pressure to blow Malinovsky's aircraft out of the sky, and Malinovsky with it. Bob lifted his thumb and used his excess speed to fly past the port side of what had until a moment before been his target aircraft and he then turned hard left again, just in case Malinovsky still harboured murderous intent.

'Thank you, group captain.' Even over the radio, the flight lieutenant's voice conveyed relief. 'I can't imagine how many forms I'd have had to fill in if one of my aircraft had shot down another and it's just nearly happened twice. Can I suggest we return to RAF Wigtown, gentlemen? I'd like us in a loose "V" formation with me between the two of you.'

Bob guessed it was about twenty miles back to the airfield and nothing more was said by any of them on the return trip. After landing, the flight lieutenant led as they taxied around the perimeter track to where the other Typhoons were parked.

The wheels of Bob's aircraft were chocked and he opened his canopy. An airman climbed onto the wing beside the cockpit and reached in to shut down the engine. Bob thanked him, then climbed out and jumped to the ground from the rear of the wing.

He then marched over to where Malinovsky was climbing out of his aircraft, noticing that Flight Lieutenant Somerset was converging with him.

'You tried to kill me, you bastard!' said Bob.

'I'm sorry, group captain,' said Malinovsky. 'I got carried away with the memories that brought back. I lost sight of you in the glare of the sun off the sea and thought I was much further behind you than I was. You must have slowed down.'

'But you must have heard me talking the group captain through his attack,' said Flight Lieutenant Somerset. 'You must have known you were much closer than you should have been. And you must have seen him in your gunsight as you fired, even if you'd lost sight of him on the approach to the range.'

'I heard you talking to the group captain,' said Malinovsky, 'but I was concentrating on what I was doing and didn't think about the implications. I'm sorry. I was just lost in the moment. I didn't see him in my gunsight until I'd already fired. He appeared from under my aircraft's nose.'

Bob caught and held Malinovsky's gaze for a moment and could see that the man was lying.

'You're lucky the group captain paid more attention to me, major,' said Flight Lieutenant Somerset. 'It only took him one turn to get on your tail and if he'd not held back, you'd be dead. For my part I'm sorry, Group Captain Sutherland. I should have seen the major was closing on you but I was focused on you and only saw him at the last minute.'

Malinvosky removed the flying kit he'd been loaned and put it down on the grass next to his aircraft. Then he looked at his watch. 'Thank you for allowing me to fly a Typhoon, flight lieutenant. It was a memorable experience and I will write up my impressions as we agreed. Perhaps we should set off for Stranraer, group captain?' The major turned and walked towards the car.

Bob saw a look of disbelief cross Flight Lieutenant Somerset's face at the speed with which the major shrugged off the incident.

Bob raised his eyebrows in response. 'Thank you, Flight Lieutenant Somerset, for the flight and the warning. That's two drinks I owe you. I'd be very grateful if you'd keep what just happened to yourself.'

'You are very welcome, sir. If I'd not seen that with my own eyes, I wouldn't have believed it. If you could put your kit down with the major's I'll get someone to sort it out.'

Not a word was said as Bob drove Malinovsy back to where they'd left the other two cars. He had been going to suggest they grab a quick lunch in the officers' mess before setting off but didn't feel hungry and didn't care how Malinovsky felt.

Bob was grateful they'd be driving to Stranraer separately. He needed time to think about what had just happened. He also needed to think about his response to it. He knew that he owed the flight lieutenant a third drink, for stopping him from killing Malinovsky.

CHAPTER NINETEEN

The Avro Anson came to a halt on a concrete parking area at the end of a line of three dark green bombers carrying what Monique recognised as US markings. She knew that Bob would have been able to tell her what they were, but Bob wasn't with her and she was surprised to realise that she missed him already.

Monique and Michael Dixon were in the seats immediately behind the pilot, a young RAF sergeant. After he stopped the engines the pilot turned around to look at his passengers. Monique could hear those behind her preparing to move towards the aircraft door.

'Welcome to RAF Nutts Corner,' he said in an American or perhaps a Canadian accent.

'Are you joking?' asked Michael.

'No, sir. I've wanted to be able to say that ever since I learned that this place existed.'

'Thank you for the flight,' said Michael.

Monique smiled at the pilot before she turned to follow the others out.

Two police cars pulled to a halt behind the aircraft as Monique stepped down to the concrete. A blond man in his forties wearing a well-worn dark grey suit got out of the driver's side of one of them and walked over to where Michael was standing.

'Are you Lieutenant Commander Dixon?' he asked.

'That's me,' said Michael.

'Good to meet you, sir. I'm Inspector Boyle. I'm with the Royal Ulster Constabulary's Special Branch. I'm sorry, but I need to see proof of your identity. Here's my warrant card.'

Michael and Monique showed the inspector their MI11 passes.

'We can vouch for the others,' said Michael.

'I've set up a meeting with my people in the offices we use in the Olderfleet Hotel, which also serves as the Royal Navy's headquarters for their port operations in Larne.'

'How far is it to Larne?' asked Monique.

'A little more than twenty miles,' said the inspector. He looked at his watch. 'The *Princess Margaret* doesn't leave until 2 p.m. We've got plenty of time to make our preparations.'

Katerina Komarova wanted to travel in the first car with Monique, Michael and the inspector. Monique wondered if she was worried that they might talk about her behind her back, before conceding to herself that they might well have done. Monique still found it hard to like Komarova and she certainly didn't trust her, which meant the conversation on the drive to Larne was stilted.

*

The Olderfleet Hotel was an imposing L-shaped stone building whose main block was four storeys in height, if you counted the slightly below-ground-floor level and the row of attic windows set into the slate roof. A side range which ran along the road they'd approached along was less grand. The inspector turned right at the corner of the hotel, revealing that it had good views over Larne Harbour to a pier, on the far side of which a large grey-painted steamer was moored.

They'd driven through the town to get to the harbour and both were busy. Inspector Boyle had difficulty finding somewhere to park and had to settle for a space between two Royal Navy lorries a hundred yards along the harbourside road beyond the hotel.

He then led the way back to the main entrance and past Royal Navy guards posted outside, who came to attention as Michael Dixon, and Monique herself, she realised, entered. The thought crossed her mind that she didn't know how to salute properly, despite having seen it done any number of times. That was a gap in her cover she'd have to ask Michael to put right before she boarded the steamer. Another guard inside checked their passes. The inspector led them down a short flight of stairs to a meeting room that looked out through criss-cross taped windows to a sunken area between the hotel and the road. The only view was of the stone wall that prevented pedestrians on the pavement from falling in.

'The navy took the rooms with the sea views,' said the inspector. 'No offence, Lieutenant Commander Dixon.'

Michael smiled. 'None taken.'

Peter Bennett and Andrew MacDonald were already sitting on one side of the meeting table that filled much of the room, sipping mugs of what Monique assumed was tea. The driver of their car had obviously been more fortunate than the inspector in finding a parking place. There were three other men in suits in the room, standing beside a side table that had an urn and more mugs.

'Can the three of you sit down?' asked the inspector, talking to the men in suits. Monique, Michael and Katerina Komarova were handed mugs and did likewise.

'There should be plenty of time for lunch on board the *Princess Margaret* before she sails,' said the inspector. 'If you agree, I think we should focus on the matter at hand.'

'Of course,' said Monique. 'You tell us what you know and we can fill in any gaps.'

‘That sounds fine,’ said the inspector. ‘My boss, the head of Special Branch in Northern Ireland, was contacted by the head of MI11, Commodore Cunningham, late last night and I was then asked to come into the office to telephone the commodore. He explained why the five of you were coming and asked for our help.

‘I understand we are trying to catch a German agent you know as Edward Daly or the Cuttlefish who is believed to be planning to travel on today’s 2 p.m. steamer sailing from Larne to Stranraer. The commodore told me that Mr Daly is a master of disguise, that he has access to a range of British military uniforms, and that he probably has a selection of identity and other documents in unknown names that he’s had professionally forged in Dublin.

‘I should say in passing that it’s not escaped us that this man probably spent last night north of the border and that he presumably has somewhere he can keep belongings and swap between the military uniforms he uses in the UK and the civilian clothes he must use in Eire. I’m afraid we’ve made no progress on that yet.

‘When I spoke to Commodore Cunningham he also told me that Mr Daly is believed to have murdered two men in Dublin yesterday and three more on a recent trip to Scotland. He is also likely to have been behind the disappearance of a naval lieutenant in Belfast earlier this month. Incidentally, I should tell you that a body turned up in the docks late last night. It had been weighted down with an iron bar and only came to the surface because it was disturbed by the propellor of a passing ship. It may take some time to formally identify the body, which was naked, even though we believe we know who it is. By my count that makes Mr Daly a murderer six times over, just in the recent past.’

'That's fairly comprehensive,' said Monique. 'It is worth adding that Mr Daly is known to speak with an Irish or Liverpudlian accent, though he might have a wider range available in his repertoire, and that he is of average height and build, has black hair and brown eyes, and is around 35 years old.'

'It's not going to be easy, is it, Madame Dubois?' asked Inspector Boyle. 'If you add to his very unexceptional description a military uniform from any of the services and well-forged papers in an unknown name, we might end up needing to check a good proportion of the men on board the steamer, both passengers and possibly even crew.'

'He does have one weak spot,' said Monique. 'He is well known to Miss Komarova and she believes she will recognise him whatever identity he has adopted and whether he is in disguise or not.'

'May I ask how well you know him, Miss Komarova?' asked the inspector.

'Well enough to know he has a scar about 10cm long across the top of his right thigh,' said Katerina Komarova.

The inspector laughed. 'You know him quite well, then. However, the scar is only going to be of help if we ask every man who matches the general description to drop his trousers, and I can't see that happening. If you can recognise Mr Daly, presumably he can recognise you?'

'This isn't my normal hair colour and this certainly isn't my normal clothing. And the last time he saw me was in Madrid. I hope I will be able to spot him without him realising who I am.'

'What can you tell us about the steamer?' asked Monique.

'I should have pointed her out when we came in,' said the inspector.

‘Is she the grey vessel moored on the far side of the pier opposite the hotel?’ asked Michael.

‘That’s right. She was built on the Clyde and launched in 1931. She was one of two steamers operating the service before the war but is now the only one available to general traffic, though unless you are with MI11 or the NKVD you need a Travel Identity Card to book passage. Other vessels are still making the crossing, but they exclusively carry military personnel and traffic, usually units or parts of units moving between Northern Ireland and the rest of the UK.

‘I will talk you through the vessel’s layout in a moment, but as I see it our main problem is going to be a feature of the ship that allowed it to transform travel on the route when it arrived. Until then it was the norm for passengers intending to travel on the 6 a.m. mail steamer from Stranraer to book accommodation in the town overnight and make a very early start. The *Princess Margaret* changed all that. As well as a range of lounge and deck areas, she was built with lots of cabins in which passengers could stay overnight before leaving Stranraer early the next morning.’

‘What do you mean by “lots”?’ asked Michael.

‘I checked this morning. She has about eighty cabins. The saloon class sleeping accommodation is divided between single and twin cabins. Steerage is less of a problem because accommodation is on bunk beds in a dormitory.’

‘That still gives a large number of private spaces in which Mr Daly could hide during the crossing,’ said Michael.

‘My thoughts exactly,’ said Inspector Boyle. ‘My starting point in thinking about this was finding a way of ensuring that our man doesn’t simply hide in a cabin for the duration. I have arranged for my two detective constables here to pose as stewards, white jackets and all. Some passengers do use the cabin accommodation for the trip to Scotland, especially if they've arrived in Larne early. My two men will spend the crossing checking on the passenger cabins to identify legitimate passengers and ensure no one is simply hiding.'

'Petty Officer MacDonald and Sergeant Bennett can assist,' said Michael. 'They can act as added security in case your men disturb someone who shouldn't be in a cabin.'

'Are they armed?'

'We all are.'

'Very well, that will allow us two teams of two checking cabins and other private spaces like crew accommodation. I assume you intend to act as security for Miss Komarova, Madame Dubois?'

'Yes, we're dressed as a pair, so might as well stay together and simply wander around the public areas of the vessel as if we're enjoying the voyage. I suggest that you and Michael play a more distant role, inspector, keeping an eye on what's going on and watching out for anyone behaving oddly as a result of what the rest of us are doing.'

'That's a reasonable plan,' said the inspector. 'The last member of my team, Detective Sergeant Duffy, who is sitting at the end of the table, will oversee security for passengers boarding the steamer. Most of those intending to travel arrive by rail and then walk the short distance from the station to the pier. He will ensure that there are no problems with the flow of passengers after the last train before the scheduled sailing time arrives. He will also ensure that none of you have any problems boarding. I should mention that the steamer will be fairly busy, which won't make our lives any easier.'

Katerina Komarova sat forwards in her chair. 'Can I ask about tickets? We believe that Edward Daly originally planned to sail tomorrow afternoon but, after the killing of the two men in Dublin yesterday, now intends to make the crossing as soon as possible. Can he sail on this afternoon's steamer with tickets issued for tomorrow's sailing?'

'That wouldn't be a problem,' said Detective Sergeant Duffy. 'Cabin bookings are tied to specific sailings but a ticket to travel would be as valid today as tomorrow.'

'I'm pleased you'll be on hand, detective sergeant,' said Monique. 'We need to make it as easy as possible for Mr Daly to board the vessel, assuming that does remain his intention. If we do anything to scare him off before he's on board and the gangplank is pulled up we lose our best chance, perhaps our only chance, of catching him. That means we need to avoid any unusual activity around the steamer between now and when it sails. For all we know, Daly could already be in Larne, having picked a vantage point from which he can watch the vessel. If we were to turn up on the pier in a couple of police cars, I think we could forget the whole thing. That's what I would do, certainly.'

'But you wouldn't have murdered six men to get to this point, Madame Dubois,' said the inspector.

'Not murdered them, no,' said Monique. She caught the inspector's gaze and he raised his eyebrows.

The inspector returned to his subject. 'We've got some deck plans of the *Princess Margaret.*' He asked one of the detective constables to roll them out on the table and proceeded to talk about aspects of the layout.

'Thank you, that was very helpful,' said Monique when the inspector had finished.

‘We should tell you that colleagues of ours and local police will meet the vessel when it arrives in Stranraer,’ said Katerina Komarova. ‘If we’ve not found Mr Daly by then we might need to keep everyone on board until I can personally clear each one of them, and if that fails we may need to search the ship.’

‘That would be hugely disruptive,’ said Inspector Boyle. ‘When weighed against that, the idea of the men in this room going round in pairs and asking each male on board to drop his trousers to see if he’s got a long scar next to his privates seems almost straightforward.’

Monique smiled, though she knew the inspector wasn’t joking. She hoped it wouldn't come to that.

CHAPTER TWENTY

Monique and Katerina gave the others a fifteen-minute lead before leaving the Olderfleet Hotel. They then walked the short distance to the railway station and followed signs to the right that directed them to the steamer pier. They'd discussed whether they needed suitcases to look the part in case the Cuttlefish was watching but decided that as WAAF officers they'd have sent their luggage ahead.

Detective Sergeant Duffy had given them their steamer tickets before he left the hotel and they had no problem gaining access to the pier. Monique was pleased that the detective sergeant wasn't anywhere obviously in sight. He looked like a policeman, even when wearing a suit.

The berth nearest the seaward end of the railway station was empty. Wooden signs promising the 'Next Sailing for Stranraer' directed them back towards the pier opposite the hotel. A couple of other people who looked like passengers were following the same trail.

To Monique's eyes, the *Princess Margaret* was a large ship. As she'd seen when arriving at the hotel, it was painted battleship grey and had a single funnel. The vessel was berthed with its bow towards them and there were streaks of rust extending down from where the anchor was held against the front of the hull to the waterline. Otherwise, it looked well cared for. She assumed the grey colour had been applied for wartime service to make it less obvious to German aircraft or U-boats. She wished the thought of an enemy attack hadn't crossed her mind. It was very unlikely, but of all the ways she could go, drowning in a torpedoed or bombed ship wouldn't be top of her list of preferences.

There was a bustle of men coming and going on the quayside. The steamer itself was held away from the concrete edge of the pier by large timber fenders and there were two gangways linking the pier to the vessel, one near the front of the superstructure and the other some way back. The latter was being used by men loading boxes, presumably of provisions, onto the steamer.

'If they use two gangways at Stranraer it will complicate the process of checking people getting off,' said Katerina.

'Let's hope we've found our man by then,' said Monique, though the thought had also crossed her mind.

There was still plenty of time before the steamer was due to depart and a steward directed them towards the dining saloon, where he said lunch was being served. A few early arrivals were already eating. The menu was very limited but the food was filling. They both skipped the starter course of a choice of soups and Monique opted for fish and chips with mushy peas for her main course. Katerina went for ham, scrambled eggs and chips. Monique wondered if she realised that the eggs were probably powdered.

'I always feel hungry before something like this,' said Katerina. 'It's the way my body responds to the tension.'

'This should keep us going,' said Monique. 'Changing the subject, I'm wondering if we might have made a mistake.'

'You mean because we're wearing officers' uniforms and travelling first class or saloon class or whatever they call it and the Cuttlefish might choose to travel steerage class?' asked Katerina.

Monique nodded. 'Yes, we might miss him altogether.'

'I've been thinking about that since we saw the two gangways. I should have seen the problem when Inspector

Boyle was talking about the deck plans. All the steerage accommodation is at the back end of the ship, while we are travelling at the front. I'm concerned that two women officers might appear unusual and attract attention if we visit the steerage class areas of the ship.'

Monique put her fork down. 'I agree that our civilian clothes might have been better but I think we'll simply have to brazen that out. We can't fail to cover a significant part of the ship because we might not fit in. Knowing Edward Daly as you do, Katerina, do you think it likely he would travel steerage class to make himself less detectable? Or is he arrogant enough to believe he doesn't need to bother?'

'The more I think about it the less I believe he will travel steerage,' said Katerina. 'We need to remember that he planned this before he knew that he had been compromised by an Abwehr agent in the SD office. We also know his uniform collection, and therefore his choice of identities, favours officers rather than other ranks. I don't believe he will try to hide in steerage or in a cabin, where he might be discovered and trapped. That leads me to suspect that he will rely on his false papers and identity to get him through.'

'What he doesn't know is that you are on board,' said Monique.

'That's right, which means that we should still have an advantage over him if he is sailing today.'

*

Monique knew it was about a two-hour crossing to Stranraer. It was a beautiful day with crystal clear light and very warm temperatures that reminded her of Malta.

She and Katerina went out onto the promenade deck to watch the *Princess Margaret* leave the harbour at Larne. The ship had become busier as the departure time approached and there were quite a few passengers out on deck. Many were men in uniform, and most of them were officers. There were a few other women on board. Some were in uniform while others, like some mainly older men, were in civilian clothes. One older woman was travelling with three well-behaved young girls. Monique guessed they might be her granddaughters. She wondered if the mix was any different in the steerage class accommodation.

Monique had seen both Michael Dixon and Inspector Boyle a couple of times since boarding but both were doing a good job of being unobtrusive. Michael was currently leaning on a railing on the harbour side of the vessel and smoking a cigarette.

'That breeze is welcome,' said Katerina.

'It is. I'm thinking that these uniforms might not have been such a good idea for another reason,' said Monique.

'I agree. No one else is removing their uniform tunics so I suppose we need to keep ours on too.'

'Have you seen anyone who looks like he could be Edward Daly?' asked Monique.

'Too many, if I'm honest. Not knowing what colour uniform he might be wearing is a real drawback. If you add the thought that Edward might have changed the colour of his hair or stuck on a moustache or beard then a lot of the men we've seen are possibilities. Some are too tall or too short. Others are obviously too young, which would be difficult to fake. I did start by discounting men who weren't on their own before realising that if I were in his shoes I'd strike up a conversation with someone else on their own, just so I didn't appear to be.'

‘I agree with you, though that is a disheartening conclusion,’ said Monique. ‘Perhaps our best hope is that Mr Daly has decided to hide in a cabin and is discovered there. Let’s do a slow tour of the ship, covering the outside and inside spaces.’

Their exploration of the steamer did nothing to change their initial view. No one stood out as behaving suspiciously and a significant proportion of the passengers could have been the Cuttlefish in disguise. Monique realised that Katerina had been hoping that she’d immediately see through any disguise that Edward Daly might wear and that she was beginning to accept it might not be as simple as that.

After two rounds of the first-class areas of the vessel, they decided to extend their exploration of the steamer to the steerage accommodation. This was accessed by crossing a gangway between the front part of the superstructure and the rear, over an area of open deck with a large cargo hatch.

Despite the efforts of the ship’s designers to keep the two classes of passengers entirely separated, Monique found the differences were not as great as she had expected. The steerage areas were less plush than the first-class areas. They were also busier and had more enlisted personnel and many fewer officers. More civilians were travelling steerage class, including several women with children. On the whole, though, she didn’t think she and Katerina stood out as obviously as she had feared they might.

Having slowly toured the rear of the vessel and stopped for a cup of tea in the steerage class saloon, they crossed back over the gangway linking the two parts of the superstructure just as the steamer passed a lighthouse off to its right.

‘I think that’s Scotland,’ said Monique. ‘We’re running out of time.’

‘How long have we got?’ asked Katerina as they strolled back along the side of the promenade deck.

‘Hello, here’s Michael,’ said Monique. He was leaning on the railing looking out to the shoreline they were now running parallel to.

‘Hello, ladies. If anyone’s watching, what could be more natural than a dashing naval officer chatting to two beautiful WAAF officers?’

He looked around. Monique had already decided there wasn't anyone else within hearing.

‘Katerina was asking how much time we’ve got before we arrive in Stranraer,’ said Monique.

‘We’ve just entered the mouth of Loch Ryan. The ship will slow down in a moment to pass through the defensive boom intended to prevent enemy surface vessels or submarines from getting in. Stranraer is at the southern end of the loch so we’ve still got a little time. How’s it going?’

‘Not well,’ said Katerina. ‘I was convinced I’d know him immediately, but there are so many men on board who might be him.’

‘That’s not ideal,’ said Michael. ‘I can add to our problems that fact that the search teams have had no joy finding the Cuttlefish hiding in a cabin, or in crew accommodation for that matter, which they’ve also searched.’

‘It’s looking as if we’ll need to have everyone cleared by Katerina after the steamer docks in Stranraer,’ said Monique. ‘That’s going to be a slow process and we’ll need to make sure there’s only one gangway operating.’

‘What worries me is that he might have concealed himself in a locker or rope store in the hope he can emerge later tonight and leave the ship,' said Michael. 'That suggests we will need to conduct a thorough search if we can't find him in any other way, which could take days to do properly.'

'And that's before we consider the possibility that he might be on a fishing boat bound for France or Norway,' said Katerina. 'I told you that the Abwehr believed he would try to come to Scotland, and that's also what I think. But if he did give up on his mission once he was compromised, we are wasting our time.'

Monique and Katerina continued their stroll around the first-class areas of the steamer but other than affording Monique good views of RAF Wig Bay on one side and the impressively large port at Cairnryan on the other, this achieved nothing.

As the *Princess Margaret* neared Stranraer, Monique saw Michael Dixon and Inspector Boyle in conversation on the promenade deck and went with Katerina to join them. To her mind, the need to agree on what they should do when the ship berthed was greater than the need to keep up the appearance that they were innocent travellers.

When they finished talking, Michael went to find the ship's radio room.

The steamer pier extended out at an angle into Loch Ryan from the east end of the town of Stranraer. There was a ship already berthed on the far or eastern side. The line of approach of the steamer made it obvious that the captain of the *Princess Margaret* intended to moor on the right-hand or western side of the pier, the side nearest to the town.

Although at first sight long and narrow, it became clear as they neared that the pier was wide enough to accommodate the substantial, corrugated-roofed shed of what the inspector said was Stranraer Harbour railway station, plus open areas to service the steamers on either side of it.

Monique listened as an announcement was made over the ship's tannoy asking all passengers to remain where they were and await instructions from the ship's crew before disembarking.

Monique's mouth felt dry as the ship came alongside the pier and was tied up, separated from the pier by wooden fenders like those she'd seen at Larne. Several cars were parked by the near wall of the railway station and she could see Bob and Major Malinovsky standing some distance apart beside two of them. Four policemen were on the quayside and she could see two more by the entrance to the railway station. She wondered what proportion of the total resources of the Wigtownshire Constabulary they represented and hoped that this wasn't all going to be in vain.

Two gangways were set up connecting the steamer with the pier, one near the front of the promenade deck at the forward end of the vessel and the second near the rear, leading from the steerage accommodation.

Monique and Katerina stood close to the head of the forward gangway and Monique watched while Bob and a policeman came aboard. Though Bob returned her smile she got the sense he was very on edge. It was hardly surprising, she was too.

Michael Dixon, Andrew MacDonald and Peter Bennett were also on the promenade deck and as passengers started to gather they directed them to form a queue three or four deep along the side of the deck next to the railings, starting next to the head of the gangway and extending back towards the rear of the vessel. All of those in the queue were male and nearly all were in uniform, both officers and other ranks.

An army captain near the front of the queue raised an arm. ‘Excuse me, but I’ve got a train to catch. Others here have too.’

‘Hear! Hear!’ added someone else in a very upper-class English accent.

‘They’re letting them off at the back!’ shouted an army sergeant. ‘Why can’t we get off now?’

Monique could hear other men muttering, She knew that stewards and other members of the steamer’s crew had passed through the vessel as it arrived, directing women passengers and any males in their early twenties or younger to go to the back of the vessel and disembark using the gangway there. Inspector Boyle and his two detective constables were doing a final sift at the top of the rear gangway before allowing anyone who couldn’t possibly be the Cuttlefish in disguise to leave the ship.

Other male passengers in both first-class and steerage had been directed to the promenade deck, where they were still gathering. Monique could imagine that the gangway linking the two areas of accommodation together was proving a bottleneck with passengers wanting to cross in both directions at the same time.

‘I’m sorry, but this is unacceptable.’ This time it was an army lieutenant colonel.

While the policeman stayed at the top of the gangway, Bob moved so he was standing opposite it, where he could be seen by as many of those in the queue as possible. ‘I hope we won’t need to keep you too long,’ he said projecting his voice. ‘I am afraid I need to ask you for a little patience.’

‘Who are you?’ demanded an anonymous voice with London origins.

Bob paused. Monique could see he was weighing up whether the man they were looking for, assuming he was on board and wasn't hiding, would have had time to make his way to the promenade deck and be in the queue before revealing his hand.

It was Michael who had suggested that Bob should board the steamer when it landed. He said that a senior officer might keep the queue calm for longer than he'd be able to manage himself. Monique thought it was a good idea.

Bob simply stood and waited and the queue quietened down. Michael, Andrew and Peter were standing at intervals along the length of the inside of the promenade deck, a little distanced from the queue along the other side of the deck. Monique could see that each had their right hand in their uniform jacket pocket. She thought the Cuttlefish would recognise that they were holding pistols, while some of the others present wouldn't.

Then Bob raised a hand. 'Thank you for being so patient. My name is Group Captain Robert Sutherland and I am the deputy head of Military Intelligence, Section 11. You have been asked to gather here because we are looking for a German spy who we think could well be amongst you.'

This caused more muttering and Monique watched as the men in the queue became visibly uneasy, with many glancing at their neighbours.

Katerina walked a few paces to stand beside Bob, where she could be seen by many of the men in the queue. Monique moved to stand on the other side of him.

'It's a bloody RAF takeover!' said the same London voice.

This time Monique heard others shushing the heckler.

Bob had at least succeeded in gaining the crowd's attention.

'I am going to ask you to move forwards slowly,' he said, 'so that you can go down the gangway one at a time.'

Monique watched as Katerina removed her uniform cap and then took off her black wig. If the Cuttlefish was in the queue and was ever going to try to make a break for it, it would be now. The theatre of the moment must have been obvious to everyone, but only Edward Daly would recognise Katerina and understand why she was here.

To Monique's disappointment, the only movement in the queue was some shuffling near the front of it. Then, one by one, Michal Dixon directed the men in the queue to walk towards the top of the gangway. Katerina held the gaze of each man as he passed and the policeman then directed him down the gangway.

Monique knew that this wasn't going to be a swift process but the men in the queue were cooperating now their exit was clear to them.

Afterwards, Monique wondered if she'd let her concentration drop for a moment. None of the men spoke as they passed under Katerina's gaze. But then, in an Irish accent, someone said, 'Hello Ludmilla. Long time, no see.'

Katerina took a step backwards but the army captain passing in front of her was quicker than her or Bob, standing next to her. He leapt forwards and grabbed her by the neck, at the same time pointing a pistol at her head.

'If anyone moves, I shoot. I know you are all armed and I know you can kill me any time you want. But if I die then so does Ludmilla. Stay there, my darling, while I come round behind you. Now, you lead us down the gangway. That's right. Meanwhile, someone can move one of those cars so it's nearer.'

Monique saw Michael move.

'Steady, lieutenant commander. I bet you're wondering whether you can blow my head off without your bullet passing through me and killing Ludmilla or my reflexes pulling the trigger and making a hole in both sides of her head. It's your call.'

Katerina shuffled awkwardly down the gangway with Edward Daly's left arm around her neck and his right hand holding his pistol to her right temple.

Suddenly there was the sound of a gunshot and Monique saw Edward Daly's pistol fly out of his hand and back towards the top of the gangway. In an instant he toppled to his left and went sideways over the handrail of the gangway, taking Katerina with him.

Monique saw Major Malinovsky walk out from behind a pile of crates on the pier with a pistol in his hand.

'They've fallen between the ship and the pier!' Monique recognised Michael's voice as he thrust something towards her.

Startled, she took it and saw it was his uniform jacket. 'What are you going to do?'

But he'd already gone over the steamer's railings. One of the men at the head of the queue dropped a lifebelt down into the strip of water created by the fenders holding the steamer clear of the structure of the pier. Then Andrew MacDonald also handed Monique his jacket and ran down the gangway to the pier before jumping into the water. Other men on the pier were gathering to help.

Monique turned around to look at Bob. She put a hand on his arm. 'Malinovsky took a shot. I think he hit Daly's right hand or his gun.'

'There's something I need to tell you about him,' said Bob, 'but not now.'

*

'There was no trace of him.' Michael Dixon was sitting in the railway station waiting room with a grey blanket wrapped around him. 'If you were an excellent swimmer, or truly desperate, you might be able to make it under the steamer into the open water of the harbour, but I'd not like to try it myself.'

'Nor me,' said Andrew McDonald. 'I only saw you and Katerina in the water before I went in. I looked around for Daly before they hauled me out but I saw nothing.

'I can't help,' said Katerina, also draped in a blanket. 'He let go of me as we fell and that's the last I can tell you about him.'

'We've got navy divers on their way from Cairnryan,' said Bob. 'We need to know if Edward Daly is dead or not. Things will be a lot simpler if we can find his body. The police have boats searching the water around the steamer and alongside the pier. They are also setting up patrols along the shoreline around the harbour to see if he emerges under his own steam or floats ashore.'

'We can be sure that he's injured,' said Katerina. 'The police noticed blood on the side of my face when you pulled me out, Michael, even after my swim, and it wasn't mine.'

'There's not much more we can do,' said Bob. 'Inspector White and Inspector Boyle were getting on like a house on fire when I left them just now. I think we can leave things to them until the morning. The police have said they will find dry clothes for the three of you, though there are no promises that they will match your uniform jackets, gentlemen. I suggest that when you've changed we drive back to RAF Wigtown to let you all have baths and another change of clothes and then a drink or two, on MI11, of course. It's been an eventful day.'

'Where's Major Malinovsky?' asked Katerina.

'I think he's headed back already,' said Sergeant Bennett. 'I saw him drive off in one of the cars.'

'When we catch up with him I want a private chat about whose side he's on,' said Katerina. 'He very nearly got me killed. He could be the best marksman in the world but hitting Edward Daly's hand or gun with a shot fired from a service pistol at that range was pure luck. He could just as easily have hit me and he could easily have caused Daly's pistol to fire.'

'I'm afraid you'll have to form a queue as I also want a word with him,' said Bob. 'He tried to kill me earlier and almost succeeded.'

Monique could see from Bob's face that he wasn't joking. She thought it best to lighten the mood. 'While you're waiting for your turn with the major, Katerina, you can tell me who Ludmilla is, perhaps over some brandy and a gin and tonic.'

'Only if there really is gin involved,' said Katerina, smiling.

CHAPTER TWENTY-ONE

As MI11 was now a car short, the police in Stranraer provided a replacement, with a driver, to run Peter Bennett and Andrew MacDonald to the sergeants' mess at RAF Wigtown. Monique drove the remaining MI11 car while Bob sat next to her, with Andrew and Katerina in the back.

'I want a bath and a change, and then something to eat and a drink,' said Katerina. 'First, though, I need to talk to Comrade Popov. Is there a secure telephone I can use to contact the Soviet embassy in London?'

Bob thought she had recovered well from nearly being shot and then having to swim for her life. He was intrigued by what happened between her and Malinovsky and wondered how that might be turned to MI11's advantage.

'I'm sure we can find you one at RAF Wigtown,' he said. 'I also need to report to Commodore Cunningham, so we can kill two birds with one stone.'

'If Katerina is going to talk to Mr Popov about Malinovsky, perhaps you should expand on what you said in Stranraer about him trying to kill you, Bob,' said Monique. 'I'd like to know what happened, too.'

Bob told them, though he made no mention of his instinctive attempt to shoot the major down in return. He thought it best if that wasn't something discussed between Katerina and Popov.

'Incidentally,' said Bob, 'while we were waiting for the steamer to arrive, Inspector White told me that they'd checked the passenger lists and someone using Lieutenant John MacKinlay's documents, and presumably uniform, sailed on the steamer from Larne to Stranraer on Monday the 14th of June. That means we know when Edward Daly first travelled to Scotland.'

'And Inspector Boyle told us that a body was found in Belfast docks last night,' said Monique. 'It's not been formally identified but I think we now know what the Cuttlefish did with the lieutenant's body.'

RAF Wigtown was again very active, with flying going on into the evening. The last mile to the airfield was along the road linking it to the domestic site and it was busy with men and women on bicycles. The guards at the main gate told Bob that the telephone exchange was in a building just behind the station headquarters and gave him directions to find it.

Bob asked Monique to drive them first to where they'd left their third car that morning, not far from the control tower.

'The car's still there,' said Michael Dixon as they rounded the corner of a hangar.

'It is, but the Airspeed Envoy's gone,' said Bob. 'Apparently, the major's not keen to talk to either of us, Katerina. Pull up next to the other car, Monique. Someone's left a note on the windscreen.'

'It's probably the station warrant officer complaining about it being parked here all day,' she said.

Bob smiled. 'Being shouted at by the SWO at Turnhouse made quite an impression on you, didn't it?' He got out and walked over to the other car, taking a piece of paper from behind the windscreen wiper. Then he walked back and bent down beside Monique's open window.

'It's from Peter Bennett. He and Andrew had the police driver bring them here rather than take them to the sergeants' mess. They've taken the car that Major Malinovsky drove back from Stranraer and, quote, "will go for a pint in the Red Lion Inn in Wigtown as soon as

Andrew's cleaned up and changed and we've had a bite to eat". Malinovsky left the car here with the key in the ignition and the door unlocked before departing in the Envoy. Peter says he asked in the control tower if the major said where he was going. He didn't. He radioed the control tower for permission to start up, to taxi and to take off and that was it. He was last seen heading north-east.' Bob looked at his watch. 'That was half an hour ago.'

'I need to talk to Comrade Popov as soon as possible,' said Katerina. 'I can't understand what Major Malinovsky is doing and have no idea where he could be going.'

'He could have turned towards London as soon as he was out of sight,' said Bob. 'I bet no one thought he was worth tracking on radar so there's no way of knowing. On the other hand, north-east is the general direction of RAF Errol, between Perth and Dundee, where he was based when Monique and I encountered him late last year. That has to be a possible destination. Let's take both cars and make our telephone calls.'

Michael drove back to the officers' mess on the domestic site to get a bath and a change of clothes while the others went to the telephone exchange. It took a short time for the WAAF flight sergeant in charge to make the arrangements Bob asked for. Then, after assurances from Bob that her call would be secure, Katerina was shown into a vacant office to contact the Soviet embassy while Bob and Monique were taken to another office at the far end of the building to telephone Commodore Cunningham. Only that wasn't what they did.

Monique looked at Bob as she held the handset to her ear. 'She's asked for Popov and they've told her to wait on the line. That's Popov now. The current countersign is the Russian for "bamboo" and "tiger". She's angry and has launched straight into a rant about Malinovsky, using terms of abuse that are quite extreme and not easily translatable. What is the man playing at? He tried to kill her and he tried to kill Group Captain Sutherland. Popov is asking her to calm down. He's asking for an account of what happened. The anger's gone now and she's talking him through what we told them after they arrived yesterday and what happened today. Now he's asked her to hold and the line's gone quiet.'

Bob found he had to make a conscious effort to breathe. Several minutes passed.

'Popov is back on the line. He's asking where she's telephoning from. She's assuring him that it's a secure line and he's telling her to be careful, telling her that she shouldn't trust us. He's saying that from what she's told him, the Cuttlefish would have got away if Malinovsky hadn't acted as he did. She's angry again, accusing him of trying to defend the man who nearly killed her. Now she's asking him if Malinovsky was acting under orders from him. He's become very defensive and he's telling her that he didn't order Malinovsky to kill you or her. She's told him that you think Malinovsky might be heading for RAF Errol. That seems to have interested him. But now Katerina is becoming defensive. It's as if she feels she might have shown too much anger or emotion and weakened her position in Popov's eyes. They've agreed that she will try to contact him again tomorrow. That's it, she's hung up, and I should too.'

They met Katerina in the corridor.

'Were you able to get through?' asked Monique.

'Yes, Comrade Popov assured me that he has nothing to do with any attempt that Major Malinovsky might have made on your life, group captain, or mine.'

‘We were less fortunate,’ said Bob. ‘Commodore Cunningham had stepped out to catch some air. Apparently, it’s as warm in London as it is here and his office can get very stuffy. I’ve agreed to ring him again in,’ Bob looked at his watch, ‘ten minutes. I suggest the two of you drive back to the officers’ mess while I make the call. That leaves me without a car but rank has its privileges and I’m sure I can get someone to run me back.’

Bob made several telephone calls after the women left. The first was to the RAF Police flight at RAF Errol. The sergeant on duty confirmed that Flying Officer Frost was still the flight commander and agreed to have him available in the office twenty minutes later.

The second was to Commodore Cunningham. Bob talked him through the events of the day, trying not to sound as guilty as he felt about failing to catch the Cuttlefish. The commodore said he would have his people ring around doctors and hospitals in south-west Scotland to ask if anyone had been asked to treat a man with an injured right hand. He would also contact the police in Stranraer later that evening, just to make sure they remembered that it wasn’t only Bob who was interested in how they were getting on. Finally, he agreed to find out as much as possible about Major Malinovsky and how he came to be working for Popov.

Bob was about to end the call when Commodore Cunningham stopped him.

‘Hang on, Bob. I almost forgot. You may recall that when we met in his office after we visited the Soviet embassy, Sir Peter Maitland said he would ask MI5 and MI6 to find out what they could about Edward Daly. I’m sorry to say that they’ve come up with precisely nothing, even with the help of the Irish Directorate of Military

Intelligence, G2, who are as keen to find Daly as we are after the murders in Dublin.

'It's as if he never existed. It's been obvious from the start that "Edward Daly" is a cover name, but they've been able to find out nothing about the real man behind the name. G2 have fingerprints from the car the second body was in that may be his, but they are of no help.'

'So we're chasing a ghost?' asked Bob.

'I'm afraid so. Take care, Bob.'

Bob then rang Flying Officer Frost at RAF Errol to talk to him about Malinovsky.

'Your timing is perfect, sir. I saw a white twin-engined aircraft land as I was coming to the office to take your call. If you hang on, I'll check it's him.'

A few minutes later he was back on the line. 'It is Major Malinovsky, sir. What do you want me to do?'

'It would be helpful if someone could keep watch on his movements, especially if he leaves the base. If he does leave, whether by land or air, then I need to know where he's gone. Be extremely careful though. He tried to kill me this morning and if he feels he's in a corner he could come out shooting. Can you tell me if No. 305 Ferry Training Unit is still based at Errol?'

'Yes, it is, sir.'

'And is Colonel Kuznetsov still the commanding officer?'

'He is, sir, though he's on leave in Edinburgh. Since that business last year I've made a point of keeping an eye on what they're doing so I know he's been away since yesterday.'

'Thank you, Flying Officer Frost, that's very helpful.'

Bob weighed up his options after talking to the flying officer. He knew that at this time of the day, the man he needed to speak to next could only be reached on an insecure line. Instead, he rang the MI11 offices at Craigiehall on the off-chance Captain Anthony Darlington might still be there. Bob wasn't surprised to find that everyone had left for the day and that his call went unanswered. He then rang the officers' mess at Craigiehall and asked them to track down Anthony Darlington. It only took them a few minutes.

Bob's final call was to the police station in Stranraer. He knew the commodore also intended to call them, but he wanted to know if any trace of Edward Daly had been found.

*

Before they left their room to meet Katerina and Michael, Bob told Monique about his phone call to Commodore Cunningham and the other calls he'd made.

She thought he'd finished and was about to brush her hair when Bob spoke again.

'The one thing I didn't tell Maurice, just as I didn't tell anyone else earlier, was that after Malinovsky tried to shoot me down, I came very close to killing him.'

'How?' asked Monique.

'Rage and instinct kicked in. I made a very tight turn and got behind him. I knew I had plenty of ammunition left after my one attack on the ground targets and all I had to do was press the gun firing button to cause both Malinovsky and his Typhoon to cease to exist.'

'Why didn't you?'

'I was starting to press the button when Flight Lieutenant Somerset realised what I intended and called me off. I owe him a favour for that, just as I do for warning me a moment earlier that Malinovsky was taking a shot at me. He saved both of our lives.'

'So no one knows about this except you, me and Adrian Somerset?'

'Malinovsky does too,' said Bob. 'I flew right past his cockpit from behind after holding back from firing. I asked the flight lieutenant not to tell anyone what happened, but it's too good a story to be kept quiet for long. Come to think of it, there may also be witnesses to my bawling Malinovsky out on the ground after we landed.'

Monique wasn't sure what to make of this. 'It might have been better if you had killed Malinovsky,' she said after a moment's thought.

'I'm not so sure,' said Bob. 'Maurice was kind enough not to point out the obvious on the phone, but I made a real mess of things today.'

'In what way?' asked Monique.

'The Cuttlefish should never have had an opportunity to take us by surprise. I was only a pace or two away, yet he was able to grab Katerina, put a gun to her head and take control of the situation.'

'It wasn't your plan, Bob. Michael, Katerina, Inspector Boyle and I cooked it up on the steamer. You were just playing the part we'd given you.'

'But I was the senior officer present. I think the mistake was letting Katerina remove her wig and expose her identity to the men in the queue. Yes, that could have caused a reaction that would have allowed us to identify the Cuttlefish. But if she'd stayed in disguise she might have been able to identify Daly without giving him a chance to plan a response.'

'We all have perfect hindsight, Bob, though you might be right about the wig. That's something I should have thought about when we were discussing what to do before the steamer berthed.'

To Monique's surprise, Bob laughed. 'Thanks for trying to draw some of the responsibility away from me. The fact remains that Popov was right when he told Katerina on the telephone that the Cuttlefish would have got clean away if Malinovsky hadn't acted as he did, however reckless that was in terms of Katerina's safety. Daly might have got away anyway, but if he's not on the bottom of Loch Ryan then at least, thanks to Malinovsky, he's got an injured hand that will make things more difficult for him and might help us track him down.'

'We need to meet the others,' said Monique, looking at her watch.

'Rather than a drink here in the mess, how would you feel about having something to eat and then driving into Wigtown to find the Red Lion Inn?' asked Bob. 'It's not far and after today it would be particularly good to drink somewhere that didn't exclude any of the team. Apart from anything else, it would be helpful to have a brief discussion about what we need to do tomorrow.'

'That sounds like an excellent idea,' said Monique.

Michael was all for going into Wigtown after a quick dinner when they met him in the mess entrance hall, as was Katerina when she appeared a moment later. Monique noted that she hadn't chosen to keep them waiting this evening, which was progress.

*

The Red Lion Inn turned out to be a small pub forming part of a run of buildings along the north side of the open area, more a rectangle than a square, that lay at the heart of

Wigtown. It looked out obliquely towards an imposingly large red brick building with an ornate tower built onto its side.

The evening was very warm. The main door of the pub stood open, presumably to help cool the interior, and there was just one window on each side of the door, both open, plus three on the upper floor. A second door, set into the left side of the frontage, also stood open and appeared to give access to a passage through to the rear of the property.

Michael led them into the hallway beyond the front door. Stairs further along the hall climbed to the upper floor. Open doorways revealed a room on either side at the front of the pub, both crowded with men and women, many wearing RAF or WAAF uniforms, sitting on benches around the sides of the room or on stools around small round wooden tables. The place was so busy that others were standing between tables or spilling out into the hallway, holding their drinks and chatting. All the wood was dark and the wallpaper and ceilings were stained brown by years of exposure to tobacco smoke, a haze of which was illuminated by shafts of sunlight coming through the front windows.

Monique realised that although the street frontage was narrow, the building was quite deep and there were more rooms behind those at the front. The pub turned out to be something of a warren, with odd nooks and corners in unexpected places. The bar itself was set behind a counter in a larger room on one side of the rear of the building. There was a mob, mainly of men but including a few women, waiting to be served at the bar, with others standing behind them making passage difficult between one end of the room and the other.

'I can't see them,' said Michael, having to raise his voice

to be heard. He turned towards an elderly woman carrying a collection of dirty glasses in each hand, holding them together with a finger inside the top of each. 'Hello. We're looking for friends. Are there any more rooms?'

'Yes.' She nodded towards the rear of the bar. 'If it's a naval man you're looking for then there's one in the skittle alley, with an RAF sergeant. That's at the back.'

'The skittle alley?' asked Michael.

'You'll get the idea when you see it.'

Michael turned to go in the direction the woman had indicated and Monique followed. Katerina was just behind her. They appeared to have lost Bob, but she was sure he'd catch up.

At the rear of the bar, a doorway gave access to a more open but equally noisy indoor area. The near end of this had bench seats around its sides. Beyond, what appeared to be an extension of the original building stretched away from the back of the pub. It was divided into two wood-floored lanes separated by a wooden structure along which a bowling ball was rolling towards them. At the far end of each lane was a set of skittles. Two mixed groups of men and women in RAF and WAAF uniforms were standing and talking. Then one of the women bowled, to the accompaniment of cheers.

'Andrew and Peter are in the corner,' said Michael.

The two men got up and came over to greet them.

'They say this is Wigtown's busiest pub and I can believe it,' shouted Peter Bennett. 'I'm not sure we'll be able to find somewhere we can all sit.'

'Is the group captain with you?' asked Andrew.

'Yes, here he is,' said Monique.

The arrival of a senior RAF officer caused the room to quieten, but only briefly.

‘We thought we’d lost you, Bob,’ said Katerina.

‘I’ve been negotiating with the landlord,’ said Bob.

‘What for?’ asked Monique.

‘There’s a snug, halfway up the stairs to the upper floor, where they turn back on themselves. It’s got a table and room for six to sit in comparative peace. I’ve also negotiated table service for only a slight premium on the drinks prices. When we need a round of drinks we pull a bell cord and someone will come to take our order.’

‘Will they bring a potty when it’s needed or do we have to find our way to the toilets?’ asked Andrew MacDonald.

Bob laughed. ‘I’m sorry, Andrew. They were asking far too much for that service.’

Peter Bennett took Monique aside as they made their way out of the skittle alley to say that he was only drinking halves of shandy and could drive them all back if they were prepared to squeeze into one vehicle. Monique thanked him but said she was happy to drive the other car.

The snug was ideal. Most of the space was filled with a fixed square table made of dark wood and there were wooden benches comfortably large enough to seat two each against the walls on three sides of it. The fourth side opened out directly onto the stairs. They could hear the hubbub from downstairs but it was quiet enough to talk. Monique had the sense that the inn’s bedrooms were on the upper floor so not many people were using the stairs.

Monique sat next to Bob on the far side of the snug from the stairs, with Katerina to her left and Michael beyond her. Peter and Andrew sat to Bob’s right.

She limited herself to a single genuine gin and tonic, and after it was served she decided to make use of it.

‘You’ve got your brandy, Katerina, and I’ve got my gin and tonic, complete with real gin. I think this is the moment you tell me who Ludmilla is.'

Katerina smiled. 'It's quite simple. Ludmilla Tolstaya was the name I was using while I was stationed in Madrid and it became the name that Edward Daly knew me by. I'm sure you must have used different names at different times and in different places.'

Monique was growing to like Katerina but she still didn't trust her, so simply nodded and smiled back.

Bob tapped the tabletop with his knuckle. 'Can I have everyone's attention for a moment? I promise not to divert you from your drinks for long, but while we are all present it would be helpful to decide how we move forward after today. I've not discussed this with any of you, but it seems to me that we've reached something of a turning point. The Cuttlefish is either dead in Loch Ryan or ashore and injured in Scotland. His body hadn't been found, by the navy divers or anyone else, when I rang the police in Stranraer earlier. But if it were to float ashore tonight then we could all go home in the morning.

'On the other hand, if he is alive, he's now the subject of a full-blown murder hunt. That means our role is going to be different from now on and we need to consider what value we can add. With that in mind, I believe that Andrew and Peter should return to Edinburgh in one of the cars after breakfast tomorrow. That will give us a functioning RAF team at Craigiehall when George Buchan finishes what he's doing with his southern opposite number. It will also allow you to pick up the threads on the naval side, Andrew, pending Michael's return. Any comments so far?'

'That makes sense to me,' said Michael. 'Andrew? Peter?'

'I think the group captain is right,' said Andrew MacDonald. 'Peter and I were able to help with the hunt for the phantom MI5 tramp and aboard the steamer. And we can always return if necessary. But I also get the feeling we are going to be a bit superfluous from now on.'

Peter Bennett nodded and Monique realised that she had too.

'We do of course need to stay on top of the police investigation,' said Bob, 'and we need to remember that in Katerina we have the only truly reliable means of identifying Edward Daly, either dead or alive. I'd be grateful if Andrew, Monique and Katerina could drive to Stranraer in the morning to find out where things stand and offer whatever help they can.'

'What about you, Bob?' asked Michael.

'I have an errand to run. I ought to be able to catch up with you in Stranraer later in the day, assuming Edward Daly's body hasn't been found by then.'

Monique knew what Bob intended to do, so said nothing.

'Anyway,' said Bob, 'There are empty glasses around the table. You're nearest to the bell pull, Andrew. Let's order more drinks.'

Monique could see that Bob was happy to have the two parts of the team together. Like her, he moved to straight tonics after one gin and tonic. Michael and Katerina were both drinking brandy and seemed to get on increasingly well with each that they consumed. Monique was relieved that Michael appeared to have overcome his grief at losing Betty Swanson, for the moment at least. She had a feeling that she knew how Michael and Katerina's evening was going to end, probably even before Michael realised. Katerina was rather older than him but he was wise enough to be able to look after himself and he wouldn't forget that while MI11 and the NKVD might be working together at the moment, it wasn't so long since he'd had to shoot an NKVD agent dead on a London street. If he liked the idea of taking an enthusiastic Katerina to bed tonight, good luck to him.

They stayed in the Red Lion Inn until closing time and then went out into the daylight. The sky was still a cloudless light blue and the sun had some way to sink before it set. Monique drove four of them back to RAF Wigtown while Peter drove Andrew.

Bob picked up a message from the mess manager's office when they got back while Katerina and Michael climbed the stairs to the accommodation together. Monique assumed they were heading for his room rather than the 'WAAF officers only' corridor where Katerina was staying.

When they were back in their room, Monique locked the door and kissed Bob.

'It seems a long time ago now, Bob, but when we arrived for our flight to Northern Ireland, you said something about helping me take off my WAAF uniform later. I know I've changed out of it in the meantime but, if you like, I'll put it back on.'

'There's no need, Monique. Helping you take these clothes off will be just as much fun.'

CHAPTER TWENTY-TWO

Bob realised that this was the first time he'd flown the Mosquito with no one in the right-hand seat. It didn't have a noticeable effect on the handling of the aircraft and he could manage without easy access to the switches on the far wall of the cockpit, except perhaps for the engine fire extinguisher push buttons. He decided that if the need arose, he'd find a way of reaching them. The fuel management controls on the rear wall of the cockpit were also hard to access as they were intended to be operated by the navigator. He knew that he wouldn't need them during the short flights he had in mind.

Bob enjoyed the trip. Conditions were excellent, though he was flying into the early morning sun. RAF Turnhouse was coming to life as he landed from the south-east, his approach bringing him in not far south of the bungalow in Corstorphine he shared with Monique.

After landing, Bob taxied around the airfield to an obvious gap in a line of aircraft parked on the grass near the hangars. He could see a police car nearby and when he turned off the perimeter track it moved to follow him.

Bob descended the short ladder from the hatch in the floor of the aircraft and turned to see his father, Superintendent David Sutherland, striding towards him in his uniform with a broad smile on his face.

'Hello Bob, how are you?'

The two men embraced.

'Well, thanks, Dad. You didn't have to come out personally.'

'The chance of seeing you twice in a week was too good to miss. Besides, Captain Darlington told me that this is very sensitive so I thought I'd do it myself. By the way, when you see him, thank him for telephoning before he came to the house last night. If he'd simply turned up on the doorstep we'd have feared the worst.'

'I take it from the message you left at the officers' mess later last night that you've found Colonel Kuznetsov?' asked Bob.

'Yes. It wasn't too hard. I think the number of Soviet Air Force colonels wandering around Edinburgh in uniform can probably be counted on the fingers of one finger. It's not as if he's being secretive about his whereabouts. He's staying with a Scottish lady at your favourite hotel, the North British on Princes Street. As I understand it, you want to be able to talk to him without anyone, especially anyone on the Soviet side, knowing that British military intelligence has been anywhere near him.'

'That's right, Dad. I've not worked out how to approach him yet, but knowing the layout of thc hotel will give me a head start.'

'I may be able to help, Bob. I'd have found him anyway, but the colonel's presence in the city came to my colleagues' attention because of an incident on Calton Hill yesterday afternoon. It was a beautiful day here and he and the lady were admiring the views when there was an altercation between him and two Polish soldiers. It came to nothing because one of my constables was on the scene very quickly and calmed things down, though not before one of the Poles had knocked the constable's helmet off. It appears they had been drinking at lunchtime and had taken the colonel's presence as an opportunity to air some highly unfavourable views about the Soviet Union.

'Frankly, it's the not sort of thing that we'd normally take any further, but it gives us a perfect opportunity to interview Colonel Kuznetsov as a witness to what happened between the Poles and the constable.'

'It does, Dad, but it's me who needs to talk to him rather than you.'

'I may be past normal retirement age, Bob, but I'm not going senile yet. I thought you might briefly resume your police career. I've got an inspector's uniform in the back of the car that I think should fit you and I'm sure you can find somewhere here to change into it. I assume you want to talk to Colonel Kuznetsov because he works for you in some way, though I don't expect or want you to comment about that.'

Bob smiled. 'When I left the City of Glasgow Police I was a detective sergeant so becoming an inspector, however temporarily, is a promotion.'

'I suspect that a direct equivalence from your rank of group captain would see you outrank me as a chief superintendent,' said David. 'But that wouldn't be in keeping with your desire for discretion. I suggest that if the colonel is in the hotel, and it is still quite early so there's a good chance he will be, you ask him to give you his statement in the police car outside. That will give you total privacy and he will have the perfect reason for having talked to you if anyone asks him. While the two of you are talking I will have a stroll along Princes Street. It's many years since I've walked the beat.'

Bob got changed in a toilet in the airfield control tower and his father then drove the police car into Edinburgh.

'This feels very strange, Dad.'

'I suppose it's a glimpse of what might have been if you'd not chosen the RAF over the police. And while your rise through the ranks in the RAF has been meteoric, I'm sure you'd have progressed beyond inspector in the police by now.'

'I was playing the game of "might-have-been" with Monique the other day,' said Bob. 'In that case, we were discussing what would have happened if I'd not been shot down and injured. I concluded that I preferred things the way they turned out. I've returned to being a policeman of sorts and I've found Monique. No other path would have brought us together.'

'She is good for you and as you know your mother and I both think the world of her. Anyway, here we are. I'll wait in the car until you come out, then I'll make myself scarce.'

'Are you just going to park here, Dad, facing the wrong way directly outside the front door?'

'It's a police car, Bob. And you're a policeman here on police business. We can park where we want.'

'The thought has just crossed my mind that they know me quite well in the hotel. What if someone recognises me and realises I'm wearing the wrong uniform?'

'Trust me, Bob, they'll only see the uniform, not the man inside it.'

Bob had a feeling that one of the two elderly ladies behind the reception desk might have recognised him, but the moment passed and after checking that Colonel Kuznetsov hadn't yet come down for breakfast, she was happy to send Bob up to his room.

Irakli Kuznetsov was wearing an open-necked uniform shirt when he opened the door, with braces holding up his riding breeches. He was a man of above-average height, dark hair and a moustache that looked just like Joseph Stalin's.

Bob held up his MI11 pass so that Kuznetsov could see it. 'I'm Inspector Sutherland of the City of Edinburgh Police, sir.' He watched as the recognition and surprise on the colonel's face were replaced by amusement.

'Hello, inspector. How can I help you?'

'Who is it, love?' asked a female voice with a west of Scotland accent from inside the room.

'It's the police.' Kuznetsov took a step back and looked into the body of the room, beyond Bob's field of view. 'I think it's about yesterday.'

'That's right, sir,' said Bob. 'I'm sorry for the inconvenience, but would you mind giving me a statement about what happened on Calton Hill?'

'As you've heard, inspector, I've got company. Is there anywhere else that we can do this?'

'I've got a police car outside the front door, sir. Perhaps we could talk there?'

Irakli Kuznetsov smiled. 'Give me a couple of minutes to put my jacket and tie on and comb my hair.'

'Of course, sir. I'll wait in the car.'

As Bob emerged from the hotel's main entrance he saw his father get out of the driver's side of the car onto the pavement. They exchanged smiles as Bob got into the driver's seat.

Irakli came out of the hotel a few moments later and walked around the car to get into the front passenger seat.

'Hello, Bob, how are you?'

'I'm well thanks, Irakli. I'm sorry to break into your stay here, especially as you have company. How are things with you?'

'They were going very well until a few minutes ago, Bob. But you've gone to a lot of trouble to talk to me without anyone knowing who you are and I'm worried about what you might have to say. Is our arrangement still in place?'

'A new identity and UK residence when you need it? Of

course, Irakli. Don't worry, I've come to see you simply to ask for some background information that won't compromise your position.'

'That's a relief,' said the colonel. 'The lady you didn't quite meet just now teaches Slavic languages at the University of Glasgow. We met at an event over there a few months ago and have since found we have a lot in common. When the time comes for me to burn my bridges with the Soviet Union and make a new beginning here, I hope that she might form part of it. I've not told her anything about my long-term plans, of course. Anyway, that's not why you are here.'

'No, I came to talk about Major Nikolay Malinovsky.'

'Can I ask why?'

Without going into any of the details of the hunt for the Cuttlefish, Bob told Irakli about his recent dealings with Malinovsky and in particular the major's attempt to shoot him down and his disregard for the safety of Katerina Komarova.

'What worries me is that I can't come up with any sensible explanation for his actions,' said Bob. 'You told me that he was with the NKVD after I met him at Errol, but he seems to be pursuing an agenda that's out of step with the head of the NKVD office in the Soviet embassy in London. When I confronted him about his attempt on my life he claimed that he'd lost sight of my aircraft and what happened was my fault for slowing down, though I hadn't. Having brazened that out, it should have been relatively easy for him to claim that nearly killing his colleague was a calculated risk that partly succeeded. I can't understand why he then went to Errol. It seems an unnecessary admission that he's in the wrong.'

'I'm not sure how much I can help,' said Irakli. 'I should

start by saying that I've never liked Malinovsky. He's a good pilot and an effective trainer of other pilots, but his first loyalty has always been to the NKVD rather than the Soviet Air Force. He left No. 305 Ferry Training Unit in the middle of the first week of May and I wasn't sorry to see him go. He was replaced a week or so later by Captain Ivan Nesterov, who is also as much NKVD as Soviet Air Force, though he's less of a shit in other ways. While that means that the NKVD still keeps a watch on what we're doing, I don't actively feel their breath on the back of my neck any more. That may be more dangerous in some ways, but it is more pleasant on a day-to-day basis.'

'Thank you, that's helpful,' said Bob. 'I still don't understand why Malinovsky left Galloway or why he's gone to Errol. If he felt he had to go somewhere, why didn't he return to London to get his side of the story on the record with the people he reports to?'

The colonel sat and looked out of the windscreen of the car.

'Are you all right, Irakli? Is there anything you can tell me about his background or his activities while he was based at Errol that might help?'

'It's probably wasting your time, Bob. He only ever spoke to me about himself once.'

'The more I know about the man, the better,' said Bob. 'It may not seem relevant to you, but it might help anyway.'

'As you wish. Major Malinovsky was told he was moving to London at very short notice and I received confirmation that he was leaving through my line of command with even less notice. I think the 1st and 2nd of May were a Saturday and Sunday. On the Monday he came to see me after lunch to say that he'd just been contacted by telephone and told to pack his bags and travel south two days later, on the Wednesday. He asked me to authorise a flight to London in one of the Albermarles to save him a long train journey.

'I'd have been happy to see him travel on a horse-drawn cart with no suspension, to be honest. But it seemed to me that it would make a good training run for one of our crews and it would also ensure that Malinovsky owed me a favour, so I agreed.'

Irakli turned to look at Bob. 'That evening, Malinovsky came to my office with a bottle of expensive Scotch whisky. He wanted the two of us to drink to the future. I think he came to my office because he couldn't get anyone else on the unit to drink with him. I liked the idea of the whisky more than I disliked the idea of his company, so I said yes. We drank his bottle of whisky between us and then started on some vodka I keep for emergencies in my office.'

'It sounds like quite a night,' said Bob.

'We were both very drunk but I kept in mind that I was drinking with a dangerous man, so was very careful about what I said to him. I could see he was being equally careful to start with and we mainly talked about flying and about our past exploits and all the friends we'd lost to enemy action or flying accidents. But as the evening wore on, he became less guarded. He'd almost passed out by the time we called it a night and I had to ask for help to get him back to his quarters. I needed a shoulder to lean on myself.

'Not long before we decided we'd drunk enough, he told me he'd had very bad news. Some months earlier, he'd received a letter from his mother telling him that her sister's son, a cousin called Maxim who Malinovksy hadn't met since childhood, had been posted to London. He said that his cousin also worked for the NKVD, though he'd joined it from the militsiya or civilian police. The two of them had been able to meet several times when Malinovsky had been called to London to report on his activities, or perhaps on mine. They'd agreed to keep their family relationship a secret from colleagues and the fact they were both with the NKVD meant that Malinovsky had been able to visit his cousin's office and meet the people he worked with.

'Late that afternoon he'd tried to contact his cousin at his office to let him know about the posting but was told that he no longer worked there. Malinovsky realised that he'd met the man he was talking to and identified himself as the NKVD friend from Scotland who had been to the office, before asking if they had a forwarding address. The man told him that Maxim was dead. He'd been killed in London the previous Friday in very confused circumstances. Malinovsky told me that he thought the reason for the short notice of his move south was because, through sheer coincidence, he had been picked to fill the gap left by his cousin's sudden death.'

Bob thought about the dates. 'Did he mention his cousin's surname?'

'No, sorry. Anyway, it was the following afternoon, the Tuesday, before I crawled out of bed. As soon as I got into the office, still feeling very rough, Malinovsky came to see me. He was very on edge and wanted to know whether he'd mentioned his family at all. I said it was all very hazy, which it was, but I did tell him that he'd talked about the death of his cousin.'

'He swore me to secrecy and I promised never to tell anyone about what he'd said, happy to add to the number of favours he owed me.'

'That's helpful,' said Bob. 'If I've got the name and date

right, I think I understand why Malinovsky tried to kill me. But I still can't work out why he flew to Errol yesterday.'

Irakli sat back in the seat. 'Perhaps he needed to give himself a little space to work out how his actions would be seen by his superiors. He could talk to people in London on a secure line from Errol while keeping a safe distance away in case what he'd done was going to land him in trouble.'

'That's a reasonable working theory,' said Bob, looking at his watch. 'I am very grateful. Perhaps you should go back up to your room so you can take your lady friend down for breakfast?'

'What are you going to do?'

'I'm going to RAF Errol to talk to Major Malinovsky.'

'Take care, Bob.'

'Trust me, Irakli, I will.'

CHAPTER TWENTY-THREE

Captain Anthony Darlington's staff car was parked near the Mosquito at RAF Turnhouse when Bob and his father returned from the city centre. The captain didn't comment on Bob's police uniform, which he changed out of in the same toilet in the control tower. Bob then said his farewells to his father before he and Anthony boarded the Mosquito.

Nothing was said as they took off and climbed.

'How did it go in Edinburgh, sir?' asked Antthony.

They were flying north over Fife and in what seemed like endless visibility Bob could see the Firth of Tay in the distance ahead. He knew that RAF Errol lay on its far shore.

'Sorry, Anthony. Let me tell you what Colonel Kuznetsov told me and see if it leads you to the same conclusion it took me to.' Bob summarised what Irakli had told him, making sure he left in the relevant details.

It didn't take Anthony long to work it out. 'Major Malinovsky's cousin was Maxim Kozlov, the man who tried to kill you and Monique with a burp gun outside Sanctuary Buildings and who was then killed by Michael Dixon after I froze. The first name matches and the date and the circumstances are right. It also goes some way to explaining why Malinovsky tried to kill you, though it might have been more logical for him to try to kill Michael.'

'I agree,' said Bob.

'Forgive me for asking, sir, but if you already know why Malinovsky tried to kill you, why are we going to Errol?'

'I want to look him in the eye and hear him admit to what he did,' said Bob. 'After my initial anger on landing, I let it go at the time because we had to be in Stranraer to meet the steamer. But I would have had it out with him later if he'd not left. I've been shot down once in my life and to my mind that's once too many.'

'What do you want me to do when we arrive?'

'You're my bodyguard, Anthony. If Malinovsky has another go at me, assuming he is still there, having someone watching my back might keep me alive. His replacement as the NKVD's eyes and ears on the unit, Captain Nesterov, might also be there, as might other members of the unit. I don't expect trouble from any of them, but you never know. If anyone does try anything, don't hesitate to respond as forcibly as necessary. I certainly will.'

The last time Bob had flown into RAF Errol he'd arrived in a spectacular manner designed to attract the maximum attention and he'd startled both the personnel in the control tower and Monique, who had been flying with him. Today he did everything by the book, gaining permission to slot into the landing pattern ahead of a Miles Master training aircraft of No. 9 Advanced Flying Unit, which also operated from Errol.

He then taxied the Mosquito around the airfield to a parking area close to the hangar that was home to No. 305 Ferry Training Unit of the Soviet Air Force.

'That's interesting,' said Bob. 'We're not their only visitors.'

'How do you know, sir?'

'We're just passing Major Malinovsky's Airspeed Envoy parked on the concrete to our right. The three aircraft lined up beyond it are Armstrong Whitworth Albemarles. That's the type of aircraft the unit is training Soviet pilots to fly back to the Motherland. Then there's the gap I'm intending to park in, and then there's an aircraft that doesn't belong here.'

'It's a Dakota, isn't it?' asked Anthony.

'Technically, it's a Douglas C-47 as it's in Soviet Air Force rather than RAF markings, but yes, you've got the right idea. Perhaps it's delivering supplies or bringing in a new batch of trainees. Incidentally, the RAF officer standing with the two airmen waiting for us is Flying Officer Frost.'

Bob introduced Anthony to Frost after they climbed out of the Mosquito.

'Welcome back to Errol, sir.'

'Thank you, flying officer. As the Airspeed Envoy is here, can I assume that Major Malinovsky is, too?'

'He's in the offices attached to the hangar, sir. We've been keeping watch as you asked.'

'We'll go and say hello,' said Bob. 'There's no need for you to accompany us.'

'Are you sure, sir? There are four men in there I've never seen before. They arrived in the C-47 about fifteen minutes ago. The aircraft crew stayed on board so I don't think they plan to be here for long.'

'Were they in uniform?' asked Bob.

'No, sir, they were in civvies. I'd have sworn that the man in charge was Lenin himself, except that Lenin's been dead for twenty years.'

'That's Yevgeny Popov, the head of the NKVD office in the Soviet embassy in London. I find it interesting that he's travelled north himself. Come on, Anthony.'

As Bob approached the main door leading to the offices built onto the airfield side of the hangar, it opened. A man in a suit emerged. He was followed by two more, closely flanking Major Malinovsky.

‘Hello Nikolay, I was just coming to talk to you.’

The major looked back at Bob and briefly came to a halt before one of the men beside him jerked his arm and forced him to resume walking, causing Bob and Anthony to stand aside.

Yevgeny Popov followed the others out and stopped when he saw Bob.

‘Group Captain Sutherland! Perhaps I shouldn’t be surprised to see you here. I have to say how deeply sorry I am about what happened when you were flying with Major Malinovsky yesterday. As you can see, I take a very dim view of what he did.’

‘You consider that to be more serious than the risk he took with Miss Komarova’s life at Stranraer?’

‘Yes, I do. That was an operational decision he took which, although highly risky, did have a partly positive outcome. I am here personally because I learned last night that Malinovsky had contacted onc of his colleagues in London and told him that his attempt on your life was to avenge the death of Maxim Kozlov. I think he was trying to find an ally, unsuccessfully as it turned out. His reason for trying to kill you seemed odd to me, as although Malinovsky moved to London to fill the gap left by Kozlov’s death, I wasn't aware they knew each other well. A little digging into personnel files last night revealed that the two men were maternal cousins.

‘As I am sure you remember only too well, group captain, Kozlov was the man who tried to kill you and Madame Dubois, who I believe has since become your wife, outside the MI11 offices in London. He was trying to kill the two of you to avenge the shooting of his lover Helena Berdyaev by Madame Dubois and, I believe, by Captain Darlington, who I’ve not had the pleasure of meeting before. Hello, captain.'

'Hello, sir,' said Anthony, keeping his face expressionless.

Popov continued. 'You may not have shot Maxim Kozlov yourself, group captain, that was the naval officer on your team, but that detail is not widely known and I am sure that when Malinovsky was able to manoeuvre so your aircraft was in his gunsights he felt it was the perfect opportunity to avenge his cousin and claim it was an accident afterwards.

'After Maxim Kozlov attempted to avenge Helena Berdyaev's death I made it very clear to my agents that that I would not tolerate any of them working on their own account. Private feuds or vendettas are absolutely forbidden. Major Malinovsky was made aware of that when he took up his post in London. Additionally, his attempt on your life broke the undertaking I gave when we met at the embassy in London to put our past misunderstandings behind us. That's not something I can afford to forgive.'

'Thank you for taking the trouble to explain,' said Bob.

'You will doubtless pass on to Commodore Cunningham and Sir Peter Maitland what I have told you, group captain. It is in my interests for them to know that I am a man of my word.'

With that, Popov turned and followed the others towards the Soviet C-47.

'With friends like that, who needs enemies?' asked Anthony.

'Indeed. He took great delight in showing off that he knew about Monique and I getting married and that he knew you by sight. The thing to remember is that although he might be considered a friend today, he could easily revert to being an enemy tomorrow. I think that before I do anything else I need to tell Commodore Cunningham what's happened. I'm sure Flying Officer Frost has a secure telephone I can use.'

*

After taking off in the Mosquito from RAF Errol, Bob climbed and headed due south, intending to keep well to the east of the anti-aircraft defences around the Forth Bridge and the approaches to it. He wanted to make landfall on the south side of the Firth of Forth at Portobello before flying in an arc around the south side of Edinburgh to land at RAF Turnhouse and drop off Anthony Darlington.

Bob employed Anthony as a lookout and with his help they spotted quite a few other aircraft as they flew over Fife, all a safe distance away. They crossed the north shore of the estuary a little to the east of Kirkcaldy at a height of 5,000 feet.

'There's another one directly ahead of us,' said Anthony. 'It's above us and flying in the same direction.'

'It looks like a Dakota,' said Bob.

'Or perhaps a C-47, sir?'

Bob could hear the amusement in Anthony's voice, even though he had his mask on.

'I should have thought of that,' said Bob. 'A Mosquito is a lot faster than a C-47. I think we've caught up with Comrade Popov, even though we gave him a lead.'

Bob climbed three thousand feet to the height of the C-47 and closed in on it.

'What have you got in mind, sir?'

'I thought we might pull up alongside and give them a wave to bid them farewell on their journey south.'

‘You’re the boss.’

The Mosquito wasn't far behind the C-47 when Bob caught a glimpse of something dropping away from the left side of it. He instinctively pulled up and to the right. ‘What was that?’ he asked.

‘It was a man,’ said Anthony. ‘I’d say it was a parachutist, but there was no static line connecting him to the aircraft. The C-47 has carried on going as if nothing happened.’

Bob tightened his turn to the right so it was possible for Anthony to look directly down towards the Firth of Forth. ‘Can you see a parachute?’

‘No, nothing, just the blue of the sea and a few boats.’

Bob continued to circle tightly while losing altitude. Neither he nor Anthony saw anything more of the falling man.

‘That was Malinovsky, wasn’t it?’ asked Anthony. ‘Killed by being tragically lost at sea while trying to escape from custody.’

‘I very much think it might have been,’ said Bob. ‘You did say that with friends like Popov, there was no need for enemies. I didn’t expect him to prove you right quite this quickly.’

‘Do you think they killed him before throwing him out?’ asked Anthony.

‘Why would they?’ asked Bob. ‘A body washed ashore with multiple injuries caused by a fall from a height into water will raise less suspicion than one with a bullet wound or a slit throat. Besides, why risk putting a bullet hole in your C-47 or getting blood on it?’

‘I’ve done some dreadful things in my time,’ said Anthony. ‘But throwing someone out of an aeroplane door is so cold-blooded it’s scarcely believable.’

‘I know what you mean,’ said Bob. ‘I doubt if anyone in the C-47 saw us, either before they invited Malinovsky to step outside or afterwards. That means Popov won’t know that we witnessed what happened. I think I need to ring Maurice Cunningham again when we land at Turnhouse.’

CHAPTER TWENTY-FOUR

It was another warm morning. Monique wondered whether the spell of what everyone agreed was most un-Scottish summer weather had somehow followed her and Bob back from the Mediterranean.

The curling stone was in place again, holding open the police station door, and Woman Auxiliary Police Constable Franklin was in her usual position behind the front desk. Monique had a sudden sense of déjà vu before realising that what she was experiencing was an actual repetition of events rather than something she was imagining.

‘Hello, Monique! How are you?’

‘I’m well, thank you Dorothy. Is Inspector White on duty?’

‘Pretty much everyone we have is on duty, with time off just to catch up on sleep. Inspector White and Inspector Boyle are both out at present.’

‘Is Inspector Boyle still here?’ asked Michael. ‘I’d assumed he would have gone back to Larne early this morning.’

‘I think the plan was for him to return if the body of the man who went into the harbour yesterday was found, but so far nothing’s turned up. His two detective constables sailed on this morning’s steamer but he’s still here. Inspector White said that when you arrived I was to take you to him. Is the group captain with you?’

‘No, it’s just the three of us this morning.’ Monique introduced Michael and Katerina.

‘Were you the lady who fell into the harbour with the enemy agent, ma’am? I was watching from the railway station. And you jumped in after her, didn’t you sir? Are you both all right?'

'We're fine, thank you,' said Katerina. 'It wasn't pleasant at the time but a drink or two of brandy later helped.'

'Should we go?' asked Monique.

At that moment, Inspector White came into the station, closely followed by Inspector Boyle.

'Hello, Madame Dubois. I'm afraid I'm the bearer of bad news. I think the Cuttlefish might have survived his swim. Let's go and talk. Dorothy, could you get someone to lay on some tea, please?'

The meeting took place in an interview room along a dingy corridor off the reception area rather than in the plush office upstairs. Monique assumed the deputy chief constable needed his office today, though she did wonder what issues he had crossing his desk that were more important or urgent than the hunt for a German spy and multiple murderer. It didn't matter as she was forming a positive impression of Inspector White.

The room smelled of stale tobacco and wasn't intended to seat five people so an extra chair had to be brought in. At least when the tea arrived it was refreshing, despite the warmth of the morning.

'What makes you think that the Cuttlefish may be alive?' asked Michael.

'We searched the promenade deck of the *Princess Margaret* after everyone had disembarked yesterday afternoon,' said Inspector White. 'It appears that the Cuttlefish was travelling without luggage unless someone else picked it up. Presumably, he kept the identity documents he'd had made in Dublin on him, in which case they might be wet by now, like his papers supporting his role as an army captain. We did however find a Webley

Self-Loading Pistol with damage to the top rear of its grip consistent with it having been hit by a bullet. There were traces of blood and flesh on the damaged area of the pistol so it appears the hand holding it was also hit. We'd believed that to be the case from the blood on Miss Komarova's face when she was rescued from the harbour, but it's good to have confirmation that the Cuttlefish was wounded.'

'My colleagues in MI11 in London have been contacting doctors and hospitals in south-west Scotland to find out if a man with an injured right hand has turned up looking for treatment,' said Monique.

'I've also asked someone to do that but will tell them to stop,' said Inspector White. 'To return to the question you asked, lieutenant commander, we had a report a little earlier that an RAF ambulance parked not far from the West Pier was broken into last night. Whoever did it took two emergency first aid kits, the sort of thing usually carried on RAF bombers or flying boats. It is of course possible that someone else did it for the tubunic ampoules in the kits.'

'The what?' asked Katerina.

'It's the name given to tins that each carry a pair of syrettes, or disposable units for injecting morphine,' said Michael. 'I get the sense you don't think it was done by anyone else, inspector.'

'No, I don't. Someone wanting the morphine would only have taken the tubunic ampoules and not the whole kits and, more tellingly, they'd not have left two other identical first aid kits in the ambulance untouched. To my mind what's even more significant is that while we were there an army corporal appeared and said that someone had stolen his lorry, a Bedford MW that had been parked overnight just around the corner. We are putting out an alert to all our men to watch out for the vehicle but it is a fairly common type and "green medium-sized lorry" isn't the most helpful of descriptions in wartime even when accompanied by the army registration number. I did briefly consider asking for military assistance to set up roadblocks on routes out of the area but if you assume the break-in and vehicle theft were done under cover of the limited hours of darkness, then the lorry could be long gone by now.'

'That's true,' said Michael. 'So our working hypothesis is that the Cuttlefish came ashore and hid up until it got dark, then broke into the ambulance before making his getaway in the stolen lorry.'

'That seems most likely,' said Inspector White.

'Bandaging his hand and dosing himself on morphine from an aircraft first aid kit can only be a temporary solution to his problems,' said Monique. 'He must still be looking for medical help. Let's hope my colleagues in London come up with something.'

'It's a miracle that the pistol didn't go off when it was hit,' said Katerina.

'It is,' said Monique, 'especially as it would have been cocked.'

'I'll kill Malinovsky when I find him,' said Katerina.

Inspector White coughed. 'Perhaps that's a thought it's best to keep to yourself Miss Komarova, especially here and in this company.'

Monique suppressed a smile and decided it might be best to change the subject. 'Have the two bodies you found in the woods been formally identified, inspector?'

'Yes, a comparison of their fingerprints with those on their military records confirmed they were Flight Lieutenant Thorn and Captain Evans. Both men were garrotted. The police surgeon can't say if they were killed at the same time or over the space of a couple of days, probably around two weeks ago. The next of kin of the two officers are being told of their deaths and I have been to see Mrs Abercrombie to tell her.'

'How did she take it?' asked Monique.

'Stoically,' said Inspector White. 'I think she'd already resigned herself to his death.'

Monique took a sip of tea before continuing. 'To my mind, the police surgeon's finding that the two men were garrotted links the Cuttlefish more firmly with the killing of the sentry on the coast south of Garlieston.'

'I agree,' said Inspector White, 'even though in other ways his death doesn't fit the pattern of the other two.'

'I accept that Edward Daly could be on the other side of the country by now,' said Katerina. 'But I don't believe that he is. Everything we know he's done in Scotland has been in this one corner of the country and I was told that he's set up a forward base here. That must have been with some purpose in mind. The injury to his hand will cause him difficulties, but I think he has a reason to remain in the area.'

'We just need to work out what it is,' said Monique.

'I've not forgotten the suggestion that the Cuttlefish has established a base somewhere nearby,' said Inspector White. 'Until the steamer arrived yesterday afternoon I had two men in and around the town asking if people remember a naval lieutenant asking about renting a property during the week he was in the country. I'll get one of them back onto that. I've also had two armed men knocking on doors in the very sparse and scattered community within a couple of miles of where we found the bodies. You may recall I wondered if the Cuttlefish knew where to dump them because he'd spotted the location while setting up a base nearby.'

'Are you calling a halt to the search for the Cuttlefish's body?' asked Michael.

'I think that might be premature until we have some sort of confirmation that he's alive,' said the inspector. 'I believe the Royal Navy divers were due back to complete their search beside the East Pier this morning, now the *Princess Margaret* has returned to Larne and vacated the berth.'

Inspector Boyle sat forwards in his chair. 'It's probably been overtaken by the theft from the ambulance and the stolen lorry but it's worth saying that with the help of the ship's crew, we mounted a detailed search of the *Princess Margaret* last night. Fully searching a ship is a big job, but I'm reasonably confident that if the Cuttlefish had somehow managed to climb back aboard, we'd have found him. My two detective constables were on board the vessel when she sailed this morning and were also part of an operation checking everyone who got off when the steamer arrived in Larne. It seemed a sensible belt-and-braces precaution.'

'Thank you, Patrick,' said Inspector White. He looked at his watch. 'I need to find out how our efforts to find the stolen lorry and the Cuttlefish's base are going.'

Monique saw Michael glance across at her.

'I'd like to talk to the navy divers if they're still at the East Pier,' he said.

'I'll join you,' said Monique, 'and I imagine that Katerina will too.'

CHAPTER TWENTY-FIVE

'It looks like they're packing up,' said Michael as Monique stopped the car in the open area of quayside between the railway station and the berth the *Princess Margaret* had used the previous afternoon.

She could see what he meant. A dark blue lorry was standing close to the side of the pier and a group of four men, two wearing diving suits without helmets, were standing and smoking at the back of it, next to a pile of equipment. Michael and Monique got out and walked over to the group, with Katerina a few paces behind.

The two men in naval uniform saluted as Michael approached.

He returned their salutes and then introduced himself. 'Who's in charge?'

'I am sir, Petty Officer Carroll.'

'Can I assume you've found nothing?'

'That's right, sir. We'll be making a full report to the police. There's quite a lot of debris on the loch floor near the pier and visibility is poor, but we're as sure as we can be there isn't a dead body down there.'

'What do you think might have happened to the man who went in?' asked Michael.

'I don't know, sir. When we arrived late yesterday afternoon the *Princess Margaret* was berthed here and we were told that four people had gone in the water and three had been saved. Were you the naval officer who jumped in after the lady?'

'He was,' said Katerina. 'And I was the lady.'

'A colleague of mine also went in to help,' said Michael.

'It was brave to jump in here, sir. With the ship being

held away from the pier by these fenders you'd have had a gap that wouldn't close, but as we found after we arrived, the currents in the water are very unpredictable if the ship moves at all. The first thing we did was check the ship's hull to see if a body had become caught up on anything, perhaps the rudders or the twin propellors, but we found nothing.'

'Could the missing man have swum under the ship and out into the harbour?' asked Michael.'Or is there any way he could have got from this side of the pier to the other?'

'The answer to the second question is no, sir. If it had been built on piles, that might have provided a way through, but it's not, and we've found no passages or culverts built into the structure of the pier that would make that possible. I'm less sure about swimming under or perhaps around the end of the steamer. Unless he had a way of boarding from sea level on the other side it wouldn't help. There are ladders at intervals along the pier, and it might be possible to hang on to a wooden fender and perhaps use it to climb out, but the police were checking all those as we arrived.'

'How about simply swimming to the pier we can see over there?' asked Michael.

'The West Pier?' asked Petty Officer Carroll. 'It must be three or four hundred yards. A competent swimmer could manage that distance in maybe five to seven minutes, though it would take longer if you were clothed. Remember that the sea was calm yesterday, as it is today, so someone swimming would be very obvious. That's a long time to spend hoping that if someone looks in your direction they will think you're a seal.

'They've gone now, but yesterday evening there were two fishing boats moored to this side of the West Pier. I'm sure the police must have searched them but there are a lot of places you could hide on a fishing boat and climbing aboard one of them would have been much easier than trying to climb up the other side of the *Princess Margaret.* I suppose that as a lot was happening on this side of the steamer to distract attention he could have swum to the West Pier without being noticed if he was very lucky.'

'Thank you, Petty Officer Carroll, you've been very helpful.'

'You're welcome, sir.'

They got back into the car and Monique drove around the harbour to the landward end of the West Pier. She and Katerina stayed in the car while Michael got out and walked along the pier. Monique watched as he stopped by a boat moored to its west side. Then he climbed down out of sight.

A few minutes later he returned to the car.

'Was that useful?' asked Monique.

'Possibly,' said Michael. 'The skipper of the fishing boat moored on the other side of the pier told me that the two boats that were tied to the side we're interested in both sailed early this morning. Though he wasn't here at the time, he said he'd been told that the police did look around all the boats moored to both sides of the pier yesterday evening but they didn't take long. I suppose that's fair enough given how much they had to do.'

'The Edward Daly I knew was a very fit and capable man,' said Katerina. 'But it couldn't have been easy for anyone to swim under or around the steamer, then across the harbour to here, and then hide in a fishing boat until it was dark enough to break into the ambulance and steal the lorry, all with what may be a badly injured hand.'

'I suppose it depends on how desperate he is,' said

Monique. She looked at her watch. 'Am I alone in feeling at a bit of a loss, as if we're simply sitting and waiting for the Cuttlefish to break cover or the police to turn up something useful? How do you both feel about visiting the woods where the Cuttlefish dumped the bodies of the two officers? It may be a waste of time but, to my mind, anything that can bring us closer to understanding him might help.'

*

Monique suggested Michael drive while she looked at the map.

'Are you sure you know the way?' he asked after they'd turned to climb a very minor road with dense vegetation intruding from both sides.

'Don't worry, Michael. It was just as bad last time. I don't need the map to find the way, I'm trying to get a sense of what's around us. The answer is not a lot, just a thin scatter of widely separated farms. It would be the perfect area to hide yourself in, yet we're less than three miles from the centre of Stranraer. Being hilly just adds to the sense of isolation. Now you need to look for a turning onto a track on the right. This is it.'

'Christ, this is rough,' said Michael.

'You can stop in the clearing ahead,' said Monique. 'On Tuesday, you could smell the death in the air before we got this far. Thankfully it seems to have gone. It's so warm today that I'd not want to have to wind the windows up.'

'Do you want to show us where Edward Daly dumped the bodies?' asked Katerina.

'Yes, if you like,' said Monique. 'The police were intending to search the area thoroughly once the bodies had gone, when they could take their gas masks off. I assume nothing significant was found.'

Monique led Michael and Katerina to where each of the bodies had been dumped.

'It might be my imagination, but I'm getting hints of the smell now,' she said. 'And the sound of flies buzzing has a sinister edge that I've never noticed before.'

'I don't think it's just your imagination,' said Katerina. 'I suppose that until there's some heavy rain to wash the traces away, this place is going to retain a memory of what you saw.'

'Should we go back to the car?' asked Michael. 'I'm not a sensitive soul, but these woods don't feel very comfortable. Have you seen what you want, Monique?'

Monique led the way back to the car and then turned to face the others. 'I'm just trying to get a sense of what happened here. The Cuttlefish must have had a vehicle at the time, just as he has now. I don't know if the theft of military vehicles is common or not, or whether any had been stolen in the area two weeks ago.'

'We can ask the inspector about any that were reported missing,' said Michael. 'Military vehicle thefts do happen. There are large numbers of cars, vans and lorries on just about any military base you care to visit. I'm sure if you picked the right one it wouldn't be missed for a while, if ever. It's going to be on someone's inventory but that's not the same as it being something an individual owns.'

'I think we should leave,' said Katerina. 'I'd not noticed until you mentioned it, but the buzzing of the flies seems much louder than it should.'

Monique was pleased that she wasn't the only one to have noticed.

*

'I've got a message for you, Monique.'

Dorothy was on her own in the reception area of the Wigtownshire Police Headquarters in Stranraer.

'What is it?'

'Group Captain Sutherland rang a little while ago from RAF Turnhouse. He said that he expects to arrive at RAF Castle Kennedy in…' Dorothy looked at her watch. 'In twenty-five minutes. He said not to worry if you're busy, he'll get someone to run him here.'

'That's only a few miles east of the town, isn't it?' asked Michael.

'That's right, sir,' said Dorothy.

'There's plenty of time, I'll go and meet him,' said Monique.

'We might as well come too,' said Michael. 'We can brief Bob in the car on the way back.'

After Michael turned the car off the main road, the approach to RAF Castle Kennedy ran along the western side of the airfield. It seemed to Monique that it was as busy as RAF Wigtown and she saw several different types of aircraft flying around in the few minutes she was paying attention.

The RAF policemen manning the main gate had never heard of Military Intelligence, Section 11, and were suspicious of a Soviet diplomat seeking to gain access. It took Michael asserting his authority as a naval officer to get them through, and even then only after one of the guards had telephoned air traffic control to confirm that a Group Captain Sutherland was due to land.

'I'm going to get George Buchan and Peter Bennett to come down here to look at this place,' said Michael as he drove through the base. 'Then they'll have heard of MI11.'

Monique smiled. 'On the other hand, though that was inconvenient, it's hard to fault their diligence.'

'True,' said Michael. 'If I've followed the directions they gave correctly, we should see the control tower ahead of us when I turn left between these two hangars. There it is.'

'Perfect timing,' said Monique. 'There's a Mosquito just landing. That must be Bob.'

Michael and Katerina stayed in the car while Monique went to meet Bob as he climbed down from the aircraft. She stood to one side while he spoke to two airmen who were placing chocks under the aircraft wheels.

Bob smiled when he walked over to her. 'Hello, my love. I just wanted to ask them to refuel the Mosquito. It's good to see you, though sweeping you up in my arms for a kiss might look a little odd. Consider it done anyway.' Then he looked over towards the car and the expression on his face became much more serious. 'Is anyone with you?'

'Michael and Katerina are in the car.'

'That's awkward. I'll talk to you and Michael later. Have you had any lunch yet? It feels like a long time since breakfast and one of the airmen was kind enough to give me directions to the officers' mess.'

Monique smiled. 'You had an early start, Bob, but it's not indecently soon for the rest of us to eat.'

Katerina had moved into the front seat of the car so Bob and Monique got into the back.

'We've decided to go to the officers' mess for some lunch,' said Monique.

'That sounds good to me,' said Michael, starting the car.

'Where have you been, group captain?' asked Katerina.

'I flew to RAF Errol to speak to Major Malinovsky.'

'What did he have to say for himself?'

'It wasn't as long a conversation as I planned,' said Bob. 'Mr Popov and three colleagues had just flown in and he was quite keen for Malinovsky to join him on an aeroplane bound for London. Beyond learning that Mr Popov took a dim view of Malinovsky's actions, it was a wasted trip, I'm afraid.'

'I'm pleased Comrade Popov took what I said to him so seriously,' said Katerina. 'The police have found the pistol Edward Daly pointed at my head yesterday and it's a miracle it didn't go off when Malinovsky's bullet hit it.'

The dining room in the officers' mess was fairly empty, perhaps because it was still early in the lunch service. That meant that they could sit at a table where they wouldn't be overheard. Monique noticed that as more people came in, they tended to favour tables as far away as possible from the one Bob had picked. It seemed no one wanted to sit nearer than they needed to an unknown group captain and his unusual group.

As they ate, Monique and Michael briefed Bob about what had happened that morning.

The lunch was functional rather than enjoyable and after they'd eaten they returned to the car.

Michael again drove, with Monique and Bob in the back. As they approached the main gate, one of the RAF policemen stepped out into the roadway in front of them and held up his hand.

'They take their jobs very seriously here,' said Michael as he halted the car. 'They made getting in awkward. You think they'd be pleased to see us leave.'

All the car windows were open and the RAF policeman walked around to the rear of the car on Bob's side and then saluted. 'Are you Group Captain Sutherland, sir?'

‘Yes, I am.’

‘The police in Stranraer have been trying to get hold of you, sir. You can use the telephone in the guardroom to call them.’

Monique watched as Bob followed the RAF policeman over to a brick building beside the main gate. Michael pulled the car over so they weren’t blocking traffic.

‘Something’s happened,’ said Monique.

Bob was back a few moments later. ‘I spoke to Woman Auxiliary Police Constable Franklin. Inspector White would like us to return to Stranraer police station as quickly as possible, pick her up and then let her guide us to where he is.’

‘Where’s that?’ asked Michael as he put the car in gear.

‘I suppose we’ll find out when we get there,’ said Bob. ‘Should we see how fast this thing will go?’

The traffic slowed down after they turned onto the main road back towards Stranraer.

‘What’s the problem?’ asked Bob.

‘It looks like RAF police are setting up a roadblock on the other side of the road, stopping everyone travelling east. Drivers on this side are slowing down to see what’s going on. It will clear as soon as we’ve passed it. There you go,’

‘Something really has happened,’ said Monique.

CHAPTER TWENTY-SIX

Katerina sat in the back of the car with Monique and Bob, which allowed Constable Franklin to direct Michael from the front passenger seat. They drove west out of Stranraer along a road that was now beginning to look familiar to Bob.

'Where are we going?' asked Monique. 'I'd be happy not to have to look at any more fortnight-old dead bodies.'

'I can't promise because I'm not sure what they've found,' said the constable. 'Inspector White and Inspector Boyle are both out at an old farmhouse not all that far from where the bodies were hidden.'

Constable Franklin directed Michael to make a series of turns on minor, hilly roads and Bob found it hard to follow where they were going. The final turn was off a heavily overgrown and very narrow paved road onto a concrete track that seemed to be disappearing between unkempt hedgerows that scraped along both sides of the car.

After a hundred yards the track ended in a rectangular open area partly covered in concrete that had a two-storey stone farmhouse on its left side, a wooden barn at the rear and a roofless and windowless range of stone buildings on the right. The rusting hulk of a tractor occupied the corner of the yard between the farmhouse and barn and piles of junk partly obscured the front of the derelict range.

The fourth side of the area was defined by a low stone wall with what once might have been a pasture beyond it that was now, literally, going to seed. A gap between the barn and the derelict range was wide enough to drive through to what appeared to be another open area in the angle between the two buildings.

While the barn and farmhouse looked structurally complete, both buildings had peeling paintwork and thick verges of tall grass and rosebay willowherb pressed against their front walls. The ruined range of buildings seemed to be filled with rusting junk and vegetation.

Two police cars and a larger van were parked nose-on to the barn and there was plenty of room for Michael to pull in at the end of the row of vehicles.

A policeman was standing next to the front door of the farmhouse and at the sound of their car doors closing, Inspector White emerged, closely followed by Inspector Boyle.

'Welcome to Upper Milldown,' said Inspector White.

'Hello,' said Monique. 'I'm told you've found something.'

'We have,' said Inspector Boyle, 'thanks to some fine police work by Thomas here.'

'That's kind of you, Patrick,' said Inspector White, 'but the credit should go to an observant constable of mine. I told you this morning that I've had a couple of men knocking on doors in the area where the two bodies were found. This place is a little over a mile in a straight line from the wood where they were hidden, though further by road. My officers came here yesterday morning and got no response when they knocked.

'This morning they resumed the process on the other side of the area and it took them until late morning before they got to the nearest neighbours to here, who are some distance away, and were told that this place has been abandoned for several years. The fine police work came when one of the constables began to wonder why the vegetation by the front door of the farmhouse had been trodden down when they first visited if no one lived here.

‘They came back and saw a fresh oil patch on the ground that they didn’t remember seeing yesterday. That’s it over there, within the barrel hoop we’ve placed to stop anyone walking over it. When they explored a little further they found that the strip of vegetation along the far end of the barn had been flattened sufficiently to allow the barn doors to open. A gap where the doors don’t quite meet allowed them a restricted view into the barn, where they saw an army lorry of the type that was stolen last night in Stranraer. While they couldn’t see the registration, that was enough for one of them to drive to the nearest telephone and alert me, while the other stayed under cover where he could see anything happening in the farmyard. Nothing did, and Inspector Boyle and I arrived with reinforcements not long afterwards.’

‘What did you find?’ asked Bob.

‘We forced open the barn doors first. The lorry is the one stolen last night. There are also signs of a second vehicle in there. Tracks leading out of a long-lived puddle caused by a hole in the roof suggest it’s a large van or utility vehicle of some sort. Then we took a look at the farmhouse. The front door was unlocked and it was clear that someone had been camping out in the house, amongst the dust and cobwebs and the tatty old furniture that still fills the place. Some cushions from the sofa are lined up on the floor and covered in blankets and there’s some very mouldy bread and cheese in the kitchen, presumably from the Cuttlefish’s first visit, along with an oil lamp and the remnants of an army ration pack. My guess is that the Cuttlefish came here from Stranraer after stealing the lorry, rested, then departed this morning in the vehicle he’d left in the barn when he was last in Scotland. He seems to have taken his uniform collection and anything else he stored here with him.’

‘If the Cuttlefish left the vehicle he was using here at the end of his first visit, how did he get into Stranraer to catch the steamer early on the Saturday morning?’ asked Michael.

‘I don’t know,’ said Inspector White. ‘We’ve never accounted for Flight Lieutenant Thorn’s bicycle. Perhaps the Cuttlefish used that to get to the steamer pier and then threw it into the loch. It’s not far and it’s mostly downhill.’

‘Is this why you’ve got the military setting up roadblocks?’ asked Bob. ‘We saw one as we came in from Castle Kennedy.’

‘Yes,’ said Inspector White. ‘He probably had time to clear the area before we found this place and there are back roads we can’t cover, but it seemed worth setting up roadblocks on main roads looking for a man with an injured right hand. Other than its likely size, we have no clue what he’s driving. Nor do we know what he’s wearing. He could be disguised as a Roman Catholic priest for all we know, but the hand is a distinguishing feature he’s not going to be able to hide easily.’

‘We were discussing vehicles earlier,’ said Michael. ‘Were any reported stolen while the Cuttlefish was first in the area? He needed one to dump the bodies and, from what you say, he then stored it here while he returned to Dublin.’

‘That’s been puzzling me, too,’ said Inspector White. ‘Nothing was reported stolen that’s not since been accounted for.’

‘I wonder how the Cuttlefish found this place,’ said Bob.

‘I don’t know,’ said Inspector White. ‘I suppose if you look at an Ordnance Survey map of Stranraer, it’s obvious that this area is close to the town, yet also hilly and sparsely populated. Perhaps when he first arrived he simply drove around until he found somewhere that met his needs?’

‘Do you mind if we take a look inside the farmhouse?’ asked Monique.

‘Ideally not all four of you, simply to minimise disturbance.’

‘Bob and I will go in,’ said Monique. Her head snapped around. ‘What’s that?’

Bob heard the sound of a police whistle coming from somewhere beyond the barn.

‘I’ve got men searching the surrounding area,’ said Inspector White. ‘It sounds like one of them’s found something. Constable, you stay here and guard the farmhouse. The rest of us will see what’s going on.’

Inspector White set off for the far corner of the barn at a pace that Bob thought was quite impressive for a man in his fifties. Not quite a run, it was still a very fast walk. Inspector Boyle and Michael ran off ahead. Bob was content to walk with Inspector White, and he saw that Monique and Katerina were doing the same. Like him, both women had their pistols in their hands.

Beyond the open area at the end of the barn, a cart track led between heavily overgrown hedgerows and then curved out of sight around a left-hand corner. Once around the corner, the right side of the track opened up into woodland. Whatever had been found appeared to be just behind the end of the hedge on the right.

When Bob reached the spot he found three police constables, Michael and Inspector Boyle standing in an arc beyond a shallow ditch that ran just behind the hedge. They were looking down at the body of a bald man lying on his back in the ditch. He was wearing a dark suit.

‘He’s been garrotted,’ said Michael. ‘Look at his neck.’

‘He’s also got a bad head injury, above and behind his left ear,’ said Monique, kneeling beside the body.

‘This killing wasn't done for a set of clothes,’ said Katerina. ‘This man is still wearing his. And he looks far taller than Edward Daly anyway.’

‘I’ve met him,’ said Inspector White. ‘He’s one of the deputy harbourmasters at the military port at Cairnryan. I’m struggling to remember his name, though.’

‘Do you mind if I check his pockets?’ asked Monique.

When the inspector shook his head she bent down and patted the sides of the dead man’s jacket and trousers before taking out a wallet and some documents from an inside jacket pocket.

‘His name is Christopher Donaldson. He’s got a National Registration Identity Card, a ration book and a Royal Navy pass.’ Monique held up the documents for the inspector to take as she looked up at Bob. ‘I’d expected to find some keys but there aren’t any in his jacket or his front trouser pockets. If we could find out how he crossed paths with the Cuttlefish, we might be closer to understanding what this is all about.’

‘It looks like you have another murder scene to manage, inspector,’ said Bob. ‘Perhaps we should divide our resources? I suggest that Madame Dubois and I go and talk to Mr Donaldson’s colleagues in Cairnryan to find out when they last saw him. Miss Komarova is the only person who can identify the Cuttlefish, so I suggest that she and Lieutenant Commander Dixon remain with you in case a suspect is stopped at one of your roadblocks.’

‘That suits me,’ said Inspector White. ‘The harbourmaster at Cairnryan is Captain Allenby. We should meet to compare notes at the police station afterwards. I suggest that Constable Franklin drives you in one of the police cars. That will free up your car for use by your colleagues.’

'Could you drop me off at Stranraer police station on your way?' asked Inspector Boyle. 'I need to catch up with my people in Belfast.'

*

Monique had seen the scale of the military port as the steamer sailed along the length of Loch Ryan the previous afternoon. She knew it comprised several long jetties running nearly parallel to the loch's eastern shore that were each attached at one end to headlands, giving huge lengths of wharfage for ships that could then be unloaded by the many cranes that had been erected along the jetties.

What she'd not appreciated from the steamer was the extent of the development on land associated with the port. There were camps full of Nissen huts as well as larger structures, all linked together by the main road and by railway tracks that ran right alongside the loch.

'Where are we going, Dorothy?' asked Monique.

'The inspector told me to take you to the port headquarters in Lochryan House. It's on the inland side of the main road towards the far end of the port, not far from the lighthouse you can see. The long building we're passing on the right is the port's administrative block, but the inspector said the harbourmaster's offices are in the old house itself, which is beyond and some way back from it. Here's the turning.'

Dorothy turned right off the main road through a stone gateway and onto a drive. Here they were stopped at a barrier manned by Royal Navy ratings with rifles who asked to see their identity papers. Beyond the barrier, the drive continued for perhaps a couple of hundred yards to a broad turning circle where Dorothy stopped the car. On its far side, a narrower ornate gateway was defined by posts that were topped off with large perching stone eagles.

Monique and Bob left Dorothy in the car and walked through the second gateway into what might once have been a fine garden. Flanked on both sides by ranges of buildings it was now given over to vegetables. Lochryan House stood beyond the garden and was an intriguing building. It appeared to combine the central section of a castle, complete with crenellations high above the upper row of windows, with flanking ranges from a more standard mansion that had grey slate roofs into which were set attic windows. These ranges advanced ahead of the central part of the house. The central frontage looked like a face with a very deep forehead and it had a door and surround that imitated a surprised mouth on a cartoon character. The house was topped off with a Royal Navy ensign flying from a rooftop flagpole.

Monique doubted if either of the naval ratings at the reception desk had seen MI11 security passes before, but one of them called someone on a telephone and then led them up the stairs to the upper floor. They passed several civilians and naval personnel, both men and women, on the way. Monique and Bob were then taken through an outer office housing a secretary to a large room at the front of the building. Monique got the impression that this offered dramatic views out over the port and Loch Ryan from its three large windows, all covered in the usual criss-cross of anti-blast tape.

The office had mainly wood-panelled walls, while one end was filled with built-in bookshelving that was only partially used for its intended purpose. The other end wall was covered with plans and charts. A Royal Navy captain was sitting at a large wooden desk with his back to the central window. He stood up as they entered, then walked around his desk to shake their hands while Bob introduced them.

'Hello. I'm Captain Allenby and I'm the harbourmaster here at Cairnryan. May I see your identity papers, please?'

Once satisfied, the captain walked back around his desk and gestured to two seats on the near side of it.

'What can I do for you, group captain?'

'What can you tell us about Christopher Donaldson?' asked Bob.

Monique sat back, content to watch.

'He's one of my deputy harbourmasters,' said Captain Allenby. 'I have two of them.'

'When did you last see him?'

'I saw him briefly first thing this morning, perhaps 8.30 a.m. There was a query about the time it would take to fix a broken crane on one of the jetties. Why are you asking?'

'I'm sorry to have to tell you this, but we think Mr Donaldson is dead. A body has been found on a farmstead on the other side of Stranraer. Mr Donaldson was recognised by the policeman leading the investigation, Inspector White, and we found Mr Donaldson's wallet and identity papers in the body's pockets.'

'My God! That's unbelievable. He was in his office when I saw him. How could he have got from there to where you say he was found?'

'That's what we hope to discover, captain,' said Bob.

'What can you tell us about Mr Donaldson?' asked Monique.

'He's very tall, is largely bald and wears spectacles,' said the captain. 'What hair he has on the back and sides of his head is prematurely grey so he looks older than his 44 years. But then you've seen him so that's not really any help. I can also tell you that he's trustworthy and reliable, bordering on indispensable. He previously did a similar job in Glasgow and has been here for two years, for most of the time it's taken to build the port and bring it into operation.'

'Can you show us his office?' asked Bob.

The captain led them to the rear of the upper floor of the house, to a much smaller and rather drab office with a single window that looked out onto what might originally have been a rear garden that merged into an increasingly steep hillside but which was now home to a collection of Nissen huts and other military buildings. The desk in front of the window was covered in piles of papers. It looked to Monique like Bob's desk after he'd let his in tray get out of control.

'This is odd,' said the captain. 'The rules are that all papers are locked away in a secure cabinet whenever an office is left unattended.'

Monique walked around the desk and looked at the document that Christopher Donaldson had left folded back on its corner staple in the centre of his desk. 'It's to do with rates of unloading grain from ships onto railway wagons. I don't think it's what we're looking for.'

'I'm sorry, but you can't do that, Madame Dubois,' said the captain.

'This is a murder investigation,' said Bob. 'What Mr Donaldson was doing when he decided to leave could be important.'

'Hello, Captain Allenby. Are you looking for Christopher?'

Monique looked up to see a dark-haired woman in her twenties standing in the doorway to the office. She was smiling, so apparently hadn't heard what Bob said.

'Oh, hello Margery. These people are with military

intelligence. When did you last see Christopher?' The captain turned towards Bob. 'Margery reports to Christopher and is one of a group of people who work in the next office along the corridor.'

'Why, has something happened?'

'Just answer the question!' said the captain, sharply.

The woman in the doorway took a step backwards, a look of something like revulsion crossing her face.

'Hello Margery,' said Monique. 'I'm sorry to be the bearer of bad news but we think that Mr Donaldson may have come to harm this morning. I can't give you any details but we need to find out as much as we can about his movements. Captain Allenby saw Christopher here at about 8.30 a.m. Did you see him after that?'

'Everyone in the main office had a cup of tea a little after 9 a.m. and I brought one in for Christopher. A few minutes later one of the ratings from the reception desk stuck his head around the door of the main office and asked where Christopher was because a telegram had been delivered and he needed to give it to him as soon as possible.

'I came with him to look for Christopher and we met him in the corridor, returning from the toilet. The rating gave Christopher the telegram and he then came into his office and closed the door, which is very unusual for him.'

'Is it normal for telegrams to be delivered here for members of staff?' asked Bob.

'No, sir, said Margery. There are lots of official signals, of course, but this was a normal Post Office telegram.'

'Do you know what was in it?' asked Monique.

'I'm sorry, no. It was in a sealed envelope. Look, there's the envelope on the pile of files on the end of the desk.'

Monique picked up the envelope and looked inside. It

was empty.

'Presumably, Mr Donaldson then went out?' she asked.

'I saw him a few minutes after the telegram arrived and he looked dreadful. He was as white as a sheet. He came into the main office and asked me to connect his phone line to the switchboard because he needed to make a secure call.'

'Do you know who he rang?'

'I'm sorry, no.'

'Usually, we only need secure outside lines to talk to the Admiralty in London or the Ministry of Supply,' said Captain Allenby.

'Do you know when he left, Margery?' asked Monique.

'I came to see if he was all right at about 9.30 a.m. and he'd gone by then. The ratings on the reception desk might be able to give you a clearer idea but there's no requirement to sign in and out, so perhaps not.'

'Thank you, Margery.'

'Where does Christopher live?' asked Bob. 'If he's been here for two years I can't imagine he stays in the naval officers' wardroom.'

'No, sir. He stays in one of the cottages on the main road through the village. He says it's ideal because it only takes him a short time to walk to work.'

'Would he walk to the village along the drive at the front, the one from the turning circle to the main road?' asked Monique.

'No, there's another way in or out at the side of the house. It cuts a corner and joins the main access to the admin building and the camp that's been built at the back of the house. Christopher would have walked that way. I'll get you the address of his cottage.'

Margery disappeared out of sight along the corridor.

Monique looked down and saw a wicker waste paper bin on the floor partly under the desk. She bent down and pulled it towards her. There was only one piece of paper in it, tightly crumpled at the bottom. As she pulled it open she saw it was a telegram, which she smoothed out until it was flat enough to read. Then she folded it in four and popped it into her handbag.

'What does it say?' asked Captain Allenby.

'Thank you for your help, captain,' said Bob. 'We don't want to use any more of your time than necessary. I'm sure the police will be in touch about formal identification of the body that's been found and about notifying Mr Donaldson's next of kin.'

Captain Allenby started to say something before appearing to think better of it. Then he turned and left.

A moment later Margery appeared in the doorway again, holding out a slip of paper which Monique took. An older, dark-haired woman stood partly behind her.

'Can you tell us what's happened now Captain Hook's gone?' Margery blushed as she remembered that Bob was there. 'I'm sorry sir, no disrespect intended. I know he's got two hands, it's just that, well, he sometimes acts a little like J. M. Barrie's creation.'

Monique wondered how to reply.

'There's no easy way to say this, but we think Mr Donaldson is dead,' said Bob. He explained why, using almost the same words as he had when talking to Captain Allenby.

The older woman in the corridor started sobbing and was comforted by Margery.

'I'm terribly sorry,' said Bob. 'We need to go, Monique. We'll see ourselves out.'

The two ratings at the reception desk didn't know what

time Christopher Donaldson had left but did say that he had seemed in a hurry.

Bob stopped and turned towards Monique after they'd descended the three curving steps outside the front door of Lochryan House. 'I think I put my foot in it just now.'

'I don't see how you could have broken it to them any more gently,' said Monique. 'I wonder whether we need to come back to talk to Margery's older friend.'

'She did seem more upset than you might expect on hearing that her boss was dead,' said Bob. 'Perhaps something was going on between her and Christopher Donaldson? Now, are you going to tell me what was in the telegram or not?'

'The actual message is just two words: "Hello Frederick",' said Monique.

'What the hell are we to make of that?' asked Bob.

'It meant something to Mr Donaldson,' said Monique. 'Perhaps we might discover what at his cottage.'

CHAPTER TWENTY-SEVEN

'The cottage we're looking for is just ahead if I've got the numbering correct,' said Dorothy. 'This is it, the single-storey building between the two houses. Is it all right for me to park right outside, sir?'

'That's ideal, thank you, constable,' said Bob. While Monique was on first-name terms with the policewoman, Bob felt it might be unwelcome if he was too informal.

Setting aside the overlay of modern military camps and harbour facilities, Cairnryan itself comprised a straggle of stone houses and cottages along the inland side of the main road. Bob had seen one pub as they drove towards Lochryan House earlier and a village shop, which couldn't be very far beyond the cottage in the direction they were facing. He'd noticed the shop because of a sign that protruded from its frontage advertising Lyons Cakes. That seemed out of place on a building that was little more than a large shed with a corrugated iron roof. The sign above the door was more prosaic and probably more accurate, offering 'Confectionery, Groceries & Tobacco'.

The dwellings in the village looked out across the main road to a tall chain link fence on its seaward side that was topped off by three strands of barbed wire. This blocked access to railway lines running along the shore. Beyond them were Loch Ryan itself and the jetties of the port, at which several ships were berthed.

The main road was busy with civilian lorries and military traffic, though its width meant there was no difficulty parking. As Bob got out of the car a goods train puffed by beyond the fence. Two men dressed like dock workers were walking along the pavement a little further along the village but, otherwise, Bob could see no people at all.

The cottage they had come to see was made of stone and comprised just a front door with a window on either side of it and a grey slate roof above. It abutted the houses on either side so there was no obvious way of getting around the back.

'How will you get in?' asked the constable. 'We know Mr Donaldson's not here.'

Monique knocked on the door while Bob tried to look in through the windows.

'The curtains are drawn, which seems odd,' said Bob.

'This is where it would have been useful to have found some keys on Mr Donaldson's body,' said Monique. 'Dorothy, if anyone asks, it might be best to say that you don't know how we got in.'

'You're not going to break the door down, are you?' asked the policewoman.

'Nothing so brutal, and the group captain doesn't need a broken shoulder. I suggest you look away for a moment.'

'Hang on, Monique,' said Bob. 'Constable Franklin, it might be best if Monique and I go in alone. Could I ask you to check if the neighbours are at home? Perhaps two or three houses on either side? We need to know if any of them saw Mr Donaldson this morning, going to work or coming back later. We also need to know if they saw anything out of the ordinary, like a vehicle parked here or anyone taking an interest in the cottage. If they ask why, say it's just a routine enquiry.'

'Yes, of course, sir.'

It only took Monique a moment to pick the lock on the front door. She obstructed Bob's view to give him the option later of saying he'd not been aware of what she'd done. Bob reminded himself that this was a skill he needed to learn.

The door opened into a darkened room. Bob had his Walther PPK in his hand as he followed Monique in.

'At least there's electricity,' said Monique as Bob heard a click and a single bulb in a floral lampshade hanging from the ceiling came to life.

They were standing in the cottage's lounge. A chair and a two-seat sofa covered in floral fabric were focused on the black fireplace and range on the left, built into the end wall of the cottage. The rest of the furniture in the room was made of dark wood and comprised a glass-fronted bookcase with quite a few books, a sideboard with a large wooden radio on it, an empty magazine rack and a small low table beside the chair. The red lino floor had a threadbare rug covering a large part of it so the lino only showed around the edges. Everything was very clean.

Bob opened a door at the rear of the lounge, beyond which was a small kitchen with a back door.

'I don't get the sense that Mr Donaldson cooked at home much,' said Monique.

She unbolted and then opened the back door and stepped out, then a moment later came back in. 'There's a tiny overgrown garden that climbs the hill behind the cottage and a semi-outdoor toilet, in a lean-to with the door immediately to the right. It looks like the only running water other than the toilet is in the kitchen sink, presumably with what comes out of the hot tap heated by the range in the lounge when the weather's not too warm to have it lit.'

They went back through to the lounge.

'I'm guessing that the other end of the cottage is the bedroom,' said Bob, opening the second internal door from the lounge.

Again the room was dark, though this time switching on the electric light had no effect.

'Hang on,' said Bob. 'I'll open the blackout curtains. There are also net curtains to stop anyone looking in from the pavement outside, as I tried to do.'

The bedroom gave an overwhelming sense of ordinariness. A dark wood framed double bed was placed next to the door against the wall shared with the lounge and a dressing table with a cloudy mirror on top sat next to the window that looked out onto the street. There was a fireplace in the end wall opposite the bed, though close enough to it for Bob to wonder how the cottage hadn't burned down. Much of the rear wall of the room was filled with floor-to-ceiling fitted cupboards, all painted in a tobacco-stained glossy cream colour, like all the skirting boards and internal doors in the cottage.

Monique went to stand in front of the cupboards, looking down as Bob heard a crunching sound. Then she looked up at the ceiling. 'Now we know why the light's not working. The bulb's been smashed and the glass is on the rug.'

'I wonder how that happened,' said Bob.

'Is it my imagination, or is that a patch of blood on the rug, next to the broken glass?' asked Monique.

Bob bent down to touch it and held up his finger. 'It's still wet.' He wiped his finger on a handkerchief. Then he saw something out of the corner of his right eye and reached out to lift the edge of the floral counterpane covering the bed. 'There's a poker lying on the floor under the bed.'

'And there's one missing from the companion set by the fireplace,' said Monique. 'I think we've discovered how Mr Donaldson came by an injury above and behind his left ear.

And how the bulb up there was broken. With an injured right hand, I imagine that Edward Daly used his left hand to hold the poker and hit Christopher Donaldson with it from behind, but also broke the bulb at the same time. I think we should leave the poker where it is. He must have had a torch available once the light was smashed.'

'Why would the Cuttlefish have then gone to the trouble of moving Donaldson out to a vehicle and driving him to Upper Milldown, only to kill him there?' asked Bob. 'Moving an injured or unconscious man couldn't have been easy. Donaldson was bigger than him, and then there's the injured hand to think about.'

'Perhaps we might find something in here to help us understand,' said Monique.

Bob watched as Monique opened each of the four cupboard doors, from right to left. The first two had deep shelving from floor to ceiling and were stuffed with bags and suitcases, with toys and games piled on the top shelf of the second of them.

Monique took a step backwards. 'Margery didn't say, but if Mr Donaldson was renting the cottage then this looks like where the owners store all the stuff they don't have a use for where they're living now.'

The third and fourth cupboard doors opened away from one another, giving a double-width space inside.

'The upper half of this is the wardrobe and there is a set of drawers below it. The upper half is very deep.'

Bob watched her push the hanging clothing to the sides.

'This is interesting,' said Monique. 'You've seen something very like this before, Bob.'

Bob stepped forwards, crunching more glass from the broken bulb as he did so.

'I have. When we found one in Strathmore Lodge in

Caithness you described it as an update of the standard issue Abwehr radios you were trained to use. Only that one was very carefully hidden in a disused fireplace behind the well-constructed false back of a cupboard. You could call this hidden, after a fashion, but it only took us a few minutes to find it. It would be quite easy to give this cupboard a false back like the one in Strathmore Lodge. It's certainly deep enough. But no one has bothered. This radio isn't what I'd call "hide it well enough to save yourself from the gallows" hidden.'

'That's a good way of putting it, Bob. There are shelves set into the back of the cupboard too, on the left side of the radio. Someone's been through them roughly or hurriedly. Books and papers that look like they ought to be on the shelves are dumped on the floor of the wardrobe. I wonder if whoever did this was after the Abwehr code book. No, that's here.' Monique had shuffled through the detritus on the wardrobe floor and held up what she'd been looking for. 'I'll take it and ask Inspector White to lock it away somewhere safe until we work out what to do with it. Ah, and hidden by the bottom of the dressing gown hanging at the right-hand end of the wardrobe is a Browning automatic pistol.'

Monique lifted the dressing gown clear. 'The pistol isn't cocked. I'm wondering if Mr Donaldson had this hidden, perhaps on one of the shelves, and grabbed it when being forced to go through the contents of the cupboard. The Cuttlefish was ready for him and hit him with the poker because it was less noisy than shooting him. That still doesn't answer your question about why he then took Donaldson elsewhere to finish him off. Perhaps he intends to return? I can't believe he does because Captain Allenby would have had someone here looking for Donaldson by the end of the day at the latest even if we'd not been to see him.'

'The radio strongly suggests that Christopher Donaldson is, or rather was, an Abwehr spy,' said Bob. 'But when you first seduced me into the select club that knows about Ultra, you told me that decryption of radio intercepts is so successful that we know with certainty that there are no Abwehr spies in the country. Those that have arrived have been detected through Ultra and turned by MI5, or executed, and the active ones now feed back the version of events that MI5 wants the Germans to believe.'

'What do you read into that, Bob?' asked Monique.

'We know that the Cuttlefish is SD rather than Abwehr and we know the two organisations are in a power struggle and actively working against each other. I'm wondering if this is evidence that the SD have established their own network of spies in Britain in competition with the Abwehr, perhaps using a means of communication we know nothing about. If so, then this could be a hugely important discovery.' Bob paused for a moment. 'Though the presence of an Abwehr radio is a little difficult to fit into that theory.'

Monique smiled. 'It has to be speculation until we find the Cuttlefish, Bob. But given that we believe Edward Daly killed Christopher Donaldson, and given how casually this radio has been hidden, and given the contents of the telegram, I'm wondering if there might be a different explanation for what's happened. It, too, would be very important and, either way, I think we need to talk to Commodore Cunningham on a secure line as soon as we can.'

'Are you going to tell me what you think is going on?' asked Bob.

‘Are you going to tell me whatever it was that you wouldn’t say about Major Malinovsky in front of Katerina earlier?’ asked Monique.

‘I will when there’s time, I promise,’ said Bob.

‘Ditto,’ said Monique, smiling. ‘Where do you think we can most readily access a secure line to call the commodore? Given what we’ve found here, I don’t think we should go back to Lochryan House to phone from there.’

‘We can call from RAF Castle Kennedy, and this uniform and the braid on the peak of my cap will ensure no one argues when I ask for access to a phone. It’s not far.’

Constable Franklin was standing outside the front door of the cottage, waiting for them.

‘I was able to talk to two neighbours or sets of neighbours out of six, sir. The others were out.’

‘I’m sorry to interrupt, constable,’ said Bob, ‘but we need to get to RAF Castle Kennedy as quickly as possible. Could you drive us there and tell us what the neighbours said on the way?’

After Bob had clarified that ‘as quickly as possible’ didn’t mean the constable needed to use the police car’s warning bell, they set off, heading south, with Monique in the front passenger seat.

‘What did you find out, Dorothy?’ she asked.

‘The next-door neighbours on both sides were out, as were those in the two houses beyond in this direction. I was able to speak to an elderly couple in the house two back towards Lochryan House, and a young lady with a baby in the cottage beyond that.

‘Mr Donaldson was a quiet man who kept himself to himself but was always friendly whenever anyone met him on the street, usually while he was walking to or from work. The elderly couple had seen him returning to the cottage this morning as they were coming back from buying milk and bread at the village shop. They knew it was a few minutes before 9.45 a.m. because they got home in time to switch on the radio and listen to the start of Harold Coombs' organ recital from the Regal in Kingston upon Thames on the BBC Home Service.

'Mr Donaldson was sweating heavily and didn't seem well. He didn't say more than "Good morning" as they passed. They were in a hurry to catch the start of the radio broadcast so didn't try to chat either. Just as they reached their house they passed a naval lieutenant walking the same way as Mr Donaldson. He appeared in a hurry to get somewhere, but still smiled and gave them a pleasant greeting as he passed.'

'Did they describe the lieutenant?' asked Monique.

'He was in his thirties and of average size and build, with black hair under his naval officer's cap. The husband thought he had an Irish accent but the wife wasn't sure as he'd only said a word or two. They agreed that the man had a bandage wrapped around his right hand.'

'It sounds like the Cuttlefish was following on foot,' said Monique. 'The couple might have been a useful diversion for him. I presume he caught up with Mr Donaldson just as he had the key in the lock of his front door. A gun in the ribs would have given him access to the cottage without making what was happening too obvious to anyone in view. What did the young woman say?'

'Because it was such a beautiful morning she'd taken her baby daughter out for a stroll in her pram. They walked past Christopher Donanldson's cottage and, further along the village, they turned left onto a lane that climbs a nice valley following the Claddy House Burn. When she came back there was an army lorry parked where I parked the police car. She remembered it because the cab door on the pavement side of the lorry was wide open and that made it difficult for her to pass with the pram.

'The lorry door was right next to the front door of Mr Donaldson's cottage, which was also wide open. As she got there, a naval lieutenant came out of the cottage. She thought he looked shocked to see her at first but was very apologetic when he realised what the problem was. He closed the lorry door to let her pass, then walked her to the door of her cottage and helped her in with the pram, even though he had a bandaged hand which was obviously causing him pain.

'She said he had an Irish accent and was very charming, if a little old for her. She offered him a cup of tea but he declined, saying he had to pick up some laundry for Mr Donaldson and then needed to take it into Stranraer. She thought it odd that a naval lieutenant would be concerning himself with someone's laundry, and that he should be driving an army lorry, but at that moment her daughter started to cry so she went to feed her.'

'Did she say what time this was?' asked Monique.

'Her mantlepiece clock was chiming 10 a.m. when she entered the front door. That's all I have to tell you, I'm afraid.'

'That's hugely helpful, Constable Franklin,' said Bob. 'It seems Mr Donaldson was followed from somewhere near Lochryan House on foot by the man who killed him, who had assumed his naval identity for the occasion. It sounds like he caught up with Mr Donaldson at the front door and knocked him out in the bedroom. He then appears to have gone to retrieve the stolen army lorry from wherever he had left it, which wasn't far away given the timings. He parked it in front of the cottage and left the passenger door open to allow him to move the unconscious Mr Donaldson from the cottage straight into the cab of the lorry. If that young mother had arrived on the scene a minute or so later, while the Cuttlefish was dragging Donaldson out, I suspect we'd be dealing with her murder too.'

Shortly after the constable turned onto the main road east from Stranraer towards Dumfries, Bob saw the traffic ahead slow down.

'I'd forgotten about the roadblock here,' he said.

Bob saw Monique smile and knew what she was about to say.

'Dorothy, if you're looking for a chance to drive on the wrong side of the road with the police bell ringing, this is it.'

CHAPTER TWENTY-EIGHT

Dorothy stayed in the police car outside the guardroom at the main gate of RAF Castle Kennedy while Bob and Monique went in. Monique was amused to see that Bob's prediction about how he would be received was spot on. The men who had been so obstructive earlier offered them tea, which they declined, and an RAF Police sergeant ushered them into a small office at the back of the building to use the phone.

Bob pulled a chair around the desk so Monique could sit close beside him and take part in the conversation. It took a few minutes to be put through to MI11's London headquarters in Sanctuary Buildings and there was another delay before Mrs Croft, Commodore Cunningham's secretary, came on the line.

'Hello, Group Captain Sutherland. How can I help?'

'Could I speak to the commodore, please? It's urgent.'

'I'm afraid he's out of the office at the moment. Are you calling on a secure line?'

'Yes, I am,' said Bob.

'In that case, I can tell you that he's been summoned to a meeting with MI5 in Sir Peter Maitland's office. He said that if you rang I should tell you that it's connected with what you are doing in Galloway and he'll need to talk to you as soon as he's back. Where are you?'

'Madame Dubois and I are at RAF Castle Kennedy, not far from Stranraer. We're not planning to stay so I'll call you again as soon as I can, Mrs Croft.'

'All right, group captain, I'll tell him when he returns. Be careful, both of you.'

Monique watched as Bob put the phone down.

‘Why do I have this feeling that I’ve missed something important?’ asked Bob. ‘You and I need to talk, Monique.’

‘We do, but first, I think we need to know if anything’s turned up while we’ve been out of touch and we also need to find out what Michael and Katerina are doing.’

‘Very true,’ said Bob. ‘We can go back to Stranraer with Dorothy if that makes sense. Let’s ring to check if Inspector White has returned from the Cuttlefish’s base yet.’

Monique again watched while Bob made the call and then moved close to him so she could hear and be heard.

After Bob had identified himself, the call was put through and she heard Inspector Boyle’s Ulster accent.

‘Hello, Inspector Boyle,’ said Bob. ‘We’re at RAF Castle Kennedy and there are a couple of things I need to pass on to Inspector White following our visit to Cairnryan.’

‘Inspector White isn’t at the station at the moment. If you tell me, I’ll pass it on when I can, though remember the line’s not secure at this end.’

‘I understand that,’ said Bob. ‘It would seem the victim was rendered unconscious at his home having been lured there from his place of work. We have witnesses who say the assailant was wearing a naval lieutenant’s uniform, though he could have changed into something else when he returned to his base. From what one witness said, his injury is causing him difficulty. We know that he drove to Cairnryan in the vehicle that was found in the barn rather than any other.’

‘Thank you, group captain,’ said Inspector Boyle. ‘Inspector White has drawn the same conclusion about the vehicle, having found blood in the footwell of the passenger’s side of the cab. You should know that the inspector has gone to Newton Stewart railway station to investigate a report of an RAF flight lieutenant with a bandaged hand buying a railway ticket to Dumfries. Your two colleagues have also gone there.'

'That's helpful, thank you,' said Bob. 'We'll send our police car and driver back to Stranraer and make our way to Newton Stewart.'

'There's one more thing you should know, group captain. Within a few minutes of my coming into the station after you dropped me off outside, we received a phone call from a man asking if we knew anything about the victim. I need to be careful here and can't give you a name, but I met this man in Belfast earlier this year and know that he is, in a manner of speaking, a colleague of yours. Should we just say that he works for a sister organisation of yours, just six numbers smaller?'

Monique raised her eyebrows at Bob and could see from the expression on his face that he had also worked out that MI11 minus six made MI5.

'What did you tell him?' asked Bob.

'We had a rather peculiar conversation, like this one, but I was able to give him the essential information about the victim. I also told him of your organisation's involvement, without directly naming names, of course.'

'Thank you, inspector, that's very helpful.' Bob put the phone down and looked at Monique. 'You look like the cat that's got the cheese.'

Monique laughed. 'I know this is your first language and not mine but do you perhaps mean "cream", Bob?'

Bob smiled. 'You already had a good idea of what's going on and that conversation has confirmed it.'

'You read me much better than you used to, Bob. I will of course share my theory with you. First, we need to set Dorothy on her way and borrow a car to get us to Newton

Stewart.'

'I agree about sending Dorothy back, but we don't need a car. I'll get someone in the guardroom to drive us to the Mosquito. It's then only a short hop to RAF Wigtown and we've got a car there. Your flying jacket and other kit is in the nose compartment of the aircraft.'

When she left the guardroom, Monique was amused to see two RAF policemen standing beside the police car and Dorothy, still sitting in the driver's seat, holding a china cup and saucer. When she saw Monique approaching she said something to the policemen and one of them took the crockery from her before they turned to walk back towards the guardroom.

Monique got into the front passenger seat.

'I think they fancied their chances,' said Dorothy.

'You could do worse,' said Monique.

'I could do better,' said Dorothy. 'I'm going out with a flight lieutenant who helps run the RAF's Marine Craft Training School at Corsewall, on Loch Ryan, out beyond RAF Wig Bay. He's a kind and intelligent man who is also very attractive. And, touch wood, he's in a post that gives him a fair chance of surviving the war. It's early days yet, but I've got high hopes for us.'

'I'm so pleased for you,' said Monique, smiling. 'Anyway, this is goodbye, for the moment at least. Thanks for running us around, but we're now going to fly to RAF Wigtown which frees you up to return to Stranraer police station.'

An RAF Jeep pulled up outside the guardroom as Monique crossed back over the road and she waved as Dorothy turned the police car around.

The driver of the Jeep dropped them off at the Mosquito and Monique followed Bob into the aircraft after donning her flying jacket, life vest and flying helmet.

'This is very warm,' she said, 'and this canopy is like a greenhouse.'

Bob smiled. 'And now you can tell me what I failed to understand at the cottage, or I'm going on strike and we'll have to sit here in all this kit with the sun shining through the canopy.'

'We can talk on the way, Bob. But let's not sit here sweltering.'

After Bob had taken off into the sun he turned the aircraft to the left until they were flying in the opposite direction. As they came out of the turn he pointed past Monique. 'Just over there, at the head of that large bay, is where Major Malinovsky nearly shot me down yesterday.'

'That's a chilling thought,' said Monique. 'Speaking of Malinovsky, what happened this morning? I promise I'll stop teasing you about Christopher Donaldson, the Abwehr and MI5, but you need to show me yours first.'

Bob hadn't fastened his oxygen mask across his face and she saw him laugh.

'All right,' he said. 'When Anthony and I arrived at RAF Errol, Popov and three men were already in No. 305 Ferry Training Unit's offices with Major Malinovsky. They emerged as we got to the door from the airfield. Malinovsky had a man on either side of him and he wasn't allowed to stop or talk to me when I greeted him.

'While his escort marched him off to the aircraft they'd arrived in, Popov did stop and was keen to tell me that he took a very dim view of Malinovsky trying to shoot me down. After Maxim Kozlov tried to kill you and me to avenge Helena Berdyaev's death, Popov made it clear to his people that they could only kill with his approval. By a remarkable coincidence that Popov knew nothing about until last night, Major Malinovsky and Maxim Kozlov were maternal cousins. Malinovsky's attempt on my life was to avenge Kozlov's death and directly broke Popov's standing orders. Popov said he couldn't afford to forgive that. He also wanted Sir Peter Maitland and Commodore Cunningham to know that he was a man of his word.'

'That doesn't bode well for Malinovsky,' said Monique. 'I'd imagine that he can look forward to being locked up in an uncomfortable space on a Soviet ship on the next convoy bound for Archangel or Murmansk and then spending the rest of his, probably short, life in a forced labour camp in Siberia.'

'He was spared that,' said Bob. 'When I was flying Anthony back to Turnhouse we caught up with Popov's aircraft, just in time to see someone fall or be pushed out of it over the Firth of Forth at a height of 8,000 feet and without a parachute. It had to be Malinovsky.'

'Seriously?' asked Monique.

'Seriously. No one on Popov's aircraft would have seen the Mosquito behind it so he doesn't know that we know. That's one of the reasons I don't want to tell Katerina. The other is that Popov made it clear to me that he approved of what Malinovsky did in Stranraer. It placed Katerina's life in grave danger but was partly successful because the Cuttlefish was wounded.'

'You're right,' said Monique 'She'd not be at all happy to hear that, which might prove useful at some point.' She paused for effect. 'Very well, I promised in return to tell you what I think is going on.'

'Thank you, Monique.'

'If I'm right, you came very close to working it out while we were at Donaldson's cottage. As you said, we know that the Abwehr have no active spies in Britain because of Ultra interceptions of radio transmissions. Any who arrive are executed or turned and the result is a network of double agents that tells the Abwehr exactly what we want them to hear. What you may not know is that this operation is run by MI5 officers reporting to what is called the Double Cross Committee.

'You and I know from what they did in Stockholm the lengths the SD are prepared to go to discredit the Abwehr. I'm sure we will find out when we talk to Maurice Cunningham, but I think that Christopher Donaldson was one of this network of MI5 double agents and I think that the Cuttlefish is here because the SD suspects the Abwehr might be losing the intelligence war with MI5. If the SD can show just how comprehensively the Abwehr has been tricked it would utterly discredit them in the eyes of those who matter in Germany. That would be a catastrophe for the Abwehr, but it would also be a catastrophe for the whole Double Cross operation and perhaps for Ultra too.'

'That sounds more plausible than my theory,' said Bob. 'It explains why the Abwehr radio wasn't well hidden. Christoper Donaldson wasn't worried about MI5 finding it because he was working for them and they already knew it was there. Presumably, "Frederick" was Donaldson's Abwehr code name. The Cuttlefish knew that and the telegram, probably sent by feeding coins into the slot in the nearest public telephone box, was intended to panic Donaldson into doing exactly what he then did. It was a trap.'

'There are gaps in the picture that Maurice might be able to fill when we speak to him, but I'm sure you're right, Bob. The stakes are extremely high.'

CHAPTER TWENTY-NINE

The staff in the control tower at RAF Wigtown were happy for Bob and Monique to use a telephone in an office on the first floor. There was less delay in getting through this time. Monique again listened as Bob was put through to Mrs Croft.

'Hello, group captain, I'm afraid you've missed Commodore Cunningham.'

'Missed him? What do you mean?'

'He returned from his meeting not long after we spoke but then went out again a few minutes later.'

'I do need to speak to him,' said Bob. 'Do you know where I can reach him?'

'You can't, not for a while. He's on his way to see you. He should be most of the way to RAF Northolt by now, with Daniel Milford from MI5 who will be flying with him. You probably know better than the commodore how long it will take them to fly to Scotland in an Avro Anson, but he said it might be two hours or more.'

'Where's he intending to fly to?' asked Bob. 'We're at RAF Wigtown now, which is slightly closer to Northolt than we were when I first called.'

'Thank you. I was hoping you'd let me have that information before he took off. If you'll excuse me I'll telephone RAF Northolt and ask them to let the commodore know where you are.' Mrs Croft rang off.

Bob held the telephone receiver in the air for a moment before replacing it on its cradle. He looked at Monique. 'Do you know Daniel Milford in MI5?'

'No, but I'll bet you a bottle of gin that he's one of the MI5 officers I talked about who report to the Double Cross

Committee. And I'll bet you a lemon to slice into the gin that it was Mr Milford who rang Stranraer police station earlier to ask about Christopher Donaldson. As soon as MI5 found out that MI11 was involved, Maurice Cunningham was hauled off to a meeting with MI5 and Sir Peter Maitland, and now Maurice and the MI5 man are on their way to see us. That seems a fairly eloquent confirmation of the main elements of our theory.'

Bob smiled. 'Thank you for calling it "our" theory, my love. The lemon is probably worth more than the gin and will certainly be far harder to find, but I'll not take you up on either bet.' He looked at his watch. 'This has all the makings of becoming an extremely long day but I think we've got plenty of time to go to Newton Stewart to find out what's happening and still be back in time to meet the commodore's aircraft.'

*

Newton Stewart railway station lay just to the north of the main road towards Stranraer and a little west of the road into the town from Wigtown. They found it without difficulty despite the wartime absence of signposts. Monique parked close to the single-storey stone station building in a car park that was largely free of vehicles, apart from an old coach that had seen far better days at the far end of the car park, a baker's van carrying adverts on its sides and a police car.

'It's quieter than I expected,' said Bob after they'd got out of the car. 'I wonder if the investigation has moved on?' He looked round as he heard a car approaching from behind him. 'I may be wrong, but I think that's Michael and Katerina.'

'It's Michael anyway,' said Monique. 'He is on his own.'

The two of them watched as Michael Dixon parked his car next to theirs.

'We were told there had been a possible sighting of Edward Daly here,' said Bob as Michael got out.

'There was,' said Michael. 'A little after 3 p.m. this afternoon, an RAF flight lieutenant with a bandaged right hand turned up at the ticket window just through there and purchased a first class ticket to Dumfries. There are only two trains that stop here each day heading in that direction.' Michael looked at a notebook he'd taken out of his pocket. 'One is at 9.33 a.m. and the other at 4.21 p.m. It looked like the flight lieutenant intended to catch the 4.21 p.m. train which gets into Dumfries at 6.21 p.m. and then carries on to Euston station in London, where it is due to arrive at 5.33 a.m. tomorrow morning.'

Bob looked at his watch. 'So it left here about an hour ago and is due to get to Dumfries in an hour from now.'

'Who noticed this man?' asked Monique. 'And did he catch his train?'

'The stationmaster doubles as a ticket seller and he noticed the way the flight lieutenant fumbled with his money when he was paying for the ticket and how his hand appeared to be causing him pain. He asked if the flight lieutenant was all right and the man thanked him for his concern but said he was fine. The stationmaster said the man had a mild Liverpudlian accent.

'At about 3.30 p.m., the stationmaster's nephew, who is a police constable based at Newton Stewart police station, came to see his uncle and have a cup of tea. I get the impression it's a daily ritual. The nephew happened to mention the roadblocks that had been set up and the hunt for a man with an injured hand and the stationmaster told him about the flight lieutenant. The constable immediately telephoned the local police station and they in turn immediately telephoned Inspector White at Stranraer police station. When a sergeant and two constables arrived from the local station as reinforcements, all armed, the RAF flight lieutenant was nowhere to be found. This was at 3.50 p.m.

'The simple answer to your question about whether the flight lieutenant caught his train, Monique, is that we don't know. Two more policemen were here by the time it left, making six in total, and none of them saw anyone other than a woman with two young children and an elderly couple board the train. Inspector White and three more men arrived in time to see the train leave and Katerina and I were just behind them, with two more constables in the back.

'A full carload of Inspector White's men are on their way to Dumfries. The idea is to hold the train there when it arrives and search it properly, using the men from Stranraer and others based in Dumfries. Meanwhile, I drove Katerina, Inspector White and one of his men to Gatehouse of Fleet station which, despite the name, is in the middle of nowhere miles from the village it's named after. We managed to get ahead of the train and I dropped them off so they could board it there. The aim is to search it en route, using Katerina's ability to identify Edward Daly to flush him out if he's aboard.'

There was a long pause. Bob saw Monique catch his eye and he knew what she was thinking.

Then she asked the question that was in both their minds. 'Did anyone stop to think that the flight lieutenant drawing attention to his injured hand while buying his ticket might be a diversion?'

'Yes,' said Michael. 'The inspector and I discussed that in the car on the way to Gatehouse of Fleet station, but we were already behind the train and he was anxious not to lose it altogether. I was much more doubtful, and said so, but it was his decision to make. As I see it, we've got nearly every available policeman in south-west Scotland converging on Dumfries, leaving the rest of the area unprotected. The Cuttlefish must have driven here, so there's no reason why, having sent the police off on a wild goose chase, he couldn't simply have got back into his vehicle and driven to wherever he wanted to be.'

'That's true,' said Bob. 'Do any other trains leave here?'

'There's a timetable on the wall over there,' said Monique.

Bob walked over with her and Michael followed.

Monique put her finger on the timetable. 'Trains also go the other way along the main line, towards Stranraer. The last of those left at 10.18 a.m. and the next isn't due to leave until 7.35 p.m. There's also a branch line that goes roughly south from here, to Wigtown and Whithorn. A train left here for Whithorn at 4.42 p.m.'

'Where will that be now?' asked Bob.

'There are six stops shown. It's timetabled to arrive at Wigtown at 4.56 p.m., at Millisle for Garlieston at 5.19 p.m., and at Whithorn at 5.28 p.m.'

'So it's pretty much got to the end of the line as we speak?' asked Bob.

'I'm afraid so,' said Monique.

'Inspector White did leave two men here,' said Michael. 'Judging from the presence of that police car, they may still be around. Let's ask if they saw anything.'

It seemed the possibility of a diversion had occurred to the two constables and they said they had carefully checked the dozen or so passengers who boarded the train bound for Whithorn. While two of the passengers had been military officers, one army and one RAF, no one who boarded had an injured hand.

When they were back outside and standing by the cars, Bob looked at his watch again. 'Commodore Cunningham is currently flying up to see us with a man from MI5. We've got time to get back to the officers' mess at RAF Wigtown, grab a quick meal and still be on the airfield in time to meet them. I'd like you to join us, Michael.'

'Of course, Bob. Is there anything I need to know first?'

'Yes, good point, Michael. I suggest that Monique drives our car while I ride with you and bring you up to date on what we've been doing. We can start with a snippet about Major Malinovsky that I don't want Katerina to know about. Her absence is also quite handy because I wouldn't want her present at the meeting with the commodore.

CHAPTER THIRTY

Bob met Commodore Cunningham and Daniel Milford when they got out of their aircraft and then drove them the short distance to RAF Wigtown's engineering squadron headquarters. Monique and Michael were waiting in the same meeting room Bob had used when the Soviets arrived. A choice of tea or coffee was again laid on.

Bob sat next to Monique on one side of the table while Commodore Cunningham and the man he introduced as Daniel Milford from MI5 sat on the other. Michael sat at one end.

Milford was a dark-haired man in his forties and wore a suit that looked like it was too warm for him or perhaps, Bob thought, the sweating was because he hadn't enjoyed the flight from RAF Northolt.

'I'll tell you why we've come to see you presently, Bob,' said Commodore Cunningham. 'The most efficient way to proceed might be for you to bring us up to date with the latest developments here.'

Bob told them what had been established about the Cuttlefish's movements since he went into Stranraer harbour, about the police discovery of the base at Upper Milldown and Christopher Donaldson's body, and about what he and Monique had found in Cairnryan. Monique then briefly outlined their theory about Christopher Donaldson's role as a Double Cross agent and the SD's efforts to discredit the Abwehr.

Michael concluded with a report of the latest possible sighting of the Cuttlefish and their suspicion that he had created a diversion. 'To bring that up to date, sir, I spoke to the police in Stranraer while Group Captain Sutherland was meeting your aircraft. They are a little out of touch but know that the train arrived on schedule in Dumfries with Inspector White on it. The most recent information they had was that a search of it was underway but, at that point, the Cuttlefish hadn't been found.'

'Thank you,' said the commodore. 'We'll fill in the picture from our side. You seem to have worked it out anyway, but I can confirm that Daniel reports to the Double Cross committee and is Christopher Donaldson's handler.'

Daniel Milford grimaced. 'I was, anyway. As background, it's worth telling you that Donaldson studied in Germany and later returned to that country to work as a junior harbourmaster in Hamburg in the mid-1930s. He married a German woman and the Abwehr tried to recruit him as an agent, presumably thinking that sooner or later he'd return to a port in Britain and might be useful to them. I say "tried" because he reported the approach to a British diplomat, who passed the information on to MI6. He's been a double agent ever since. His German wife was, ironically enough, killed in the Clydebank Blitz in March 1941.

'Throughout his time in Cairnryan, he's operated as the controller of a phantom network of non-existent agents. This is a typical pattern for the Double Cross agents and allows us to feed false intelligence to the Abwehr on a wide range of subjects. I know that Donaldson recorded detailed information about his agents in a black leather-bound notebook he kept with his Abwehr radio. It helped to maintain the mythology if he was consistent about their ages, backgrounds and circumstances when reporting intelligence they had supposedly passed to him for onward transmission. Did you find anything like that at his cottage?'

'No,' said Monique. 'But I wasn't looking for it. I was

after the Abwehr code book, which I found and kept. I'll let you have it at the end of the meeting, just so you know where it is.'

Bob went to pick up his teacup, then thought better of it. 'If the Cuttlefish is trying to prove the Abwehr's intelligence network is being manipulated by MI5 then, as I see it, he has two possible approaches open to him now. The first is to find the people who the Abwehr believe worked for Donaldson as agents. Do you have a list of who they are meant to be, Daniel? We don't need their inside leg measurements, but names and locations might allow us to work out where the Cuttlefish could go next.'

'None of them have real names,' said Daniel Milford. 'They only have code names. But I do have a list I can let you have, group captain. I'll not waste time telling you how sensitive it is because it's entirely possible that Edward Daly already knows what's on it, either from Donaldson's notebook or from whoever in the Abwehr has been passing information to the SD.' Milford took an envelope out of an inside pocket and passed it over the table to Bob.

'You said the Cuttlefish had two approaches open to him, Bob,' said Commodore Cunningham. 'What's the other?'

Bob could see the commodore already knew what he was going to say. 'If the SD knows the identity, the Abwehr code name and the location of one Double Cross agent then they might have the same information about more of them. It's possible that instead of going after the lower-level agents who were meant to be reporting to Donaldson, the Cuttlefish might decide instead to go after more of the real Double Cross agents. Are there others in the area?'

'We're ahead of you on that one, group captain,' said Milford. 'The next nearest to here are in Ayr and Dumfries, with others on Clydeside and in Glasgow, as well as in Leith and Carlisle. However, that isn't your problem. Special Branch officers from the relevant police forces should already be with each of those men or women. They will stay with them until we've found the Cuttlefish. The aim is to keep them alive and keep them sending an uninterrupted stream of carefully concocted reports to the Abwehr.'

'If buying a train ticket to Dumfries was a diversion by the Cuttlefish then it was a clever one,' said Monique. 'It raises the threat that he might be going after the Double Cross agent located there, assuming he knows of their existence.'

'That's true,' said Milford. 'I'll look at increasing that agent's protection, just in case. Losing one of them is already a serious blow.'

'But as far as MI11 is concerned, you want us to focus on the fake agents who supposedly reported to Donaldson,' said Bob.

'That's right,' said Milford.

Commodore Cunningham pushed at his cup and saucer awkwardly, as if he was unsure how to phrase what he wanted to say. 'Bob, there's one more thing I need to tell you, and this comes directly from Sir Peter Maitland. It is possible that Edward Daly already knows enough to cause huge damage to Double Cross and possibly to Ultra. That means…'

There was a long pause.

Monique smiled grimly. 'What you're telling us, commodore, is that when we catch up with the Cuttlefish we are not to take him alive.'

'That's it, exactly. I can't let you have a written order to that effect, but it is an order, nonetheless. Can you live with that, Bob?'

'If I'd been told when I was offered this job that I'd ever be given an order like that, I'd have turned it down, sir. But a lot's happened over the intervening months and I'm not the same man I was then. I can't guarantee we'll catch the Cuttlefish, but we will do our damnedest, and I will ensure that we don't take him alive. Having said that, if he was on the train to Dumfries then the Cuttlefish may already be in police custody. If so, I'm afraid you will have to look elsewhere to find someone prepared to silence him permanently.'

'Thank you, Bob,' said the commodore. 'And I understand your last point.'

'Can I ask Daniel a question?' asked Monique.

'Of course,' said the commodore.

'Was it you who Christoper Donaldson rang after he got the "Hello Frederick" telegram?'

'He tried, but I was out of the office and so were my immediate colleagues. My phone was answered by someone in a nearby office but in an unrelated area of work who happened to be passing my door. They wrote down a message for me. The message was just a single word, a codeword meant to be used only in the most extreme of circumstances when an agent believes they are in immediate danger. Its significance wasn't recognised by the person who took the message so nothing was done about it.

'I was out of the office for longer than planned. When I read the message I tried to contact Donaldson at the port headquarters in Cairnryan. Someone else picked up his phone so I rang off. I then called the police station in Stranraer. When I said who I was they put me on to a Royal Ulster Constabulary Special Branch inspector who's working with them. I had met him in Belfast not all that long ago and he remembered me. It was awkward because it was an insecure line but he told me that he'd just returned to the police station from a murder scene and that Donaldson had been the victim. He also told me in a roundabout way that MI11 was involved in the investigation. That's when my boss rang Sir Peter Maitland. The rest you know.'

'Thank you,' said Monique.

'Is there anything else you need from us, Daniel?' asked Bob.

'If you could ask the RAF to lend me a van, something with a lockable rear luggage area without windows, that would help.'

'Can I ask why?'

'I need to tidy things up at the cottage Donaldson was using in Cairnryan and will drive over there this evening. I particularly need to remove the radio and find the notebook in which he kept details of his agents if it's still there, though I have a feeling it isn't. Do you happen to have the key to the cottage?'

'Sorry, no,' said Monique. 'There were no keys on Donaldson's body so I suspect the Cuttlefish has them. You should take care in case he's doubled back having laid a false trail in Newton Stewart, though you don't need me to tell you that. I can't see him returning to Cairnryan anyway given that he knows Donaldson will have been missed by now. And you might want to make sure you've got a torch. It stays light until late here at this time of year but the lightbulb in the bedroom was broken when Daly attacked Donaldson and you might not want to keep the blackout blinds open and take the chance of someone in the street seeing what you're doing through the net curtains.'

'Thank you. I'll find a way in, just as you did, Madame

Dubois. I will also need to talk to the harbourmaster at Cairnryan, Captain Allenby, though that might need to wait until tomorrow morning.'

'There's one other thing,' said Monique. 'We got the sense Donaldson might have formed a relationship with a colleague, a dark-haired lady aged around forty who works in the next office. She became very upset when she heard about his death.'

'I'll talk to her to see if Donaldson told her anything he shouldn't have done,' said Milford.

'I've got the plane and pilot waiting and will return to Northolt,' said Commodore Cunningham. 'That will leave you unencumbered in your efforts to find the Cuttlefish, Bob.'

'And kill him,' said Monique.

Bob saw Maurice Cunningham wince.

*

After the meeting, Monique drove Commodore Cunningham the short distance back to his waiting aircraft and Daniel Milford made a phone call to arrange increased security for the Double Cross agent in Dumfries.

When Milford finished his call, Bob asked a corporal he saw in the corridor how to get to RAF Wigtown's motor transport section. As it was just around the corner, he suggested to Milford that they walk.

The MT section turned out to be much like equivalent units on every other RAF station Bob had been based at or visited. Two rows of sheds faced each other across a broad concrete yard in which vehicles of all types were parked.

The evening shift was busy and the flying officer in charge, who had seen Bob talking to Group Captain

Belmont in the officers' mess bar two nights earlier, was very happy to help. He produced a form he wanted Milford to complete and then handed over the ignition and door keys for an RAF van with an enclosed load area and no windows behind the front seats.

After Milford drove off, Bob walked back to the engineering squadron headquarters and found Monique and Michael in the meeting room.

'I've got bad news,' said Michael. 'I've telephoned Stranraer police station again and they've heard that the search of the train in Dumfries was completed without finding any sign of Edward Daly.'

'I think we expected that anyway,' said Bob. 'What about Katerina?'

'The police are driving her back, though she might not be here until later.'

'I suppose it would have been far too easy for the Cuttlefish to be arrested on the train,' said Bob. 'Right. If it's going to be our job to focus on Christopher Donaldson's stable of phantom agents, we'd better see what we've got to work with. Excluding Katerina from this when she returns is going to be awkward, but we need to avoid mentioning this document or its significance to her.'

He took the envelope Daniel Milford had given him out of his inside pocket and extracted a single piece of paper from it, which he opened and laid flat on the meeting room table. Monique and Michael stood on either side of him, so they could also see.

'Is that it?' they both asked, simultaneously.

Bob turned the sheet of paper over to find the reverse was blank, and then back again. 'Yes, that's it. I'd laugh if I didn't feel so deflated. I'm sorry I didn't open it when Daniel Milford was still here.'

‘It may not be that bad,’ said Monique. ‘Yes, I think I expected more than…’ she paused for a moment, ‘…twelve agents. I also expected more information about each of them. Let’s look at what we do have. Each has a code name based on a German female given name with a unique first letter, starting with Astrid and working through the alphabet to Liesl.’

‘What concerns me is how sparse the information is about each of them,’ said Michael.

‘The Double Cross agents probably don’t need more than this to allow them to function,’ said Monique. ‘Remember that these aren’t real people. Take Dagmar for example. He or she works at the explosives factory at Carsegowan Moss, north of Wigtown. Helga is a retired railway worker who has a house overlooking Stranraer harbour. Jutta is a farm worker who works on a farm next to RAF Castle Kennedy. Katja is a civilian motor engineer employed at RAF Wig Bay. Liesl is a fisherman who works out of Portpatrick, and so on. This gives a perfectly good starting point for fake intelligence to be sent back to the Abwehr by the Double Cross agent running the network. It sounds like Christopher Donaldson added more background detail as he went along, and recorded that in his leather-bound notebook so he could ensure he was consistent in future reports supposedly originating from individual agents.’

‘That worries me,’ said Bob. ‘If Edward Daly found the notebook, does he already have sufficient proof for his needs? Can he show that these agents are fake without needing to investigate any further?’

‘Hopefully not,’ said Monique. ‘If Christopher Donaldson had any sense, and we have to remember that he was a double agent for a long time, he’d have written his notes about his phantom agents as if they were real people but kept them anonymous and untraceable. Daniel Milford talked about the notebook containing information about the phantom agents' ages, backgrounds and circumstances. That might allow the Cuttlefish to come closer to working out who they ought to be, but hopefully not close enough. I think he's still got work to do before he can prove those individuals don't exist and the Abwehr is being duped.'

'I accept all that,' said Bob. 'Monique, you've had more experience of this sort of thing than Michael or I. If you were the Cuttlefish and knew what was typed on this list, what would you do now?'

'I'm not sure,' she said. 'I think this is the wrong place to start.'

'What do you mean?' asked Michael.

'Wouldn't it be much better to focus on the Double Cross agents themselves? If you could induce one or more of them to admit they are double agents working for MI5, and perhaps sign statements to that effect, then surely that's all that's needed? It's pure speculation, but perhaps Daly took Donaldson's unconscious body back to Upper Milldown in the hope he could make him talk, then killed him when he didn't recover consciousness.'

'I agree with your logic,' said Bob. 'But MI5 and Special Branch are looking after the Double Cross agents. We've been charged with getting ahead of the Cuttlefish as far as Donaldson's phantom network is concerned. I don't think we've got the option of telling Maurice Cunningham and Sir Peter Maitland that there's no point, even if that's what we believe.'

'So what should we do Bob?' asked Michael.

'I'm exhausted,' said Bob. 'Let's sleep on it, perhaps after a drink in the officers' mess bar.

'That sounds like an excellent idea,' said Monique.

'Hang on,' said Michael. 'It doesn't help us catch the Cuttlefish, but have you noticed anything about the locations on that list?'

'You obviously have,' said Monique. 'What is it?'

'The match is far from perfect, but there's a good overlap between locations for non-existent members of Christopher Donaldson's phantom network and places where the presence of the mysterious MI5 tramp was reported.'

Bob thought he could see what Michael had in mind. 'Are you suggesting that Donaldson went to look at some of the locations used for members of his phantom network while disguised as a tramp so he could make the reports he was passing to the Abwehr more believable?'

'I was, but it doesn't work when you think about it,' said Michael. 'In his official capacity, he'd have been able to visit most of those places, the explosives factory perhaps excepted, without taking the huge risk of pretending to be an MI5 agent who was pretending to be a tramp, who would simply look to almost everyone he encountered like an enemy spy. It must be a coincidence.'

'With Donaldson dead, we're never going to know,' said Monique. 'But it is an interesting idea. Should we go and find that drink, gentlemen? I think I might have gin in all of my tonics tonight.'

CHAPTER THIRTY-ONE

Monique sat back in the car and watched the pleasant Galloway scenery pass by as Bob drove. It was another superb morning with clear blue skies and the temperature was already climbing. Monique's experience of Scotland was too limited to judge for herself, but everyone she heard talking about it said how remarkable the weather had been. Most then went on to predict its imminent collapse into thunderstorms, but that hadn't happened so far.

Monique looked across the car at Bob. She knew she was on his blind, left, side so he probably wasn't aware she was looking. They had been married for a day less than four weeks and she wanted to shout with joy at the idea of spending her life with him. She wondered if anyone else had ever had such an eventful start to their married life. First Malta, then Bamber Bridge, and now the Cuttlefish.

They'd not drunk much in the officers' mess bar the previous night. Katerina had been very subdued when the police dropped her off. She soon disappeared with Michael, presumably intending to make the end of her day more pleasurable than the rest of it had been. When the two of them appeared together at breakfast, Katerina was bright and bubbly and it seemed that Michael's restorative powers were undimmed by his rejection by Betty Swanson.

An early night had also allowed Bob to exercise his restorative powers and Monique smiled at the memory.

'A penny for your thoughts.'

She realised Bob had turned his head to look at her and had caught her smile.

'I was just thinking about going to bed with you last night. Thank you.'

'Thank you, too,' said Bob. 'It's what newlyweds are meant to do, isn't it?'

'I'd like to think we'll still be doing it long after we're newlyweds.'

'Me too.'

They lapsed into a comfortable silence for a mile or two.

'At the risk of introducing less pleasant thoughts, what do you think of Michael's idea?' asked Bob.

'It's a good one,' said Monique, 'and not just because we want to keep Katerina away from the whole subject of the Double Cross agents. The charade about buying a ticket to Dumfries was intended to be a diversion, and we know that a train to Whithorn left Newton Stewart twenty minutes after the train to Dumfries. What if Edward Daly did somehow get on board without the remaining policemen seeing him? There aren't many stations on the line. Michael and Katerina visiting each of them to ask if anyone saw a military officer with an injured hand when the train arrived is a good use of their time.'

'You stopped short of saying it, Monique, but I get the sense you think that might be more worthwhile than what we're doing.'

'You really are getting better at reading me, Bob. But given what we've been ordered to do, I agree with you that the best approach is to talk to Daniel Milford in Cairnryan. He's seen the Double Cross system in operation and might be able to offer some ideas about using the list he gave you to close in on the Cuttlefish. When you suggested it, I was worried we might pass him as he drove back to RAF Wigtown and have a wasted journey. Having talked to the police in Stranraer we at least know he's gone back to the cottage this morning with Inspector Boyle.'

Neither of them said much for the rest of the drive.

As they approached Christopher Donaldson's cottage, Bob slowed down to let two large military lorries coming the other way pass and then pulled over to the wrong side of the road where he parked nose-on to a van painted in RAF blue grey.

'I assume that's Daniel Milford's van,' said Monique.

'It is.'

The cottage door was opened by Inspector Boyle in response to Bob's knock.

'Come in, both of you. Close the door behind you. Daniel found most of what he wanted yesterday evening but we're staying in the same hotel in Stranraer and after a few pints in the bar last night I was rash enough to offer to help him give the place a more thorough going over this morning.'

Monique looked around the lounge, which had changed considerably since she'd last seen it. 'Including lifting lino and floorboards and looking behind skirting boards,' she said.

'That's right, Madame Dubois.' Daniel Milford had appeared in the doorway leading to the bedroom. 'I wanted to be certain that the notebook I talked about had been taken by the Cuttlefish. If that meant pulling a few things to pieces then so be it. We started in the lounge and moved on to the kitchen and toilet and, no, despite my best hopes, Donaldson didn't hide it in an oilskin package in the high-level cistern.'

'Which is why you're now in the bedroom,' said Monique.

'That's also right. The cupboards are the biggest challenge. I emptied everything out last night, including a lot of stuff that can't be Donaldson's which I think came with the cottage. But the one time I visited him here I had the impression he kept the notebook near the radio so we've been going over the cupboards with a fine-tooth comb.'

Monique realised the implication of the grin on Daniel Milford's face. 'You've found it, haven't you?'

'Yes, just now in a void behind the bottom drawer beneath the wardrobe. It was a bit of a stretch to reach, but then Donaldson was a tall man with longer arms than me.' Milford held up a grubby black leather notebook.

'That's good,' said Bob, 'but it's not why we came to talk to you. Can I assume that Inspector Doyle knows what Donaldson was doing here and why?'

'I do,' said the inspector. 'Daniel told me last night. I had to find a secure phone at the Stranraer port headquarters this morning to ensure that my Special Branch colleagues are fully protecting Double Cross agents in Northern Ireland. I know we think the Cuttlefish is on this side of the North Channel but it's better to be safe than sorry.'

'After you left RAF Wigtown, Daniel, I opened the document you gave me,' said Bob.

'What did you make of it?'

'We concluded that we had been sent on a wild goose chase,' said Monique. 'Twelve female code names and twelve very brief descriptions and that's it. Now the notebook has been removed from the equation, the best information the Cuttlefish can possibly have is the Abwehr's version of the list you gave us. There's no way that he can use that to try to gather evidence that the Abwehr has had the wool pulled over its eyes by MI5.'

'Is that all?' asked Milford.

'No,' said Monique. 'We also concluded that the Cuttlefish's only realistic chance of success is to go after the Double Cross agents themselves. Moving Donaldson from the bedroom of this cottage to a lorry parked outside must have been very difficult, especially given Donaldson was physically bigger and Daly had an injured hand. But let's assume his strategy was to force Donaldson to talk when he had him back at Upper Milldown. Once he got him there, he realised that he'd hit Donaldson harder than he intended and he wasn't going to regain consciousness quickly, if at all. Daly therefore killed him and dumped his body there.'

'That would fit with what we know from the scene,' said Inspector Boyle. 'The best guess is that the lorry was reversed along the track behind the farm and then Mr Donaldson's body was simply dragged out very close to where it was found.'

'I need a straight answer,' said Bob. 'Are we wasting our time with the list you gave us, Daniel?'

'You should take the honest answer to that question as a compliment, group captain. As we thought it likely that the Cuttlefish would have a copy of that list or something very like it, we had to test what he might be able to discover from it once he was in the area.'

'So MI5 set MI11 a puzzle that you believed made no sense?' asked Monique.

'It was the best way to be certain that it didn't make any sense to the Cuttlefish. Your team has a very high reputation with the powers that be in British military intelligence, group captain. It was felt that if you couldn't make sense of the list then no one else would either.'

'I've heard some backhanded compliments in my time,' said Bob, 'but that may top them all. Did Maurice Cunningham know that you were setting us up to fail?'

'No, that was agreed with Sir Peter Maitland before

Commodore Cunningham joined the meeting.'

'That's something, at least,' said Bob. 'What do you expect us to do now?'

'What would you be doing if I'd not given you the list?' asked Milford.

'Half my team, if you include the NKVD stray we've acquired, is currently checking railway stations on the line from Newton Stewart to Whithorn to see if the Cuttlefish boarded a train that left twenty minutes after the one the police thought he'd caught to Dumfries. I will go and see how they're getting on.'

'I'm sorry if you're angry about this, group captain,' said Milford. 'It really is useful to know that the Abwehr's list of agents won't be of help to the Cuttlefish. When we've finished here I'll go to Lochryan House to talk to Captain Allenby and the lady you mentioned.'

Daniel Milford turned back into the bedroom. After a moment, Bob turned and walked out of the cottage. Monique followed.

'Don't take it badly, group captain,' said Inspector Boyle, who had also come out onto the pavement. 'There's a saying where I come from that you should count your rings and your fingers after you've shaken hands with MI5.'

Bob smiled. 'It's been good to meet you, inspector, have a safe journey home.'

Bob was quiet after he turned the car around and drove back through Cairnryan.

'You didn't tell the inspector that my home department is MI5,' said Monique, smiling.

'No, it seemed best to leave him with the last word. I might need a friend on the Emerald Isle one of these days.'

*

Bob turned off the main road and soon afterwards passed Kirkcowan railway station. As they entered the village itself, he realised that a red light on the top of the dashboard was flashing.

'That's the radio, Bob!' said Monique.

Bob saw her reach under the dashboard and pull out what looked like a bulky telephone handset on the end of a coiled wire.

'Hello. Yes, it's Monique. Hello, Michael. Where? Can you say that again? Wigtown railway station?' She looked at Bob. 'Perhaps twenty minutes.'

Bob saw her return the handset to its cradle.

'I take it we're going to Wigtown railway station,' he said.

'We are,' said Monique. 'I think Michael wanted to say something else but the signal died.'

As Bob drove into Wigtown, Monique started to give directions. 'It's only a one-inch map so the detail is lacking, but we should find our way to the central area with the Red Lion Inn on its northern side. Then we turn right to pass in front of the large building opposite, then left alongside it. That's it. Now we turn right at the end. The railway station should be at the bottom of this road. That might be handy, we've just passed the police station on our right.'

'The rather gothic building with all the looming chimneys?' asked Bob.

'That's the one. And the railway station's just beyond the junction ahead of us. I think that's the entrance. There are Michael and Katerina.'

'And on the other side of the car park are two police cars and a Humber heavy utility car with RAF markings,' said

Bob.

'Perhaps that's why Michael looks like the cat that's got the cheese,' said Monique.

Bob laughed. 'You're never going to let me forget that, are you?'

Bob pulled up next to Michael's car and got out.

'Hello, Bob,' said Michael.

What's going on?' asked Bob.

'Katerina and I did what we agreed at breakfast,' said Michael. 'We drove down to the far end of the line, at Whithorn, and worked our way back via each of the stations that the 4.42 p.m. train from Newton Stewart stopped at. The distances aren't large and, fortunately, there is a late morning train that comes down the line from Newton Stewart, so none of the stations had been abandoned by their staff.

'Less fortunately, no one saw anyone resembling our man. I made a point of asking about the two military officers who were seen boarding at Newton Stewart and can tell you that the RAF officer got off here and the army officer went to the end of the line at Whithorn, which is what you might expect given this is the closest station to RAF Wigtown and Whithorn is the nearest to Cairn Head. Neither of them, or anyone else, seemed to have an injured hand. It occurred to both Katerina and me that at a couple of the stations it would have been perfectly possible to get off the wrong side of the train, climb down to the track and avoid being seen by station staff, but there was nothing to suggest that anyone did.'

'So why are we at Wigtown station?' asked Bob.

'This was the first stop for the train yesterday after it left Newton Stewart,' said Michael. 'Katerina and I talked to the stationmaster and a porter and heard about the RAF officer with the uninjured hand getting off yesterday afternoon's train. They had nothing else to tell of any interest. Then we came back to our car. I'd not noticed it when we went in, but something caught my eye about the Humber utility car over there. We went back into the station and asked about it, and were told it had been there since yesterday afternoon, though no one saw who was driving it or where they went when they got out.

'If you look around, it's obvious that this isn't exactly a convenient car park for the town, and there's plenty of parking there anyway. It just seemed odd. While Katerina and I were looking around the Humber the rear load area door sort of fell open, even though neither of us had touched it. Inside was a leather suitcase. Inside the suitcase was a damp and tatty army officer's uniform with possible bloodstains on the right sleeve. It had been rolled up in a towel. The suitcase also contained a naval officer's uniform, some shoes and underwear, some toiletries and a shaving kit, as well as parts of an RAF first aid kit and identity documents in several names. We called the police from the railway station and they arrived in no time at all as the police station's only just up the road.'

'Am I the only person in the team who doesn't know how to pick a lock?' asked Bob.

'That was me,' said Katerina, smiling. 'Michael can't either.'

'Well done, both of you,' said Bob. 'It appears that the Cuttlefish performed his diversion at Newton Stewart and then drove here. He would have had plenty of time to get here before the train arrived, so could have boarded it here. Except no one saw him doing so, or getting off anywhere else. We know an RAF officer got on at Newton Stewart and got off here, so that couldn't have been the Cuttlefish, even ignoring the injured hand.'

'He obviously intends to come back to the car,' said Monique. 'Everything he needs to carry out his mission is in that suitcase. We need to get the police to pull back and set up a 24-hour watch on the Humber and sooner or later they will catch him. I have more difficulty working out why he's done what he's done. As things stand he only has the uniform he's wearing, without even a bar of soap or a shaving brush. Where's he gone, and why?'

'That's the really important question,' said Bob. 'Have the police said anything about the Humber itself, Michael? It's got an RAF registration. The Cuttlefish has had that vehicle for over two weeks. It seems odd no one has reported it missing.'

'I'll talk to the sergeant who's currently in charge,' said Michael. 'He said Inspector White was on his way from Stranraer but might be some time, so I'll get him to pull his men back and keep watch until we can agree on a plan with the inspector.'

Bob looked at his watch. 'Let's go back to RAF Wigtown so I can call Commodore Cunningham on a secure line and bring him up to date. We can then come back here and talk to Inspector White. Monique, if you can drive Katerina, I'll ride with Michael and tell him about our visit to Cairnryan.'

CHAPTER THIRTY-TWO

The drive from the railway station wasn't far, but Monique and Katerina were still some way ahead of Michael and Bob by the time they reached the main entrance to the technical site and airfield at RAF Wigtown.

Bob had taken Monique to one side as they were about to leave the station and told her to meet him at the telephone exchange on the base. He thought Katerina might take advantage of being there to ring Yevgeny Popov at the Soviet embassy in London and, if she did, he wanted to listen in again.

Security had been tight when the little convoy of three MI11 cars first arrived at RAF Wigtown on Monday, with papers being checked and a phone call made to someone higher up the pecking order. But, since then, Monique had grown used to being waved through. There were times when being noticeable was beneficial and she and Bob were both, in different ways, noticeable.

This time, however, the RAF police corporal manning the barrier didn't lift it. Instead, he raised his hand to indicate that Monique should stop.

Monique's window was already wound down to counter the heat of the day and the policeman walked round to her side of the car.

'I'm sorry ma'am. I've got an urgent message for Group Captain Sutherland. I can see he's not with you. Do you know where he is? The guards at the gate to the domestic site are also looking out for him.'

'He should be here shortly. I can take the message if you like.'

'I'm sorry, ma'am, it's addressed to him. If I lift the

barrier, would you mind waiting in the pull-off area over there?'

'Not at all.' Monique did as instructed.

'What do you think it is?' asked Katerina.

'It's probably Commodore Cunningham wanting to know what's happening.' She glanced in her mirror. 'Here are Bob and Michael now.'

Monique turned round in her seat to watch as the RAF police corporal gave Bob an envelope. Michael then pulled in behind Monique's car.

'Let's find out,' said Monique, getting out of the car.

Bob was looking at a piece of paper when Monique arrived at his side window.

'This is intriguing,' he said, passing it to her.

Monique looked at it. 'It's handwritten, marked as extremely urgent and addressed to you, Bob. It's from Flight Lieutenant Somerset. It says that he has information he believes is critically important to national security and, as he knows that you are with military intelligence, he would like you to call on him at the 175 Squadron office on the airfield as soon as possible.'

'We'd better find out what he wants,' said Bob. 'He didn't strike me as a time-waster so we need to treat this at face value. Monique, you drive and I'll show you the way. Michael and Katerina can follow in this car.'

Bob directed Monique onto a road that led around the edge of the airfield.

'Do you think including Katerina is a good idea, Bob? Adrian Somerset was there when Major Malinovsky tried to shoot you down. What if this has something to do with that?'

'That's a good point,' said Bob. 'Michael and Katerina can wait outside until we know what's going on. This is where we want to be, the grey building on this side of the line of aircraft.'

'Are those Typhoons? I've seen them flying around the area but never close up. They look brutal, don't they?'

'They do. I described them as beasts the first time I saw them this close.'

Two pilots in full flying gear emerged from the building just as Bob and Monique approached, stepping aside to make way for them.

'I'm looking for Flight Lieutenant Somerset,' said Bob. 'Is he here?'

'Yes, sir,' said one of the pilots. 'Turn right along the central corridor and his office is at the end.'

Bob led the way. The door at the end of the corridor was closed and Bob knocked on it. Monique noticed that it carried the words 'Flight Commander' on a little wooden plaque, but no name.

Adrian Somerset opened the door. Monique saw a look of relief cross his face. 'Group Captain Sutherland, thank you for coming. Please, come in.'

Monique followed Bob into the office. There were two windows, one on the end wall and the other looking out at the aircraft parked nearby. A desk was set near the corner formed by the walls with the windows. The wall with the door set in it carried a large blackboard divided into a grid that obviously had something to do with the operation or servicing of the aircraft. The other windowless wall was covered with a large map of south-west Scotland, in front of which was a large but very battered leather sofa.

A matching armchair had been placed at an angle to it. This was almost immediately behind the door and as Adrian closed it Monique saw a very striking young woman stand up from the armchair. She had red shoulder-length curly hair and though her eyes were red and puffy, they were still as startlingly green as any Monique had ever seen. The woman wore a creased floral blouse and beige skirt and seemed to be in her late twenties.

'Would the two of you mind sitting on the sofa?' asked Adrian. 'I'll pull the chair to this side of the desk. Can I introduce Doctor Grace Sullivan?'

Monique saw Bob glance at her as they sat down and knew he wanted her to take the lead.

'Hello, Dr Sullivan,' she said. She introduced Bob and herself. 'Please call me Monique. Can I call you Grace?'

The woman nodded.

'Thank you. Was it you who asked Adrian to contact military intelligence?'

'Yes, it was. I work as a doctor in the auxiliary hospital at Galloway House, which is near the coast just to the south of Garlieston. Adrian and I met when he suffered a head injury while playing cricket a couple of weekends ago. We got on well and agreed to have lunch together at the hotel in Garlieston on the following Friday, which was two weeks ago today.

'When he was driving me back afterwards, we were stopped and I was asked to look at a body that had been found as the tide went out in Garlieston Bay. I later discovered that this was Private Stanley Young, who had disappeared while on guard duty at a coastal lookout a couple of miles further south very early on the Wednesday morning. He had been garrotted.'

There was a long pause. Monique wanted to get Grace talking again so floated an ambiguous question the woman could interpret as she wished. 'How did you come to be here?'

'I rang Adrian from the hospital earlier this morning and

asked him to meet me in Garlieston. He heard what I had to say and thought I should come here while he contacted you.'

'What is it you want to tell us?' asked Monique.

'You've probably guessed from my accent that I'm from Eire. I came from a well-off family. My father was an eminent lawyer who died before his time from a heart attack. I studied medicine and became a doctor. I'm working at Galloway House because I heard they had a post available that came with its own cottage, which is in the grounds near the walled garden. That matters because my mother had a stroke early last year and needs a lot of care. I was always closest to her after Father died and I thought that the cottage would allow me to practice as a doctor while also caring for Mother.'

Grace paused for a moment before continuing. 'I have three older brothers. The youngest of them became a fisherman, much to my mother's displeasure, while the middle one married into a wealthy farming family, which she thought was slightly more worthy. The oldest one, Edward, was influenced by my mother's strong anti-English political views and became involved with some very dubious people. Rather than study in Dublin, he wanted to go to a German university and then spent much of his time abroad, doing God only knows what.'

'Can I stop you there?' asked Monique. 'Is your oldest brother in his mid-thirties with dark hair and of average height and build?'

'That's right. He's 34.'

'And does he have a scar about 10cm long across the top of his right thigh that he tells people he acquired in a sabre fight?' asked Monique.

'How on earth do you know that?' asked Grace. 'Do you

know him?'

'I've only met him in passing, but I have a Soviet friend who got to know him well enough in Madrid to learn about his scar. She knew him as Edward Daly, which is also the name he's been using recently. Look, Grace, I'm sorry to cut your story short, but do you know where your brother is?'

'Yes, he's at Broom Cottage, where I live with my mother. He's heavily drugged, so won't be leaving in a hurry. He arrived last night with a badly injured right hand, asking me for help. He wouldn't say what happened, but I think he was shot. The side of the hand below the base of the index finger and above the base of the thumb is in a bad way and I think he'll be lucky ever to regain full use of it.'

Monique could feel Bob move on the sofa next to her and was growing impatient herself. 'Do you mind if we stop there?' she asked. 'It's imperative we take your brother into custody and we need to leave immediately. We have two colleagues outside, including the Soviet lady I just mentioned. I suggest you come with us, Grace, and we can hear the rest of what you've got to say on the way.'

'I should come too,' said Adrian Somerset.

'Just ensure you stay out of the way when we get there, flight lieutenant,' said Bob, opening the office door.

When they got outside, Bob strode over to where Michael and Katerina were standing by their car.

'We know where he is. He's heavily drugged but I don't want to take any chances. Michael, find the officer commanding the RAF Regiment unit here. There must be one. Pass on to him my direct order that he has ten minutes to assemble twenty of his men, fully armed, with two lorries and set them on their way to Broom Cottage, which is near the walled garden in the grounds of Galloway

House, close to Garlieston. Then I want you to let Inspector White, or whoever is available in the Wigtownshire Constabulary, know that's where our man is before you and Katerina head there with all speed.'

Meanwhile, Monique was chaperoning Grace into the back of the other staff car and Adrian into the front passenger seat. She wanted to find out as much as she could from Grace and knew that once they arrived at Broom Cottage the chance might have gone.

Bob was an excellent driver in daylight, but Monique tried not to think about the speed they were going as she braced herself to avoid sliding around on the back seat.

'I think you only told us part of your story, Grace, back in Adrian's office. What else should we know?' asked Monique.

'Edward turned up last night wearing an RAF flight lieutenant's uniform. I know that he also visited Mother just over two weeks ago, and stayed over on the Tuesday night of the week Adrian and I had lunch together. I was on night duty in Galloway House so literally only met him as he was leaving the next morning. That time he was wearing a naval officer's uniform but driving an RAF vehicle, which he'd left out of sight just around the corner from the cottage. That seemed very odd, but he's my older brother so I didn't question it.

'I've been aware over the last couple of days of a search for a military officer with an injured hand and gather that both the police and military intelligence have rung the hospital to see if one has turned up needing treatment. It was obvious to me when Edward arrived last night that he was the man everyone was looking for. But he was exhausted and he needed medical help so I gave it to him, even though it meant going back to the hospital to steal bandages and drugs.

'I've told you about the severity of the injury, and when I took another look at it early this morning it seemed even worse. He needs an operation on his hand and while I could probably perform it, it would have to be done in the hospital rather than in the cottage.'

'What caused you to contact Adrian?' asked Monique.

'I let Edward come out from under the sedation this morning, though I kept him on the morphine for the pain. I wanted to discuss his hand with him but he strayed off the subject in a very uninhibited way.'

'How?' asked Monique.

'He tried to taunt me that Mother supported his anti-English and pro-German politics rather than my more pragmatic approach to the world. He told me that he was in Scotland on a secret mission that could transform Germany's ability to conduct the war. He also said that on his last visit, Mother told him about top secret work being done by the British military along the coast here. She sees very few people so I don't know where she got that from, it certainly wasn't me. Edward said that he had more important things to do in Scotland, but to humour her he had taken a walk along the coast south of here in the middle of the night. He'd not seen anything of interest and had returned for a few hours of sleep before he had to leave.'

Given the point at which Grace had started her story in Adrian's office, Monique thought she knew where this was going. 'What happened then?'

'I sedated Edward again. The more rest he gets the more chance he has of recovery. But then I began to think about what he'd said about his previous visit to the cottage. I went through his uniform tunic pockets and found this.'

Grace opened her handbag and took out a brown

envelope, which she passed to Monique.

Monique peered inside. Then she reached in to pick up what was there, before she worked out what it was and snatched her hand back.

'What is it?' asked Adrian.

Monique realised that Grace hadn't shown it to him. 'It's a length of braided telephone handset cord strung between two large chromed ballbearings. It's a garrotte.'

'That's exactly the sort of thing that was used to kill Private Stanley Young,' said Grace. 'What Edward didn't tell me, but I'm certain about, was that on the night walk he took to humour our mother, he encountered and killed a sentry, who I then attended when his body turned up two days later. Whether Edward is my brother or not, I can't live with that. That's why I contacted Adrian.'

'Thank you, Grace,' said Monique. 'This must be very difficult for you.'

'Has he killed anyone else?' asked Grace.

'Are you sure you want to know?' asked Monique.

'Yes, I am.'

'Very well. As far as we are aware, he killed a naval lieutenant in Belfast before his initial trip to Scotland. It was his uniform that Edward was wearing on his first visit to the cottage. Then he killed an RAF flight lieutenant and an army captain in or near Stranraer later that week, both of them for their uniforms and identity documents as they looked like him.'

'My God! Is that it?'

'I'm sorry, no. Edward then returned to Dublin, where he killed an elderly man who had forged documents for him and a German agent who was spying on Edward's arm of German intelligence for a competing one. Then, yesterday, he murdered one of the deputy harbourmasters at

Cairnryan.'

'I was going to ask you to promise not to harm him, but now I'm not so sure,' said Grace.

Bob had to stop the car at a security checkpoint. After he pulled away Monique caught his eye in the driving mirror.

'You took his garrotte,' said Bob. 'Does Edward have any other weapons you know about, Grace?'

'He had a pistol when he arrived last night,' said Grace. 'But when I left this morning I took it and threw it into some bushes a good way from the cottage.'

'Thank you,' said Bob. 'If he's drugged, sedated and unarmed, taking him into custody ought to be relatively straightforward.'

Monique wasn't superstitious, but she found herself wishing Bob hadn't said that.

CHAPTER THIRTY-THREE

Bob stopped the car on the road in front of Broom Cottage. Looking across the car and out of the window, Monique could see it was the sort of place she sometimes dreamed of sharing with him after the war was over. She knew nothing about gardening, but the pink roses climbing up the left-hand side of the cottage made her think she might want to learn. It took a conscious effort to return to the reason why they were there.

'Where's your brother?' she asked.

Grace took a moment to respond. 'He's in what is usually my bedroom, behind the left-hand dormer window. The other bedroom is my mother's. That's all there is upstairs.'

'What's the layout like downstairs?'

'Beyond the front door is a narrow hallway. That's where the stairs are and it also leads to a kitchen and a bathroom in an extension at the back. There's a door on either side of the front of the hallway. The one on the left leads into the sitting room. The one on the right leads into the dining room, though we never use it and everything in there is covered in dustsheets.'

'Is your mother mobile at all?'

'It varies. Sometimes it's possible to help her down the stairs to the sitting room and she spends time listening to the radio there, in front of the fire if it's cold. On other days she's barely able to get out of bed. This morning I left her upstairs, after making sure she had a drink of water and a sandwich if she needed them, and checking that her chamber pot was empty.'

'So, to reach Edward we simply go in the front door, up

the stairs and turn left?' asked Monique.

'That's correct. You will need help and a stretcher to move him.' Grace looked at her watch. 'I'd expect him to be out cold for another couple of hours at least. Here's the front door key. Please try not to upset my mother.'

'We'll do our best,' said Monique.

Bob got out of the car and Monique followed him through the gate in the low stone wall dividing the road from the cottage's front garden. As they approached the front door, Monique took her pistol out of her handbag and she saw that Bob had drawn his too. She hoped Grace wasn't watching but thought she probably was.

Monique unlocked the front door and Bob opened it with his free hand, allowing it to swing back. The stairs climbed the right-hand side of the hallway and Bob started up them slowly. Monique realised how quiet everything seemed. She'd heard birds singing outside the cottage, but here there was no sound at all beyond the ticking of a clock in the sitting room. One of the stairs creaked as Bob put his weight on it and he stopped moving. Then he started to climb again.

'Grace, is that you?'

Grace's mother sounded very frail.

'Grace, stop fooling around. Edward, are you there?'

Both doors from the tiny landing at the top of the stairs were closed. Monique watched as Bob gently opened the one on the left with one hand while holding his Walther PPK ready in the other. A wooden double bed was placed against the back wall of the room, just far enough away from the door to allow it to open fully. There was a lump in the bed but as Monique walked into the room she realised they'd been duped.

'He's gone, Bob.'

Bob reached down and pulled back the bedding, revealing a rolled-up quilt placed there to give the impression the bed was occupied.

Monique heard the front door slam, then turned and ran back down the stairs, hearing a woman's voice shouting outside as she neared the bottom.

She pulled open the front door and ran to the car.

'Where is he?' she asked.

She heard Bob behind her.

'He ran off in that direction,' said Adrian Somerset, pointing to the back of the car. 'He came out of the cottage and ran towards us. I took the key out of the ignition and threw it out of my window to stop him from taking the car. He had a pistol and I thought he was going to kill me, but Grace stopped him.'

'He must have hidden a second pistol in the cottage,' said Grace. 'I think he's gone to Galloway House. You saw it in the distance when we were driving through the grounds, but it's not far from here if you follow the path you can see through the trees.'

'You stay here, flight lieutenant,' said Bob. 'There's a pistol and ammunition in a case under the seat you're sitting on. Make sure Dr Sullivan is safe if her brother returns. When my colleagues arrive, tell them where we've gone. When the men from the RAF Regiment arrive, get them to set up a cordon around Galloway House to ensure that Edward Daly, or Edward Sullivan, can't get out, and have them send for more help so we can search the place properly if we need to.'

'Come on, Bob,' said Monique, turning towards the start of the path Grace had indicated.

Bob easily kept up with her as they ran through what in other circumstances would be a beautiful area of woodland.

‘He could hide and double back,’ said Monique.

‘I know,’ said Bob. ‘If so, at least Adrian Somerset’s armed now. For the moment let’s just assume the Cuttlefish has done the obvious thing and headed for somewhere he can easily hide and where he can access medical supplies. Do you think Grace was lying about expecting to find him out cold?’

‘I don’t think so,’ said Monique, starting to feel breathless. ‘Perhaps he’s developed a habit and, as a result, Grace underestimated how much morphine or whatever else he needed to keep him under. As I know all too well, spying and drug addiction can go hand-in-hand. I think we’re there.’

They’d arrived at a crossroads of paths. Ahead of them, the one they’d been following continued a short distance to an open gate in a low, ivy-clad stone wall.

‘I can see him, Monique!’

Beyond the wall and gate, an open area that might once have been a lawn extended as far as the south end of Galloway House. Two large reddish stone ranges of the building were connected by a lower structure that was bowed out towards them. At the right-hand corner of the building, ornate stone steps led up to a balustraded balcony at the first-floor level. A figure wearing an RAF uniform was just reaching the top of the steps.

‘He appears to be labouring badly,’ said Bob, ‘But he’s done well to stay that far ahead of us. He’s gone. There must be a door there.’

‘At least we know he’s not doubled back,’ said Monique, setting off towards the corner of the building at a run.

The balcony at the top of the steps gave access to Galloway House via an open French window. Inside was a large room with impressive windows facing to the south and the east. It might once have served as a dining room or ballroom but was now being used as a hospital ward. Only a few of the dozen or so beds were occupied and a young man with his arm in a sling was sitting up in one of them and pointing with his other arm towards the ornately-framed door on the far side of the room.

'He went that way, group captain!'

Bob ran towards the door and Monique followed, smiling at the young man as she passed him.

Beyond the door was a maze of corridors and side rooms. Bob slowed to a walk as he began to look into each of the rooms in turn.

Suddenly there was the sound of a gunshot from somewhere ahead of them and a woman screamed. Monique moved ahead cautiously, with Bob just behind her. The corridor opened out into a double-height room housing an impressive staircase that wrapped around three sides of the square space before connecting with a gallery running high along the inner wall of the room.

Monique walked through an arch to find herself in what had to be Galloway House's entrance hall. The walls and the ceiling were covered in decorative plasterwork and the gallery that was reached from the top of the stairs continued across the upper part of the rear of the hall.

Monique took all this in in a glance, but her attention was drawn more to the army sergeant lying on his back on the floor. There was blood on his tunic and the floorboards next to him and two nurses were crouched beside him.

One of them, a blonde woman in her twenties, looked up at Monique. 'He's been shot in the shoulder.'

The front door burst open and Michael Dixon came in with his pistol drawn. Katerina Komarova was just behind him, also holding her gun.

‘Flight Lieutenant Somerset said you were here and we heard a gunshot as we pulled up outside,’ said Michael.

‘Where’s the man who shot him?’ asked Bob, looking at the nurses.

‘He went that way,’ said the second nurse, pointing behind her, towards the north end of the house.

‘What’s along there?’ asked Bob.

‘More rooms that were once grand. It’s a real warren and it’s on three or four floors connected by lots of staircases. There’s a large billiard room on the lowest floor at the north end of the house itself, but then there are ancillary buildings beyond that.’

‘Michael, you come with me,’ said Bob. ‘Monique, can you and Katerina keep this central part of the house secure until the RAF Regiment arrives? I hope they will have sent for reinforcements. It’s going to take a lot of men to search this place thoroughly.’

Bob turned and ran into a corridor leading out of the far end of the entrance hall. Michael followed.

Monique turned to the nurses tending to the wounded man. ‘What happened?’

The blonde woman answered. ‘We were just leaving. An RAF flight lieutenant ran into the entrance hall brandishing a gun. The sergeant came in through the front door at the same time and moved towards the flight lieutenant as if to try to stop him, and was shot for his troubles.’

‘Will he be all right?’ asked Katerina.

‘He’s not going to die if we can stop the bleeding, but that’s not quite the same as “all right”.’

Monique heard what sounded like a scuffle from somewhere above them and then a loud grunt and a thud. She looked at Katerina and then ran for the bottom of the staircase in the adjoining room. She heard Katerina behind her as she ran up the stairs two at a time.

The gallery at the top of the stairs didn't only carry on across the top of the back of the entrance hall, it also became an upper-floor corridor that seemed to run through much of the length of the building.

Looking to the south, back towards the cottage, she could see a body lying on the floor. 'Someone else has been hurt up here!' she shouted as she ran towards a figure she could now see was moving.

It was a grey-haired man wearing civilian clothes. 'He hit me with his gun before I realised what was happening.'

'Where did he go?' asked Monique.

'I'm sorry, I don't know. I think I lost consciousness.'

An older nurse was coming towards them along the corridor.

'Have you seen an RAF flight lieutenant with a gun?' asked Monique.

The woman shook her head. 'What's happened?'

'He's been hit on the head.'

'Monique,' said Katerina.

Monique looked at her. Katerina was pointing to a doorway behind them that opened onto a narrow staircase that led upwards. Monique stepped inside and looked up. She heard a door bang somewhere above her.

Katerina turned to face the nurse. 'Where does this staircase go?'

'Up to the upper floor and attic rooms in this main range and the roof. We don't go up there much.'

'Thank you,' said Monique. 'If you see a group captain or a lieutenant commander looking for a fugitive, please tell them that we think the man we're after has gone up to the attic. Come on, Katerina.'

The staircase was as confined as it had looked and the

lighting was poor. Monique got her torch out of her handbag. The stairs turned back on themselves repeatedly. At what must have been the floor above where they'd started, there was a door on one side with a handle covered in dust that didn't look like it had been used recently. It felt like a longer climb to the next level. Here they emerged onto a small landing that had a door on the left and another ahead of them. The only natural light came from a small and grubby skylight in the roof above. In the beam of Monique's torch, it was obvious that no one had used the door on the left recently. The handle of the door ahead of them, on the other hand, had a coating of dust that was disturbed and partly removed.

'He went this way,' said Katerina. 'The hinges are on this side so the door opens inwards. You open it, Monique, and I'll go through.'

'The Cuttlefish may be waiting for us on the other side,' said Monique.

'I know. But even though we never knew each other's real names there was once something between us, however briefly. He could be expecting me, but he might still pause for longer before shooting than he would if you went first.'

'Are you sure?' asked Monique. 'You told me that his last words to you in Madrid were that if you ever saw each other again, one of you would have to kill the other.'

'Yes, but this way we stand a better chance of him dying rather than me. Or you, for that matter.'

Monique shrugged, then leaned past Katerina to grasp the door handle. She pulled the door open while Katerina pressed herself against the side wall to avoid blocking it. She'd half expected a squeal of rusty hinges, but it opened nearly silently. With the door fully open, Monique could see what lay beyond.

After the darkness of the stairs, it took a moment for her eyes to become accustomed to the glare of the sun reflecting off the light grey covering of a flat roof. Katerina edged out onto the roof, her gun pointing to the right. Monique followed, focusing her attention to the left.

'He's not here,' said Katerina.

The flat roof formed a broad semi-circle around the edge of which was a heavy and very ornate stone balustrade. They had emerged from a doorway towards the southern end of a blank stone wall that closed off the semi-circular area from the rest of the roof of the building.

'I've not seen the east face of Galloway House,' said Monique. 'I wouldn't mind betting that its central section curves out to form a large semi-circular bay, and this is the roof of it.'

'The wall behind us doesn't reach as far as the balustrade at its southern end,' said Katerina.

Katerina led the way around a corner. The balustrade continued on their left, defining a narrow strip of roof between it and, on their right, the stone structure at the top of the stairs that they'd emerged from. Ahead was the start of the gentle slate-clad slope of the main roof of the house. The most obvious feature in that direction was a massive chimney stack, built end on to them. Two more chimney stacks of similar bulk lay across the line of the ridge of the roof off to their left.

Monique caught a glimpse of movement from the nearest of the two. Before she could react, a shot rang out and Katerina screamed and doubled up, then collapsed. Monique threw herself down next to the Soviet woman. The balustrade was built on top of a stone base that was some eighteen inches in depth. If the Cuttlefish was hiding behind the chimney stack then the stone base of the balustrade offered them some protection. On the other hand, it also meant they had to keep extremely low to avoid exposing themselves.

Monique shuffled around so she was facing Katerina, who was lying on her back with her arm across her middle and breathing heavily. A large bloodstain on her midriff was growing visibly.

'How bad is it?' asked Monique

'It caught my side. It feels bad, but I think it's just a large flesh wound.'

Monique turned and tried to see more of the roof but must have raised her head too far because there was another shot. This one chipped off a piece of the balustrade very close to her.

'You should keep your head down,' called a man with an Irish accent.

'And you should have drowned in Stranraer harbour,' shouted Katerina.

'Are you still with us, Ludmilla? I'm usually a better shot than that. That's what comes of having to shoot left-handed, I suppose.'

Monique wondered if she could move far enough without being seen to allow her to pop up from an unexpected position and take a shot at him.

'I recognised both of you on the steamer,' called the Cuttlefish. 'How could I not recognise my lovely Ludmilla after you took your wig off? That was a nice touch, by the way, almost worthy of me. But I also recognised you, Vera Eriksen.'

Monique felt a sense of shock. She had no recollection of ever having met Edward Daly or Edward Sullivan or, for that matter, any Irishman working for any arm of German intelligence who could possibly be the man now on the roof of Galloway House.

'I followed you and the group captain back to your hotel in Stockholm from the Grand Hotel. We never did find Maximilian von Moser after he disappeared in Gothenburg. There was no evidence that he'd been killed in the house fire, and then you reappeared in Stockholm as if nothing had happened. What did you do to him, Vera?'

There was the sound of another shot, this time from a different direction. Monique twisted around and saw Bob kneeling with his pistol extended in front of him, held in both hands. He'd taken a shot through the balustrade from near the corner leading from the semi-circular roof.

Bob stood up, then returned his Walther PPK to his shoulder holster. Monique cautiously stood as well. She could see a body lying across the ridge of the roof of Galloway House, next to the chimney stack. Blood was running down the slope of the near side of the roof and Monique could see that the body was missing part of its head.

'He was too busy talking to pay attention to what was going on,' said Bob.

'Thank you, Bob,' said Monique. 'Now can you get help? Katerina's been shot.'

Bob looked towards them and then turned and ran back out of sight.

Monique crouched down beside Katerina and gently lifted the side of her blouse, causing her to scream. 'You're right, it's a mess but it's relatively superficial. Bob's getting help. If I sit down against the wall you can lay against me and we can bunch up my skirt to try to stem the bleeding. That's right.'

'Did you get him?' asked Katerina.

'Bob killed him.'

‘Thank him for me, Monique. I think he saved both our lives.’

‘I’m not sure,’ said Monique. ‘The Cuttlefish was as pinned down by us as we were by him. I’d have worked something out, given time.’

Katerina laughed, then groaned. ‘Please don’t make me laugh. Was Edward right?’

‘About what?’ asked Monique.

‘About you being Vera Eriksen?’

‘It was a name I used for a while, yes.’

‘I remember things like that. When he said it, I knew the name rang a bell from long ago. There may be other women with that name, but were you once married to Count Sergei Ignatieff?’

Monique hadn’t been expecting that. ‘Yes, I was.’

‘Perhaps I shouldn’t tell you while you’re helping keep me alive, but I’m truly sorry.’

‘Sorry about what?’ asked Monique.

‘It was me who entrapped him in 1936. I was assigned to investigate his activities. What he told me while we were in bed together got him arrested and then shot as a spy. I want to be honest with you, Monique. Please don’t hate me.’

‘Don’t be sorry, Katerina. He was a bastard who was better off dead.’

‘I suppose it meant that you were free to marry the gorgeous group captain,’ said Katerina.

‘It was a little more complicated than that but yes, eventually I did. I can hear someone coming. They’ll look after you.’

EPILOGUE

Bob, Monique and Michael returned to the officers' mess at RAF Wigtown so Monique could get a bath and change before they all ate a late lunch. Monique and Michael then drove the two cars back to Edinburgh. After a long conversation on the phone with Commodore Cunningham, and a shorter one with Wing Commander Bernard Spencer, the station commander at RAF Turnhouse, Bob flew the Mosquito back on his own.

Bob spent most of the next day, Saturday, in his office at Craigiehall writing a detailed report of everything that had happened. Monique and Michael both helped, and Joyce Stuart came in to type up their joint efforts.

Joyce also came in on Sunday, to help Bob tackle the paperwork that had accumulated during his absence. With Michael also away from the office the previous week, the new system of delegation had largely ground to a halt. Monique wasn't happy to lose a Sunday with Bob but took the opportunity to visit Betty Swanson at the Haymarket Station Hotel. She told him afterwards that Betty had heard she would be joining the Women's Auxiliary Air Force within a few days. When Bob asked, Monique said they'd not talked about Michael at all.

On Sunday evening, Bob and Monique enjoyed dinner together at the North British Hotel on Princes Street. It was only after they returned to the bungalow in Featherhall Crescent that he told her why he'd been so keen to clear his paperwork.

Bob had been worried that the weather was showing signs of breaking down over the weekend, with thunderstorms on Saturday evening and rain on Sunday morning, but Monday dawned bright and sunny. There were a few more clouds than the previous week, though not many, and the winds were light. They drove to RAF Turnhouse and loaded two small travel bags into the luggage compartment behind the rear cockpit of a de Havilland Tiger Moth two-seat open-cockpit biplane training aircraft that was waiting for them. The aircraft was on the inventory of RAF Turnhouse and Bernard Spencer had been happy to loan it to Bob for what he had in mind.

With both of them togged up in their leather flying jackets and helmets, goggles, scarves and gloves, Bob helped Monique into the front cockpit of the Tiger Moth. He then got into the rear cockpit and started the engine with help from an airman who manually swung the propellor.

It was years since Bob had last flown a Tiger Moth, but he found it was like riding a bicycle. Some things you just never forget. They took off to the north-west and continued in that direction. Bob knew that they were flying an aircraft that would be instantly recognised by even the most myopic anti-aircraft gunner for what it was and, with that worry gone, he stayed low as they kept the River Forth off to their right and then passed south of Stirling and over the Trossachs. He gave a running commentary of where they were over the intercom for Monique's benefit.

After climbing a little, he suggested that Monique might like to take the controls. The Tiger Moth was a superb basic trainer and thousands of pilots had had their first experience of flying in the front cockpit of one. Monique took over and they did a few gentle turns, each time coming back to the course that Bob wanted to fly. He was pleased to find she had a natural empathy for the aircraft. She flew it for longer than Bob had intended before he took back control.

After passing over Oban, Bob flew at low level along the Sound of Mull, a route he'd last flown in a Sunderland flying boat the previous September. When he saw the lighthouse at the tip of the Ardnamurchan Peninsula passing on their right, Bob checked his note of the course they needed to follow. This was just habit as there was no real need. He could see the outline of their destination in the distance ahead. He knew that on a different day, with poor visibility, if he got their heading wrong their next landfall would be in Greenland. Only it wouldn't, as they'd have run out of fuel long before getting that far.

Bob had never seen the beach airport near the northern end of the Isle of Barra but he'd read about it when scheduled air services began in 1936 and it had always been an ambition of his to visit. He'd borrowed the Tiger Moth partly because it would be an enjoyable alternative to the Mosquito and partly because it would allow Monique to try her hand at flying. Mainly, though, he'd borrowed it because he'd been told that no one had ever landed a Mosquito on Barra's sand runways and being the first to try might not be a good idea.

The tide was out, as he'd been told it would be, and Bob landed the Tiger Moth without difficulty. He didn't know what to expect, but a couple of men were on hand to tie the aircraft wings to anchor points set into the upper edge of the sand, near the small airport building. It clearly got windy here.

The taxi Bob had arranged had seen better days, but he knew it was only about seven miles around the island to Castlebay so if the worst came to the worst he and Monique could hitch a lift or walk. The Castlebay Hotel was home to the four officers in charge of the RAF radar station located in the north-west of the island but was otherwise open for normal business and had been happy to find a room for Monique and him. When he'd mentioned on the phone that they would be there on honeymoon, he was promised the best room. This turned out to have panoramic views over the village and harbour, including a ruined castle on a tiny island in the bay from which, he imagined, Castlebay took its name.

The next few days were idyllic. There was always more cloud than the previous week, but blue skies still predominated. With a persistent but gentle breeze, it never got uncomfortably hot and the midges were never intrusive. Bob and Monique enjoyed food that was better than he had anticipated on a remote island and there was plenty to drink. He'd not expected to find champagne, so wasn't disappointed when there was none. Their bed didn't squeak so they were able to enjoy the traditional pursuits of a honeymoon couple without worrying they were disturbing other guests or residents.

On their first day, they simply wandered around Castlebay, drinking in how quiet it was, other than an odd grating noise that Bob was later told was the call of the corn crake. These birds seemed to be everywhere.

On Tuesday they explored Barra on a motorcycle an RAF officer based at the radar station who they'd met in the hotel bar offered to lend them. Monique drove while Bob sat behind her, their flying jackets, helmets, gloves and goggles proving perfect for the purpose. On Wednesday a fisherman took them out to the ruins of Kisimul Castle in the bay, and then across to the island of Vatersay.

Thursday was another perfect day, with fluffy clouds and only a little wind. Monique drove Bob to the airport on the motorcycle and they then set off in the Tiger Moth. This time Bob headed north, flying at extremely low level above the magnificent white beaches and turquoise sea that formed the western fringe of South Uist and Benbecula, where they had to watch out for aircraft flying to or from the RAF airfield on the island. Then it was on to North Uist before turning more to the north-east as Bob stayed low over Berneray and the beaches of South Harris, which surpassed anything they'd seen until then. He climbed to give them views of the mountains of North Harris before following the north-west coast of Lewis as far as the lighthouse at its northern tip, the Butt of Lewis.

After turning south, he flew down the east coast of Lewis as far as RAF Stornoway, where he landed and arranged to have the Tiger Moth refuelled.

Monique and Bob enjoyed an excellent lunch in the officers' mess with the station commander, Group Captain Tom Erickson, who they both knew. His posting to RAF Stornoway had been extended for longer than originally planned. His daughter Helen, who Monique had saved from Soviet agents and a predatory London policeman in late April, was doing well in her medical studies. On the other hand, his marriage to her mother, whose top secret work and ill-advised affair with a Soviet spy had caused some of the problems for their daughter, was effectively over.

Afterwards, Bob and Monique flew back down the rockier and in places hilly east side of the archipelago, concluding with an overflight of Eriskay as Bob turned to make his approach to Barra Airport. The tide was much further in this time, but there was still plenty of room to land a Tiger Moth.

The last night of their deferred honeymoon was bittersweet. Their stay had been so wonderful that neither wanted it to come to an end.

On Friday they flew back to RAF Turnhouse and then

went to the MI11 offices at Craigiehall to find out what had been happening in their absence. Joyce and Michael had achieved wonders in keeping Bob's paperwork down, for which he was hugely grateful.

Joyce also told him that Commodore Cunningham had arranged for an aircraft to fly him, Monique and Michael to RAF Northolt on Monday, for a meeting with the commodore and Sir Peter Maitland.

That left the weekend free. On Saturday morning, again with Bernard Spencer's blessing, Bob took Monique for her first flying lesson in the Tiger Moth they'd flown to Barra and back. She was as good a pilot as he'd hoped and so enthusiastic that what had been intended to be a one-hour lesson lasted for over two.

Afterwards, Bob presented Monique with her own Royal Air Force Pilot's Flying Log Book, or 'Form 414', to allow her to record her flying. Plans to give her a second lesson on Sunday fell foul of torrential rain, so they visited his parents in Cramond instead.

*

'This is the only street in the country where you have to drive on the right,' said the corporal driving the army staff car that had met them at RAF Northolt.

'Why is that?' asked Monique from the back seat.

'They say it goes back seventy years, ma'am, to when they built the Savoy Theatre. Horse-drawn cabs could drop fares off at the theatre, which is on the right here, and then they could pick up a new fare from the Savoy Hotel as they turned around in front of it at the end, ahead of us. They also say that every London cab that's ever been made has had to have a turning circle small enough to get around the roundabout in front of the hotel. They were less careful about the design of military vehicles, so it might take me a turn or two to make it round. Here we are.'

'Thank you, corporal,' said Michael as he got out of the front passenger seat.

Bob and Monique joined him on the pavement outside the hotel's entrance. The huge canopy extending out over the turning circle kept them dry, but Monique could hear the rain beating down on top of it.

Monique raised a hand in thanks as the car pulled away, though she doubted if the driver saw her.

'If that corporal needs a job when the war is over, he's got all the chat he needs to become a London taxi driver,' said Michael.

Monique saw Bob smile before he spoke. 'I'm intrigued to know why we're meeting here. Come on, let's go in and find out.'

They were directed to a very plush room on the first floor of the hotel with a rectangular table that was covered in purple cloth and had ten matching chairs around it. They were the first to arrive. While Bob and Michael chatted, Monique looked at a line of three pictures of London hanging on one long wall. There were three more on the opposite wall and Monique found herself wondering whether they were original paintings or reproductions. As they were displayed behind glass, it was hard to tell.

After a moment, she felt herself becoming detached, thinking back to her wonderful stay on the Isle of Barra with Bob. It was a complete surprise, as was his suggestion that she help fly the Tiger Moth on the way there. The flying lesson on Saturday had been a revelation and, for the first time, she truly began to understand the joy of flying that was so central to the soul of the man she'd married.

The door opened and Sir Peter Maitland walked in, followed by Commodore Cunningham.

'It's good to see you all and thank you for coming,' said Sir Peter. 'I hope the two of you had a better honeymoon this time than you managed originally.'

'Yes, thank you, sir,' said Bob. 'The company and weather were perfect and Barra was sublime.'

'And I didn't turn up to spoil it,' said Maurice Cunningham, smiling.

'Coffee and cakes will be served in a moment,' said Sir Peter. 'Don't overdo the cakes because lunch will be served after our meetings are over. Please sit down..'

Monique caught the significance of the plural and immediately understood why they'd been brought to the Savoy Hotel rather than to Sir Peter's office or the commodore's. She saw Bob smile and realised he'd noticed, too.

Bob, Monique and Michael took three of the seats on one side of the table while Sir Peter and Maurice Cunningham sat on the other.

After the waiters had left and the door was closed, Sir Peter put his cup down on its saucer. 'I would like to thank all three of you for a job very well done. Finding the Cuttlefish and ensuring the danger he represented was brought to an end was a huge achievement, especially as MI5 were playing silly buggers over the list of phantom agents they gave you.'

Monique was sitting to Bob's right and caught his eye as he glanced at her. She could tell that he, too, was thinking that Sir Peter had been party to what MI5 had done, but this didn't seem the moment to object to a little rewriting of history.

Bob sat back in his chair. 'Thank you, sir. As you'll have

seen in our report, I killed the Cuttlefish because he was shooting at Monique and Miss Komarova. I'm not so sure I'd have been able to obey an order to kill him had he, for example, already been taken into police custody.'

'That does you credit, Bob,' said Sir Peter. 'But it's academic because that wasn't what happened. With that in mind, you will recall that when I offered you this job it was on the basis of a temporary promotion to group captain that would be made permanent after a year. In light of your performance since you took up your post last October, it has been decided to make your promotion substantive with immediate effect.'

Out of the corner of her eye, Monique saw a look of surprise cross Bob's face.

'Thank you, sir,' he said.

Sir Peter smiled. 'Now, the reason why I've brought you here is that we will shortly be meeting Yevgeny Popov and Miss Komarova and neither Maurice nor I want either of them anywhere near our offices.'

Sir Peter looked at his watch. 'I'd like to use the time we have before they arrive to clear up a couple of points I don't want to discuss in front of them and set some ground rules. First, given the way things ended, there is no need to mention Mulberry, even though we know that Edith Sullivan, the Cuttlefish's mother, actively encouraged him to report what was going on in the area to his employers in the Sicherheitsdienst or SD.'

'What will happen to her and Grace Sullivan?' asked Monique.

'As I understand it, Dr Grace Sullivan was pivotal in our locating her brother,' said Sir Peter. 'She deserves nothing but thanks. The mother is more of a problem but I'm told she's largely immobile and may not have long to live. The decision has been made to do nothing about her.

‘Moving on, I also don’t want any mention in front of our Soviet allies of the Double Cross agents and especially not of Ultra. As I read your report, you were able to manage Miss Komarova’s involvement in a way that meant she was not aware of those issues.’

‘We did, sir,’ said Bob. ‘As far as Mulberry is concerned, I mentioned in my report that the Soviets have a good idea that something is going on along that coast. But they don’t appear to know any details and we tried to keep it that way.’

‘Good,’ said Sir Peter. ‘Does anyone have any comments or is there anything else we need to cover now?’

Michael coughed.

‘Ah, yes,’ said Sir Peter. ‘Bob, you were open in your report about Lieutenant Commander Dixon becoming close to Miss Komarova while you were in Galloway.’

‘I can’t imagine her being so open in her report to Popov, sir,’ said Michael.

‘I’m sure you’re right, lieutenant commander. I suggest you do nothing and the rest of us say nothing to enlighten Mr Popov in case he doesn’t already know.’ Sir Peter looked at his watch again. ‘Maurice, would you do the honours?’

Commodore Cunningham left the room. When he returned a few minutes later, he was followed by Yevgeny Popov and Katerina Komarova.

Katerina beamed and came round the table with her arms open wide. For a moment Monique thought she was heading for Michael, beyond Bob. Instead, she stopped and embraced Monique, very gingerly. ‘It’s good to see you.’

‘How are you, Katerina?’ asked Monique.

‘Recovering. Thank you for helping when I was shot.

Thank you too, Group Captain Sutherland, for killing Edward before he could kill us.'

There was a reshuffling to allow Yevgeny Popov and Katerina Komarova to sit in the two central seats on one side of the table. On impulse, Monique sat next to Katerina. Bob looked at her, then paused for a moment before he went to sit next to Popov.

Monique saw Sir Peter smother a smile as he, Maurice and Michael sat on the other side of the table. More coffee was served, but no cakes this time.

The meeting that followed was largely taken up by Monique, Bob and Michael giving a highly edited version of their report, and Katerina doing, presumably, the same. The meeting still went on for longer than it should and Monique was grateful that she'd taken two cakes when they were offered because lunch seemed to be getting no closer.

She was almost caught by surprise when Sir Peter drew proceedings to a close with a slightly wordy tribute to the benefits of joint working between allies and Yevgeny Popov responding in similar terms.

Then Sir Peter announced that they should move to an adjoining room for champagne cocktails and lunch.

As they stood, she saw Bob turn to face Povov. 'I forgot to ask, how is Major Malinovsky getting on?'

'When we met at RAF Errol I expressed my deep regret that he had tried to kill you,' said Popov. 'In the circumstances, it was felt best that he should return to the Motherland.'

'That's fair enough,' said Bob. 'I hope you didn't make him swim.'

Popov's back was turned to Monique but she still saw the way he stiffened, as if someone had inserted a poker somewhere very personal. She sensed that he wanted to know how Bob had found out what happened to Malinovsky, but couldn't ask in case he'd misunderstood what Bob meant. This time she saw both Sir Peter Maitland and Maurice Cunningham suppress smiles. She had the feeling that lunch was going to be rather awkward.

AUTHOR'S NOTE

This book is a work of fiction and should be read as such. Except as noted below, all characters are fictional and any resemblances to real people, either living or dead, are purely coincidental.

Likewise, many of the events that are described in this book are the products of the author's imagination. Others did take place.

What has become known as 'The Battle of Bamber Bridge' happened on the night of the 24th to the 25th of June 1943 and was largely as described, albeit with some changes to aid the flow of the narrative. The characters involved in my account of the battle are fictional, though they had real counterparts. The broader British response to what took place is conjecture on my part. After many of the black soldiers involved were convicted by US courts martial, General Ira C. Eaker, commander of the Eighth Air Force, stepped in to moderate the judicial response, improve the quality of officers and integrate some of the racially segregated units: all in a not entirely successful effort to prevent recurrences of the unrest elsewhere.

Development work on Mulberry harbours took place along the coast from Garlieston to Cairn Head and many of the descriptions used in the book of places or incidents, such as the testing of the Swiss Roll in Garlieston Bay, are drawn from contemporary accounts or photographs. The existence of an MI5 agent disguised as a tramp who wandered the area testing military security was accepted as fact by some people at the time.

Trains have a role to play in this book. The timetables quoted are as set out in the June 1943 edition of

Bradshaw's Guide.

Let's move on to the characters who appear in the book. Some of them could be associated with real people because of their roles, like the harbourmaster in Cairnryan, police officers and the commanding officers of various military units. The characters who play those roles in this book are not based on their real-life counterparts and are fictional. Minor characters are also entirely invented, as are members of Military Intelligence, Section 11. The Soviet agents are fictional, as are the Cuttlefish and the rest of the Sullivan family.

Group Captain Robert Sutherland is also an invented character, though he has a career in the Royal Air Force that will be recognised by anyone familiar with the life and achievements of Squadron Leader Archibald McKellar, DSO, DFC and Bar. Bob Sutherland's family background and pre-war employment were very different to Archibald McKellar's, but the two share an eminent list of achievements during the Battle of Britain. Squadron Leader McKellar was tragically killed when he was shot down on the 1st of November 1940, whereas the fictional Group Captain Sutherland was only wounded when he was shot down on the same day, allowing him to play a leading role in this book and its six predecessors.

And Madame Monique Dubois? She is a fictional alias for a real woman. The real Vera Eriksen, or Vera Schalburg, or take your pick from any number of other aliases, had a story that was both complex and very dark. She disappeared during the war after the two German agents she landed with at Port Gordon on the Moray Firth were tried and executed by the British for spying.

A hint of Monique's story emerges from the pages of this book but to get a fuller picture you should read my first novel, *Eyes Turned Skywards.*

Military Intelligence, Section 11, or MI11, was a real organisation that had a responsibility for military security. Its organisation and other aspects of its operations described in this book are entirely fictional.

The Security Service (MI5) and the Secret Intelligence Service (SIS or MI6) both existed, and both continue to exist at the time of writing.

The success in intercepting German communications encrypted by Enigma machines was much as outlined here, under the code name 'Ultra'. There was also a Double Cross Committee overseeing the running of double agents who had originally been identified and apprehended as a result of Ultra intercepts.

Let's now turn to places that appear in this book. Galloway House exists and was an auxiliary hospital during the war. It was generally as described, though the nearby Broom Cottage is an invention. I am grateful to the owner of Galloway House, Kamal Hanif OBE, for showing me around his amazing home and I hope he forgives any liberties I have taken with the layout.

Garlieston was generally as described at the time and the Galloway Arms Hotel existed. It has since become the Harbour Inn, which has proved a great place to stay while researching this book. Nearby Cruggleton Church is real and is just as chilling as described in the story. Cairn Head was home to a military camp in World War Two much like the one that appears in this book and the nearby pierhead and floating pier are shown in contemporary photographs.

RAF Wigtown, RAF Castle Kennedy and RAF Wig Bay were all real places and all were generally as I describe them. The flying operations at RAF Wigtown and the problems encountered there were again as they appear in this book. There was a deployment of Typhoons from 174 and 175 Squadrons at the base at the time the story is set. Descriptions of flying the Typhoon are based on accounts written at the time. There was a Red Lion Inn in Wigtown during the war and it had a skittle alley. Other elements of its internal layout are imagined.

My descriptions of Cairnryan and Stranraer are based on contemporary sources and photographs and that includes the arrangement of the piers and railway station in Stranraer as well as the military port and Lochryan House in Cairnryan. The cottage in Cairnryan is not based on a particular building but there are a number like it. Upper Milldown is fictional but the landscape west of Stranraer is generally as described. The Wigtownshire Police Headquarters was on Lewis Street in Stranraer, on a site now occupied by a fire station.

The sea route between Stranraer and Larne was served by the *Princess Margaret* at the time the book is set and the steamer's layout was generally as described. That is also true of Larne and the Olderfleet Hotel. Large parts of the latter were later demolished.

Craigiehall, west of Edinburgh, was taken over by the army during the war and later became the main army headquarters in Scotland until its closure. The presence there of part of MI11 is fictional. The North British Hotel in Edinburgh became the Balmoral Hotel some decades ago. RAF Turnhouse became Edinburgh Airport after the war and the original runways are no longer in use.

Featherhall Crescent in Corstorphine exists, divided into northern and southern arcs, and it is home to bungalows like the one lived in by Bob and Monique. Theirs is a typical example rather than a specific house. The Haymarket Station Hotel is fictional.

Bo'ness in the 1940s was a very different and much more industrial place than it is today and was generally as described in this book. Corvi's was there at the time and remains there today, home to the best fish and chips I've ever eaten.

Barra, Barra Airport and the Castlebay Hotel were much as they appear in the book. The flight into the world's only beach airport offering scheduled flights remains an unforgettable experience.

To conclude, in my view a fiction writer should create a world that feels right to his or her readers. When the world in question is as far removed in so many ways, some predictable and others not, as 1943 is from today, then it is inevitable that false assumptions will be made and facts will be misunderstood. If you find factual errors within this book I apologise and can only hope that they have not got in the way of your enjoyment of the story.